I0535401

THE CONCERT KILLER

By

RJ McDonnell

© 2011

Killeena Publishing

Copyright © 2011 by RJ McDonnell
All rights reserved.

No part of this book may be reproduced in any form or by any
electronic or mechanical means, to include information
storage and retrieval systems, without the expressed written
permission of the publisher, with one exception: Reviewers
may quote brief passages.

Killeena Publishing
PO Box 3611
Scranton, PA 18505

2nd edition
This book is a work of fiction. Any similarity to real people,
alive or dead, is purely coincidental and not intended by the
author.

Printed in the United States

ISBN: 978-0-9814914-5-5

www.rjmcdonnell.com

rj@rjmcdonnell.com

Chapter 1

Virginia Tolliver couldn't stand another day of being known to her classmates as *most likely to become a nun.* Senior year was underway and she was still living up to the first six letters in her name. There was no shortage of opportunities to unlock her chastity belt. Except for a slightly pug nose, she was a natural blond beauty. But high school boys could never satisfy her lofty expectations. She wanted a man whose appeal would rival the hunks in her favorite romance novels. The lead singer in Concierge Lover was such a man. When she read that his band would be performing in the area she invested most of her savings in a beautiful pink mini-dress and a professional makeover. She saw enough groupies on television to know where to go and how to act after the show.

A man with the intense gaze of a hunter sat in his white sedan looking through a small pair of binoculars. He watched six groupies gathered near the stage entrance to the amphitheater where the concert headliner's bus would soon be entering. His eyes were drawn to a blond tart wearing a sheer pink mini-dress. He knew instantly that she would be the one.

He tailed her from a safe distance after the bus arrived. Her outfit made this task exceptionally simple. Throughout the warm-up act and the main show he watched as she drank four beers and danced with rowdy boys and other slutty girls on the lawn behind the permanent seats. When the band finished, she clapped wildly and glanced back at the restroom. He knew that her main concern would be to primp for the band. While the rest of the concert-goers roared for an encore, he finger-combed his brown wig, adjusted the prosthetic breasts he wore under his light gray v-neck sweater, and followed the groupie into the cinderblock women's room. Upon entering, he heard a stall door close, squatted for a moment and, glancing under the stall doors, confirmed that they were alone. He was momentarily disgusted by the array of toilet paper, discarded cups, and paper towels that were strewn about the floor. Before rising, his nostrils flared as he became aware of a puddle of vomit below the sink nearest to him.

He went into the stall at the far end of the restroom so that he would pass the pink trollop as he exited. He sat on the toilet, bent forward, and carefully removed his long brown wig. Underneath was a plastic zip-lock bag containing a pair of latex gloves and a single sheet of paper folded into thirds. After putting on the gloves, he looked down at the paper which displayed the words, "Concerts are Evil," written across the top in newspaper clippings. Below were the headlines of three murders he committed over the past three months. The police were obviously too stupid to recognize the connection, so he decided to point them in the right direction. At the bottom of the note he taped his signature, "The Concert Killer."

He quietly removed four pieces of masking tape from the bag and taped the paper to the back of the stall door, wrinkling his gloves as he smoothed the tape. He placed the wig back on his head, making sure it completely covered his short black hair. He heard the tart's toilet flush and her stall door open.

Virginia was nervous and starting to have second thoughts about turning her fantasy into reality. The beers bolstered her courage, but she couldn't stop thinking about her little sister, who wanted to be just like her. And, did she really want to share this experience with the guy she'll eventually marry? Could she live with keeping it a secret?

Staring at herself in the restroom mirror, Virginia concluded that her plan was a mistake. She focused on her bright red lipstick with the suggestive name, grabbed a tissue, and began quickly rubbing it off, as if once removed she could return to her old self.

From his front pocket, the Concert Killer pulled out a small blackjack that belonged to his grandfather, a deputy sheriff from Eureka, CA. It was about six inches long and was comprised of a leather handle and a small oval of iron wrapped in leather. His grandfather used it to knock out pugnacious drunks who refused to go peacefully.

He slid the metal bar, unlocking the door, and exited. A row of eight sinks and mirrors lined the wall opposite the stalls. He planned on using a diversionary tactic so that the groupie wouldn't see him swing the blackjack. But she was so engrossed in working on her lipstick that the ruse wasn't necessary and she never saw it coming. He connected with her right temple and she dropped instantly, bouncing her chin off of the sink. Holding her by the calves, he dragged her to the stall he had used, circled 90 degrees to his left, and pushed her to the toilet, head first. Noticing that her dress was now up to her waist, the Concert Killer pulled it down over her white panties, flipped her over, and adjusted the back of her dress. He then straddled her, grabbed her blond hair, and shoved her face into the toilet with all of his might. She regained consciousness briefly, but the blow weakened her and he had no trouble holding her down until she was dead. He left her facedown in the toilet bowl.

As he exited the stall he wiped down the handle and inside latch bar that he touched before donning the gloves. Another adjustment to her dress was necessary. He removed the gloves, flushed them down a different toilet, using a single knuckle on the handle, and walked out of the restroom. The band started playing another encore song and everyone's attention was directed toward the stage.

Chapter 2

Calvin Dawson is one of the top concert promoters in Southern California. I've known him since the year I graduated from high school. During that ten year period, I considered him a wealth of knowledge on all facets of the music scene. He's in his early 40's but looked five years younger when I last saw him over the summer.

"You sounded very upset on the phone," I said, gesturing to the chair across from my desk.

"Do you mind if I shut the door?"

"No problem."

This seemed like an odd request since my administrative assistant, Jeannine Joshlin, was the only other person in the office, and Calvin knew that she did all of my research.

He sat down and slumped forward. "I have some very disturbing news and I need your help."

"What's going on?"

"Two nights ago a woman was murdered at a concert I promoted in Irvine. The killer left a note taking credit for another three murders that took place at other concert venues in California over the past three months. This is my worst nightmare," he said, and rubbed his face with both hands.

"Do the police have any suspects?"

"No one had a clue that they were related until now. Two were men and two were women. One was strangled, one was shot, one was knifed, and the most recent victim was bludgeoned and drowned in a restroom toilet."

"Were they all in Southern California?" I asked.

"No. The first was in San Francisco, the second in Sacramento, the third in Oakland, and the last one, as I said, was in Irvine."

"I can see how the different MO's would keep the cops from connecting them."

"Not only that, two were killed inside the concert venue and two happened in the parking lot; one before the show, one afterwards, and two during."

"It almost seems like the killer went out of his way to keep the cops from recognizing the link. How did he announce that he was responsible?"

Calvin reached into his pocket and produced a copy of the note that was taped to the restroom stall. "The cops showed it to me yesterday, and I reproduced it as best I could."

I read the note and placed it on my desk. "How can I help you, Calvin?"

"Right now I'm dealing with four different police departments. I was told that a statewide task force has been formed, but I doubt that keeping me in the loop will be a priority for them. I met with my three partners yesterday and we want to hire you to be our liaison with the police. We don't expect you to solve the case. We need to know that everything is being done to protect the safety of our customers."

"If I'm not satisfied that the police are on the right track, do you want me to pursue leads and try to find this guy?"

Calvin replied, "We're in a real bind here, Jason. There's nothing that we'd like more than to see him get caught as soon as possible. We'll pay any travel expenses and won't have a problem with you investigating as long as you keep us up on what's going on."

Over the next ten minutes I copied the business cards of the detectives from each police department as well as

Calvin's contacts within those departments who handle the assignment of police personnel to concert venues.

"Do the police want to keep the link out of the press?" I asked.

"Some think we'd have a better chance of catching the killer if we go public. Others feel it could shut the concert industry down in California and he would just take his show on the road out of state. The L.A. police commissioner said that law enforcement has an obligation to tell concert-goers that they could be in danger if they attend a show. But the consensus is that the cops would have a better chance to nab him if they zero in on his habits, have limited concert offerings in the major venues, and stack these places with undercover cops," Calvin said.

"Who's coordinating the case?"

"For right now it's the Highway Patrol."

"Are they expecting the perp to get a speeding ticket leaving the scene?"

"That was my initial response too. But I found out that they coordinate statewide criminal investigations and have almost 7,000 sworn officers. I told them I was expecting the FBI. Apparently they won't be officially involved until the Concert Killer crosses state lines unless CHP asks for help."

"Is San Diego PD involved?"

"All of the cities with major concert venues have assigned a rep to the CHP's Task Force. I'm not sure who your local guy is, but Lieutenant Dean Casey is running the show from CHP headquarters in Sacramento. You've got a copy of his card."

"What do they think about the perp's headline, *Concerts are Evil*?"

"Most of the cops believe the guy is a major nut case. That helped me sell my colleagues and the police on working with you. They like the idea that you have a couple of degrees in psychology and know the ins and outs of the music business from your years as a club musician. Do *you* have any ideas on the note?"

"Not yet," I said.

Calvin stood up, extended his hand, and with a weak smile said, "By the way, congratulations on having Kelly move in with you. I told Kayleigh and she's dying to meet her."

"I'm sure we'll be seeing a lot more of each other until this guy is caught. We'll have to get them together," I replied, and Calvin departed.

I called Jeannine into my office to get her started on researching the four murders. She was a former client from my two-year career as a mental health counselor. During that time, and for eight years prior, I was the lead singer and rhythm guitarist for a local band. The bassist from my last band, Tsunami Rush, recently told me that he thinks Jeannine looks like Reese Witherspoon. While her Obsessive-Compulsive Disorder severely curtailed her relationship with men for several years, she has been dating Michael Marinangeli, the former lead guitarist from Tsunami Rush, for over a year.

As she entered my office, Jeannine was followed by her German Shepherd puppy, Hoover. I discovered in my first couple of years as a private investigator that the office can occasionally be a dangerous place. I bought the dog for her so that he could be trained to become her guardian while I'm out in the field. I also bought one from the same litter for Kelly.

"I want you to do an Internet search and copy everything that was written on all four murders. Then check the obits and try to get contact info on the victims' family members," I said.

"Why do you need to talk with them?"

"Two reasons. First, I want to find out if any of the vics mentioned being followed in the days prior to the murder. The killer might pick his victims at random when he gets to the shows, or he could be casing the advanced ticket windows and stalking them prior to the concerts."

"That makes sense." Jeannine bent down and picked one of Hoover's hairs off of the carpet. "What's the second reason?"

"I'll be looking for a common thread that might tie the murders together. His note said, 'Concerts are Evil.' I can't help but feel like he's got some kind of agenda. I want to start by gathering as many bits of information as possible. We can sort them out later."

She pinched another dog hair from the carpet as she was getting out of her chair and said "Come, Hoover." She walked back to her desk displaying her usual perfect posture. Hoover walked alongside her, stride for stride with his head held high.

Private investigating is a unique business in many ways. But the one thing it has in common with the rest of the business world is the importance of networking. This is especially true when it comes to interacting with police departments. Having no police contacts in any of the cities where the murders took place put me at a disadvantage. Calvin said the various departments agreed to work with me as the liaison to the major independent concert promoters of California, but that doesn't mean they will share the information I'll need to understand the big picture.

I phoned SDPD homicide detective Walter Shamansky, who worked with me on the two biggest cases of my two-year career. Instead of the normal phone salutation Shamansky asked, "Which band, and what happened?"

"It's not a band this time. I was hired by four California concert promoters to look into the concert killings."

"Why did they pick you? The closest the killer has come to San Diego is Irvine. That's 75 miles from here."

"One of the promoters is an old friend. He told me that CHP put a statewide task force together encompassing all of the cities that have concert venues. I was hoping, after your two recent music industry cases, that the brass picked you be our local rep."

"The luck of the Irish isn't happening today, Duffy. This is the first that I've heard of the task force. I just learned about the killings at roll call this morning," said Shamansky.

"Any chance you could find out who's the local rep and give me an intro?"

"Doing favors sure does work up an appetite." Shamansky is a big fan of a fine dining establishment on La Jolla Boulevard, about a half-mile from my office.

"Does lunch at Larabee's work for you?" I reluctantly asked, knowing I would be parting with a wallet-sized photo of Ulysses S. Grant.

"Tomorrow at noon," he said, and disconnected.

Over the remainder of the day I read everything Jeannine could find on the four murders. Not only had the killer varied his method of murder for each kill, but the victims themselves were extremely dissimilar. They included a banker, a beer vendor, a roadie, and a high school senior dressed like a groupie.

I reached the three detectives assigned to the Northern California murders and arranged to meet with them individually on Wednesday and Thursday. Jeannine took care of the travel and lodging arrangements.

Chapter 3

I spent Tuesday morning listing similarities and differences in the four murders. It was hard to get past the notion that the killer did a brilliant job of making the murders appear unrelated, only to leave a note connecting the dots. Why?

Jeannine spent the morning searching the net for serial killers with constantly changing MOs. She found that while it is uncommon, there are several documented cases. Almost all of those who were captured said they did so to keep the cops from making the connection. One particular sicko said he just wanted to try all of the tools in the toolbox. But he was a big fan of capture and torture, which rules out the copycat possibility for the Concert Killer.

At noon, I ascended the picturesque hillside terrace leading up to Larabee's restaurant, overlooking the Pacific Ocean. Their personable mid-60s hostess greeted me by name and directed me to a window table. Five minutes later, Walter Shamansky walked into the dining room arm-in-arm with the hostess. Despite his 57 years, Shamansky looked like he could go ten rounds with a guy half his age. Maybe it was his shaved head that made me think of a boxer.

"I see you're wearing your court suit and a smile. That's a first," I said.

"It's an afternoon session," he said. "Call me at the end of the day if you want my take on courthouse coddling."

"What's going on with the task force?"

"First things first, Jason. I heard the chef added a couple of new appetizers."

It's best to work around Shamansky's palette when seeking favors and information. Upon arrival, our waitress kissed the top of Shamansky's head and gave him a detailed description of the new menu items. The entire staff is eternally grateful for his work in catching an embezzling partner and saving their business.

After placing our orders Shamansky said, "You're not going to like what I've got for you."

"What is it?"

"The local task force is being headed up by your old friend, Detective Dan Darden."

Darden was forced to transfer out of Metro, the hub of power in the department, after we crossed swords on a recent case.

I said, "I thought he was shuffling papers at a community outpost."

"One of his political connections waved a campaign contribution at the right hack and Darden got recommended for the assignment by the mayor himself."

"Does this mean I'm flying solo on this one?"

"Not entirely. Before coming over here I popped into the captain's office and reminded him that I worked a couple of homicides relating to the music business over the last year," he said.

"What did he say?"

"He tap danced around the political implications to make sure I knew what I was getting into."

"Did he put you on the task force?" I asked.

"No. But he did me one better by assigning me to work with them in an advisory capacity while reporting directly to him. I won't be involved in the day-to-day activities and won't be coordinating with any law enforcement personnel in the other cities. You'll be on your own with them. If we get a vic in San Diego all of that could change. But until then, I wouldn't count on too much."

The Concert Killer thought of himself as a successful businessman. He grew up on a farm in a strict Fundamentalist

Christian home with a loving mother and a father who took a *fire and brimstone* approach to parenting. As a senior in high school he finally rebelled against his father's many rules, and moved out of their house shortly after graduation. His work ethic and knack for writing award-winning scholarship essays helped him to earn a degree in Business Administration. That same work ethic and wordsmith prowess served him well in developing sales skills. It didn't take long for him to achieve financial success.

In spite of the fact that he was killing people, he didn't think of himself as a bad guy. *Concert Killer* had the ominous ring that was needed to instill the desired effect, but he thought of himself simply as CK.

Sitting in front of his laptop, CK read every article he could find on Saturday's murder. He was disappointed that the press didn't reveal his note or the fact that the police were looking for a serial killer. But he planned to provide many more opportunities for the press to make the connection. He opted not to contact them directly because he didn't want to be perceived as a publicity seeker.

Chapter 4

I took an early commuter flight on Wednesday and arrived at SFPD at 9:00 AM, after checking into a downtown hotel. Detective Ike Rappaport met me at the front desk and escorted me to a small interview room.

"We use this room for vics and family members. It doesn't have a two-way mirror," Rappaport said.

"Then what's that?" I pointed to a mirror on the far wall.

"It's just for show so nobody messes with the mug books or does anything stupid while they're left alone."

"What can you tell me about the Delainya Tanner case?"

Rappaport ran a hand through his thick brown hair with a few flecks of gray. He actually had more gray in his eyebrows than on his head, which I found very unusual.

"She was found in the parking lot near the stage entrance. The coroner approximated the time of death at one hour after the concert. The maintenance staff was cleaning up the lot when a custodian spotted her three hours after the show."

"Was she out in the open?"

"She was in an empty parking space between a car and an SUV. A pickup truck was parked behind her, so the body wasn't in plain view."

"Why were all of those cars still there three hours after the show?"

"She was near the stage entrance. That's where the employees park. They were still cleaning up, counting money, and taking down the stage."

"I read The Examiner's account of the crime. What else can you tell me?"

Rappaport rubbed his prominent chin and slid his hand down his throat. "The ligature marks on her neck made it clear that she was strangled by a man. I was floored when I got the word that it was the work of a serial killer. It felt like a crime of passion to me."

"Who did you look at?"

"The family told us about a boyfriend, but he came up clean."

"Was he at the concert?"

"No, he worked late that night. A coworker corroborated his story."

"What was your theory before the serial news broke?"

Rappaport said, "Delainya Tanner worked her way from bank teller to assistant loan officer in three years. That's pretty fast track for her bank. When we found her, she was dressed in an outfit that didn't look like anything a loan officer would wear. I got the feeling she was dressed by the killer after the fact."

"So you thought it was somebody she worked with at the bank?"

"It wouldn't be the first time a pretty young girl slept her way up the ladder."

"Was there anything else that supported that theory?" I asked.

"The coroner found some light bruising around her crotch. He called it signs of heavy-handed foreplay."

"Maybe the boyfriend likes it a little rough."

"He claims they hadn't had sex for a week. Apparently, he cancelled a vacation because of a work-related matter, and she had been holding out on him ever since."

"Do you think there's any chance the domestic squabble escalated?" I asked.

"The boyfriend is your classic Type A workaholic. I'd say that relief from stud duties *was* his vacation." Rappaport's serious expression never changed.

"I don't quite see where you're going with your theory, Rappaport. Are you saying you think her boss from the bank choked her in the parking lot?"

"The boss who signed off on her promotion has an alibi. But help can come from a lot of sources. There's also the possibility that she facilitated a loan that she shouldn't have. Or, maybe she was having an affair with someone at a higher level than her boss. My theory was that she broke some bad news to the perp after the concert and he didn't take it well."

"OK, I can see how you got there. What are your thoughts now that the serial killer posted his note?"

"I'm thinking she was still cheating on her boyfriend. But it could have been a case of being in the wrong place at the wrong time. Maybe she and her lover go back to his vehicle for a little backseat boogaloo. When they're done, as she's walking back to her car, the perp strangles her and drops her behind the pickup truck."

"Why wait for an hour after the show? I'd think opportunities would be pretty slim at that hour."

"It was his first kill. By that point there weren't a lot of witnesses around. If the right circumstances presented themselves he could do it with little chance of getting caught. If not, there were plenty of other concerts over the summer," Rappaport replied.

I needed to kill a few hours before meeting with the primary investigator for Murder #3 in Oakland, and returned to my hotel. After entering notes on my interview with Rappaport, I reread the newspaper articles on victim #3, Daryl Harris, and formulated questions for Oakland Detective, Maurice Johnson. I tried my best not to prejudge any conclusions before meeting with the detective, but the contrast between the two cases weas glaring. The only commonality that I could spot was that they both took place at a concert venue, and they were both supposedly committed by the same perp.

It took just over a half-hour to get from the hotel to Johnson's stationhouse in Oakland. Maurice Johnson was a 6'2", 200 lb. African-American detective working in the environment that spawned the Oakland Raiders. I expected a tough as nails, no nonsense, streetwise, throwback to the 60s with a bronzed rubber hose mounted to his cubicle wall. Instead, I met a *Don't Worry, Be Happy*, dreadlock-wearing, casual dude with the smile of a stoner. If he owned a rubber hose it was probably attached to a hookah.

After the self-introductions I asked, "Are you working undercover?"

"I used to work narco a few years back, but I've been in homicide for the past four years." Noticing my expression he added, "I guess you're wondering about my Rastafarian look."

"It's not quite what I expected."

"I tell the brass that it puts the bad guys off their guard. But actually, Oakland Homicide is a very high stress assignment. Half of the department is on the Maalox and martini diet. I choose to surround myself with natural stress reducers, like healthy food and the music of the Marley family."

"I played in a band for 10 years before becoming a PI. I think you've got a terrific approach. What can you tell me about Daryl Harris?"

"Dare me?" he asked.

"OK, I dare you to tell me about Daryl Harris," I said, wondering if I had jumped to conclusions about Johnson's approach.

Johnson grinned and replied, "That's his nickname, Daryl "Dare Me" Harris. He was a part-time roadie, part-time

L.A. club bouncer. I've been working with Detective Celia Bains of LAPD, who said Dare Me tossed rowdy drunks out of a hardcore club on a nightly basis. Apparently, Dare Me was well-known for his combative nature."

"I assume it was his roadie job that brought him to Oakland."

"He worked for the hardcore band Flex-N-UR Face. They were the warm-up act the night he was killed."

"I read all of The Tribune's articles on the murder. What can you tell me that didn't make the papers?"

Johnson replied, "I thought you were the liaison for the promoters. What do you need that for?"

"As far as I can see, I'm the only one in the field right now pulling these bits of information together. I'm planning on meeting with the head of the task force tomorrow. I expect that he'll want the cooperation of the promoters in canceling scheduled shows to narrow the number of possible targets. The more I know about how this guy operates, the more likely it is that we'll pick the right venue to catch him."

"Duffy, you seem like a decent guy, but then so do half of the perps I bust. How do I know that if I give you this info it's not going to wind up in some sensational rock station concert promotion?"

"You could call Detective Shamansky of SDPD. I worked with him on the Terry Tucker murder last year."

"Hang on a minute." Instead of picking up the phone he turned to his computer and browsed for over five minutes. "The Union-Tribune says you were responsible for busting the bad guys on that one."

"Shamansky played a big part in that case. I've got his number in my phone," I said, and flipped it open.

"That won't be necessary. Here's what went down. Harris was the only roadie for his band. When the Flex set was over, the headliner's backline techs helped Harris clear the stage. They just tossed everything into the Flex truck for Harris to sort and secure later. Harris drove the truck off of the loading dock, parked it in the lot, locked up, and helped the stagehands set up for the headliner."

"Harris hung out with some of the backline techs until the band started playing an ear-splitting opening number. He then returned to his truck. It looked like he was in the process of opening the padlock on the back door when the perp shot him in the eye from just a few inches. The coroner dug out a .41 caliber bullet, probably from a derringer, which wasn't recovered."

"Were you surprised by the serial killer's note?" I asked.

"Bains and I thought the motive was revenge. We figured it was one of the guys he beat up bouncing at the L.A. club. A lot of people in the club knew about his gig with Flex-N-UR Face. We thought the perp picked an out-of-town show to divert suspicion. For the last three weeks Bains has been running down leads on guys that got bounced shortly before the murder."

"Once you found out it was part of a serial case, did you look to see if the perp took a souvenir?"

Maurice replied, "I thought of that and reviewed his personal effects. The band members already told me he didn't wear any jewelry, except a skull ring and a Casio watch. They were both still on the body. I sent his wallet down to Bains, who is going to bring it to his brother to check out. They were pretty tight."

"Where does the investigation go from here?"

"Before the big news broke, me and Bains were looking at a meth-dealing biker named Jimmy DeLong. We know that he left L.A. the day of the murder and didn't return until the following day."

"Did you check his alibi for last Saturday night?"

"Bains is working on it. But even if he was in lock-up the nights of the other murders, we're still going to follow up. Just because a perp takes credit and photocopies some news headlines doesn't mean it's a sure thing he popped all four of them."

I considered going to Fisherman's Wharf for dinner, but Johnson's speculation that the Irvine perp may have confessed to crimes he didn't commit meant I needed to do some extensive work on this puzzle. I opted for a family restaurant where I'd have plenty of room to spread out my file folder. I reread the accounts of murders two and four as I waited for my meal. If I were in Johnson's shoes I wouldn't be inclined to abandon my working theory and prime suspect based solely on the word of a guy who was probably trying to mislead the police.

During dinner I focused on how Johnson's theory might fly with the task force leader, Dean Casey, whom I would be meeting tomorrow afternoon. In my two years as an investigator, I had yet to work a case in conjunction with the Highway Patrol. I kept thinking about watching reruns of the TV show CHIPS with my dad when I was in junior high. I expected that Dean Casey would be nothing like Eric Estrada.

Chapter 5

I arrived at Sacramento PD barely in time for my 10:00 AM meeting with Detective Harry Lutz. Ten minutes after I checked in with the sergeant at the front desk a muscular man in a charcoal suit walked up to me.

"You must be Duffy. I'm Harry Lutz," he said in a surprisingly congenial voice.

He escorted me to the detectives coffee room, poured two cups, set a bowl of sugar packets and powdered non-dairy creamer in front of me, and asked, "How much do you know already?"

"I read that the vic ran a beer concession for the past five years. He was a family guy with no known enemies. The promoter told me his throat was slit from behind and you managed to find the knife," I said.

"That's pretty much it in a nutshell."

"Can we expand on the nutshell version? I can't picture how a beer vendor gets his throat slit during a show, and nobody sees anything."

"He had a girl who worked with him. The featured band just started playing its second song when one of the kegs ran out. The vic, Brian Winslow, unhooked the dry keg and carried it to his truck behind the concession stands. When he set the keg down to open the truck, the perp knifed him," Lutz said.

"Did it look like he took any souvenirs?"

"No, but he did something we kept out of the papers that was pretty unusual."

"What's that?" I asked.

"He cleaned his knife on the back of the vic's shirt."

"What did it look like?"

"He made an X," Lutz said, "like he was cleaning one side at a time."

"Where did you find the knife?"

"He threw it down a Porta-Potty."

"What made you look in there?"

Lutz replied, "The entrance to where the vic parked his truck was visible from the last two Porta-Potties. I thought we might be able to get a witness who saw the perp come out from behind the concession stands. So I asked the other vendors if they remembered anything that stood out about the people standing in line for the toilets. Two of them said there wasn't anybody over there after the main act hit the stage."

"You thought it might be a good place to get rid of the weapon before walking past security at the exit," I surmised.

"Exactly. So I had them strained and we got it."

"Was there anything unusual about it?"

"It's probably the most common hunting knife on the market. I think every Wal-Mart in the country stocks them."

"I don't suppose you found any prints or partials."

"Forensics found a little bit of blood at the hilt, but other than that they didn't find shit." Lutz paused and smiled. "Bad choice of words. They actually found plenty of that, but no usable trace."

"Were you able to get any footprints from the scene?"

"No. It was a gravel road and it hasn't rained up here in months. The sprinkler system keeps the lawn looking great, but it doesn't run behind the concession stands."

"What do you know about the vic?"

"Like you said before, he's a family guy. No known enemies. One of the female cops interviewed the girl who worked with him in the booth. She was pretty cute. I thought maybe a jealous boyfriend could be involved if they were having an affair. But she said he talked mainly business and occasionally about his son's Pop Warner football team. She was broken up about him, but also concerned about finding another job."

"One last question: Were you surprised when you found out we were dealing with a serial killer?"

"Not at all. In fact, I speculated about that possibility with my lieutenant over a month ago when I couldn't find even a hint of a motive. The vic had $200 in his wallet that wasn't touched. To be honest with you Duffy, it was a relief when the news broke about the serial killer."

At 2:00 PM, I was escorted into the office of Dean Casey at CHP headquarters. Casey was in his sixties with snow-white hair, a ruddy complexion, and a curdled milk look on his face. The office décor suggested that our tax dollars were certainly not wasted on creature comforts at this locale.

"Thanks for seeing me on such short notice," I said. "I'm sure you've been swamped."

"Is it your vast experience at working serial cases that tells you how busy I've been?" he asked. One white caterpillar eyebrow arched while the other one dropped and narrowed.

"I met with Detectives Rappaport, Johnson, and Lutz since yesterday morning and I'm finding a lot of conflicting information."

"Are those detectives planning on coordinating concert schedules with you? Because, as far as I'm concerned, the extent of your involvement in this case is restricted to helping the police limit the number of concerts until the killer is found. Do we understand each other?" Casey asked.

I was obviously talking to a bureaucrat with a two-by-four up his ass, looking to minimize my role. "I'll be glad to help out in that capacity. But I was also employed to do whatever I can to help put this guy away as soon as possible."

"You're not a sworn officer, Mr. Duffy," he said, folding his hands on the desk. "As such, I consider anything you do above and beyond the purview of acting in the role of concert liaison as interfering with a police investigation. Do I make myself clear?"

I'm normally a firm believer in the notion that you can catch more flies with honey than you can with vinegar. But, when the honey becomes little more than a gooey mess, sometimes you just have to get out the fly swatter, take a couple of swings, and hope for the best.

"Lt. Casey, as a sworn officer isn't it your duty to uphold the laws of California as defined by the legislature?"

"What's your point?"

"The laws relating to a citizen or company's right to hire a licensed private investigator is one of the laws of the land that you were sworn to uphold, is it not?" I asked, without the smug expression I was repressing.

"I don't like you or your kind, Duffy. You waste valuable resources, tip perps through the press, and are generally a pain in my ass. You are correct. You do have the right to ask questions. Just as *I* have the right to not waste *my* time by answering them. I also have the right to share my feelings on the subject with the other members of the task force," he said, and stood up.

I remained seated. "To catch this guy as soon as possible you need the concert promoters to limit your targets so that you can get adequate coverage at those venues. Do you really think the best way to gain their cooperation is to blow off their representative?"

He replied, "I have a sneaking suspicion that their priority is to lose as little money as possible and not the stroking of your ego. Right now we're keeping the serial connection out of the press in exchange for the promoters' cooperation in limiting shows. If I decide that the promoters aren't cooperating to my satisfaction, I have options. I could call a press conference this afternoon and tell the public to stay away from all concerts unless they want a slit throat, a wrung neck, a bullet hole in the eye, or to get drown in a fucking toilet! Now, get the hell out of my office and don't come back!"

Mounted on the wall behind Casey's desk was a plaque with the CHP motto, *Safety, Service, Security.* I stood up and pointed at the plaque.

"You may want to get your triple S motto updated. It feels more like two S's will do the trick in here." Achtung, Herr Casey.

Chapter 6

It was a very productive day for CK. Business was going well and the upcoming concert schedule was looking very promising. Another soul would lay claim to martyrdom before the pagan holiday of Halloween.

He was currently in a suite at a five-star resort in Pasadena that represented the finest of luxury accommodations in the North L.A. area. CK realized that most commoners would believe that such a display of opulence would be equated to the excesses of the Patricians that Jesus drove out of the temple. He believed that wealth was God's way of rewarding His favorites. CK's female minister was his lighthouse on a raging sea when he first moved into the city. Her sermons inspired him to embrace creature comforts as an affirmation of God's love. Of course his father would consider this way of thinking to be nothing short of heresy. But CK was his own man. He no longer cow-towed to his father's fundamentalist ways.

CK carried one of the straight-back chairs from the dining area to the balcony entrance and set it sideways so that the beautiful view of L.A. could be seen over the seat. He reached into his wallet and removed a crisp new dollar bill. He folded the bill in half, and positioned the halves at a 90 degree angle on the chair so that the Eye of Providence, atop the pyramid in The Great Seal, faced him as he knelt before it. He read aloud the Latin words below the pyramid, "Novus Ordo Seclorum," then translated it to, "New Order of the Ages." There was indeed a new world order. It did not include outmoded ideas and archaic values. He believed that if the meek will indeed inherit the earth it won't be until it's as used up as a post-menopausal harlot. It was unfortunate that his father clung to manmade church laws that only served to hinder the new world order.

The sins of his father disappeared, as did the vista of L.A., as CK focused on the eye at the top of the pyramid. His hands separated from the praying position and extended outward as he emptied his mind to receive God's grace. His posture corrected to a perfect position and his breathing became slow and deep. His eyes wanted to close, and narrowed to slits, but they never strayed from the Eye of Providence. After ten minutes he lay prostrate in front of the Eye and wept into the carpet. He did not weep for his sins. He did not weep for his victims. He wept for all of God's children who failed to find their way into His state of grace in spite of the multitude of signposts put in their paths on a daily basis. Music was the devil's portal into the souls of the young and impressionable.

CK walked to the marble table beside his bed, picked up a book, placed it on the wide balcony railing, spread his arms, and began reading aloud from the profit Nahum.

"The Lord will take vengeance on his adversaries, and he reserveth wrath for his enemies. The Lord is slow to anger, and great in power, and will not at all acquit the wicked."

Chapter 7

I sat at my kitchen table on Friday morning enjoying breakfast as I brainstormed questions to ask Detective Michele Ko of Irvine PD. Jeannine tried setting up a morning meeting, but the best Ko could do was to see me at 1:30. I was hoping Lt. Casey hadn't informed her of my leper status as yet.

"How do I look?" Kelly asked, breezing into the kitchen wearing a short skirt that matched her chestnut hair. "Today's the field trip to Scripps Aquarium."

"You better stay away from the shark tank. If they get a look at those legs they might go into a frenzy and traumatize your second graders."

"Ha, ha," she replied. "I forgot to tell you last night, I invited your parents over for dinner tomorrow night."

"Then I expect you to handle all of the repercussions that go along with the invitation."

"Don't worry, I'm cooking and I'm sure your mom will help with the clean-up."

"That's not what I'm talking about," I said. "The last time they were over I got inundated with decorating, home improvement, and gardening suggestions from Mom."

"I'll be glad to have those conversations with her." Kelly walked over, bent down, and gave me a kiss goodbye. "I'm stopping at the store on the way home tonight. What would you like for dinner?"

Holding the hem of her miniskirt between my thumb and forefinger I replied, "How about a couple of shark steaks?"

She slapped my hand and said, "Bottom-feeders," before walking away.

I was in the middle of briefing Jeannine on the highlights of my trip and assigning corresponding research projects, when Detective Johnson called.

"I gave you a lot of info on Wednesday and I need something in return."

"What can I do for you?" I asked.

"Bains just found out that our biker suspect used to work for your employer, CLAM Concert Promotions. Actually, that's not true. He worked for the L in CLAM, Lonnie Cancelli, before they formed their partnership."

"What would you like to know?"

"I want to find out what kind of work he did. If he was on the security staff, are they still wearing the same shirts? And, were there any of his old coworkers on payroll the night of the murder?"

"I'd like answers to those questions myself. How did Bains discover that DeLong worked for Lonnie?"

"She has a fine looking biker cousin who knows Jimmy from one of her favorite bars. He's been a busy guy lately, recruiting his own little band of buffalo soldiers. The cousin said that she interrupted a business meeting when she visited his table, and everybody shut up, which was very out of character for Jimmy."

"I'll call you as soon as I get some answers," I said, and hung up.

Jeannine asked, "Anything important?"

"Absolutely," I replied. "Detective Johnson didn't say a word about Lt. Casey telling him to freeze me out. So I'm guessing my meeting with Detective Ko is still a go."

I called Calvin to see what he could learn about DeLong, but settled for leaving a message.

When I arrived at Irvine PD, Michele Ko led us to an interrogation room without offering coffee or casual conversation. She was in her early 40s with ink-black hair cut just above her shoulders, and she looked very worried.

"First, I need to know if you are friends with Chief Considine," she said.

"I never met the man. Is there a reason that I should know him?"

"I'm under the microscope on this one. The chief didn't like the idea that I made detective and he wants me out. That's why I got this case dumped in my lap. As soon as something goes wrong, I will be blamed as the one who screwed up."

"How long have you been a detective?"

"Since the end of June. I'll bet you think I am too inexperienced to handle this case. Well let me tell you something—"

I held up my right hand. "I'm 28-years-old and I deal with that kind of shit all of the time. Does your chief have something against Koreans?"

"I think it's more like the good old boys don't like being told they have to induct a female into their little fraternity."

I thought that Irvine was much too large of a city to just now be getting around to promoting women into the detective ranks. But I wasn't about to start an argument.

"Detective Ko, I met with the detectives working the Concert Killer case in San Francisco, Oakland, and Sacramento. I have a pretty good feel for where they're at in their investigations. I'll be glad to share what I've got with you."

"Why?"

"I believe that the more we cooperate the sooner this guy gets taken down."

Over the next hour I laid out what I had learned so far. Of course, I skipped the part about Dean Casey wanting to minimize my role, but was otherwise very forthcoming. When I finished, I asked what bits of information her department withheld from the newspapers.

"We found a funny looking partial print on the toilet in the stall next to where we found the victim. Forensics thinks he flushed the gloves and used a knuckle on the handle."

"I don't suppose there's any kind of database for knuckle prints."

"No, but if we get it narrowed down to a few suspects it could be very helpful."

"Did you find anything else, Michele?"

She took a deep breath and turned away. "I think that's all I can say at this time."

"C'mon, Michele. I gave you everything I know."

"The chief told me not to tell anyone. This is the kind of thing he could hang me out to dry on if he found out I disobeyed his orders."

"How's he going to find out? I'm certainly not going to tell anyone."

Michele glanced briefly at the mirror on the wall of the interrogation room and said, "Be sure to keep me posted on any new developments." As she stood she added, "Why don't you give me one of your business cards. If I don't hear from you in the next couple of days I'll call to see what you've learned."

It seemed strange that she suddenly got paranoid about what she said in front of the mirror, especially after saying that her chief was setting her up to fail. I opted to tread lightly, gave her the card, and respected her silence as she led me out the front door of the stationhouse. She looked like she was going to say something when we got outside, but then glanced back over her shoulder at the desk sergeant, shook my hand, and quickly walked back into the building.

I got as far as the nuclear power plant at San Onofre when my phone rang. Without identifying herself, Michele said, "In the stall with the knuckle print, Forensics also found a hair from a brown wig. Don't tell anybody." She hung up before I could reply.

At 4:30 PM, I was reviewing an Orange Country Register article on murder #4 when Calvin returned my call.

"Where are you at with the case?" he asked.

I spent the next half-hour summarizing the five meetings. I skipped the part about Detective Ko's political uncertainty within the department. I don't like asking friends to keep secrets, especially from their business partners who have a major stake in everything relating to the investigation. If, for example, Lonnie were to call Irvine PD and request a more experienced investigator be assigned to the case, I could end up getting shut out by all of the assigned detectives and task force members without the help of Dean Casey.

"Kayleigh and I are hosting a little backyard barbecue on Sunday afternoon. The other three partners in CLAM will be there and I was hoping you and Kelly could make it," Calvin said.

"I'll have to check with the social activities director. But barring another commitment, we'd love to attend."

"Good. Kayleigh has been giving me hell for not introducing her to the woman who got you to settle down."

"I'm not married yet, bro," I replied.

"We're getting started at 2:00 PM. You've been up to my place in Rancho Palos Verdes. Do you remember the directions?"

"All the way to the mail box with the wah-wah pedal on top. How could I forget?"

"One minor request. I'll brief the partners on what you told me today. If there are any new developments feel free to tell them individually, but we're keeping the grisly details from the significant others as much as possible," Calvin said.

"I understand. While you're talking with the partners be sure to ask Lonnie to get me everything he has on Jimmy DeLong. I'm swimming upstream with this CHIPPER who's in charge of the task force. If I come through for Johnson in Oakland it could go a long way toward building a relationship with the other detectives. I'll see you on Sunday."

Chapter 8

Shortly after I graduated from high school I was recruited to play in a band that was the brainchild of lead guitarist, Michael Marinangeli. As a huge Eric Clapton fan, Michael loved the idea of how the bands "Blind Faith" and "Cream" were super-groups comprised of the best of the best. He selected three teenage San Diego musicians, all recent grads playing in different bands, to form a local super-group heading into our college years. That's how Tsunami Rush was born.

We played together for almost eight years. It was a lot of fun for most of that time. But later our enthusiasm waned when we came to the realization that none of us possessed a talent for composing music. Always running with other people's ideas didn't appeal to me. When I initiated the break-up, our drummer told me he was about to do the same thing, and our bass player revealed that the band was keeping his girlfriend from accepting his marriage proposal. Michael continued on with other groups until he finally made it with the headliner, Doberman's Stub. He's also been Jeannine's boyfriend for over a year.

When I tried to compose music, I would look for a place inside of myself where that spark of originality was conceived. I'd look for those two chords that became three and four. I tried writing poems that would fuse with the music to combine like an egg and sperm, giving life to original masterpieces. It never happened. Sure I wrote songs; probably more than 100 over the years. But I never felt that any of them would take off. I wasn't compelled to call the rest of the band members and insist that we practice immediately so that we could polish our first big hit.

When I became an investigator all of that changed. As early as the start of my apprenticeship program, I began to come up with theories that were completely original in terms of deductive reasoning. I discovered that I could think like a criminal, attributing that skill to endless hours of watching prime-time cop dramas with my SDPD detective father. It was about the only thing we had in common. Dad hated the fact that I played in a rock band. Almost all of our conversations ended in fights unless we were speculating on a whodunit. Mom would occasionally join us on those days where the beginning of each commercial break was like the bell to start a three-minute round of verbal boxing. I'm not quite sure if Mom was a master of misdirection or if my father realized how much our fighting was upsetting her, and played along out of love and respect.

I didn't ask Jeannine to come into the office on Saturday morning. I needed quiet time to process all of the information I gathered and open my mind to theories that would dictate how I'd proceed with the case. After reading my notes from the detective interviews, I began pacing from room to room. Something was brewing and I needed more room to think it through.

I left the office and walked north on La Jolla Boulevard until I could cut down to the scenic walk along the beach. Looking out over the rocks and sand just south of La Jolla Cove, I tried to reconcile some very incongruous facts. Not only were all of the MOs different, but two of the detectives couldn't believe the murders were committed by a serial killer and two accepted it as a very logical conclusion.

The words on the killer's note, "Concerts are Evil," kept flashing in my mind. I sat on a bench overlooking a group of surfers waiting for a wave in relatively still waters. Suddenly, an idea hit like a giant wave coming out of nowhere. What if the killings were done by different members of a religious cult with a common purpose? It would explain the different MOs, the different locations, and especially the "Concerts are Evil" headline.

I walked back to the office at a very brisk pace. Should I call Dean Casey and show him the kind of value I could bring to the investigation, or would he dismiss the theory simply because it was mine. It was almost noon and the sun was burning off the coastal haze. Approaching an intersection near my office, I spotted Jeannine cleaning up after Hoover. She lives in an apartment less than a block from the agency.

"Jeannine, are you up for earning some overtime this afternoon?"

"What's going on?"

"I need research on religious cults that don't like rock music," I said.

"How about if I run home, eat my lunch, and meet you in about 45 minutes?"

"You're the best, Jeannine."

Hoover barked once and wagged his tail.

Mom and Dad arrived for dinner at 7:00 PM. I told Kelly that I needed some alone time with Dad and felt the best time to do so was as soon as Mom uttered the words *Home Improvement Network.*

Unfortunately, she did so before I could get everyone situated on the couch with a cocktail. Kelly opened her mouth to dutifully play her part, but heard the timer go off in the kitchen before she could speak.

"I've got to get that," Kelly said.

"Do you need any help, dear?" Mom asked.

"I'd love it, Molly" she replied, and all was right with the world.

"Dad, did you ever work on a task force headed up by CHP?" I asked.

"A few times. They usually hold down the fort until the FBI takes over."

"Did you have any problems with the CHIPPERS?"

"I worked about six of those cases. Twice CHP ran the case from beginning to end and there were no problems. But the other four times it was nothing but trouble. It was like having a substitute teacher in high school. They felt like they weren't getting the respect that they deserved because the cases had FBI written all over them, and every cop in the stationhouse knew it."

"Aren't they supposed to do everything they can until the case is taken over?"

"Being a lifetime member of the law enforcement community I hate to admit it, but there can be a lot of animosity between different agencies. It doesn't help that most FBI field agents are usually dismissive of the hard work done by the departments they just scooped. Some guys have thick skins after getting burned multiple times. I take it you're running into one of those problems," Dad said.

"I got major attitude from a Lt. Dean Casey in Sacramento a couple of days ago."

"Tell me about your case."

Before I could do so, Kelly and Mom came out of the kitchen carrying steaming trays, and Kelly announced, "Dinner is served."

Remembering Calvin's request to keep the significant others away from the details, I initiated a conversation about Kelly's class field trip to Scripps Aquarium. Dad was decidedly more interested in the Yankee pot roast than the story, but Mom hung on Kelly's every word. I hoped Mom had finally run out of stories about my 2nd grade experience, and was momentarily relieved when she started out saying, "When Jason was in 3rd Grade." But then she went on to tell about the day I ripped the seat of my pants on the playground, told my teacher when I got back into class, and suffered the indignity of having her probe the gaping hole while my classmates laughed.

"You poor dear," Kelly said, patting my forearm.

I glanced at Dad to see if I could get some guy support. But after sticking his foot in his mouth about my relationship with Kelly over the summer, he gave a look that said: *You're on your own, son.*

I said, "I was a trend-setter. After that, showing maximum boxer shorts became all the rage." This got both women carping all the way through dessert without further embarrassment.

When dinner was finished Kelly looked out over the dining room table and said, "The girls did all of the cooking and set up."

To his credit, Dad replied, "Just before we sat down, Jason started asking me about the case he's working. If you two wouldn't mind, I'd like to pick it up where we left off."

"Come on, Kelly. I'll tell you a story that will make the ripped pants seem like a fond memory," Mom said with a big smile.

"Do tell," Kelly said, lifting a serving platter from the table and carrying it into the kitchen.

I grabbed a couple of beers and we walked out to the backyard.

Dad said, "With a name like Dean Casey I wouldn't be surprised if one of my friends knows the guy."

"Are you saying the long arm of the Irish Mafia reaches all the way into the CHIPPERS?"

"If you keep using that term my network of contacts isn't going to reach anywhere for you, buddy-boy."

I hadn't been buddy-boyed in almost five years. "Sorry Dad. I couldn't agree more. It's terrific to have lots of friends."

"I'll ask around and see if anybody knows him."

CK's lower lip was sore after intentionally losing a round of golf at the Riviera Country Club to a prospective client with a 20 handicap. His prayers for patience and humility were answered over dinner when he signed a contract that put him over the top on his quarterly business goal.

It was barely 9:00 PM and CK felt it was the perfect opportunity to scout concert venues. No martyrs would be offered up this evening. Tonight was a time to plan. Since his hotel was near the Rose Bowl, that was his first stop. Although he visited the stadium on one prior occasion, he never studied it with his new purpose in mind. Upon arrival, he parked his car and checked out the entry and exit points. He hoped there would be some type of scheduled activity so that he could get a look at the interior, but the facility was closed.

Then an idea occurred to him. He took out his iPhone and learned that USC was playing a football game at the Coliseum. CK arrived shortly before the game ended.

After most of the fans departed he made his way into the seating area and took a leisurely tour of the facilities. Twice he was stopped by staff members, and explained that a credit card fell out of his pocket while paying a vendor. Both were fine with allowing him to continue his search.

As thrilled as he was to have such fine access, CK found the Coliseum to have too many disadvantages. The building was very old and had narrow walkways. It also had too many blind spots where security or police could pop out at any moment. In addition, it held over 90,000 people. The kinds of bands that would be booked into a facility this size would undoubtedly make for very few alone moments with potential martyrs. In addition, with USC across the street there would be a lot of witnesses continuing to party in the parking lot, as they were doing right now. Then there was L.A. traffic to lend further complications. Even though CK considered L.A. to be badly in need of a demonstration of God's ability to smite sinners, and where better than a facility named after an ancient hub of martyrdom, He certainly didn't want His instrument on earth to be imperiled in the process.

Chapter 9

On Sunday morning, Kelly asked if we could leave for Calvin's barbecue a half-hour early. When I asked why, she simply said she wanted to show me an interesting place along the way and that it was a surprise.

Jeannine had enthusiastically agreed to dog-sit for the afternoon. She was very interested in seeing the pups from the same litter keep up their familial relationship.

Kelly wanted to give our puppy a cute name, while I pushed for an intimidating moniker that would convey the serious job he was expected to perform. I thought Saber was a fine name, but Kelly hated it. I suggested we compromise with a name that honored the breed and its German roots, while also recognizing the dog's American home. Kelly began calling him Colonel Hogan, and it stuck.

When I advised Jeannine on how to pick an appropriate name, I stressed the fact that the dog was to be her protector, someone she relied on every day to keep her safe and secure. In retrospect, I can understand how an Obsessive-Compulsive person could attribute those qualities to the name Hoover. I immediately regretted my response when Jeannine asked what I thought of the name. I never should have said, "It sucks," especially while sitting next to Kelly in her sturdiest pair of high heels.

After dropping Colonel Hogan off, I selected an MP3 mix on the stereo that I knew Kelly would enjoy, and considered what could be accomplished talking with Calvin's partners.

"How did you come to be friends with Calvin?" Kelly asked.

"A few months after Tsunami Rush formed, Calvin started booking us as the warm-up band for concerts in San Diego."

"Your friendship seems like more than a business relationship."

"To me, Calvin represents what's right with the concert industry. He volunteers for charity events. He fights against unaffordable ticket prices. And, he brings shows to small cities that are usually ignored by the corporate promoters," I said. "He's also a good listener, and gives good advice."

When we transitioned from Interstate 5 North to the 405, my focus switched to Kelly's surprise. Her evasiveness led me to believe it would be a mildly unpleasant experience, such as an antique store, or possibly an exhibit of 2nd grade art through the ages. Whatever it was, I felt I could suck it up for a half-hour. WRONG! A weekend-long chick flick marathon would have been preferable to this surprise.

She directed me to The Wayfarer's Chapel, also known as The Glass Chapel, located about three miles from Calvin's house. It's actually a beautiful structure, designed by Frank Lloyd Wright's son, Lloyd. It was built in the middle of a grove of redwood trees and featured a spectacular view of the Pacific from its front steps. It seemed that everywhere we turned we saw beautiful vistas and horrifying brochures describing it as the perfect venue for a wedding. For a guy who just moved his girlfriend into his home two months ago, it was a runaway train and I was feeling tied to the railroad tracks.

I did my best to focus the conversation on everything but weddings. My knowledge of architecture was tapped out after a couple of minutes. I mentally zipped through the Simon & Garfunkel song *So Long Frank Lloyd Wright* hoping to glean a conversational side-trip. But the best I could come up with was to ask her if she thought Frank's son, Lloyd, was a middle child. I took a picture of Kelly hugging a redwood.

If worst came to worst I could email it to a Greenpeace recruiter and hope for the best. It's not that I don't love Kelly. Actually, I'm crazy about her. It's more that I'm still feeling like my father forced us onto the runaway train in the first place, and I like doing things on my own terms. Fortunately, she let me talk her out of a walk through the gift shop.

Calvin's house was as breathtaking as the Glass Chapel. It's nestled into a steep hill overlooking the Pacific, with a clear view of Catalina Island. Kayleigh answered the door and scored a lot of points by not implying that Kelly had finally gotten the playboy of the western world to settle down. They hit it off immediately and Kelly was quickly whisked away for the grand tour while I showed myself to the back deck where the party was underway.

Calvin stood talking to a petite woman in her mid-20s in front of my favorite swimming pool in the world. It's shaped like the neck of a bass guitar, with four thick black lines creating five swimming lanes, spanning about 50 feet. Thin black lines intersected the lanes to resemble a guitar's fret board, and circular abalone inlays dotted the third, fifth, seventh, and ninth frets. The double dots at the twelfth fret marked the far end of the pool. The head of the guitar was a combination spa and underwater bar, with four underwater barstools in the alcoves outlining the guitar keys. Three feet above the spa was a redwood deck that was just high enough the see out over the Plexiglas that sheltered the pool from the coastal breeze.

"Jason, I want you to meet Ashley Talbot," Calvin said, and we shook hands. "Ashley is a partner and the A in CLAM."

She said, "Calvin told us about how you solved the Terry Tucker murder case."

"With a lot of help from my friends," I said, laying my hand on Calvin's shoulder. "Were you into Terry's music?"

"I mainly handle emo, soft rock, and acoustic solo acts," she said, brushing her dark bangs away from her eyes.

Calvin said, "If you read Rolling Stone's recent article on artists that actively support the Green Movement you have a good idea of the bands Ashley promotes."

"I take it you're committed to the cause," I said.

"Aren't you?" she asked. "It needs to be everyone's responsibility if you really care about what your children and grandchildren will inherit."

I replied, "You're preaching to the choir, Ashley. Right now, I have a bucket in my shower to catch the runoff. I use the reclaimed water to fill my toilet tank." I didn't tell her that the bucket went in only after the faucet started leaking and I never got around to fixing it.

"Good for you, Jason. I'll have to start doing that myself. What a great idea," she said.

Calvin said, "I'm going to introduce Jason to Mark. Will you excuse us?"

Walking toward the deck I asked, "Isn't she a little young to be in your line of work?"

"She has an MBA from Wharton, and a daddy who's very rich and very well connected in the business world."

"Does daddy have any nasty enemies?"

"I don't know. Why do you ask?"

"That's what I do now, Calvin. I ask questions. Most of the answers I get aren't worth a floor full of ticket stubs, but every now and then I find a backstage pass that makes it all worthwhile."

"There's Mark over on the deck. His forte is Christian rock, so mind your manners."

Calvin made the introductions and excused himself to attend to hosting duties. Mark was tall with a slender build, light skin, and spoke softly with a mid-western accent.

"I certainly wish we were meeting under different circumstances, Jason," he said.

"I agree."

"Calvin speaks highly of you. I hope you can keep the police moving on finding the killer. Do you have any leads yet?"

"I met with the primary detective from each department, as well as the head of the task force. The murders have very little in common aside from the fact that they've all taken place at concert venues."

Mark asked, "What do you think about that?"

"It doesn't make sense. Normally, the main reason the killer would change his methods would be to throw the police off of his trail. But then, why leave a note taking credit for all four?"

"Do you or the detectives have any suppositions?"

"The detective in Oakland believes the Irvine killer may be taking credit for crimes he didn't commit."

"Why would he do that?"

"For the same reason the police get false confessions for practically every murder. He may have claimed to be a serial killer to throw the police off from his real motive."

"Is that what you think?" Mark asked.

"Right now, I'm at the stage where I'm keeping an open mind to all of the possibilities. Let me ask you a question, Mark. What did you make of the note stating that concerts are evil?"

"Did Calvin tell you that I primarily promote Christian rock shows?"

"That's why I'm asking you this question. I was hoping you might know of a religion or sect that has it in for the concert industry."

"There are definitely some religions that believe rock music is the work of the devil. I'm sure you know that several acts try to promote that image. But religions are based on love of God and espouse respect for all of Gods creatures."

"Yes, but the evening news reminds us of how extremists kill in the name of God every day."

"Do you actually believe these killings were the work of an organized religion?" he asked, using a loud voice for the first time.

"As I said, I'm just considering all possibilities at this point. But with each of these murders having such a unique signature, I can't discount the possibility that they were the work of different killers with a common purpose. Not an organized religion, but it certainly could be the work of a radical sect," I said.

Mark took a deep breath and looked skyward.

Calvin returned to the deck, put a hand on each of our shoulders and said, "It sounds like you two are having a lively discussion."

Mark said, "Your friend has a rather disturbing notion that the murders could be the evil doings of a misguided religious sect. While I don't discount the possibility, I'm afraid it's put me in a mood where I need some quiet time to myself. If you don't mind, I'll be taking my leave, Calvin."

I said, "It's just one theory, Mark. I didn't mean to upset you."

"You're just doing your job, Jason. As a partner, it needed to be brought to my attention. But I am who I am, and right now I need to pray that you're wrong." Turning to Calvin he added, "Please express regrets for my early departure to your lovely wife." He then left without saying goodbye to anyone else.

"Sorry, Calvin. I haven't seen that kind of response since Tsunami Rush played a Black Sabbath song at the Sacred Heart church picnic."

Walking toward the edge of the pool, Calvin asked, "Have you ever considered a Dale Carnegie seminar?"

Our awkward moment was interrupted by the return of Kelly and Kayleigh from their tour. Kelly said, "Calvin, your home is stunning! And look at this pool!"

"The concert industry has been very good to us." Turning to me he added, "At least up until now."

Before I could respond we got splashed by Lonnie, who made his grand entrance to the party by doing a cannonball dive next to our group. He then pulled himself up onto the cantilevered deck and ran his fingers straight back over his scalp, pushing his dark brown hair into place. After doing so, he looked like a 40 year old Christopher Walken.

"This is the quiet and shy member of our group, Lonnie Cancelli," Calvin said. "Lonnie, this is our private investigator, Jason Duffy, and his girlfriend, Kelly."

Lonnie looked toward the house and crooked his finger at a blonde wearing a thong bikini, too much makeup, and too much silicone. When she joined us Lonnie said, "This is Chanel, like the perfume." He then turned to her and said, "Why don't you jump in the pool and wait for me while I talk some business."

"I can't swim," she replied.

While the attention was on Chanel, Kelly leaned over and whispered, "She certainly doesn't need a floatation device."

I stifled a laugh, cleared my throat, and avoided eye contact with Kelly.

Lonnie sent her off to the bar and said, "I think we should hire the Hell's Angels to stand guard at our concerts until this psycho is caught."

Calvin replied, "Just what we need, another Altamont. That'll certainly be reassuring."

Lonnie squared his shoulders to Calvin and expanded his chest. "Altamont happened a very long time ago. I'd say it's time they got a second chance."

Calvin said, "Not in my lifetime."

I jumped in and said to Lonnie, "How about if we take a little walk and I'll fill you in on what's happening with the case?"

We walked to the far end of the property and I summarized my meetings. "The Oakland detective is interested in a former employee of yours, Jimmy DeLong. He fought with the victim a couple of weeks before he was killed, and swore revenge."

"I canned Jimmy over a year ago. He's an OK guy, but he just wouldn't stay straight for the shows. I have a strict policy of no drugs or alcohol until after the venue is cleared. Jimmy's a tweaker and probably always will be."

"Do you think he's capable of violence?"

"He wouldn't be on my security staff if he wasn't. But he's not a master criminal by any stretch of the imagination. There's no way he could have gotten away with four murders without fucking up. Even if he did just one of them he'd be bragging about it to anybody who'd listen."

"Were you serious about wanting to put Hell's Angels on the security force?"

Lonnie laughed, "No, I've been busting Calvin's balls ever since he made me agree to accept Saint Mark as a partner. I'm surprised he isn't here yet."

"I'm afraid I scared him off with a theory that the killings could be the work of an extremist religious sect."

Lonnie laughed so hard that the rest of the party looked our way. "They say the fun doesn't start until the guests get loaded. I've got to start showing up on time."

"It's just one of several theories at this point. I didn't think he'd get so upset."

"Don't worry about stepping on a few toes. If the cops decide to tell the press about the serial killer we're gonna get castrated at the box office. You do what you have to. Just make sure this guy gets put out of business fast."

Before we left the party I told Calvin that Lonnie wasn't serious about hiring the Hell's Angels.

"Don't be so sure," he said. "Lonnie's forte is metal and rap. He had some pretty mean metalheads working for him when we formed the partnership. Even worse, he had a few security guys wearing gang colors at his rap shows."

"Why did you bring him into the partnership?"

"Lonnie has a long history of financially successful shows. In tough economic times it helps to have a hard-line contract negotiator."

"He looks like the kind of guy who'd party with the band after the shows."

"You got that right. I know that he drinks too much, and suspect he's into chemicals, too."

"I don't suppose he met Chanel at a local Mensa meeting."

"You know how this business works, Jason. Most of us have exposure to all of the vices. It's just a matter of degree as to whether we become self-destructive. Lonnie plays it close to the edge, but from what I've seen and heard, he's never gotten in over his head."

"That's good to know," I said.

The rest of the afternoon was primarily social. It was obvious that Kelly and Kayleigh were becoming fast friends. But the specter of the Concert Killer loomed like a drunken uncle cleaning his gun by the side of the pool.

Chapter 10

CK began his week with a very productive business meeting in San Diego. Afterwards, he checked into a suite at Loews Coronado Bay Resort. Once he unpacked, he reclined on his pillow top mattress bed and reviewed the upcoming concert schedule in the San Diego Reader. After a few minutes he found what he was looking for – a techno concert at a large outdoor venue in Oceanside. His next target would be a drug pusher. He hoped to find an ecstasy dealer, and felt a techno band would provide a very good opportunity.

He removed a crisp one dollar bill from his wallet and set it on top of his hotel multimedia cabinet. He placed a phone directory under it so that the Eye of Providence was at his eye level.

He said, "There are 13 steps to the top of the pyramid. By the time we truly see eye to eye, the unholy temples of devil worship will be closed forever. Those easily swayed by sinners will understand Your power and embrace Your love. Amen."

He briefly flashed on the eyes of his first victim as he choked the life out of her. "Your death won't have been for naught."

I called Maurice Johnson to tell him about my conversation with Lonnie. "I hope you had a restful weekend, detective."

"I don't know who you pissed off, Duffy. But I've been ordered to only talk with you regarding the scheduling of concerts. You're on somebody's shit list and I don't plan to join you."

"That's too bad," I replied. "I met Lonnie Cancelli yesterday afternoon. I thought you'd be interested to hear what he said about Jimmy DeLong. Or did the head of the task force convince you to forget about your suspect?"

"I had a little run-in with the feebs earlier this year. My lieutenant caught a load of crap for backing me up. He's not up for round 2, and I don't feel like becoming a crack-house specialist."

"When did the FBI take over the case?" I asked.

"They haven't done it yet, but they will. Dean Casey is like one of those guys you pay to stand in line for you. He'll do some grunt work until there's a break in the case. Then the feebs will swoop in, snatch the case, and kick him to the curb."

"Why is he being such a hard-ass about working with me?"

"Because there's no upside for him. I don't know that guy personally, but I'd guess he's looking to make it to his retirement with minimal risk. The feebs aren't gonna want to get involved with a PI. In Casey's eyes, anything you could contribute isn't worth the possibility of him looking bad to his boss."

"So are you and Bains going to forget about Jimmy DeLong?"

There was a moment of silence. "Bains understands the political bullshit that goes on. I'm sure she'd welcome a call from you. But I can't be trading any more information."

"Just so you know, Lonnie said DeLong is capable of a revenge kill, but totally incapable of shutting up about it afterwards. He also said Jimmy's not too bright and would never be accused of being a master criminal. He had a hard enough time remembering the dos and don'ts of concert security," I said.

"Thanks, Jason. I'll pass it along to Bains. Good luck," he said, and hung up.

I tried calling Detectives Rappaport and Lutz, but got routed to voicemail. I suspected that Caller ID was working against me. I did manage to reach a stressed-out Detective Ko in Irvine. All she said was, "I can't talk to you," and hung up.

While contemplating my next move, Hoover walked in and gave me a sympathetic expression. "Any good ideas, Hoover?"

He gave a small whine and ran the side of his face across my leg. Jeannine entered the office and said, "Hoover, you know you're not allowed to wander in here." The dog immediately assumed the *heel* position. "Good boy," she said.

"Did any of the concert venue security videos come in over the weekend?" I hoped the detectives followed through on my request before getting the word from Casey.

"As a matter of fact, you have packages from San Francisco and Sacramento."

"Give Cory a call and see if he can come in and start combing through them for anyone who looks suspicious."

Cory works part-time as a photographer and stake-out specialist. Like Jeannine, he was also a former client from my days as an outpatient mental health counselor. Cory suffers from Tourette's Syndrome and blurts obscenities at times when he would normally be inclined to speak. In the interest of good taste, Cory's comments are always paraphrased.

"He didn't stop by on Friday for his paycheck, so I'm expecting him any minute now," she said.

"Great. Have him jump right on it. Then I want you to start looking for media stories on any of the partners in CLAM."

"Including Calvin?"

"If our perp is targeting the concert industry, maybe he has a grudge against one of the partners. Calvin's a great guy, but who knows what could set off the kind of person who would murder four people. Check everybody out."

Before Jeannine could reply, Hoover barked once and turned toward Jeannine's desk. She followed his lead and departed.

I reached Shamansky at SDPD Metro Division. "I'm getting shut out by the bureaucrat who's running the task force."

"Darden just told me. When he was walking to my desk I was sure they put him on Prozac from the expression on his face."

"I'm glad to hear my fan club is alive and well. But I'll feel like I'm working without a computer if I can't talk with the lead detectives. Do you have any suggestions?"

"The guy who's shutting you out is named Dean Casey. Correct?"

"Yes."

"What ethnic origin is that name?"

"Irish. I already asked Dad to reach out," I said.

Shamansky replied, "You follow up with him and I'll see what I can do on this end. But don't get your hopes up. Darden's not the kind of cop who'd forget about a vendetta for the sake of his case."

"What about his transfer out of Metro?"

"As long as he's heading up the task force he can set up his HQ wherever he wants. Right now he's got the Special Detail room at Metro. If the Concert Killer strikes in San Diego, I'm sure he'll get upgraded to the Commissioner's conference room."

"Call me if you hear of any major developments," I said, and hung up.

I phoned Mom and got invited to lunch. Mom is a willing co-conspirator when it comes to enlisting Dad's help on a case. Over the ten years that I worked as a professional musician, my relationship with Dad could be described as *very strained*, at best. Mom's thrilled that we finally found something in common, but she's decidedly less than thrilled with the dangers I've encountered as a PI.

I arrived at my parents' house on the edge of the Little Italy section of San Diego at 12:30 PM. Dad's head was under the hood of his green 1995 Buick Riviera.

"Hi Dad. Whatcha doin'?"

"Waiting for you to tell me what you want," he replied, as he used his forearm to wipe sweat off of his brow.

"Don't you think it's possible that this might just be a social visit?"

"Not without your better half," he said. "Hang on. Is it politically correct to call Kelly your better half when you aren't married?"

Whenever I start to believe our relationship is improving, Dad gets a bug up his ass and pisses me off all over again. My automatic pilot was telling me to get back in my car and find another way to work the case. His meddling in my relationship with Kelly caused major problems over the summer. But I flashed on how I'd be letting Calvin down if I allowed my father's cantankerous nature to keep me from fixing a big problem.

"Is Mom inside?"

"Where else would she be? Do you think she went to the beauty parlor after you invited yourself over for lunch?"

Mom was in the kitchen cooking three burgers. "It smells great in here, Mom."

"Hello Jason. Lunch will be ready in about five minutes," she said. "Did you talk with your father on the way in?"

"Are you kidding? He's acting like he misses the old days when our Cold War was raging."

"You need to cut him a little slack today. Bob Kerrigan called about an hour ago and told him that O'Malley's doctor sent him for a biopsy last week."

"I'm sorry to hear that, Mom. Maybe I should just forget about asking for help and give him a couple of days."

"I know your father better than anyone. He'll stew about this until he hears back on the test results unless he has something more important to work on. When he helped you with the other cases it was like he was back on the force. Find a way to ask him today and you'll be doing both of us a big favor."

When lunch was over I followed Dad back to the Riv. "Did you get a chance to look into Lt. Casey?"

"You just asked me about it on Saturday night," he replied.

"I was hoping that the owner of your favorite bar might be a relative."

"Casey Dunn?" he asked.

"I assumed Casey was his last name."

"If you plan on earning a living as a detective you're going to have to learn not to make assumptions. Has anything changed since Saturday?"

"As of this morning, Casey has declared me persona non gratis."

"Why?"

"The detective in Oakland said it's because the FBI will probably be taking over the case and he doesn't want to look like he needed help from a PI."

"Do you feel like you were making any headway?"

"Definitely. The killer hits a different city each time and uses a different MO. I was the only one to interview the primary detective on all four cases."

Dad said, "OK. I'll make some calls this afternoon. I'm sure San Diego Metro's been alerted."

"Our old friend Darden is heading up the local task force."

"Another politician's ass smells like Darden's lip balm. What else is new?"

"Shamansky got himself named as an advisor to the task force. He can pass me some information, but he'll be limited with Darden back at Metro."

"I think you should work the case as if you won't be getting any cooperation from the boys in blue. Even if I find a friend of Casey's, the file's probably going to get passed to the FBI as soon as the perp starts killing out of state," Dad said. "I'll call you if I make a connection."

When I returned to the office I found Cory reviewing a video surveillance tape. We converted his darkroom into an office after our newest equipment upgrade changed Cory's opinion on the quality of digital photography.

"I want you to concentrate on the crowd at the Sacramento show," I said. "The San Francisco vic was killed in the parking lot and there weren't any cameras on the lot. I doubt if the killer entered the venue."

Amid a tangle of curse words, Cory asked if he should be looking for anything specific.

"The beer vendor was set up to the right of the stage. Start with the assumption that the perp was in the Lawn Section and he was alone. Look for a guy who's spending a lot of time looking to the right of the stage. The bathrooms and other vendors are down there as well, so wait and see if a girlfriend or buddy with a beer shows up before you ID someone as a possible suspect."

Around 3:00 PM I took a caffeine break as Cory was emerging from his office to do the same. Hoover cruised over to see what was going on and if it involved food. When I asked Cory how the search was going, something interesting happened that significantly changed our office dynamic. Every time Cory blurted an obscenity, Hoover barked over it, effectively censoring Cory perfectly. I could tell by the look in Jeannine's eyes that she was surprised, and this wasn't a trick they were practicing at home. However when Hoover looked at her, she smiled like a proud mother. I offered to continue the conversation in my office, but Cory declined and appeared thrilled by the new development. It was uncanny how the dog could anticipate every foul word and otherwise be perfectly quiet.

As hard as it was to focus on what Cory was saying, I learned that he identified a few possible suspects. A little over an hour later Cory showed me a digital mug book he created on his computer.

"Is there any way you can use software to project what these guys would look like without hats and facial hair?" I asked.

Cory said that he'd try to find out what the police use, and would get started on the project tomorrow. Hoover could be heard from the reception area at all the right moments. Cory smiled and asked if I thought Jeannine would allow him to take Hoover for walks.

"I don't have a problem with it as long as I'm around the office. Remember, the reason Hoover's here is to serve as her watchdog."

Chapter 11

Tuesday was one of those frustrating days where much was done and little accomplished. I was feeling the pinch from being shut out by the task force. The only break came late in the day when Dad called.

"It looks like I may have some good news for you, son. I asked around about Dean Casey and Fallon told me he thought O'Malley knew him."

"That's great, Dad. Do you think he's up to making the connection?"

"Your mother called Dorothy and she thought it might take his mind off of the tests. He's supposed to get the word any day now and he's been going nuts waiting. She asked me to come over for lunch tomorrow. I'll give you a call as soon as I get home."

After bashing into brick walls all day, I was frustrated. The best way I know how to release that frustration is through music. When I got home, Kelly had dinner cooking and was in the bedroom reviewing projects done by her 2nd graders on a breakfast-in-bed tray table. I gave her a quick kiss, closed the bedroom door on my way out, turned on the air conditioning, and closed all of the windows. Then I powered up my amp, plugged my mic into the stereo, and cranked up a CD. After a couple of minor adjustments to my amp and B string, I was shredding along to the Jimi Hendrix version of *All Along the Watchtower* and leaving my frustrations behind.

Just as I closed my eyes and started to soar, the stereo suddenly went silent. I opened my eyes and saw an angry Kelly staring at me from the other side of my mic stand. Kelly and I have been dating for over two years, but living together for just over two months.

"What are you doing?" I asked, in a tone that told her I was as pissed as she looked.

"You saw that I was grading papers! How can you expect me to work when you're shaking the walls?"

"I had a bad day. I need to get it out of my system."

"Then take Colonel Hogan for a walk. I can't concentrate while you're peeling the paint."

Unfortunately, I replied, "C'mon Kelly, how hard can it be? They're only 2nd graders."

It would serve no purpose to go into the details what followed. Suffice it to say that Kelly ate her dinner on the bedroom tray table and I woke up with a stiff neck after sleeping on the couch. Colonel Hogan did get a nice long walk. I didn't want to be one of those parents who put the children in the middle of a domestic dispute.

I left for the office at 6:30 Wednesday morning, still in a bad mood after a hot shower and two ibuprofen tablets did little for my stiff neck. Adding a cold shoulder to the mix was more than I was willing to endure. After two years of hearing how Kelly dealt with her alcoholic brothers, I had a strong feeling that the silent treatment was on the breakfast menu. So I opted to test the theory that absence makes the heart grow fonder.

The main advantage to getting into the office early was reaching Detective Bains before roll call at LAPD. While Shamansky could keep me up on what was happening in San Diego, Bains was my direct link to one of the four detectives actively working the case.

"Detective Bains, this is Jason Duffy in San Diego. I wanted to make sure Detective Johnson passed along the info I got from Lonnie Cancelli on Jimmy DeLong."

"Johnson tells me that Casey issued a gag order to the task force as far as you're concerned," she replied.

"I wasn't cc'ed on the memo, but we've definitely lost that lovin' feeling."

"So, you're calling me looking for a back door into the task force?"

I said, "I wasn't aware that you're a member of the task force."

"As a matter of fact, you're right. I'm not on the task force and, like you, I'm none too happy with Casey's edict that they won't be looking at Jimmy in connection with the case. I guess you could say we're both being shut out."

"What's your take on Cancelli saying Jimmy doesn't have the smarts to pull it off, or the willpower to shut up about it?"

"Let's call him Lonnie. The CLAM acronym makes scorekeeping easier," she said.

"Fine."

"He's right about Jimmy having a big mouth and a love for all things pharmaceutical. But Jimmy's also a guy with big plans."

"How so?"

"Jimmy's been actively recruiting his own little biker gang for the past couple of months. I think he fancies himself on par with a small Mafia family, and is doing what he can to grow his organization."

"From what Lonnie said it doesn't sound like he grasps the concept of *Omerta*."

"Silence isn't necessarily as big of a virtue when you're in the recruiting phase of building your organization. Lonnie sees him as a braggart. I see him as a politician looking to grow his base."

"Just how big is Jimmy's family?" I asked.

"Right now he's got four full-time members, another four or five who will party with them on a regular basis, and a few more that will join him for specific jobs, like drug scores."

"How do you see the concert murders fitting into the equation?"

"The vics look pretty random on the surface. The only common denominator is CLAM. How well do you know Lonnie?" she asked.

"I met him for the first time over the weekend. My connection is through Calvin. I've known him for years."

"Mind if I ask how you met him?"

"I used to play in a band. Calvin liked our sound and scheduled us as the warm-up act for some of the groups he brought to San Diego. I handled all of the contracts for our group and we hit it off. If you're thinking Calvin is involved in something illegal, you're off the track."

"I don't know very much about Calvin, but Lonnie has been on my radar screen for the last two years. Nothing indictable, but his lifestyle and associations tell me he wasn't earning merit badges in his youth."

"CLAM is a marriage of necessity brought on by a combination of the economy and the mega-corporations taking over the concert industry."

She replied, "That explains a lot. I couldn't figure how Mark Danby got mixed up with a guy like Lonnie."

"Where do we go from here, Detective Bains?"

"I've been doing some undercover work at a biker bar where Jimmy hangs out. I might ask you to come and join me some night, so you better start calling me Celia. I'll let you know if I hear anything that connects Jimmy to the murders."

At 4:30 PM Jeannine was on a restroom break when the phone rang. Before I could finish giving the company salutation I heard, "God damn! Mother fucker! …"

"Cory?" I asked, thinking his voice sounded different.

"Don't you know your own father's voice by now!"

"What happened, Dad?"

After another two minutes of expletives and very little content I said, "Dad, I'm coming over now. I'll see you in about 20 minutes."

My mother met me at the front door. "What's going on, Mom?"

"O'Malley agreed to talk to Lt. Casey over lunch with your father. Just as your dad was about to leave, O'Malley's doctor called with the test results. The cancer's malignant and it's too far advanced to do anything about it."

"No wonder he's so upset."

"That's just the half of it," she said. "O'Malley called back around 3:00 to say your father should expect a call from Lt. Casey at any minute. O'Malley also told him how much it helped getting the bad news on a day when he could get one more shot at helping to solve a crime. I'll let your father tell you what Casey said."

"Thanks, Mom. I'm very sorry about O'Malley."

When I walked into the backyard I saw something I hadn't seen in over 10 years. Dad was vigorously going at his Everlast heavy punching bag, slung over a branch of the oak tree in the middle of the yard. He looked like Rocky Balboa in the 12th round with Apollo Creed. I stood behind the bag and held it in place while Dad took a couple of final swings.

"Mom told me about O'Malley. I'm really sorry."

"We all gotta go sometime, son." Dad slammed his fist into the bag.

"I know," I said, "but cancer is sure a tough way to check out."

"He's not doing the chemo or radiation. He said the doctors call it fighting, but he sees it as lingering, and he'd rather go out on God's schedule."

"Maybe if they caught it earlier," I said. Dad gave me a look that said I was too young to understand his point of view and moved on.

"That Dean Casey is a piece of work."

"What did he say?" I asked.

"The sonofabitch told me O'Malley should go fishing and keep his nose out of police business now that he's out to pasture."

"Did you say anything about O'Malley's condition?"

"Screw him!" Dad drove hard into the heavy bag, sending it into my gut.

"I wasn't expecting that one," I said, straightening up gingerly. It was the closest Dad came to a smile.

"Then get the hell out of the way if you aren't going to make yourself useful."

"I need your opinion, Dad. How much trouble could Shamansky get into if I ask him to get me the security video from Irvine?"

"If the video showed somebody following that girl into the bathroom I'm sure they're already all over it."

I told him about what Cory was planning with the Sacramento video. "If we could find a match to any of those suspects it could give us our first solid lead."

"I doubt if that enhancement software would hold up in court, but it could be a decent steppingstone to getting on the right track. If Shamansky goes along with it, you should make a copy and get the original back to him as soon as possible. You can be sure Darden will be watching everything Shamansky does with the case."

"Good point. I'll ask Shamansky to make the copy so the original never leaves his possession."

"Now get over here and hold Casey still while I finish him off. Then I'll be finishing off a case of Guinness Stout." Switching to an Irish brogue he added, "So I suggest you head home to that fine Irish lass of yours and let me cry in me beer."

I refrained from saying that my fine Irish lass probably had *my* picture on a heavy bag in our backyard. So I said goodbye to Mom, assured her that everything would be OK, and departed. I wanted to tell her to come over if Dad got too loaded, but I had no idea how things would play out with

Kelly and didn't think she needed any more problems laid at her feet.

When I got home there was a note on the refrigerator in thick blue marker pen: *I'm going out with a couple of the teachers after PTA tonight. Don't wait up.*

I took it to mean I was expected to sit home and think about our relationship and what it would be like if she wasn't there. Hey, we've only been living together for two months. I called Shamansky and arranged dinner at a restaurant that was less pricey than his usual haunt.

Over dinner, Shamansky agreed to my proposal after I sweetened the deal by saying I'd give him credit for the find if Cory turned up a match. It was the only way to keep him out of trouble.

I got home around 10:00 and Kelly was still out. After starting my day at 5:15 AM I felt like I'd be at a distinct disadvantage if Round 2 broke out, so I called it a night. My stiff neck thanked me for a return to my firm mattress and favorite pillow.

Chapter 12

When I woke up on Thursday morning my second favorite pillow had a note on it stating that one of the parents couldn't make PTA last night, so Kelly was meeting her before class. I started wondering if problem avoidance was an Irish trait or a coping mechanism common to all ethnic groups. I was jarred out of my moment of introspection by Colonel Hogan, who just learned how to get his paws up on the bed.

As I went through my morning routine, thoughts of relationship problems gave way to the uncomfortable feeling that I missed something important when talking with Celia Bains. The more I replayed our conversation in my head the farther I got from the answer.

CK was going through his morning routine as well. He concluded his prayers by asking God to help him ink his deal by the close of business tomorrow. That would work out perfectly with his plans for the techno concert on Friday night. He waited a month in between each martyr in the past. But his urge to speed up the process was very powerful. After staring at the Eye of Providence for ten minutes he noted how the width of the pyramid lessened as the structure built from its base toward the eye. He concluded that his plan was built on a solid base so he needed less time to prepare for each sacrifice. Besides, it was the weekend before Halloween and disguises and outrageous behavior would be the norm. Removing a drug dealer from society on the eve of a pagan holiday seemed like a fitting way to emphasize his message.

I spent the morning at my office having Jeannine research media coverage of Calvin's partners. Lonnie received the most coverage by a long shot. The press portrayed him as a player with a knack for bottom-line profitability. A few lawsuits were filed against him over the years, but none of them made it through a trial. A couple of stories hinted that Lonnie's friendship with the gangsta rappers helped him to reach favorable settlements with the petitioners.

All of the articles about Mark portrayed him as a wonderful person. Most were found in Christian publications. Ashley was usually described as a liberal friend of many causes, but the question of her daddy's money and lifestyle made a few journalists question her motives and sincerity.

As I was getting ready to make a lunch run, Celia Bains called. "I need a big favor and I need it now."

"What's going on?"

"Jimmy DeLong and three of his buddies just met with Lonnie at a biker bar in L.A. Lonnie gave Jimmy a thick envelope, about the shape of a stack of bills, and asked him to deliver it to a guy in Ocotillo Wells. My partner and I have to testify at a trial in two hours. Can you make a run to the Sidewinder Lounge, see who shows up for the money, and get a license plate number?" she asked.

"What makes you think this has anything to do with the case?"

"Jimmy's got a new member in his gang."

"So?"

"Think of this biker gang like the mob. Right now Jimmy has a crew. He'd like to have his own little branch of the family and is in the process of recruiting new members."

"What's interesting about the new member?"

"He has a tattoo of a derringer on the back of his neck."

"Now that is interesting. What about the rest of the crew?" I asked.

"There were four of them at the table when Lonnie showed up. One of them wore a knife on his belt."

"Could you hear what Lonnie was saying?"

"His head was turned away from me. I couldn't hear him until after he stood up to leave. He said, 'Tell him to meet me at the Sidewinder Lounge, just this side of Ocotillo Wells, at three o'clock.' Five minutes later the boys walked out the door and I called you. Any chance you could pass yourself off as a biker?" she asked.

"I have a Metallica T-shirt and black jeans at home."

"Toss in a studded belt and a pair of boots, and you're all set."

"I haven't seen any mug shots. How will I know what Jimmy looks like?"

Bains laughed and said, "You're gonna love this. He's got a tattoo on the inside of his left forearm that says, *DeLong Rider Club*."

"Is that his gang's name?"

She replied, "I hope not. The D is shaped like a circumcised penis in profile."

"Just what I need: A four-hour round trip to keep tabs on Jimmy DeShlong. You'll owe me for this one, Celia."

"I know. I should be getting out of court around the time they hit the bar. Call me as soon as you've got a plate number. I'll tell you who it is and where it leads."

"I also want the 411 on derringer neck and anything that Maurice Johnson passes along on the case."

"You got it, Jason. Be careful. Jimmy's still looking to prove he's lead dog material. If he figures out you're watching him he could turn you into a dune buggy speed bump." She hung up before I could reassure her with false bravado.

At 2:30 PM I pulled into a parking space at the Sidewinder Lounge, with an early 70's Plymouth Duster on my right and six motorcycles on my left. The bar was in the middle of the desert, on the outskirts of town, with no other buildings in the area and virtually no cover to discreetly watch the lot. My only option was to hang out in the bar.

Foregoing my usual favorites for the sake of blending in, I ordered a Bud from a redhead in her mid-thirties after taking a seat at the far corner of the bar where I could see the door, tables and most of the stools.

"I haven't seen your face in here before," the bartender said. "I'm Lacey."

"Jason," I said, and nodded.

"We get mainly bikers in this place."

"What gave me away?"

"The sneakers. What brings you to town?"

Glancing around the room I spotted a small bandstand in the corner, complete with amps and instruments. "I'm playing a gig at a house party on the Salton Sea later tonight."

Lacey looked like she was going to ask another question when a burly patron pounded his empty beer mug on the bar and thundered, "Lacey, get your ass over here."

I said, "They say it's great to be wanted."

"Then this is the place to be. We get enough of them to fill a post office bulletin board," she said, and drifted toward her customer. Another rap on the bar hastened her pace.

The crew at the other end of the bar kept her tied up until Jimmy and his posse arrived and sat at a table about 15 feet away from me. Derringer neck ordered a pitcher and four mugs. Jimmy's back was to me, but I instantly identified him by his dickhead tat. It reminded me of the Surgeon General's warning on cigarette packs.

After pouring the pitcher, Lacey returned to talk music. About ten minutes later a guy in blue jeans, a dark sport jacket, and an aqua T-shirt walked in and sat in the vacant chair next to Jimmy. It looked like they knew each other, but weren't old friends. Using Lacey's footwear evaluation technique I determined that there was now a third four-wheel vehicle in the lot.

Since they were both facing away from me, I decided it would be a good time to score the license plate number for Bains.

"On to the next watering hole," I said to Lacey, dropping a tip on the bar.

Sure enough, a black Chevy Blazer was on the left end of the lot, ten bikes away from my RXS. I walked quickly behind the SUV. As I read the plate I heard a strange noise coming from the far side of the vehicle. Glancing to my left I saw an arc of yellow liquid stream past the rear bumper as I heard a gruff voice say, "What the fuck!"

I did an about-face and was half-way back to my car when I heard, "Hold it right there, asshole," followed by the unmistakable sound of a round being chambered in a pistol. I raised my hands and froze. Assuming my captor was on a cell phone I heard, "I just caught somebody snooping around the Blazer."

A few seconds later, Jimmy, his crew, and the winner of the Sonny Crockett look-alike contest came storming out the front door.

"Who the fuck are you?" Jimmy asked.

Knowing they'd be looking in my wallet soon, I was glad I stashed my PI license in the car. "Jason Duffy. What's going on?"

"You tell us," said Sonny.

"I was about to head out when I decided to take a piss and looked for a place where I couldn't be seen from the highway. When I got over there I heard your buddy doing the same thing and turned around."

Jimmy moved in on my left side and asked, "Why didn't you just join him?"

"Call me old fashion, but I never do the piss-buddy thing till the third date." Jimmy responded with a punch to my gut.

"Not here," Sonny said. "Let's bring him out back."

We walked to a spot between the back door and a dumpster, with Jimmy giving me a shove three times along the way.

"You want to rephrase your answer?" Sonny asked.

"OK, the truth is I can't go when somebody's watching. I get pee-shy. It's embarrassing. So, I just turned around," I said, trying to look ashamed.

Jimmy said, "I think maybe I'll just beat the piss out of you so you don't develop any bladder problems."

A ray of sunlight blinded me for a second. When my eyes readjusted, knife-dude was fondling a pearl-handled blade and flashing a set of teeth that were screaming for a cleaning. "If that don't work I could C-section his bladder."

"Who sent you out here?" Sonny asked.

"I just stopped at the bar to get a drink."

Jimmy said, "Let's throw him in the back of the Blazer and do a little off-roading toward Borrego."

As Sonny pondered Jimmy's suggestion, Lacey walked out the back door and asked, "What the hell are you doing to this poor guy?"

Jimmy replied, "He was stickin' his nose where it don't belong. I think he was spying on us."

Lacey said, "He's a musician on his way to play a party at the Salton Sea."

Jimmy plucked my wallet out of my back pocket and read my driver's license. "You're a long way from San Diego, Duffy."

"I go where the gigs are."

Jimmy asked, "If we walk out front to your car are we gonna see your guitar and amp?"

"They're in the equipment truck," I said.

Jimmy said, "Maybe if we take that ride out into the desert we can find the equipment truck."

Sonny elbowed Jimmy and nodded at Lacey.

Jimmy said, "I been workin' with bands for years and you don't look like no musician to me."

Lacey said, "We have the Twister's gear set up inside. Why don't we let him show us that he's who he claims to be?"

Sonny said, "Good idea. Bring him inside."

As we walked in, Lacey spotted the mug-banger leaning over the bar, helping himself to a refill of his beer.

"That's gonna cost you double, douche bag!" she yelled.

Sonny looked relieved when I powered up the PA and an amp. After strapping on a battered Telecaster and making sure it was in tune, I launched into the old Guns & Roses song, *Welcome to the Jungle*. I don't have Axl Rose's high-pitched voice, but transcribed into a lower key, I ripped through the intro and transitioned into powerful vocals. About half-way into the song, the beer burglar plunked his large frame on the drum stool and did a credible job of laying down the beat.

When we finished, Jimmy walked over to me clapping his hands. His smile quickly faded and he said, "I want you to keep on playin' till we're out of here at least a half-hour. I got some friends in this bar that'll be watching." He shot a glance at the drummer and scanned the bar.

"Why?" I asked.

"I don't want any assault complaints called into the cops while I'm still in the neighborhood."

"We were just getting to know each other. No harm done. Forget about it."

Jimmy said, "I'm gonna go have Lacey bring you a beer like we're good buddies. But if you quit playing a minute shy of that half hour you'll never make it to the Salton Sea." Jimmy turned to the bar with a big smile on his face and yelled, "Lacey, I want to buy my new buddy a beer."

Since getting the plate number to LAPD wasn't a time critical matter, I went along with Jimmy's request. After I finished, I ordered another beer from Lacey and went to the restroom where I called the number in to Celia's voicemail.

"You should stick around and give The Twisters a few lessons," Lacey said.

I sat down in front of my beer. "What's up with Jimmy?"

"He's an asshole."

"Does he come here much?"

"Every Saturday night for the last couple of months. He's got a girlfriend on the other side of town."

"Does he always have his posse with him?"

She replied, "You aren't planning on doing something stupid like picking a revenge fight, are you?"

"I make music, not war. I was just wondering if he acted as tough when he didn't have his back-up."

"Clarkie's been comin' here even longer. His girlfriend is roommates with Jimmy's girl."

"Which one's Clarkie?"

"He's the bald guy with the little gun on the back of his neck," she replied.

I headed east out of the parking lot to see if I could spot any of the four bikes that were parked next to the Blazer, but no luck. I kept going until I picked up the road to Interstate 8 and headed for San Diego.

When I passed San Diego State University and started down the hill into Mission Valley, I glanced at the clock on the dashboard, realized Kelly would be home, and was clueless about what to say to her. My instincts told me it was time for a visit to my mentor.

Bernie Liebowitz is the owner of my favorite club, The Dali Lama, Yo Mama. He's also a 70-something former agent who got out of the recording industry because he hated the way record companies screwed their young talent. As a club owner, Bernie took a liking to me and helped Tsunami Rush to go as far as we could possibly make it without any writing talent. He's also the guy who introduced me to Calvin and probably knows the rest of the CLAM partners.

Happy hour was in full swing. All of the barstools were taken and the tables nearest the bar were buzzing. A solo guitarist/singer was performing, and a happy hour buffet of pizza, wings, celery and dip was stationed in a neutral corner.

From behind, a familiar female voice said, "Please don't tell me the Russian Mob is back in town with a contract on you."

I turned around and said, "I should be so lucky. This time it's my Irish girlfriend who put out the contract. How are you doing, Jasmine?"

"Better than you. I'm working the other end of the love train, and it feels pretty good for a change."

"Who's the lucky guy?"

"A Navy pilot stationed at North Island. I'll give you the details if you hang around long enough for the crowd to thin out. Do you want me to tell Bernie you're here?"

"Thanks, Jasmine. That would be great."

I managed to squeeze in between two patrons and scored a bottle of St. Pauli Girl beer before Bernie greeted me and led them back to his office.

I said, "Happy hour entertainment and munchies. I like it."

"The crowd seems to like it too. We just started happy hour karaoke on Tuesday nights about a month ago and that's bringing them in as well."

The office décor was every bit as inviting as always. Bernie was set up to conduct business at a beautiful teak desk, while band members and assorted guests amused themselves with a pool table and an exceptional sound system. I could live in this room. If I didn't straighten things out with Kelly it might be my best alternative.

"You look like you've got something on your mind, Jason," Bernie said.

"I have a few questions about the concert promoters Calvin is working with, but my girlfriend problems seem to be dominating my thoughts."

"Are you still with Kelly?"

"She moved in with me a couple of months ago. At first, everything was going well. But making music is still an important part of my life, even if I'm not a performer anymore. I don't think she gets that, and I'm worried it might sink our relationship."

Bernie said, "It sounds like something specific happened recently. Why don't you tell me about it?"

I gave him the details on the homework incident and a couple of other times that she asked me to stop playing.

When I finished, Bernie stood up and walked around the room with the fingers of both hands tented in front of his mouth. He then sat on a stool next to the pool table.

"I was married to a wonderful woman for 26 years. She died about 10 years before I met you, Jason. In those days there was no moving in together before getting married, so there were a lot of adjustments in the first year."

"How could she not get along with a nice guy like you?"

"I wasn't born a nice guy. In fact, when I married Doris I was pretty full of myself. A couple of months before we were married I signed a guy who was touted to be the next Roy Orbison. He had a five octave range, Elvis's looks, and the women would faint if he made eye contact. Record companies were calling me with bona fide offers. I thought I was pretty hot shit."

"Doris must have been happy about your success," I said.

"She was thrilled for me. But it didn't take long before she saw what it did to me. I'd get home from club dates at 3:00 AM and crank up the music. Doris was a nurse and worked first shift. She didn't like that I kept waking her up, and liked it even less when I wouldn't shut it off and come to bed."

"What did you do?"

"At first, I told her she should quit her job and we'd start raising a family. Then she pointed out that babies liked getting woken up in the middle of the night even less than she did. After a couple more weeks of me ruling the roost, Doris said that she thought maybe getting married was a mistake"

"What happened?"

"I poured my heart out to a guitarist's wife and she told me to buy a pair of headphones. It saved our marriage."

"Who was the big star you represented?" I asked.

"You never heard of him. He did the backstage horizontal bop with the wrong guy's wife and woke up in Doris' hospital with a crushed voice box, a flattened nose, and two broken hands. If it wasn't for Doris' nursing job we never would have been able to pay our bills."

"Thanks for sharing that, Bernie."

"I suppose you want to hear about Calvin's partners now."

"Whatever you can tell me."

"Not as much as you'd think. I never worked with Mark or Ashley. Calvin and Lonnie both book club tours, but I think Mark and Ashley have always stayed with concert promotions."

"Don't they work the clubs?"

"We have a reputation as a rock and metal venue. Neither of those two handle our kind of bands."

"What about Lonnie?"

"My natural inclination is to say: Calvin's a friend. Lonnie's his partner. If you can't say something nice about somebody, don't say anything at all, and leave it at that."

I said, "But you know that your good friend wouldn't be asking if he didn't have a really good reason."

"I'd feel a lot better if you'd give me an inkling of what that reason might be."

"Have you read about the murders at concert venues in San Francisco, Sacramento, Oakland, and Irvine?" I asked.

"I was hoping they weren't connected."

"I need you to keep this confidential, but Calvin and his partners hired me after a note was found in Irvine claiming responsibility for all four."

"What does this have to do with Lonnie?"

"Oakland PD has a suspect that used to work for Lonnie. An L.A. detective saw Lonnie give him an envelope around noon, and I saw him pass the envelope to a suspicious character a few hours ago. They caught me getting the guy's license plate number and I almost took a one-way ride into the desert."

Bernie said, "I've booked several acts through Lonnie since opening here. Frankly, he's a pain in the patoot. He acts like we're best friends when we're alone hammering out a deal. Then, a few days later, he'll question my integrity in front of his talent to make himself look tough and act like he's doing me a big favor by playing at a club instead of an arena. As far as I'm concerned, he's as two-faced as they come."

"Do you think he's into drugs?"

"Unless he's into sniffing powdered doughnuts, I have no doubt."

"Can you think of any way these murders could possibly help his business?"

"My knee-jerk response would be to say, no. Scaring the public away from shows could be devastating to his bottom line. But then I have to ask myself about how his deal is structured with Calvin and his other partners."

"I'm not following you, Bernie."

"I don't see Lonnie getting into an all-for-one and one-for-all relationship with that group. He might do it with Calvin, but the term *strange bedfellows* springs to mind when I think of Mark and Ashley. What if controlling interest in their organization is based on performance over the first year?

Mark and Ashley's shows are likely to get crushed by this news. But, do you think gangster rappers and hardcore fans are going to be scared away by the threat of violence? I'd guess the danger factor would probably improve the gate for those shows."

"Once again, my mentor walks me out of the forest," I said, and stood up.

"What's your next move? A call to Calvin?" Bernie asked.

"Actually, I'm headed to the mall to find a good set of headphones. Thanks, Bernie. I'll tell Calvin you were asking for him."

Chapter 13

The combination of a near-death experience and my talk with Bernie put me in the right frame of mind to patch things up with Kelly. When I walked in the door last night with a dozen roses, a *Best Teacher in the World* coffee mug, and my new headphones, she looked genuinely relieved. After growing up in a family with two alcoholic parents and two older brothers with the same affliction, Kelly Kennedy didn't get much in the way of appropriate role modeling when it came to domestic disputes. So she retreated and hoped for the best. When she explained these things, I felt badly about letting it go on for so long, although the make-up sex was spectacular. The 2nd grade class clowns could have a field day if they only knew their teacher's state of mind.

I called Celia Bains shortly after arriving at the office.

"Did the license plate tell you what you wanted to know?"

"It's actually taking me in a surprising direction. I hope I didn't cause you too much trouble," she said.

I was curious about what she learned and needed a favor. So I gave her the long version of what happened, emphasizing the one-way ride to the desert and editing out the pee-shy ruse.

"Who owns the SUV?" I asked.

"His name is Aaron Tesslerod. He's a professional bodyguard. We're trying to track down who sent him on the errand."

"What's surprising about this new direction?"

"My sources tell me Tesslerod works exclusively with white-collar types. Finding him in a biker bar is like running into Jimmy at an L.A. Chamber of Commerce dinner."

"Once the bartender saw us out back he definitely wasn't enthused about Jimmy's suggestion to give me a permanent sand nap."

"Tesslerod's used lethal force in the past, but it was cleared as being justifiable. My partner is checking some sources to see if we can get a handle on his client list."

"I found out that derringer neck is called Clarkie. Maurice Johnson wanted to know if any of Jimmy's old security staff friends were working Oakland the night of the murder. I called Calvin on my way back from Ocotillo Wells. He said they have a Doogan Clark on their security staff roster, but he didn't work the Oakland show, and is coded to only be called for SoCal shows."

"I'll let Johnson know the next time I talk to him," she said.

"I need a favor."

"After nearly fertilizing a cactus for me, I guess you're entitled."

"I need the security video from Irvine. Can you get it for me?"

She replied, "I can try. What are you looking for?"

"Common faces in the crowd that may have been keeping an eye on the vics or kill zones," I said.

"I hope you've got a lot of popcorn."

"Better yet, I've got a video expert who will be reviewing it for me." I was glad I wouldn't have to ask Shamansky.

We agreed to keep each other informed on how our leads panned out.

Seconds after hanging up, Hoover started making an unusually high-pitched combination of barking and whining. I followed the noise to the kitchenette, where Jeannine was pulling on a pair of disposable gloves. Hoover continued to make his unique noise as he nervously paced in front of a poop that was half-on and half-off of the newspapers.

Jeannine looked up and said, "Hoover's terribly embarrassed. He's usually very accurate."

I looked at the newspaper and saw a large ad for a re-issue of Disney's *Lady and the Tramp*. "Maybe he didn't feel right crapping on Lady," I said, hoping to get a laugh. Instead, Jeannine agreed and heaped bountiful praise on Hoover for being such a young gentleman.

By 4:00 PM CK was feeling like God had just shown His appreciation for his efforts to shut down the concert industry by helping him to land his second major contract in two weeks. Between the deal and tonight's concert at Leatherneck Park in Oceanside, he was feeling like a very powerful man. That high was short lived as his cell phone vibrated and he checked the caller ID.

"Yes, Father," he said.

As usual, his father began the phone call with a reading from the Bible. Upon concluding the reading, his father said, "The devil will be everywhere in the cities this weekend, my son."

"Is he not also in the country, Father?" CK asked.

"We country folk spend more time in church and less time giving ourselves over to the urges of the flesh."

CK said, "The Lord has been instrumental in helping me to succeed in business."

"I don't believe there are many Patricians seated at the right hand of the Father in the kingdom of heaven."

CK wished he could find a way to explain about how he was going to shut down the concert industry. But he knew his father would instantly start lecturing on the Sixth Commandment, *Thou Shall Not Kill*. So he simply asked, "How is Mother?"

"She's nearly worried to death that you'll lose your soul associating with the godless masses in the city," he thundered.

"It's not where you are, it's who you are. You and Mother did a wonderful job instilling a set of morals and values that don't change with my address."

His father began citing verses from the Bible, and CK tuned him out. He removed a dollar bill from his wallet, and stared at the Eye of Providence until his vision went out of focus. When he heard his father pause, CK said, "I have to go, Father. May the Lord be with you."

"And also with you, my son," he replied.

CK changed out of his business suit and into a pair of black jeans, a USMC sweatshirt, sneakers, and tucked the bill of a red Semper Fi cap into the back of his pants. He then pulled a yacht club windbreaker over the sweatshirt to wear through the resort lobby. He had made a reservation under an assumed name at a cheap motel in Oceanside, not far from the Marine base. This is where he'd change into the Halloween costume he would wear to the concert.

Kelly reminded me at least three times during the month that her high school friend, Lynette, was working at a haunted house in downtown San Diego throughout the Halloween season. I called at lunchtime and asked if she wanted to go see Lynette tonight. She was thrilled that I was paying attention. Lynette told her that if we went through the haunted house at the back end of the first group, she'd be able to chat for a minute and was looking forward to meeting me. Kelly thought the box office opened at 6:00 and the first tour went through at 6:30. I made reservations at a nice Italian bistro in the Gaslamp Quarter, not far from the haunted house, for 7:30.

Kelly suggested we wear Halloween costumes in keeping with the spirit of the weekend. But knowing that the restaurant would not be catering to revelers, I told her we shouldn't compete with Lynette's outfit and should probably dress in the kind of casual clothes that horror movie victims wear.

Just before 6:00 we arrived at the box office, only to read a sign that it opens at 6:30. After a quick scan of the immediate area, I spotted a Hooter's nearby and suggested we kill the half-hour by getting a drink.

"You were doing so well, up to this point," Kelly said.

"Oh, c'mon. It'll be fun."

"Fun for you. This was probably part of your plan all along"

"I'm not the one who said the box office opens at 6:00. I'll bet the waitresses are dressed up for Halloween."

Kelly reluctantly went along with my plan and, sure enough, the waitresses were in Halloween costumes. Our waitress was dressed in what appeared to be official USMC underwear, with a few cuts and tucks to the boxer shorts. Kelly landed a kick to my shinbone after I saluted her and said, "Private Pleasure reporting for duty, sir!"

After she took our orders and retreated to the bar, Kelly said, "I'll bet you're a riot at the tittie bars."

"I don't go to those places, except when I'm tailing someone for work or providing moral support at a bachelor party."

"I saw how you looked at her," Kelly said in a teasing manner.

"Just because I'm on a diet doesn't mean I can't look at the menu." Classic quotes, like classic rock, can be timeless.

"Unless you want to switch to the *No Fun Diet* I suggest you be mindful of your eyes when she returns with our drinks."

"I'll stare at the floor as a sign of my true devotion to you, my love."

Five minutes later our saucy soldier returned. True to my word, I held a $20 bill in my hand as I stared at her feet. "What color nail polish is that?" I asked.

"It's camouflage, to go with my outfit," she replied. "Do you like it?"

"I don't think it's such a good idea."

"Why not?" she asked.

Looking into her eyes for the first time since she returned, I replied, "You don't want the boys calling you *camo toes*, do you?"

My smile turned to a grimace as blood rushed to my shinbone.

The Jarhead Inn was everything CK expected. The desk clerk wasn't the least bit surprised when CK said he didn't have a credit card, but pulled out a small roll of twenty-dollar bills. The room would be $49.95 for the night.

"I'll need $100 security deposit if you don't have a card," he said.

"Right," CK replied, and peeled off five bills from his roll. "I like to get an early start in the morning. What time does the front desk open?"

"6:00 AM, sir," he said.

"Banker's hours," CK said. "Are you OK with settling up right now if I let you keep the balance of the deposit for your trouble?"

"Yes, sir! That would be fine, sir!" the clerk said enthusiastically.

CK walked a block and a half to his car, returned with his suitcase, and carried it up a flight of exterior stairs to his room. After placing the suitcase on the floor at the foot of the bed, he closed the curtains and turned on all of the lights. He then dropped to his knees near the head of the bed, and with his fingers interlocked on the bedspread he recited the Lord's Prayer aloud. Then he took a very hot shower, dried himself thoroughly, and stretched out naked on his bedspread for the next hour, staring at the ceiling. Statements such as: "I am a soldier in the Army of the Lord," and, "Tonight I am the physical embodiment of the wrath of God," were recited over and over.

CK arose from his bed at 7:30 PM and removed a costume from his suitcase. First, he put on a pair of red boxers. Over them he wore a pair of bellbottom blue jeans. He considered a similar pair with embroidery around the bottom hem, but decided against them to avoid standing out in the mind of one of the motel guests, should he be seen leaving for the concert. CK pulled on a T-shirt with the word "Nahum" stenciled in an abstract font across the front of its tie-dyed pattern. He then added nondescript socks and a new pair of cheap sneakers he picked up at a discount retailer in the South County.

He removed a long black wig he purchased in Los Angeles the previous week. Then he pulled a black cigar tube from the suitcase. Black electrical tape held one end of a small chain to the cigar tube, while the other end was attached to a black alligator clip. CK put on the wig, pulled it back into a ponytail, and used a black band to hold it in place. He then removed the wig, clipped the cigar tube into the ponytail, and tied the bottom end with a second band. He added a third band in the middle to make sure the tube didn't poke out of the tail. A tie-dyed headband was removed from the suitcase and put in his pocket. He placed a fake beard, spirit gum, and a change of clothes in a Marine backpack he acquired at a military surplus store.

CK pulled a crewneck USMC shirt over the tie-dyed shirt. Then he carefully wound the ponytail on top of his head and placed the large red Marine cap over it. He felt for both ends of the cigar tube, to make sure the hat's shape wasn't distorted.

He removed a dollar bill from his wallet and a black pen from a suitcase pocket. Starting at the bottom of the Great Seal, he drew a black line through the lower four rows of pyramid blocks. He drew a broken line through the fifth row and said, "There are 13 rungs on my ladder. As I ascend these steps, help me to be worthy to enter Your kingdom."

CK left his motel room at exactly 8:00 PM and trotted down the stairs. When he reached the bottom he heard, "Hey soldier, what's the hurry?"

He spun around and saw a hooker in her early thirties standing in the doorway of the motel room at the foot of the stairs. All she was wearing was a miniskirt-length red T-shirt that read *I'd rather be screwing a jar.*

CK asked, "Isn't there a man in your life who would rather see you dead than giving away your favors?"

"I ain't givin' nothin' away, soldier. It'll cost you fifty bucks if you want any favors from me."

CK briefly considered citing scripture on how a harlot could still attain the kingdom of heaven if she would only repent. But a voice within reminded him to stay focused on one mission at a time.

"I'll save my fifty for the collection plate."

"You do that," she said, "and I'll save my pussy for after you get drunk. Knock four times if Mr. Seagrams changes your mind."

Chapter 14

Dale Ebonrite worked most of the shows at Leatherneck Park that attracted a teens and twenties crowd. He was thrilled that tonight's show featured a techno band since his biggest profit margin came from selling ecstasy - the drug of choice for this crowd.

Leatherneck Park was Dale's favorite concert venue. It's the home of the Oceanside Leathernecks minor league baseball team, which goes out of its way to attract a family-oriented following. Behind the stands, down the right field line, is a children's playground which is within the concourse, but sealed off from the rest of the park to make it easy for parents to keep an eye on their kids without worrying about wanderers, perverts, or drunken patrons. A small restroom is located adjacent to the playground, which is where Dale handles all transactions. His friend on the security staff was well connected and always managed to get assigned as the sole protector of that section. He kept his distance to avoid scaring off customers, but remained close enough to call Dale on his cell phone if one of the few Oceanside police officers assigned to the show happened to wander his way.

As usual, Dale planned to start dealing as soon as the warm-up act kicked off. He would quit around the third or fourth song of the headliner, then watch the show and troll for latecomers and those who wanted to double their pleasure. Business was brisk during the warm-up act and the break that followed. Two of his regular customers had bought him beers, which he finished just after the headliner took the stage.

CK stopped his car in front of a vacant elementary school on his way to Leatherneck Park. Pulling his backpack up from the passenger seat floor, he removed his USMC shirt, and attached his beard with spirit gum. He then made sure his wig was straight, added the tie-dyed headband, and tucked the Marine shirt and cap into his bag.

He arrived inside the park 45 minutes after the warm-up was slated to begin. He immediately ordered two beers and began cruising the concourse. After a few minutes he found what he was looking for – a group of three girls in their late teens. They were dressed in bee costumes, that is, if bees suddenly decided to adopt a sexy look and spend the day at the beach.

"Hi girls," he said.

"Want to help us get our buzz on?" asked the queen bee.

CK shared one of his beers and asked if they knew where he could score some X. They told him they weren't into it, but would pay him to buy them more beer. He told them he could get in trouble for that, but allowed them to keep the one they were passing around.

A few minutes later he hit the jackpot. He saw two girls wearing glo necklaces and sucking on lollypops shaped like baby pacifiers. His online research told him these items were very common among ecstasy users. For a mere two sips of beer he was directed to the playground and told to say: *Heather said to get me rolling.*

By the time he got over there he could hear instruments being tuned and knew that the break was nearly over. He stood in the concession line nearest the playground and thoroughly inspected the surrounding area for security cameras. The only one he could see was aimed at the concession stands, so he pretended to reach for his wallet, checked his other pockets, and left the line without angling his face toward the camera.

Surveying the playground, CK saw about 10 people crowded around the swing, so he veered away and found a spot that was reasonably well lighted and away from the crowd. He pulled a piece of paper from his pocket and studied his notes on the names and opening lyrics of the headliner's top songs.

As the band started playing, he saw several people leave the playground area. Concerned that the dealer might close up shop to see the band, CK took another pass by the playground and saw three people bopping to the techno beat next to a playground swing. He decided that techno music made him feel less like dancing and more pressed to get on with his mission.

After glancing at his notes once again he saw a Halloween reveler with gigantic lips and teeth painted across his face, emerge from the bathroom. CK backed off and waited. He discretely removed the cigar tube from his ponytail, then slid a capped syringe from the tube and put it in his pocket. When the next song started he recognized it as the third one on his list, and certain to draw the fans into a sight-line to the stage. Sure enough, he saw four people run from the playground.

As CK entered the playground he saw a guy of about his same age sitting on a swing. He was aware of CK's presence, but acted very casual.

"Heather said to get me rolling," CK stated with a smile.

"Step into my office," Dale said, gesturing toward the restroom.

"Don't mind if I do."

When they got inside, Dale asked, "Straight X, or would you prefer kitty flipping?"

Time constraints trumped CK's curiosity about the nature of kitty flipping. "Straight X."

"They're fifteen each. How many do you want?"

"Two ought to do me," he replied. "But before we do this I gotta ask you a question. I've been having a problem getting my girlfriend to put out. Do you think your X will do the trick?"

Dale replied, "You want some advice from the love doctor? Hang on a minute. I gotta take a piss." He then turned his back on CK and stood in front of the urinal. As soon as the dealer faced the wall, CK removed the syringe from his pocket and pulled off the cap.

Dale said, "Your girlfriend wants it just as bad as you do. She's just being controlled by the guilt that her parents are laying on her. The X will make that guilt roll away."

"I gotta piss too," CK said, as he approached Dale.

When Dale started to zip up his pants, he glanced over his right shoulder just in time to catch sight of the syringe. His right forearm caught CK just below the elbow. Dale pivoted on his left heel, and tried to spin away. But he was pinned against a small tile wall that separated the urinals from the sinks.

CK used his legs, left shoulder, and arm to hold Dale against the wall while he gripped the syringe in his fist with his thumb on the plunger. Dale put his right foot against the wall behind him and pushed. He expected his assailant to back up. But 18 years of farm chores built a lot of muscle mass. All Dale's move managed to accomplish was to cause a blue drip to form on the tip of the needle, which was now just an inch from his eye.

"Take the cash and the stash. You know I'm not gonna report you," Dale said in a strained voice.

"Not interested, pusher," CK replied.

"You're that girl's brother. You can't blame me. She told me she was buying the ten hits for a party. I couldn't know that she'd take them all herself. You gotta believe me!"

CK lowered the syringe a couple of inches. "So, you're not just a pusher, you're also a murderer. The devil's got a special place for guys like you."

Dale desperately tried a head-butt move that he had seen in 100 movies. CK responded by pulling his head and shoulders back while keeping his hands in place. He also instinctively closed his eyes and turned his head. Before they reopened CK felt a tremendous weight pull his hands down.

For a moment he couldn't comprehend what had happened. The pusher briefly convulsed on the floor while facing the tile wall that was at his back. A final spasm whipped the pushers head around and CK saw the syringe sticking out of his nostril. Dale had impaled himself on the needle as he finished the head-butt.

"That must be the kitty flip."

CK peeked out the restroom door, then returned the syringe to the cigar tube and stuck it in his pocket.

He then removed a note that said $X=V$ from his back pocket and dropped it on the floor. After adjusting his wig in the mirror he glanced at the dealer and said, "Nice doing business with you."

Aside from the Hooters detour, the evening went very well. I convinced Kelly's friend that she nearly threw my heart into arrhythmia when she came out of nowhere in makeup and clothes that made her appear to be a pre-Technicolor, black & white zombie. She was as elated as an aspiring actress could be over her rave reviews.

Kelly and I discussed our domestic spat shortcomings over dinner, but in a positive way that made us feel like we were moving forward in our relationship. We stopped for a couple of drinks at Dick's Last Resort after dinner, where the people-watching on Halloween weekend made the Star Wars Bar look pedestrian.

We were home before midnight and headed straight to bed. Normally, Kelly's prep routine takes twice as long as mine and I'm in bed long before she emerges from the master bathroom. But I let her know I was taking the dog out to the backyard to be sure she was in bed first.

Earlier in the day I found a Big Bad Wolf rubber mask in the garage. After a little digging I also found the Granny outfit that Kelly wore in a school play last year. While Colonel Hogan did his business I put on the outfit, cued up an old Sam the Sham and the Pharaohs CD, and put the CD remote in the apron pocket. I left the mask off until the last possible second, since prior experience taught me it didn't take long for a rubber mask to make my face look like I just ran the Calcutta Marathon in record time.

After a couple of minutes the main light in the bedroom was replaced by Kelly's blue meditation light. When Batman sees the Bat Signal he knows to get ready for some action. Kelly's meditation light was my Bat Signal. Yes, I knew I'd be getting lucky with or without the costume and soundtrack. But as any guy who's ever taken his girlfriend to the back row of a drive-in for a horror film will tell you, a well-timed scare can be a powerful aphrodisiac.

I turned off the rest of the lights, moved to the left of the bedroom doorway, pulled the mask over my head, and pressed *play* on the CD remote. Right after Sam the Sham sang, "Who's that I see walking in these woods? Why it's Little Red Riding Hood," I pounced on the bed and let rip with a powerful, "Aaaaahhhhhooooooooooooooo!"

Kelly shrieked the scream of an amused participant. A second later the phone rang three feet to her left and it scared the shit out of her. I was hoping Caller ID would allow me to stay with Plan A. I'd been dying to launch into my parody as Sam sang "What big eyes you have" but it was not to be. Detective Walter Shamansky would be calling at that hour for only one reason.

Chapter 15

I arrived at Leatherneck Park just after 1:00 AM, called Shamansky, and met him at the police barricade spanning the right field entrance. Beyond the barricade I could see a night construction lighting tower pumping out enough wattage to give me a tan.

Shamansky moved the sawhorse police line out of the way long enough for me to enter. He then returned it as a press photographer tried squeezing in.

"Stay close to me, Darden's here," he said.

"You don't suppose he's holding a grudge."

"Let's keep the bullshit to a minimum. He's running the show and won't put up with any distractions, especially from you."

"Out!" yelled Darden, as soon as he saw me. He then turned to his partner and added, "This guy nearly got me killed a couple of months ago."

"The captain said he could be here," Shamansky said.

"This is my scene and I say he's out," Darden said in his high pitched voice, taking a step closer to Shamansky.

Shamansky pulled out his phone and said, "I'll get him out after you wake the captain up and tell him why you countermanded his directive in the field. Otherwise, back off and let us do our jobs."

Darden said, "He's your responsibility, Shamansky. Make sure you both stay out of my way."

Shamansky grumbled to me about departmental politics as we walked over to the swings. When we arrived he said, "It looks like the vic was a drug dealer. We found ecstasy and ecstasy with ketamine in his pocket. The body's in the restroom by the urinals."

"It looks like a pretty sweet set-up for a dealer. No cross-traffic, no vendors nearby. Is there a security camera covering this side of the concourse?" I asked.

Shamansky pointed in the direction of home plate and said, "That white wall over there is the far end of the concession stands. There's a camera above the right field gate that doesn't cover anything beyond that wall."

"How many Oceanside PD officers were assigned to the show?"

"Only four: two in the parking lot and two inside. As you know, most of the security is handled by a paid staff."

I said, "I'm thinking the dealer might have used a lookout. If we don't spot the killer on the video, we might be able to ID the lookout."

"I'll ask the captain to have an extra copy made. I don't think we should rely on Darden passing anything along."

"At what point in the show was the body found?" I asked.

"The main act took the stage at 9:20 and the body was found around 10:00."

"Did they stop the show?"

"No. By the time the scene was secured the show was almost over. Oceanside PD felt the perp was already gone and the chance of somebody getting hurt in a panic stampede was too high."

"Good call," I said.

"What was the gate attendance?"

"Around 8400."

"Techno is bigger than I thought."

Shamansky said, "The crime scene people are still in the restroom, but we can see most everything from the doorway."

He was right. The victim was lying in a contorted position in front of the urinals, facing away from them.

"Any new developments?" Shamansky asked the supervisor.

"We found several small droplets of a blue liquid in front of the sinks," she said.

"Any prints?" he asked.

"No."

"Cause of death?"

She replied, "The cause isn't apparent. But, the coroner will be checking for a hypodermic puncture wound in his first pass."

Leaning in to get a better look, I was suddenly elbowed in the solar plexus, careened into the doorframe, and slid to the floor.

"Out of our way, Duffy," squeaked Darden. "You too, Shamansky."

I looked up and saw Michele Ko, the Irvine detective, standing next to Darden. I gave her a wink and she quickly looked away.

Darden said to Ko, "We found the note on the floor below the paper towel dispenser."

"What note?" asked Shamansky.

By this point I was on my feet. Darden held up the note, which was now encased in clear plastic.

"What does it mean?" asked Ko.

Darden replied, "X=V sounds like part of an algebra problem to me. Did you have any math-related clues in Irvine?"

I said, "X is the slang for ecstasy, which is what the dealer was selling. V is the Roman numeral five, as in murder number five."

Michele returned my wink and gave me the smallest hint of a smile.

Darden asked, "Why leave a note stating the obvious?"

Shamansky said, "He wants to make sure he's given credit. That was the purpose behind his last note."

"If he wants credit, why hasn't he gone to the press?" Ko asked. No one answered.

Darden said, "Make sure you don't run your mouth to the press, Duffy."

"I work for the promoters. The last thing they want is to scare off their paying customers."

Darden said, "Maybe we should rethink going public. Our obligation is to protect the people."

"It's not your call," said Shamansky. "As long as the head of the task force says to keep a lid on it, that's what you do."

Darden replied, "Maybe it's time a little birdie started whispering in that chipper's ear."

I said, "Be sure to give him a little peck on the lobe for me, Darden. I'm outta here."

Chapter 16

Kelly woke me at 11:00 AM Saturday to say Calvin was on the phone.

"I know you were up until all hours, so I won't keep you very long. How about if Kayleigh and I take you and Kelly to dinner at Grant Grill around 7:00 if I can get a reservation? Afterwards, we can go across the street to Horton Plaza and let the girls window shop while you fill me in on the murder."

"Sounds like a plan."

"I'll call back if I can't get 7:00. Otherwise, we'll pick you up at 6:30."

I spent the rest of the day doing domestic chores while mulling various potential suspects and motives. I forced myself to focus on Calvin's partners since I could get some answers about them in a few hours. After my experience with Jimmy DeLong, Lonnie was definitely a person of interest. But I couldn't connect him to a religious motive. Maybe it was a ruse. If not, Mark certainly gave me the impression he was a true believer. But it seemed that his concerts would be hit the hardest financially by a serial killer on a mission from God. Ashley was a wild card. I hoped Calvin could make her decidedly less enigmatic.

Shortly after 7:00 we were seated at Grant Grill in one of San Diego's most historic hotels, the US Grant. I ordered the estancia grass fed strip loin, while Kelly selected the Julian pear & duck confit tart. Despite the fact that the menu was teeming with pretentious lingo, I couldn't bring myself to engage the waitress in snappy repartee. Viewing a young corpse in the middle of the night was having an undesirable side effect.

Judging from Calvin's color and manner, he was internalizing the murder as well. Fortunately, the women were happy to carry the conversation as their friendship blossomed. I was enthralled with Kayleigh's tales of being the bass player in an all-girl band. One story was funnier than the next. Instead of matching stories from my years with Tsunami Rush, I prompted Kelly to share some moments that helped our hosts get to know her better.

After a round of decadent desserts and coffee, we aimed our sauce-laden bellies at the Horton Plaza shopping center and managed to waddle across the street without getting sideswiped. Kelly and Kayleigh understood that the men would be tailing them at a distance while conducting shoptalk.

I laid out the crime scene for Calvin without bringing up the Darden complications, other than to mention his desire to go public.

"Do you think he can sway the task force to go in that direction?" Calvin asked.

"He's an asshole, but a well-connected asshole. You should get in front of it if you have any influence with the powers that be."

We paused while Kayleigh pointed at an outrageously expensive sleeveless white evening gown. Calvin smiled and shook his head. Kayleigh contorted her face into an exaggerated pout for a moment, then beamed at Kelly.

"I think I'm being set up," Calvin said.

"Pro beach volleyball players could take lessons from those two," I replied.

"Back to the investigation," he said. "Where are you at?"

I gave Calvin an overview, ending with Lonnie's connection to Jimmy DeLong. "I'm not sold on the fact that Jimmy or Lonnie had anything to do with the murders, but I have a few questions for you that could help me eliminate suspects."

"Shoot."

"Lonnie's clearly the wildest of the four of you in the CLAM consortium. Do you know anything about his parents or any religious experience he may have mentioned?"

"I think you're barking up the wrong tree on that one. I don't know anything about his parents, but I can tell you that he was against bringing Mark into the fold because he thinks religion has blinded him to the realities of the business world."

"It sounds like Lonnie's pretty down on religion."

"Definitely."

"Enough to make religious fanatics the fall guys if he has a financial motive?"

"What possible financial motive could he have? The murders could ruin us."

"By us you mean CLAM. What if Lonnie wants out? What if a serial killer at concerts is a plus for heavy metal and rap shows, while putting alternatives like Christian rock out of business?"

Calvin rubbed his face with both hands. "We began operating as a limited partnership in January. Since Lonnie and I are older and more established, we brought more to the table than Mark and Ashley. We share expenses and revenues, but not equally. Performance at the gate plays an important role in the profit split."

"It looks like I can't eliminate Lonnie based on motive."

"Also, the partnership is renewable annually."

"Does that mean at the end of your fiscal year, if there are partners who aren't pulling their weight, you're free to reconfigure the relationship?"

Calvin nodded sorrowfully and said, "Yes."

"Thank you!" shouted Kayleigh from twenty feet away as she grabbed Kelly's hand and ran into Nordstrom.

I said, "Now that you're worried on two fronts, let me ask you about Mark. Is there any chance he could be affiliated with a fanatical sect?"

"I honestly don't believe so. When I think of a fanatic I see someone with a *glass half empty* attitude. Mark is an optimist and a humanitarian."

"Have you ever seen a serial killer's neighbor being interviewed?"

"*He was such a nice guy.* Sure, I've seen them. But Mark is also a Ten Commandments guy. Breaking *thou shall not kill* is a ticket to hell in his book. There's nothing on this earth that would motivate him to take a pass on heaven."

Suddenly, a horrifying yell rang out less than five feet behind us. Clearly startled, we spun around in time to see two kids dressed in *Scream* costumes running toward the escalator.

"I thought there was another murder right behind us," Calvin said.

"I thought Kayleigh just showed you the Nordy bill," I replied.

When we got home from our outing I wasn't in the mood to reprise my Big Bad Wolf routine. The element of surprise was gone. Instead, I asked Kelly to play granny wolf. She was going along with the idea until I told her what came after, "What big teeth you have."

I actually did have some fun with the outfit on Halloween night when the neighborhood kids rang my doorbell for their annual sugar fix. Kelly answered the door cleverly disguised as her alter-ego, Marilyn Munster. After making a fuss over their costumes she excused herself to get the candy. But instead of amiable Marilyn, they got a well-timed *aaaaahhhhhhooooooo* as I leaped into the doorway. At least five of them ran away without collecting their booty, but with a terrific story to tell their friends.

My enjoyment of the festivities came to a halt when I walked outside to check on the candle in our jack-o-lantern. As I leaned down to see how much candle was left, a loud roar hijacked my attention. I turned around and saw four large motorcycles parked across the street. Each biker's face was painted like a member of the band, *Kiss*.

The one who dressed like Gene Simmons flicked a lighter, turned, and huddled with the other three. When he turned around, all four threw M-80s into my yard. After the explosions and screams from several children, they revved engines, popped wheelies, and rocketed up the street at a speed that was way too fast for a Halloween night.

Chapter 17

The next ten days were relatively uneventful. It was a time when Jeannine helped me to bring order to a growing mountain of data. Since Cory's darkroom was converted into an office we added a rolling two-sided corkboard. On one side Jeannine listed the victims across the top. Below she added dates, venues, band genre, weapons, occupation, and other demographic items.

On the other side she listed potential suspects across the top, leaving room for additions. We opted to keep the board in Cory's room since three out of our four employers were on the list. I did my best to learn their whereabouts on the night of each murder. Ashley was the only one I cleared through this process.

I coordinated with Celia Bains three times during this timeframe. I called her the day after Halloween to tell her I thought Jimmy was trying to *Rock & Roll All Night* in my neighborhood. She didn't have a tail on him, but confirmed that he wasn't at his favorite L.A. watering hole that evening.

She called back a week later and asked me to find out who insured the CLAM concerts. After I asked why, she said she'd tell me when she had the information.

Calvin does a little tour planning and contract negotiations for bands on the side. He was in Texas putting a deal together when I called. He wasn't able to answer my question until he returned to his office files because CLAM used different insurers depending on the venue, band, and expected attendance.

I was about to call it a day on Wednesday, the 9th, when Calvin called. "I can't believe I didn't see this before.

We used the same insurance company for all three of the shows we promoted when there were murders. What's the connection?"

"The detective who's following Jimmy DeLong asked the question. She told me she'd let me know when I had the information. I'll call you back."

Two minutes later I connected with Bains. "All three CLAM shows were insured by Gordian C. Knox Insurance."

"Does CLAM use them for all of their shows?" she asked.

"No. In fact they spread their business over several different insurers. Apparently, the insurance companies that cover concerts have unique formulas for assessing risk. While they combine most of the same risk factors, they weigh them very differently," I said.

"I don't get it," she said.

"Let's say ABC Insurance covered 10 concerts last year and processed a total of one claim – a senior who fell at a 50's show and needed hip replacement surgery. So they bump their rates for 50's shows. But, XYZ Insurance settled with the parents of a kid who broke his leg in a mosh pit at a hardcore show. They might drop their rates for 50's shows to try to attract an older demographic, and jack their rates on hardcore and metal. Smart promoters shop the rates."

"So, the odds are pretty long that this is a coincidence?" she asked.

"I'd say so. What about the two shows that CLAM didn't promote?"

She replied, "They were covered by the same insurer, but not the one CLAM used. It would be a full house if we were playing poker."

"What got you on to the insurance company tie-in?"

"I should probably flesh this out a little more before I start drawing any conclusions," she said.

"C'mon, Celia. You're overdrawn at the favor bank. It's time to make a deposit. It's not like I'm taking this to the press," I said.

"Yes, but you are working for CLAM."

I told her about my *suspects* board and assured her that Lonnie would be kept in the dark on this matter.

She said, "The bodyguard you met in Ocotillo Wells is working for a guy named John Murray. He's no longer affiliated, but used to be a partner in an insurance company that underwrote a lot of concert policies."

"Not Gordian C. Knox, by any chance?" he asked.

"Actually they're more like an insurance company to the insurance companies. They're called Diversified Risk Insurance Group. I don't have their client list, but I've got a contact inside the company who will confirm or deny an affiliation."

"I take it the company that insured the two shows that CLAM didn't produce is on the client list."

"You are correct, sir."

"Anything else?"

"Just a thought," she said. "Why don't you give your favorite bartender in Ocotillo Wells a call and ask her if Jimmy and his posse showed up in costume on Halloween night."

"You should be a detective."

"Call me when you find out and I'll let you know what my contact says about CLAM's insurer."

Chapter 18

I knew something was wrong the instant I walked into my office on Thursday morning to a ringing phone and the number 7 flashing on the answering machine. Since Jeannine was outside with Hoover, I picked up.

"Duffy Investigations."

"Jason, its Derek," said my former band mate from Tsunami Rush. "Did you read the article on the concert killings in San Diego Sound Scene this morning?"

"I just got in. What does it say?"

"It says a serial killer is working the California concert circuit. There are some grisly details on five murders over the past four months."

"What made you call me, Derek?"

"The article says you've been working with the police on behalf of CLAM to do a hush-hush, behind the scenes investigation."

"Holy shit! Who wrote the article?"

"Dee Martin Sandler," Derek said.

"Damn! He's the most credible writer that I know on the free press circuit."

"Just how well do you know him?"

"Well enough that if you Google me you'll find an article he wrote about my appearance with Doberman's Stub last year."

"I take it the cops are going to think you're the leak."

"Especially my number one fan. This is a disaster."

"Let me know if I can help."

"Thanks, Derek."

I sent Jeannine over to Schlotzsky's Deli for a copy of the paper as soon as she walked through the door. I listened to the messages while she was out. Darden didn't identify himself, but simply said, "Merry Christmas. My present came six weeks early this year."

When Jeannine returned I read the article. The other surprise that Derek didn't mention was the theory that the killings could be the work of a radical religious sect. Since this was my theory, I started listing the people I told when Jeannine said Shamansky was on the phone.

"Where the hell did they get that story?" he asked emphatically.

"I have no idea. I haven't talked to the guy in over a year."

"He certainly knows about you and your connection to the case. He also seems well versed on your theory."

"My initial theory," I corrected. "I haven't mentioned it to anyone since my encounter with Jimmy DeLong."

"Do you think Jimmy's in on it?"

"There are a lot of things that don't add up about this case. Jimmy's name keeps popping up. But if he's involved, he certainly isn't the brains behind a religious sect."

"I overheard Darden planning your character assassination this morning."

"Will you give me a heads-up if there's anything I need to worry about?"

"Heads-up," Shamansky said, and disconnected.

I called Calvin and summarized the article. It was decided that Calvin would meet with his partners and get back to me.

I debated whether or not to call Dee Martin Sandler. I needed to find out the identity of the mole, but doubted that Sandler would reveal his source. I also assumed that the mainstream press would be in touch with him throughout the day, and decided that a call might fan the flames.

The other issue was that I respected Dee and didn't want to lie to him. At first I was a little surprised and perturbed that he hadn't called to confirm the story before going to press. Then it dawned on me that Sandler realized it would put me in a precarious position with my employers and the police. We weren't such great friends that he'd kill a free press story-of-the-year to help me avoid a career setback. More importantly, I was sure he believed that concert-goers absolutely needed to know of potential dangers at the shows.

Calvin phoned shortly after noon to say Lonnie sent out a press release categorically denying the veracity of Sandler's story. He called it "irresponsible journalism, using sensationalist tactics to try and build his reputation." Lonnie followed up with phone calls to his best mainstream print and radio contacts in L.A., San Diego and San Francisco.

Calvin said, "He's putting his rep on the line to sell the denial. How does that jive with your suspicion that he could be involved?"

"Before I answer, let me ask you this: How will your insurance rates be impacted once it becomes known that a serial killer might be in the audience?"

"They'll go through the roof. If we can't find a company to cover us, we won't get permits for any shows."

I said, "So, the concert killer could actually kill the industry here in California."

"At least as far as the independent promoters are concerned. I'm sure the big monolith corporations that not only promote but also manage bands and control ticket sales could certainly force insurers to cover California shows or be dropped from their bid list."

"Is there any chance somebody on the inside at one of the corporations could be involved?"

"You're asking the wrong guy that question, Jason. I've considered them the Evil Empire for so long I couldn't possibly give you an objective answer."

"But you agree that they would benefit more than anyone from the independent promoters being squeezed out in California."

"Definitely. But I can't see a whole region being in on a conspiracy."

"What about a rogue salesman, or a manager about to lose his job if he can't get his numbers up?"

"You may need a bigger corkboard, Jason."

As the day progressed it became clear that Lonnie's PR campaign convinced the mainstream press that Dee Martin Sandler's story was nothing more than a publicity stunt contrived by the free press. I cringed when I saw Sandler grilled by a reporter from a local network affiliate. It came down to the reporter trying to force Sandler to give up his source to prove his credibility. Sandler wouldn't cave, but used his moment in the spotlight to warn the public to use extreme caution when attending shows, both inside and outside of the venues.

Just before I left the office for the day I glanced at my To Do list and realized that I needed to call Lacey, the bartender in Ocotillo Wells. Using my cell phone to avoid having Duffy Investigations show up on caller ID, I reached her on the fourth ring. After a minute of shameless flirting I told her I thought about coming out to see her on Halloween night but was concerned that Jimmy might be there.

"It's a good thing you stayed home. He was here and dressed up like Gene Simmons from *Kiss*. Every time I leaned over the bar he tried poking me in the boob with his foot-long rubber tongue. I nearly broke a beer bottle over his head."

I told her I would stop by again, soon. Then I called Kelly to make sure the doors and windows were locked. Too bad Colonel Hogan is still a pup.

Chapter 19

The first thing I did on Friday morning was to call an annoying, yet brilliant client from my days as a mental health counselor. Drayton Claymore is as paranoid as a teenage boy dating a hitman's daughter. But he knows more about the latest high tech security equipment than most of the R&D department heads who develop the technology. I helped him land a job with the top security firm in Southern California, but learned over the summer that one of Drayton's other quirks got him fired.

On the sixth ring he mumbled, "Hello."

"Drayton, its Jason Duffy. Don't tell me I woke you up on this beautiful morning."

"OK, I won't."

"How would you like a job setting up a security system at my house?" I asked, but there was no response. "Drayton? Are you with me?"

"She looked just like my mother. How did you do that?"

I yelled, "DRAYTON, ITS JASON! WAKE UP! SIT UP IN BED AND OPEN YOUR EYES!"

"Jason?"

"Yes, Drayton. I need you to set up a security system at my house. Can you get started on it today?"

"Sure. First thing in the morning," he said. "Can you give me a wake up call?"

"It's after 9:00. This *is* your wake up call. How soon can you meet me at my house?"

"I'm sorry. I was having a really vivid dream."

"You aren't staying up all night spying on your neighbors again, are you?"

In a voice that told me he was finally awake, but not necessarily being truthful, he said, "I learned my lesson. I'll never do that again."

"I live about 20 minutes from your house. Can you meet me at 11:00?" Drayton agreed and I gave him directions.

I found Jeannine in Cory's office staring at the victim chart. "Any thoughts I should know about?"

"I don't like the way we've set up the board. I can't get the occupations to line up in the little blocks under the victims' names. The roadie and groupie are fine. But the beer vendor, loan officer, and drug dealer just won't fit," she said.

"Feel free to abbreviate."

"I don't see why we need the occupations at all. I tried to correlate them by occupation and, no matter how I look at it, I can't figure how a loan officer fits into the equation," she said.

Touching the chart I said, "Look at the weapons column. The drug dealer was shot up with drain cleaner. The groupie was drowned in a restroom, a well-known spot for sex at a concert. The roadie was shot in the eye with a derringer. Did he see something he wasn't supposed to? The beer vendor's throat was slit. He won't be pouring alcohol down anyone's throat anymore."

"What about the loan officer?" she asked.

"Maybe he saw her as the concert-goer, not a bank employee."

"Why choke the concert-goer?"

"Possibly so she can't tell other people what a great time she had at the show," I said.

Jeannine picked one of Hoover's hairs off of my sleeve. "You've given me a lot to think about."

I arrived home at 10:45 AM and found myself standing in front of my liquor cabinet. I'm really not much of a drinker. But in the 20-minute ride from my office I kept thinking about how much I disliked the therapy sessions with Drayton. He used to try to turn everything I said into a pun or a joke. It was probably just a manifestation of his condition which was never accurately diagnosed. But it made for some very long and painful sessions. I walked away from the liquor cabinet when I realized I'd need to have my wits about me if I wanted to understand Drayton's security techno-speak.

At exactly 11:00 my chimes rang. When I opened the door Drayton said, "Avon calling," and began examining the deadbolt. Drayton is 6'4" and weights about 150 pounds. He has a hawk's nose, turquoise eyes, and a habit of running his hands through his long dirty-blond hair.

"What do you think?" I asked.

"You're not the straw house piggy, but you're not the brick house piggy either. I guess that makes you the stick house piggy."

"No way! I was the big bad wolf a couple of weeks ago for Halloween," I said. Drayton looked momentarily confused while I glanced at the liquor cabinet and wondered what might have come out of my mouth if I hadn't abstained.

"So, you decided to call your old buddy after the door failed your huff and puff test?"

"All kidding aside, a motorcycle gang showed up at my house that night, and I want to make sure my girlfriend doesn't get any surprise visitors."

"Ah, the lovely Kelly. I remember her from the album release party last summer."

"Thanks again for your help on that case. The security system you installed in my office probably saved Jeannine's life."

"The world would be a lesser place without Little Annie Fannie. Glad to be of service. What did you have in mind for your house?"

I told him how much I could afford and Drayton started drifting through my living room like he was Adrian

Monk doing his trance-like assessment while his arms floated in front of him. The trance abruptly ended when he walked in front of the French doors leading to my enclosed patio and Colonel Hogan barked at him. His startled reaction was so intense that I was afraid he might have wet himself.

"That's Colonel Hogan. Are you OK?"

"Yes, but for some odd reason, dogs don't seem to like me. Can you tie him to a tree or something?"

Unless it's raining I keep the door to the enclosed patio open during the day so that Colonel Hogan has access to the fenced back and side yards. He wasn't thrilled about being restricted to ten feet of rope and barked constantly whenever Drayton was in sight.

It's best to spare you the details of Drayton's recommendations. Basically, he proposed cameras aimed at the front and back of the house that work like motion sensor lights. But instead of a light going on, a bell would sound on my computer, and the image that tripped the sensor would appear on the screen. A third mini-cam would be placed on a harness collar that Colonel Hogan would wear. This one would be activated by barking instead of motion. I'd be able to view them from my office and mobile phone screens. In addition, he proposed installing panic buttons that auto-dial 911, enabling the operator to hear what's going on in the house.

I gave him a blank check made out to his favorite electronics store and he said he'd be back around 2:00. As soon as he departed I hopped in the RXS and drove to my parents' house just in time for lunch.

Mom spent most of our meal describing my sister's kitchen remodeling project. Dad and I did our best to appear interested but unenthusiastic. It was our polite way of letting her know not to volunteer us for any construction-related activities. When lunch was over, Dad and I went out to the backyard.

Dad said, "It sounds like you've got a leak. I heard about the music paper mentioning your name."

"I think Lonnie's damage control headed off any big problems for the moment."

"So, what brings you over here today?" Dad asked.

I told him about Jimmy DeLong's Halloween visit and Drayton's involvement. Dad met Drayton on a case over the summer.

Dad said, "I have to admit, when I first met that guy I thought he should be living in a padded room. But the way he set up your office was brilliant."

"I'm glad you feel that way, Dad, because I need you to keep an eye on him this afternoon while he does the installation. I have some things to do that can't wait until tomorrow. But every time I think about Kelly getting ambushed I lose focus. Can you help me out?"

"Oh, Jeez! You know I'm not good around those kinds of people."

"I'm sure you'll do just fine. You didn't have any problems last summer."

"You know he's going to say something to piss me off. Remember how he kept talking to me like I was Frasier Crane's father? And besides, it's Veteran's Day. I'm sure a lot of old friends will be heading to Casey's Bar early today."

"I'm sure you put up with a lot worse when you were on the force. If you don't want to do it for me, do it for Kelly."

"I thought Lisa's kitchen remodel was the worst thing I'd get roped into this afternoon," he grumbled.

"Wait until you see what Drayton's going to be doing. You'll be fascinated. He's even putting a mini-cam on Colonel Hogan's collar."

"Isn't that what got him fired from Kitzer & Kitzer?"

I looked at my watch. "If you're not going to do it I'm going to have to start rearranging my day."

"Alright. I've got your house key in the kitchen. I'll be there by 1:45."

"Thanks, Dad. Any news on O'Malley?"

"Not good, son. Keep him in your prayers."

As I walked into Duffy Investigations, Jeannine said, "I've got the insurance company information you asked about."

"Bring it into my office."

She handed me a file folder before sitting in the chair across from my desk. I noted that there were about 10 pages in the file.

"Can you give me a brief summary of what's in here, Jeannine?"

"As you know, John Murray was partners in Diversified Risk Insurance Group. They insure independent insurance companies."

"What got John bounced from the partnership?"

"The official line was that he left the company to pursue other opportunities."

"How original. Did you get a chance to check the business chat rooms?"

Jeannine replied, "I floated the question on a couple of boards, but no replies yet."

"Try putting *Diversified Risk Insurance Group sucks* into a search engine. If it brings up a forum in the first three pages, ask the same question. People who are pursuing legitimate opportunities don't need bodyguards."

"How would using a potty-mouth expression help to find out what happened?"

"Disgruntled former coworkers and unhappy clients like to express their dissatisfaction. By putting the word *sucks* in the search engine you tap into that group. Were the two insurance companies that covered the five murder venues both using Diversified Risk for reinsurance?"

"Yes, but that's not very unusual. They're the top reinsurer of concerts west of the Mississippi." Hoover nuzzled Jeannine's calf for attention. Holding her finger by his nose she said, "Manners."

"I need you to check John's police record, credit rating, and see if you can find his resume in an online executive search database. Also, if Diversified Risk Insurance Group is a publically traded company, take a look at their SEC filings and analyst reports."

"Anything else?"

"If Cory's in his office will you send him in?"

"He never went home last night."

I plucked the file labeled *Video Perp Possibilities* from my desk drawer. If Jeannine is ever cured of her Obsessive-Compulsive Disorder I'll have to hire an assistant's assistant.

I could tell from the cadence of Cory's F-bomb entrance that he was excited. I surmised the surveillance video from Leatherneck Park that Shamansky dropped off yesterday afternoon was the cause of Cory's enthusiasm.

"You look like you're busting to tell me something. Why don't you go first."

Cory led me back to his office where he showed me a split screen close-up of two men with vaguely similar features. One looked like a transvestite while the other appeared to be a hippie. The transvestite looked like he was wearing a brown wig, reminding me of my call from Detective Ko. Cory told me the next picture would be a split screen of the same photos after using his disguise removal software. The resemblance became striking; maybe not admissible in court, but striking nonetheless.

"What's that word on the front of the hippie's shirt?" I asked.

Cory said that he framed the spot on the video where it was most visible and tried enhancing it. But the best he could do was to identify the first letter as a capital "N" and the last as a lower case "m."

"Good work, Cory. I want you to tail John Murray. He has an ex-mercenary bodyguard who's loosely connected to a biker gang, so be extra careful."

I felt like Cory's discovery could be my ticket back into Dean Casey's good graces. Realizing that the direct approach was unlikely to produce results, I called Shamansky and summarized the findings.

He replied, "I wouldn't send Casey a *friend request* just yet."

"Why not?"

"First, Irvine and Oceanside are just over a half hour apart. There could have been a lot of people at both shows," Shamansky said.

"Power pop and techno fans? I don't think so."

"Some people go to shows for reasons other than the music. Maybe a tranny on the prowl likes to experiment with different crowds."

"He looked more Haight-Ashbury than RuPaul at Oceanside."

"It was Halloween. Dean Casey wouldn't go out on a limb that thin for a former partner."

"So I'm supposed to sit on a picture of our top suspect?" I was clearly irritated.

"I'm just telling it like it is."

"The guy was facing the playground when the video caught him."

"That should put him in line at one of the concession stands. Am I right?" Shamansky tried sounding more sympathetic than skeptical.

"So, you don't think it qualifies as a solid lead?"

"I think you should work it for all it's worth. It's just not enough to get you on the other side of the stone wall that's facing you with the boys in blue right now. If I can lend any detective skills let me know," he said, and hung up.

Exiting my car, I heard Dad screaming. "Claymore, when I find you I'm gonna shove one of your namesakes up your arse and throw you out the window!"

"What's going on?" I called.

"I'm about to cure your old patient with a frontal lobotomy!"

"Calm down and tell me what happened."

In an even louder voice Dad yelled, "Get the hell out of my way! I'm gonna kill him!"

I clamped an arm around my father's shoulder, spun him toward the door and said, "You need to get out of here and calm down. You look like you're about to have a stroke. I'll take care of whatever it is that Drayton did."

Cooperating, but still shouting, Dad added, "If anything about me shows up on the Internet that asshole goes in the ground!"

After I shut and locked the door I heard Dad yell, "Dead man walking!" before he burned rubber pealing out of the driveway.

"Drayton?" I used a soothing tone.

I poked my head in my old office that now served as the storage room for Kelly's excess furniture.

Drayton whispered, "Is he gone yet?"

"He's gone. Now come out here and tell me what happened."

Drayton wiggled out from under a love seat in the far corner. "I know this looks bad right now, but I may have recorded the funniest thing that will ever appear on YouTube." At the threshold to the office door he asked, "Are you sure he's not out there?"

"Didn't you hear him leave? He burned through more rubber than a downtown pharmacy on days when the fleet comes in."

Drayton walked to the roll top desk at the back of the living room where I now kept my computer. "Oopsie," he said. A hammer was embedded in the monitor. "I have a laptop in my car."

Once it was up and running he said, "I'm not exactly sure of how to monetize huge numbers of Internet hits, but I know we're sitting on a goldmine."

"What are you talking about?"

"I told you about how I was getting a special harness for Colonel Hogan that would hold a camera and a microphone. I figured if there was a problem outside that wasn't visible to one of the cameras, the dog would be on it and you'd see it from inside the house or on your computer at work."

"What happened to my father?"

"While I was checking out the system, nature called and Colonel Hogan followed him into the bathroom."

"And you caught him with his pants down?"

Drayton covered his face with both palms and inhaled deeply. "There's no way I can describe this. You have to watch the video." Not waiting for an acknowledgement he tapped his keyboard.

Sitting to the left of the camera, Dad was on the throne and made a couple of squinty faces that I didn't find particularly amusing. As I was about to admonish Drayton for his sophomoric prank I heard my father say, "Colonel Hogan, that's what you're supposed to do on the papers." The camera tilted, which meant that Colonel Hogan was giving his *I don't understand* response.

I saw the four sheets of newspaper I placed on the bathroom floor earlier in the day. Dad proceeded to circle the papers three times before assuming a squatting position. He didn't actually go on the papers. But his enthusiastic instructions and Rodney Dangerfield smile was a gut buster. I didn't want Drayton to see me laugh, but containing my emotions was an impossible task. First my stomach started to quiver. Then my shoulders began to bob up and down.

"Let it out, Jason. You're liable to shoot an aneurism if you stifle that laugh any longer."

I lost control. I laughed so hard that tears streamed down my cheeks. I nearly had my emotions back in check when Drayton said, "We could probably Photoshop a happy face over his naughty parts and be good to go." My relapse lasted nearly three minutes.

Finally I said, "All copies of that video need to be permanently deleted right now."

"Are you kidding? We could be millionaires in less than a month."

"What good is money if you're too dead to spend it?"

"Your father wouldn't actually kill me. He was a cop."

"I never saw my dad look that upset or say the things he said. I don't think he'd actually kill you, but I guarantee you something very, very bad would happen to you."

"A rich man can buy his way out of almost anything."

"Drayton, you got in trouble with the police for spying on your neighbors because your paranoia made you suspect that they were watching you. If you release this video I can assure you that every cop in San Diego with an Irish last name *will* be watching you."

"What can they do?"

"How many times could you live through a night in the drunk tank with a bodybuilder who calls you Honey Buns?" As Drayton stared blankly I added, "Right now Dad's putting his plan together. You might not even make it home before the Friendly Son's of St. Patrick start filling out your dance card.

As Drayton's crossed legs slid from the traditional male *ankle on knee* to the female *don't look up my address* position, I knew the matter was settled.

Chapter 20

I walked into CLAM's office suite in downtown L.A. at 10:00 Saturday morning. Calvin met me at the reception counter and ushered me into his office as Lonnie's voice boomed from the conference room 40 feet away.

"Lonnie's going to call for your head at the meeting," Calvin said.

"It sounds like I wasn't the only one to get a license plate out in Ocotillo Wells. I think the bodyguard got mine too."

I brought Calvin up to speed on the Lonnie, John, Jimmy connection.

"Do you have any idea what they're up to?"

"I've got Jeannine and my contact at LAPD looking into the circumstances surrounding John's departure from Diversified Risk. When I find out it should tell us a lot."

Calvin's phone buzzed. "We'll be there in a minute, Ashley."

I said, "I'm going to keep John's name out of our conversation today."

"Lonnie's a pretty persuasive guy. I've only got one vote."

"If I have to look like the bad guy for a while, so be it."

The conference room held a table for 16. Lonnie sat at the head of the table and faced an attentive Ashley. Mark sat across from her with his elbows on the table and his palms supporting both jaws. As I took the seat next to Mark I noted that his index fingers were covering his ears. *Hear no evil.*

"Let's get started," Lonnie said. "I asked all of you to come in today to discuss the public relations disaster that just hit us. Obviously there's a leak that needs to get plugged right away."

"I agree," said Calvin.

Lonnie replied, "Glad to hear it, Calvin. Jason, you're fired. Now get out of here while we figure out how to clean up your mess."

Calvin said, "Jason, you're not fired. This is a partnership, not a dictatorship."

Lonnie stood up and leaned forward with his knuckles on the table. "Why don't we take a vote right now?"

"That's another sign of bad leadership, Lonnie. Issues get discussed before they're voted on," Calvin said.

"What's to discuss? I read quotes and speculation that sounded exactly like what Jason told me at your barbecue."

I said, "Just because I came up with an idea that I shared with all of you doesn't mean I'm the only one who could have passed it on to Dee Martin Sandler."

"Why would any of us pass it on? It could kill our business."

"Having a killer on the concert scene would certainly gut ticket sales for Christian rock, and I'm guessing that Ashley's green band fans would stay away in droves. But I don't see it as an equal deterrent to gangster rap and heavy metal fans. In fact, it could be an attraction that generates lots of free publicity."

"We're a partnership, Duffy. If one loses, we all lose."

"All of the partnerships I've seen in the music business have been performance-based. Will you all get an equal slice of the pie when your partnership renewal date comes around if Mark and Ashley's numbers fall off a cliff?"

Looking at Calvin, Lonnie asked, "How does he know about our partnership contract?"

I replied, "I'm over here, Lonnie. My mentor is Bernie Liebowitz. He's been writing music industry contracts since before you were born. He explained how you probably structured your partnership."

Ashley said, "Lonnie tends to jump to conclusions."

Lonnie sat down and tilted his legal pad. "You want facts? Try these on for size. Fact: Dean Casey sent out a memo instructing all police personnel to stop cooperating with Duffy. Fact: Dean Casey doesn't like Duffy. Fact: The lead investigator in San Diego, Dan Darden, doesn't like Duffy and would love to see him off of this case. Fact: If the task force decides to go public we probably won't be able to get insurance and, as you know, no insurance means no permits. And finally, fact: Duffy has a personal relationship with Sandler and clearly the least to lose by going public. I think he did it as a ploy to try to flush out the killer."

Mark bolted out of his chair. "I did it! I called Sandler. I couldn't live with the idea that innocent people were being slaughtered while we failed to warn them of the risk. It's a sin that we didn't tell them as soon as the killer left the note in Irvine."

Calvin said, "Jason, I need you to wait for me in my office for a few minutes."

Fifteen minutes later I was called back into the conference room. Mark was no longer in attendance.

"Have a seat, Duffy," said Lonnie, tapping the back of the seat Mark had occupied. Instead, I returned to the chair opposite Calvin.

Ashley pursed her lips to stifle a smile.

Lonnie said, "One down, one to go."

I said, "You got your mole, Lonnie. Why don't we put our heads together and come up with a game plan on how to proceed."

"I say we proceed with a vote to fire you. Our little discussion is over. Now it's time to purge two bad apples and get back on good terms with the police. I vote that Duffy is out."

Calvin said, "I watched him solve the Terry Tucker murder case and think we're very lucky to have him on the team."

Lonnie turned to Ashley and said, "It's up to you, sweet cakes. If you think that telling the police to shove it up their ass will help our business, then vote with Calvin. If you want to save our business by playing ball with the boys in blue, then vote with me."

Ashley pushed away from the table and walked to a service cart where she twisted the cap off of a bottle of water. She then stood next to Lonnie, put her hand on his shoulder and said, "I'm with Calvin on this one, sweet cakes. Meeting adjourned."

Chapter 21

I called Shamansky after reading my email on Monday morning. "I received an anonymous tip over the weekend that the task force is now being assisted by an FBI profiler."

"Your resources reach into the department. I'm impressed," Shamansky replied in mock surprise.

"I thought I'd get your take on the swami's prowess."

"This is not a conversation I want to have from my desk in the squad room."

I said, "I'm guessing the timing might be better around the noon hour."

"Did you ever consider a career in profiling? I'll bet your predictive powers will guide you to the perfect location, as well."

"I predict that if *you* make the reservation at Larabee's we'll get in a lot closer to noon than if I make the call."

"I'll see you there," Shamansky said, and hung up.

The Concert Killer also opened an interesting email that morning. He had set up a Google Alert for an exact match of the words *Concert Killer* and read the Dee Martin Sandler article. Afterwards, he used his search engine to research Jason Duffy. Upon reading interviews with two of Jason's former clients, Chelsea Tucker and Max Varner, he grew concerned.

CK found much to dislike about Jason Duffy. First, he was a former rock musician who probably stirred a huge number of vulnerable young souls with the devil's music. Second, he took up an adversarial position to himself, the Lord's instrument on earth. The police cannot be blamed for pursuing him. They are merely doing their jobs. God will reveal His plan to them in His own time. The final reason the Concert Killer disliked Duffy was noted by Sandler when he wrote of the longstanding relationship between Duffy and concert promoter Calvin Dawson. His father often said: *Tell me who your friends are and I'll tell you what you are.*

CK could live with the notion that the police will eventually stop him. Law and order should rule the land. But God's laws need to be first and foremost. He was confident that once his motivations were revealed that other like-minded disciples would pick up the banner and continue to slaughter the evil rock concert industry. If Duffy were to foil his plans it's possible that the media would glorify an ex-rock musician and the martyrs would have died in vain. That could not be allowed.

I was surprised to see only one table of al fresco diners as I entered Larabee's, an upscale La Jolla restaurant with an exceptional view of ocean waves meeting a large outcropping of rocks. Upon entering the half-empty dining room I wondered if I was missing a major news event.

"What happened to the big crowd?" I asked Shamansky after the hostess departed.

"The owner told me that most of his regulars are so concerned with stock market fluctuations that they won't leave their business news shows or computers long enough for a leisurely lunch. At least they're still filling the room for dinner."

After Shamansky schmoozed with our waitress and commiserated about the drop-off in business, I asked, "What did you think of the Feeb's profile?"

"Jason, you're asking about one of my fellow law enforcement professionals. I expect you to show the proper respect."

"Excuse me. What did you think of the FBI profile of the Concert Killer?"

Shamansky smiled, nodded, and replied, "It sucked."

"Care to elaborate?"

"Like you, they're assuming he's a religious fanatic. I'd say that's a 50/50 proposition at best. He could just as easily be misleading us to keep from getting caught. I didn't see any clues at the first three murder scenes that supported the religious angle. Did you?"

"I reread my notes yesterday and kept coming back to something Detective Lutz said about the knife used to slit the beer vendor's throat. He told me the killer wiped the blade in an X pattern on the vic's back. What if the killer was making the sign of the cross instead of just wiping the blade?"

"I think you might have something there, Jason. But, if he's using religion as a diversion instead of being a true believer, it doesn't help us much."

"So, what are your biggest problems with the profile?"

Shamansky said, "I can't go along with the profiler's age range of late 30s to mid 50s. It assumes that men don't get motivated by religion until later in life."

"I'm always looking at social networking websites when I work missing persons and divorce cases. A lot of guys in their 20s and 30s are very open about their religious affiliations and activities. What else don't you like about the profile?"

I was perplexed by Shamansky's change of expression until our waitress placed lunch in front of us and ran her perfectly manicured nails along his cheek.

"Enjoy," she said, and pivoted toward the kitchen.

I allowed Shamansky to savor his moment before asking the question again. He ignored it and popped a pork medallion into his mouth.

After five minutes of hearty eating and kitchen door watching, Shamansky was ready to resume the conversation.

"Every serial killer profile I've ever seen labels the perp as a sociopath. No conscience, no regrets. It's how they can go from one atrocity to the next without sickening themselves. With your degree in psych I'm not telling you anything you don't already know."

I said, "But the word sociopath didn't appear in this profile. Do you think they believe sociopaths can't practice religion?"

"The FBI is a very politically conscious agency. There are many people of faith in high places. I couldn't help but feel like the profile was more about not stepping on powerful toes than about the true psychological make-up of our perp."

We finished our entrees in silence. When coffee was served, I asked, "Does lunch come with the Shamansky profile?"

"It's not my case and I'm not an official member of the task force, so I haven't given it as much thought as usual."

"But…."

"I get the feeling that we have a very atypical situation on our hands. I'm afraid profiles based on prior experience might do more harm than good, especially considering the religious angle and its political implications, not only with the FBI but with the other agencies and investigators on the task force. I'm currently looking into who benefits by what's going on."

"Are you talking about somebody at one of the big corporate concert promoters?"

Shamansky replied, "If the independent promoters go out of business somebody makes out like a bandit. I intend to find out specifically who has the most to gain."

"I ran that idea past Calvin recently. He said he couldn't make an objective comment on the subject due to his strong dislike for their monopolistic business practices."

"I wouldn't mind picking his brain on where I could get started in pinpointing which salesman, manager, and regional director benefits the most."

I agreed to let Calvin know Shamansky would be calling and gave him the phone number. "Now I've got a request for you. Would you call Lutz, tell him about my sign of the cross theory and see if he'd be willing to meet with me later this week?"

"Another road trip?"

"I think there's a reason it started in NoCal and moved south. I got the impression at the Oceanside crime scene that the task force isn't working that angle."

"I'll call Lutz if you do something for me."

"Name it."

Shamansky stood. "Leave a $20 tip today. Cassandra looks like she hasn't been eating right. I'd hate to see our waitress lose her figure to an economic downturn."

When I sat at my desk in the mid-afternoon Hoover slunk into my office and began a mournful whine.

"What's the matter, boy?" I asked.

The young German Shepherd responded by looking back at the doorway.

I followed him past the unstaffed reception desk to Cory's office. Jeannine sat in front of the *victims* corkboard, crying into a tissue.

"What's the matter, Jeannine?"

"I'm not sure. I'm getting depressed and I don't understand why."

"It hasn't been very long since you nearly died. Maybe it's just starting to hit you. It could be post traumatic stress."

She replied, "It feels more like I'm letting you down. I keep looking at that board and I know I missed something."

"I get that feeling all of the time when I'm working cases. I see it as a good sign."

She dropped her tissue into a waste basket. "Really?"

"I think it means that I'm on the right track and getting closer. Did you have any more thoughts on your idea that the victims are related in some way?"

"You're not going to want to hear this, but sometimes my Obsessive-Compulsive symptoms include getting stuck on a thought that I keep coming back to over and over."

"What are you repeating to yourself?"

"It's going to sound stupid."

"Tell me."

"The victims are either random or they aren't. I've repeated that phrase to myself at least a thousand times this week. I know I should be doing other things. If you had a different assistant she'd be giving you the kind of research that would help you to solve this case."

She pulled another tissue from a nearby box and sobbed loudly. Hoover ran his face along the side of her knee and whined.

I put my hands on her shoulders and said, "I just told Shamansky that I'm going back up to NoCal this week because I think there's a reason the killings started there. You gave me that idea when you pointed out that there could be some kind of relationship that connects the victims. They're either random or they aren't. My next move is to try to answer that question."

"So I helped?"

"You got stuck because you thought I was missing an important question that needed to be answered."

"It felt so unnatural and unproductive."

"Suppose Hoover heard somebody prowling around outside your apartment door and started barking. Let's say you misinterpreted, and told him to be quiet. Wouldn't you want him to keep barking until you understood that it was a warning?"

"I wouldn't tell him to be quiet. Just like I'm your assistant, Hoover's my assistant."

"OK, Jeannine. How about assisting me by reviewing everything we have on the Sacramento murder, putting it in a file for me, and including any questions that come to mind? I may get another sit down with Detective Lutz."

"C'mon Hoover. We have work to do."

Chapter 22

Returning to the home office after a couple of weeks of luxury hotels on the road was a comedown for CK. On a staff of 24, he and three other account executives were granted five star accommodations on the road. The corporate Director of Sales would be picking two account reps to handle national accounts, one from each side of the Mississippi River. CK's only competition for the promotion came from Shane Wesley, whose territory encompassed Oregon and Washington. Despite the fact that CK and Shane were light years ahead of the other salesmen, they still were required to work from cubicles, separated by a six foot aisle. Both coveted the change in status and private office that would accompany the promotion.

"Are you still out there preaching to the prospects, Cali-boy?" Shane asked.

CK replied, "Ye of little faith will be toiling at the cubicle farm while I pray my way to the top."

"Maybe you better get off your knees and make a few phone calls. I just passed you for the quarter."

"It's going to work out like all of your trips to Las Vegas. At some point you're sure you'll come out a winner. The next thing you know, you're scratching your head and looking in your empty wallet wondering what went wrong."

Shane said, "I'll tell you what's wrong with your plan. Eventually one of those holy roller CFOs that you've been selling to is going to figure out that you and your *God wants you to buy from me* sales pitch is full of shit. Once the media gets wind that you've been milking the true believers, you're going to screw things up for everybody here."

"Envy is one of the seven deadly sins. I'm willing to share my good fortune with you, Shane. I can help you to make God your real sales manager. All it takes is a little faith."

"Make God my real sales manager? I can't believe this company lets you represent them in the field."

"Come back, Shane. Come back to the Almighty."

"I think your Almighty is the almighty dollar. Leave me alone."

On Tuesday morning I received a call from Shamansky. "I talked to Harry Lutz this morning and he'll see you tomorrow, but he doesn't like it."

"I'll bet he liked my tip about the bloody sign of the cross."

"It's the one and only reason you get to buy him an early lunch. He'll meet you at Templeton's Café on Prescott at 11:00. I gotta run."

Next on the agenda, I called Detective Ike Rappaport, SFPD.

"Duffy, I thought it was made clear that I can't talk to you."

"We're both in the information collection business. I've been working this case full-time since we met. Don't tell me you're going to let a bureaucrat tie your hands on a case," I said.

"If you have a problem with that particular phrasing let me put it to you this way: I won't be breaking a direct order to help you out. Good luck. Catch the bad guy. Don't call back." Click.

When the front door is locked it's time to try another entrance. I succeeded in setting up a meeting with Jorge Martinez, the bank supervisor of victim #1, Delainya Tanner. Martinez also agreed to allow me to use a private office to talk with the coworker who accompanied Delainya to the concert. Unfortunately, I only got as far as voicemail when I tried to reach the boyfriend, Luke Milner.

I didn't bother to call Detective Johnson since he already made it clear he wouldn't be sharing information. Besides, Celia Bains would keep me apprised of any new developments from the dreadlocked detective.

Kelly was excited about a dessert she was planning to make for our Thanksgiving dinner at my parents' house on Thursday. I was pleased that she and my mother were getting along so well.

We were about to turn in for the night when the phone rang. Remembering the call around the same hour on Halloween weekend, I expected to hear Shamansky's voice when I answered. Instead, the caller asked for Kelly.

Listening to one side of the conversation I learned that Kelly's brother, Danny, was involved in a fist fight with her father at a local bar and both were in jail. After hanging up she said, "I need to go."

"I'm going with you."

As I drove to the jail in downtown San Diego, Kelly explained that this would be her fifth trip to the jail for similar charges. In a matter-of-fact manner she told me what we should expect in terms of bail, bondsman, hearing, paperwork, and time. However, as the *to do* list ended she became angry. After venting for a few minutes she told me how much she appreciated that she wouldn't have to go through the process alone this time.

"The worst part happens after they get released and have to go back to the same house while they're still mad at each other," she said.

"Will your brother, Sean, be able to keep them in neutral corners until they cool down?"

She replied, "I'm sure Sean stayed at the bar and will keep drinking until he passes out. His only contribution will be if I don't have to deal with him too."

"Will your mother be any help?"

"At first she'll appear to be helping me. If I yell at my brother she'll say, 'Listen to your sister, Danny.' But as soon as I'm gone she'll suggest that they bury the hatchet over a bottle of Bushmills."

"My mother says the road to hell is paved with good intentions," I said.

Working through the *to do* list took all night. The arraignment of Michael and Daniel Kennedy took place at 7:20 AM. My flight to Sacramento was scheduled to leave at 9:15. As soon as the arraignment was over I said, "I've got to get home and shave before my flight."

"What about my family? I thought you were going to give me a hand with this," Kelly said.

"Shamansky barely managed to get me a sit-down with the detective handling murder #3. The meeting happens in Sacramento at 11:00 this morning. If I don't show up I lose my only cop contact in Northern California."

"Can't you reschedule it for tomorrow?"

"This guy didn't want to meet with me in the first place. It's a one-time offer. Kelly, you've been through this with your family on numerous occasions. If I thought you couldn't handle it I'd be there for you. I have every confidence in you."

"I wish I could say the same about you," she said, and walked away.

I rationalized that guilt and a temper were to be expected from an Irish girlfriend. I couldn't rationalize letting Calvin down or possibly allowing a serial killer to claim more victims because my girlfriend wanted me to reprise my role as a counselor.

Chapter 23

I suffered from coffee breath and a headache when I walked into Templeton's restaurant in downtown Sacramento. I hadn't pulled an all-nighter in quite a while and was sure my eyes looked like I had smoked my breakfast. As I wandered through the restaurant hoping to find the men's room I heard, "Sit down, Duffy."

I slid into a booth across from Harry Lutz. "Thanks for agreeing to the meeting."

"You look like shit."

"I was up all night on a family matter. What's been happening since our last meeting?" I asked.

"Before we get into that I want you to know two things. First, I don't agree with how Casey is freezing you out. The bloody cross helped to confirm something I found out a week after your last visit. If it was up to me I'd be fine with you helping us. That said, on to my second point. It's not up to me and I can't afford to get caught bucking the department. I'll answer your questions today, but this will be our final communication unless your status gets changed. Do we understand each other?"

"Absolutely. What did you find?" I asked.

Before Lutz could respond, a waitress took our orders.

"I got a call from Sharon Winslow, the vic's widow. She told me she visited her husband's grave that day and noticed a religious medal stuck in the ground."

"She didn't mention it to me when I spoke with her," I said.

"Why did *you* call her?"

"I called most of the family members listed in the obits to find out if the victims mentioned being followed between the time they bought their tickets and the night of the shows."

Lutz looked perplexed.

I said, "I was hoping the killer was staking out the advanced ticket windows of the venues to pick his victims and following them home."

"Maybe there *is* a brain behind those bloodshot eyes," Lutz said.

"What was on Winslow's medal?"

"It was a St. Blaise medal. Do you know who that is?"

"I know that the Catholics bless throats on St. Blaise Day."

"And Winslow's throat was cut."

I asked, "How did St. Blaise die?"

"He was tortured and beheaded."

"Was he considered a martyr?"

"Definitely. What does that have to do with anything?" asked Lutz.

"I'm not sure – maybe nothing. Was the medal purchased locally?"

"It's sold at all of the religious retail stores. A clerk at Berean Christian Stores told me it's big with throat cancer patients and the parents of kids with strep throat and tonsillitis. There's probably over a million of them floating around."

"Was Brian Winslow a church-goer?"

"The widow said they attended St. Paul's Methodist Church every week."

"Did you find out if anything was left at the graves of the other victims?"

"They all got the fine toothed comb treatment but nothing turned up. They also got staked out to no avail."

As we finished lunch I asked, "Are there any theories floating around about a common denominator that could tie the victims together?"

"Do you think the victims aren't picked at random?"

"I'm not sure. I was just wondering if anyone else was pursuing that angle."

"Not to my knowledge." Lutz stood up. "Thanks for the freebie. It's been nice knowing you."

I bumped my knuckles together and frowned. I knew I missed an opportunity to ask an important question, but was too tired to think clearly.

Before I left the restaurant I was able to connect with the victim's boyfriend, Luke Milner, who agreed to meet me for a drink at 6:30. I called Jeannine and asked her to get me on a later flight. I'd call Kelly with the change of plans when I got a chance.

Jorge Martinez directed me to a wing chair in his office at 2:30 PM. He was in his late 30's and very well-groomed.

"Mr. Duffy, I'm pleased to see that someone is looking for Ms. Tanner's murderer. Tell me how I can be of assistance."

"You could start by telling me about Delainya's work history here at the bank."

"Ms. Tanner started working for us shortly after graduating from high school three years ago. She worked as a teller for a little more than two years and was promoted to Assistant Loan Officer at the beginning of this year."

"How would you describe her as an employee?"

"She was dedicated, hard working, and ambitious."

"Ambitious in what way?" I asked.

"She enrolled in community college courses to improve her banking skills about a year ago, and did everything since then to prove herself worthy of being promoted."

"Was she ambitious when you first hired her?"

"Ms. Tanner has matured quite a bit since she was hired."

"What was she like before she matured, Mr. Martinez?"

He replied by pressing his lips together and looking down at his desk.

I added, "I know it's uncomfortable to speak ill of the dead. But if it will help to catch her killer I'm sure Delainya would want you to be completely honest with me."

"In her first year or so, Ms. Tanner showed a pattern of Monday absences. She also submitted a number of requests for time off on Fridays, and her error count was noted as unacceptable in one of her reviews."

I said, "So, she was a party girl who came to the realization that hard work and perseverance would be a better way to go?"

"I'd say that's a fair assessment."

"What turned it around for her?"

"Ms. Tanner never confided in me. However, I had occasion to meet her gentleman friend at the bank's holiday party last year, and I believe he's had a profound impact on her motivation."

"What's he like?" I asked.

"Mr. Milner struck me as smart, charming, well-mannered, and very personable. About an hour after we met I ran into him at the salad bar and he asked me what Delainya needed to do to advance at the bank."

"What did you tell him?"

"I suggested a community college banking curriculum and recommended that she volunteer for more Saturday hours?"

"How did he respond?"

"He thanked me, gave me one of his business cards, and told me to call him if I ever needed any assistance in keeping her on the right track."

"Did he come across as controlling when he said that?"

"Quite the contrary, Mr. Duffy. I felt like he was expressing a willingness to help and sincerely looking out for her best interests."

"Did you ever have occasion to see Delainya outside of the bank, other than the holiday parties?"

"No," Martinez said, and looked at his watch. "I'm afraid I have another appointment coming in soon."

"You mentioned that I could meet with Delainya's coworker that went to the concert with her," I said.

"Amanda Dorian. Her break starts at 3:00."

Martinez led me to a small private room that appeared to be used by safety deposit box renters. After bringing a second chair into the room he said, "May you enjoy the good fortune of a man on a righteous quest," and departed.

Amanda appeared in the doorway dressed in a manner that could be best described as borderline acceptable for the banking industry. I got the impression she was headed straight to happy hour after work. Her long black hair was pulled into a French braid and her bangs were ruffled by her eyelashes every time she blinked.

"Have a seat, Amanda. Thanks for meeting with me."

Her smile conveyed that she was more focused on my looks than the fact that I was there to discuss her dead friend.

"Don't mention it."

"I understand you and Delainya were pretty close," I said.

"We went to high school together and started working here about the same time. It was awful what happened to her."

"Did she mention any problems she was having with anybody at the bank? Maybe someone whose loan didn't get funded, or a customer who asked inappropriate questions?"

"Lainy never told me about anything like that."

"How was she getting along with her boyfriend?"

Amanda glanced at the ceiling before answering. "OK, I guess."

"I take it you don't get along with Mr. Milner," I said.

"He's alright if you're looking for a workaholic that wants to change you into a corporate wannabe."

"What kind of band did you and Delainya see the night she was killed?"

"It was an emo band called Aorta Event Invitation. Have you heard of them?"

"Not yet. Did you and Delainya go to many concerts?"

"We used to before she started dating one of the Brooks Brothers. When her wardrobe went resort casual I thought she went over to the dark side forever."

"How is it she went to a concert without her boyfriend that night?"

"She got tired of staying home alone on weekend nights. We didn't go out very often. It was more like the occasional *once more for old time's sake* adventure."

"Did the cops show you any pictures?"

"They tried to right after it happened and I freaked. But Detective Rappaport got me to come into the stationhouse a couple of weeks ago and I answered a few questions for him," Amanda said.

"Did he ask you about the clothes she was wearing?"

"That was the first thing he asked about. He thought the killer dressed her up to look like a slut. What a douche bag. Rappaport's wife probably wears babushkas."

"Was her outfit from before she started dating Luke Milner?"

"That's right. She was a lot of fun back in the day. She'd still cut loose every now and then, but it was never quite the same."

"How so?"

"I could tell she was getting serious with him and felt guilty going out without him. It just wasn't as much fun as the old days."

"How did you two get separated after the show?"

Amanda crossed her ankles and squeezed her knees together. "I met a guy I liked and told her I was gonna rearrange the fillings in his teeth. She told me not to worry about her, that she'd get home fine."

A mascara stream darted for her chin.

I was feeling the effects of my all-nighter. I realized that I should be asking questions to pinpoint why Delainya had been selected as the *concert-goer* in the victim link theory that I kicked around with Jeannine. But I sensed that my opportunity was slipping away. Amanda looked at her watch and told me her break was over.

I arrived at Starbucks 15 minutes before I was scheduled to meet with Luke Milner. I sat at an indoor table with what I hoped would be enough high-test caffeine to defibrillate my sleep-deprived brain.

Prompt to the minute, I spotted the silver and blue tie that Luke told me to look for as he strode to the back of a short line. I gave him a wave when he walked away from the counter. Luke appeared to be in his mid-20s. His cordial smile faded the instant he sat down.

"It's about time somebody did something to find Delainya's killer."

"Has Detective Rappaport been keeping in touch with you?" I asked.

"Before I start answering any questions, I want to know who hired you." Luke's tone was decidedly adversarial.

"I'm working for the concert promoter."

"It sounds like they're expecting to get sued."

"This particular promoter is known throughout the industry as one that consistently exceeds the security mandates for every concert at every venue. Hiring me is just one more example of going above and beyond expectations to provide a safe and secure environment," I said.

"Are you a detective or a PR man?"

"I'm a guy who wants to find Delainya's killer and I'll need your help to make that happen."

Luke rolled his shoulders, glanced at his watch and said, "I have to get back to my office in a half hour. What do you need to know?"

"Were you two living together at the time of her death?"

"We each kept our own apartments, but spent quite a bit of time together."

"Would you say you're pretty familiar with most of her friends?"

"Yes and no. She made several friends since we started dating, and I know them quite well. However, she was still in the process of transitioning away from her high school friends when I met her, and I don't know those people at all."

"Did you know she was going to the concert with Amanda Dorian?"

"No."

"Was it like Delainya to keep secrets from you?"

"She wanted us to go away for the weekend. I thought I was going to be able to do it until two weeks before the concert. I picked up a business referral and things started happening at a very fast pace."

"What line of work are you in, Luke?"

"I'm with a company that converts fleet operations from gasoline or diesel fuel to liquefied natural gas. I work with trucking firms, taxi cab companies, package delivery corporations – any operation that cares about the environment and wants to save money."

"It would help if you could take me through your recollection of the day she died."

"We watched a movie at my apartment on Friday night and she stayed over. Since it was Saturday I slept in until 6:30, showered, dressed, ate breakfast, kissed her goodbye, and went to the office."

"Did she eat breakfast with you?"

"She was sleeping in. She woke up long enough to say, 'Bye, honey,' after I kissed her on the forehead."

"Did you talk with her on the phone at any time afterwards?"

"That was the last I spoke with her."

"Were you surprised to find out she went to the concert?" I asked.

"Very much so. I know that most men my age go to concerts on a regular basis. I came from a poor family. I wanted an education, so I worked a full-time job through college. I didn't have time for extracurricular activities, Mr. Duffy. We never even talked about going to a concert."

"How about if you tell me what you think happened, Luke?"

After a deep breath he said, "I got used to an 80 hour work week in college. I couldn't shut it down. I think Delainya got fed up with me being gone so often and called an old friend to have some fun without me. I can't say that I blame her."

"Detective Rappaport told me they cleared you of any wrong-doing." Luke nodded and took a drink of coffee.

"He told me they found drugs in her system. I can tell you in all certainty that I never saw her on drugs. But who knows. Maybe she gave in to peer pressure and went along with her friend because she was mad at me."

"Do you think she might have used drugs before you met her?"

"I got the impression from Detective Rappaport that her old friend was no stranger to the drug party scene."

"You never used drugs with her?" I asked.

Luke held up his Starbucks cup. "This is the strongest drug I've ever used. I can't speak from experience, but I'm told people do things that are totally out of character when they take a hard drug and don't have a tolerance built up."

In spite of the triple espresso, I was crashing. I knew that a couple of delicately worded follow-up questions might possibly help me rule out an affair with a fellow bank employee. But I was too frazzled to press on. I decided to try one last ploy to see if I could get a reaction.

"There was one little break in the case that could help tremendously when the police start bringing in suspects."

"What's that?"

"The coroner was able to calculate the killer's exact hand size from the marks on Delainya's neck."

My brain cells momentarily rallied as I watched for any kind of body language affirmation that Luke was worried. He was either innocent or excelled in the art of self-control.

"I suppose that will help. But regardless of whether the killer is caught or not, I'll always know that my neglect played a significant role in her death."

I said, "I know you're beating yourself up over not being there for her. But I've got to tell you, I think your company's role in getting our country off of foreign oil and into a fuel that is so abundant here in the US is very admirable."

"I'll try to remember that tonight when my guilt does battle with my rationalizations."

I fell asleep on the flight back to San Diego. At one point I woke up from a dream that seemed important. I couldn't recall any details, but was certain it related to the victim theory.

Chapter 24

I was jarred out of a sound sleep on Thanksgiving morning by the distinct sound of pots and pans rattling in the kitchen. I suspected it was Kelly's way of telling me to get up and finish our fight. I felt an obligation to accommodate her after our Halloween Eve dinner where we promised to work through our differences in a timely manner. I found her in the kitchen with a pan in each hand.

I said, "Is it Thanksgiving or did I sleep straight through to New Year's Eve."

"Excuse me. I thought you might have a passing interest in what's been happening with my family."

"Are you the same woman who forbid her family from calling before 9:00 AM because she wasn't going to get caught up in their drunken drama anymore?"

"Danny's facing attempted murder charges."

"Did you get him a lawyer?"

"Like you care." Kelly tossed the pans into a cabinet.

"I went without sleep the night before four important meetings in Northern California to give you moral support. Now you're giving me a ration of shit for not blowing off the meetings too?" I was getting hot.

"You're the one with the psych degrees. I sure could have used some expert advice when dealing with those idiots."

"I'm not a counselor anymore."

"You could have used your training to help straighten things out yesterday. It was a crisis."

I said, "There are no quick fixes."

"In the last week I've heard you say a dozen times that you've got to catch 'em in the act and respond immediately if you want to change the behavior. Yesterday they were caught in the act."

"I was talking about training your puppy. What did you want me to do, smack your dad on the butt with a rolled up newspaper?"

"It's the same principle. They were caught in the act and embarrassed. If anybody had a chance of talking some sense into them it would have been you after that arraignment."

"I was obliged to be at those meetings. I'm a PI now. Calvin is counting on me."

"What about your obligation to me? Shouldn't I be able to count on you? If you really loved me you wouldn't have skipped out on me."

"That's unfair. I'm trying to shut down a serial killer. The result of those meetings could save a life."

"You've been on the case for over a month. I don't think one day is asking too much."

"Let me ask you this: If you were at SeaWorld with your 2nd grade class and I called and said you had to abandon the kids and come home immediately because I needed you, would you do it?"

"Don't be ridiculous."

"It's only ridiculous because I'd never ask you to do it. There's no way I'd get to reschedule with Detective Lutz. He told me something very important. The guy I'm after has killed five people so far."

"I know my family is screwed up, but they count too."

"Alcoholics change after they've hit bottom and decide that swearing off is the only way to go. Nobody talks them into it. The decision comes from within. There are no magic words that counselors use to make the light bulb appear over their heads."

"Well, I could have certainly used your support," she said in a cooler manner.

"I stayed up all night and conducted those meetings with my frontal lobe tied behind my back."

Kelly gave a thin smile. "I know. But I'm still mad at you."

We arrived at my parents' house at 2:00 for Thanksgiving dinner. My sister and her family always share this feast with her in-laws and have Christmas dinner with Mom and Dad. I expected Dad to be a bit morose because of his friend's deteriorating condition, but I had no idea he would be totally sullen. He gave us a nod and a small wave as we walked through the living room, and immediately went back to watching the football game on television without a word.

When we reached the kitchen Mom explained that Dorothy O'Malley called early in the morning and asked if Jim would join her husband and Bob Kerrigan in watching the ten o'clock game at their house. He returned home in a cab at 1:30.

"I'd say he's half in shock and half in the bag," Mom said.

It was the least festive Thanksgiving I ever remember spending in that house, or anywhere for that matter. Dad acted like we were being disrespectful whenever anyone initiated a conversation at the dinner table. Afterwards, Kelly helped Mom with the cleanup and I watched part of the second half of the game with him. At one point I tested the water to see if he was interested in talking. But it was painfully obvious that he was in a *do not disturb* mood.

Chapter 25

I was surprised to find Shamansky chatting with Jeannine when I entered the office on Friday morning.

"Have you come to invite us for a ride in the Crown Vic this morning?" I asked.

"No can do. I'm out of duct tape. Can I have a word with you, Jason?"

Shamansky closed the door to my office. "I met with the insurance agent who wrote the policy for the Oceanside concert on Wednesday."

"It wasn't by any chance our friend John Murray?"

"No, but Murray just happened to give him a call the week before the show and asked him to email the contract up to his office in Monterey."

"Was that an unusual request?" I asked.

"It was a very unusual request. Murray told him he used to write concert policies for his last company and wanted to see how it was done at his new place of employment."

"It seems more than a little odd for a reinsurer to make this kind of request of a client. What do you think?"

"It appears to take coincidence off of the table. But, then again, Murray made partner at a very young age. He's barely in his mid-thirties and looks a lot younger than that. He may just want to get back into concert insurance for the backstage passes."

"Do you still think there could be a tie-in with a national concert promoter?" I asked.

"They look like the big winners if your friend's company goes belly-up. It's possible that Murray gets an exclusive if he helps eliminate the competition. After taking a demotion from partner at the top reinsurer, down to sales agent at a lesser company, he may be looking for a way to supplement his income."

"Do you know why he uses a bodyguard?"

"I haven't interviewed him yet for three reasons. First, it's Darden's case and I'd be obliged to report it. I don't want that idiot scaring him into a rat hole. Second, I don't want Murray to know he's on my radar screen yet. And third, he's based out of the Monterey office. So, regular surveillance and snitches are not an option."

"I'm guessing you didn't just drop by to give me a report."

"I found out Murray will be at a weekend commercial insurance conference at La Costa, starting this afternoon. I'm on good terms with the concierge. She's willing to let Cory pose as event photographer. I didn't mention his Tourette's because I assume you still have the camera with the mouthpiece."

"We do, but I think you'll need to send someone along with him to field questions and special requests."

He asked, "Did you know that your poor deprived administrative assistant has never enjoyed the benefit of a weekend at La Costa?"

"I should be flogged."

"Is Cory here?"

"I'm expecting him at noon."

"The conference registration starts at 3:00 PM. I can stop back around 1:00 to give them some instructions on what I need."

"Since I'll be footing the bill for their overtime, how about if you share a little on what you found out about the corporate promoter angle?"

He said, "I just came up with a contact at ConcertMaster and have a phone meeting in about an hour. I'll bring you up to speed when I return."

On his way out the door, Shamansky whispered in Jeannine's ear and she smiled as she held my gaze. Two outpatient mental health clients in a high profile role at a luxury resort. What could possibly go wrong?

Jeannine spent most of the morning on the computer trying to find out why John Murray lost his partnership status and was now working in a sales capacity for another company. Despite her best efforts all she learned was that sealed court records relating to Murray existed, but the reason for the secrecy remained unknown. She found absolutely no press coverage on whatever incident precipitated his fall from grace.

I spent my morning coming up with my own agenda for Jeannine and Cory. I listed all of my questions regarding the relationship binding John Murray, Lonnie Cancelli, Jimmy DeLong and Aaron Tesslerod together. I also considered the plusses and minuses of using my B&E skills to take a look around John's room while he attended the conference. The Tesslerod factor and my unfamiliarity with the La Costa burglar alarm system were the major deterrents.

I had a brief phone conversation with Mom. She found out after we departed that O'Malley agreed to try an experimental procedure that was considered very high risk. He told Dad that he wasn't interested in being a burden to his family, trying to eke out a few more months of pain and suffering for all parties concerned.

Jeannine managed to learn that John Murray functioned primarily in the role of rainmaker while at Diversified Risk Insurance Group. This seemed highly unusual for a young executive.

She found a trade article from two years ago that talked about how John's business book was a model of diversification. Where many commercial insurance firms establish a niche within an industry or two, John attracted clients from across a broad spectrum of business sectors. The author of the article felt that this level of diversification would indemnify the company against catastrophic losses from sudden downturns in such areas as real estate, technology, or the financial institutions. I concluded that John was a very good salesman (even in the role of partner), and this level of diversification would make it more difficult to determine how Tesslerod fit into the picture.

Shamansky arrived on time, carrying a small three-ring binder. I waved him into my office to talk prior to assembling the staff.

I said, "I want to remind you that Jeannine's doctor said she should keep away from high stress situations. Her health needs to be the top priority."

"I was there, Jason. She won't be in the least bit of danger."

"Just so we're clear. If I hear anything in your instructions that I find questionable regarding her assignment, I expect you to back off and find another way."

"Agreed."

"Why aren't you doing this yourself, or bringing in another detective from the department?"

"I'll answer the second part of your question first. If I ask the captain to assign anyone to La Costa I'd be required to tell him which case it related to, and he would have to report it to Darden. Within minutes, he'd be pumping me for everything I have on Murray and probably pull him in for questioning before he unpacks his suitcase."

"Your answer to the second part of the question makes perfect sense."

Shamansky said, "As to the first part, I have a prior commitment. Can we just leave it at that?"

"Are we talking prior commitment as in a weekend getaway with the woman of your dreams, or as in another suspect you don't want to tell me about?"

"I don't like rolling out half-baked theories. It's like taking a half-baked loaf of bread out of the oven and poking at it."

"You told me earlier that you just made a contact at ConcertMaster, and would bring me up to speed on your conversation when you returned."

"You're not going to leave it alone, are you?"

"C'mon Shamansky, the loaf's already out of the oven."

"Since I'm a man of my word, I'll give you the facts but not the speculation. ConcertMaster has an employee named Matthew Manning who's responsible for booking most of their acts into California venues. I'm going to be taking a closer look at him this weekend."

"You're holding out on me, Shamansky. You said facts. That single fact alone wouldn't be enough to keep you from working La Costa yourself this weekend."

He pushed his shoulders back and stretched his neck. "I think we've shared enough for one day."

"Do you realize I have to pay Jeannine and Cory time-and-a-half on Saturday and double-time on Sunday."

He shook his head.

I added, "Not only that, knowing that Tesslerod will probably be there, I'm sure I'll be up there both days to make sure Jeannine isn't getting into trouble."

He looked at his watch.

"I was more than willing to go along with a tit-for-tat arrangement, but I'll be damned if I'm paying double-time for a shit-for-tat deal." Looking at my watch I added, "What's it gonna be, Shamansky? My time is valuable, too."

"I'm sure you know that ConcertMaster recently merged with a huge band management corporation. When that happened, Manning was put in charge of the teenage Christian rock band, Divine Guys Dance."

I asked, "The altar boy band?"

"They're not actually altar boys. In fact, they're not even Catholic. But yes, that's what the press calls them."

I whistled and said, "Holy shit."

"I think you can see why I need to follow up on Manning right away."

Shamansky gave Jeannine and Cory a binder that included a floor plan of La Costa and a set of written instructions. He asked Cory to take pictures of Murray whenever he engages in one-on-one conversations.

Jeannine's job is to look especially fetching to keep everyone from noticing where Cory is pointing his camera. She will also serve as Cory's spokesperson at all times.

After Shamansky departed I explained to Jeannine the logic of her going home and changing into a sexy top with a short skirt. I also explained that she would be in the middle of a large group of salesmen at a convention, and that her outfit would be like waving a red cape in front of a bull. Cory listened with his eyebrows locked in the arched position as I suggested a series of lines she could use to pointedly, yet politely, dissuade unwanted suitors. I also told her that if anyone laid a hand on her she was to tell them her boyfriend was the San Diego County Ultimate Fighting Champion. I made her promise to call me and point out anyone who touched her if she encountered a problem. My last bit of instruction involved telling both of them to stay in well-lit and populated areas regardless of John Murray's movements.

Cory bypassed valet parking and found a space at the back end of a self-parking lot, near a copse of trees separating the lot from the golf course.

"Are you sure Hoover's going to be OK in the back of the van?" Jeannine asked.

Cory told her that half of the floor was covered with papers, that he opened the side and roof vents, and that since it was almost December there was no chance the van would overheat.

Jeannine gave Hoover a warm hug, followed by a serious talk, while holding his snout between her thumb and index finger. When she closed the door she heard him give a mournful high-pitched whine. She walked to the side window, tapped on the glass, shook her head, and Hoover stopped whining. He only barked one more time as they crossed the lot, and that coincided with a Cory F-bomb.

Jeannine took a deep breath as she entered La Costa's reception area, and exhaled audibly. Cory held his camera and mouthpiece to his face. A busman directed them to the concierge desk where she introduced herself to an attractive woman in her mid-40s. The pleasantries of the moment screeched to an immediate halt when she introduced Cory, who let two and a half no-noes escape before jamming the mouthpiece back into place.

Jeannine quickly said, "Cory's from a small town on the outskirts of Andorra. Unfortunately, some of their words sound like English curses. That's why he wears the mouthpiece. He actually said that this handsome resort is only matched in beauty by its lovely concierge."

She replied, "Nice try, sweetie. Tell Shamansky that one dinner isn't going to cover this favor, and make sure your buddy keeps his pie-hole plugged or I'm back to schlepping crème brulees."

The conference registration desk was set up in the Costa Del Sol section of the resort in a long hall with vaulted ceilings. Wearing the credentials provided by Shamansky's friend, Jeannine and Cory floated between the front desk, registration area, and a cocktail party at the Garden Pool Event Courtyard. Cory spotted John Murray picking up his event pass at the Costa Del Sol Perfu at 4:30 PM. Since he wasn't carrying a suitcase they assumed he had already checked into his room. The poolside garden provided excellent cover for covert observation and photography. John made their job less difficult by accepting a seat at a table for eight.

At 6:30 the hostess announced that a buffet was being served outside the ballroom. John excused himself from his cocktail friends and sought out an acquaintance already in the buffet line. Once they filled their plates, John directed them to a table for two on the periphery of the ballroom. Cory found a spot where he was able to zoom in on a lanyard around the neck of John's dinner guest.

Cory volunteered to check on Hoover, and see if he'd be interested in watering any of the trees behind the van. Jeannine, knowing that Cory's Tourette's Syndrome is always a problem in crowded men's rooms, assured him she'd be fine for a while.

She was watching Murray when a salesman holding a margarita tapped her on the shoulder.

"I've seen you on TV," he said.

"You have me mistaken with someone else."

He used the condensation from his glass to slick down a rebellious tuft of hair. "You were an underwear model for Victoria's Secret. You were my absolute favorite."

"That wasn't me."

The salesman reached behind her and lightly touched the side of her skirt. "I'll bet if I took a little peek I'd see the pair you wore on the runway."

Jeannine replied, "I'll bet after my boyfriend shows you how he won the County Ultimate Fighting Championship you'll be lucky if you can open your eyes wide enough to get a peek at the instruments in the ICU."

The salesman removed his hand and said, "On second thought, you were the gal holding up the round cards at the fight. My apologies."

Following dinner, John worked the room until he retired to his villa at 10:30 PM. Jeannine was fairly certain he wasn't headed to bed, but decided it was best to adhere to the plan, and they called it a night.

Chapter 26

Early Saturday morning Jeannine gave me a report on John's activities while Cory downloaded photos to his office computer.

Jeannine said, "I'm sorry we weren't able to give you more. I'm sure he didn't go to bed before 11:00."

I handed Cory a camera with a night scope attached.

"You're right. He met with Tesslerod and a guy I didn't recognize. Cory, will you see if you can do anything with the picture I shot with the scope before you head up to the breakfast buffet?"

Cory grunted, knowing that I have trouble shooting moving subjects in the daylight. Ten minutes later we were looking at a somewhat blurry profile of a bald man, probably in his late 40s, wearing glasses with thick dark stems and a collared business shirt. The stems of the glasses totally obscured his eyes. Cory's attempt to comment on the shot prompted so much barking that I sent them on their way.

The breakfast buffet was a disaster for team Duffy. Jeannine's Obsessive-Compulsive Disorder got the better of her as she cleared crumbs, discarded empty sugar packets, and constantly realigned the pastry until the concierge relegated her to *time out* in a small office in the administrative wing.

Cory decided to take Hoover for a walk among the pines that bordered the south golf course. But as he approached his van he spotted John Murray handing a ticket to a valet attendant. He tailed John a few miles up Interstate 5 North, and exited at Carlsbad Village Drive. He made a left, and drove another half-mile to the coast where he found street parking in front of a restaurant. John walked across Route 101 and headed north on a scenic walkway overlooking the ocean. Cory put on a herringbone beret and a pair of sunglasses. With Hoover leading the way, Cory maintained a distance of about 50 feet until Hoover became enamored with a young black Labrador Retriever attached to a rather fetching woman who, like Cory, was in her early 40s.

"Well aren't you precious?" she said.

Cory was tongue tied, which was a very good thing. He wasn't sure if she was addressing him or Hoover.

"You can't be more than a few months old," she said.

As Cory spoke, Hoover barked over each and every curse word.

The woman looked deeply into Cory's eyes and smiled. She then tapped his ID badge from the conference and said, "It was a pleasure meeting you, Cory. I hope to see you again." After a finger wave and another smile, she resumed her walk in the opposite direction.

Cory was dumbstruck. If a cop saw his expression at that moment he'd have been given a sobriety test. However, the smile disappeared the moment Cory realized that John Murray was nowhere in sight. He checked the beach and continued on for five blocks, but to no avail. He walked inland one block to a street that featured a couple of sidewalk cafes, but still no sign of him. Cory thought if he staked out John's car he might return with whomever he was meeting. But when he reached Carlsbad Village Drive, John's rented Lexus was gone.

When Cory returned, Jeannine was standing in the parking lot.

"Where were you? Jason called a half hour ago and needs you to take some shots."

Cory explained about his experience, focusing on Hoover's role in his most intimate encounter with a woman since his photography school fling with a deaf girl.

"Jason wants us to look for reps from Gordian C. Knox Insurance and Keagle Insurance Associates. They're the two companies that covered the Concert Killer shows. Jason's especially interested in finding out if John Murray meets with any of their reps."

Cory put his arm around Hoover's neck and rested his cheek on top of his head.

Except for a minor incident that followed the hotel staff putting out a large bowl of chips and dips, the day was uneventful until high tea was served at 4:00 PM.

John struck up a conversation with a rep from Gordian C. Knox. They were in a fairly busy breezeway on the patio, and Jeannine was able to get close enough to eavesdrop.

After snapping a couple of pictures of the rep, Cory strolled around the room taking random shots. He didn't want John getting suspicious. He bit down on the camera mouthpiece when he saw Aaron Tesslerod in his viewfinder, watching Jeannine spy on his boss. Cory froze when he saw Tesslerod walk directly toward Jeannine.

Cory had been a victim his whole life. He was currently at his maximum weight of 140 pounds, and developed a violence phobia somewhere around the 50th time he was beaten up as a child. He asked himself what chance he'd have against a professional bodyguard, even if he didn't have every fiber of his being telling him to RUN AWAY!

Tesslerod approached Jeannine from behind and clamped his powerful hand around her wrist.

"I know what you're doing?" he whispered in her ear.

Jeannine tried to cry out, but one of her many phobias left her incommunicado. She briefly flashed on waking up in a hospital bed, emerging from a catatonic state brought on by high stress. She took a deep breath and tried not to panic.

Tesslerod quietly said, "We're gonna take a little trip up to my room. If you make any noise it will be the last sound you ever hear."

Suddenly, out of nowhere, Tesslerod was hit by flashing strobe lights. As dusk shrouded the patio, Tesslerod and Jeannine were now the focus of everyone's attention.

Cory yanked the mouthpiece out and yelled, "Orlando Bloom," along with half of a four letter word before reinserting his mouthpiece.

Over the excited buzz of the crowd, Jeannine shouted, "Would anyone care for a photo with Mr. Bloom?"

Tesslerod immediately released Jeannine's wrist and shielded his face with his arm.

"I have to go," he shouted, and walked away.

Jeannine announced, "If Mr. Bloom comes back be sure to let us know and we'll be glad to take a souvenir photo."

After scanning the crowd for about a minute she spotted John Murray 40 feet away. He was on his phone and staring at her.

Jeannine led Cory to the concierge desk, where Shamansky's friend arranged for two large busmen to accompany them to the van. Cory spotted Tesslerod sitting in the Lexus he had tailed earlier in the day. After quietly conveying this information to Jeannine, she used her charms and good looks to get the busmen to detain Tesslerod.

The Lexus was backed into a space four slots closer to the exit in the same row as Cory's van. One of the busmen stood in front of the Lexus as the other tapped on Tesslerod's window. When Cory began pulling out, Tesslerod revved his engine, startling the blocking busman. But to his credit, he backed up only a step, and stood his ground. Tesslerod allowed the Lexus to lurch forward to within a few inches of the busman's knees. As Cory's van passed in front of them, I was on their tail and stopped in front of the Lexus. I beeped and waved the busman over to my driver's side window, away from Tesslerod, who was blocked now on all four sides.

While Tesslerod blasted his horn, I used my hand as a stop sign and continued asking the busman for directions.

When Tesslerod stayed on the horn, I moved my right hand from the stop position to a cup around my ear. When Tesslerod realized that the horn wasn't going to intimidate me into moving he jumped out of his vehicle, but Cory was long gone. Just as Tesslerod ran around the RSX, I pulled out. He sprinted back to the Lexus, but was once again frustrated as I observed the five mile per hour speed limit through the parking lot. When we finally reached a spot wide enough for him to pass, I flipped him off, obscuring the bodyguard's view of my face.

Chapter 27

CK called his boss early Monday morning and told him he would be out of town, pursuing a lead he networked over the weekend. Considering his track record, the boss didn't object.

A close inspection in the hotel mirror told CK that the San Diego Gas & Electric Company uniform he had stolen off of a backyard clothesline over the weekend was close to his size and wouldn't merit a second look. He struggled for a few moments with the moral justification for what he was about to do. Noticing a slight slump in the mirror, CK straightened to perfect posture and began to hum *Onward Christian Soldiers.*

At 12:30 PM Mom received a call from Bob Kerrigan's wife. She said that Bob went over to the O'Malley's home to watch the Chargers game yesterday and had been drinking ever since. He took a cab to Casey's Bar an hour earlier and was in very rough shape. Their son, Dennis, was on duty with SWAT and couldn't take the time off. Mom agreed to send her husband over to help his ex-partner.

Molly Duffy didn't meekly state the problem and suggest that Jim lend a hand. She made it very clear that Jim was only to answer the call if he could swear to her that he wouldn't end up crying in his beer all afternoon on the stool next to Kerrigan. At first it looked like Jim was going to respond by going on the counter attack.

But he held his tongue and replied, "I'll be fine."

Ten minutes later Mom heard a knock at the door.

"What can I do for you?" she asked the man in the San Diego Gas & Electric uniform.

"I'm with the Smart Grid Conversion Team. I'm here to check on the compatibility of your electrical system with the new meter you'll need for the upgrade."

"I'd rather you do this while my husband is home," she said.

CK replied, "I can go on to the next house if you want. But this first round of site inspections and upgrades is free. After today it will cost you at least $2,500 to get the very same upgrade. It's going to be mandatory for all of our customers by this time next year."

"I didn't hear anything about this," Mom said. She went on to tell him about how it was proper procedure to inform customers about such an unexpected visit.

While she talked CK noticed a framed *Meritorious Conduct Citation* given to Detective James Duffy. His eyes rested on a foot-high, black, metal sculpture of *The Maltese Falcon.* It looked to be the perfect size and weight to serve his purpose.

CK said, "We sent you an insert with your bill last month explaining the upgrade and the fact that we would be starting the process this month. Didn't you read it?"

"Everybody throws those inserts away. I'm surprised I didn't hear about it from any of my friends."

"Actually, today is our first day in the field. The program planners decided to start with the oldest neighborhoods in town to get a handle on how much work needs to be done. Little Italy was right at the top of the list."

"You'd really charge me $2,500 to come back later?" she asked.

"Sorry, ma'am. As far as I know, if you pass on the survey, you pass on the freebie. Maybe that will change in the future. But considering how much this upgrade is going to cost SDG&E, I doubt it."

"All right, come on in," she said, stepping back from the doorway.

He was pleased to see no one on the street as he closed the door. Mom stepped quickly as she led him through the house and out the back door. CK wanted to collect some information before he would need the black bird.

Mom rounded the corner to a walkway along the side of the house and pointed to the main breaker box.

"Everything's right there."

CK didn't want Mom to go back into the house and make any phone calls. He opened the breaker box and saw what he was looking for.

"Like most folks, you have hand written notes on masking tape next to the switches. I'm going to need you to read them to me in just a minute or two." He wrote a few numbers on a clipboard form he created over the weekend.

"Those are interesting gloves you're wearing," she said.

"It's the latest in safety equipment for electricians. They're ultra thin for maximum dexterity and more shock resistant than anything that's ever been on the market."

Over the next five minutes he unclipped his form, flipped it over, drew a schematic of the breaker box, and asked Mom to read the tape for each breaker.

When they finished he said, "I have to pull the plate off of two of your receptacles in the house. I need to see where your dryer goes into the wall and maybe look at the one out by that beautiful statue of the Maltese Falcon you have in the living room."

Upon entering the laundry room CK said, "My wife and I are expecting our first child in April."

Mom brightened for the first time. "That's wonderful."

"We've been looking to buy a house for the past couple of months and we're considering Little Italy. Do you think it would be a good place to raise a family?"

Mom spent the next ten minutes telling him about her children. CK mentioned that he saw the citation in the living room and asked if her son followed in his father's footsteps. Mom gave him several details.

"Would you like to know when we're going to be at your son's house for the upgrade survey? It could save him a lot of money if somebody's there to let us in."

"Absolutely," Mom replied.

CK pulled out his smart phone and asked, "What's his street address?"

Mom gave him the info and CK tapped keys. "It looks like he's scheduled for January 15th. If you like, I can put a note in the system while I have it up. What time does he usually get home from work?"

"Around 5:30, if he doesn't have anything important to do on a case."

CK finished his note and popped the phone in his pocket. "I requested a time after 5:30. Now let's take a look at that receptacle in the living room."

Mom led the way as CK stared at the back of her head. Glancing at the crucifix on the kitchen wall, he decided that she seemed like a good Christian woman. He'd give her a final earthly reward for her faith by striking her just once on the back of the head to make sure the mourners could see her in an open casket. While he unscrewed the receptacle plate in the living room, he stared at a graduation picture of Jason and imagined how his expression would change when he looked in that casket.

CK's only regret was that he couldn't leave any message letting Jason know that it was his consorting with the devil's minions that caused his mother's death. The purpose of today's sacrifice was to distract and punish Jason. A connection to the Concert Killer might bring unwanted heat from the task force, since the victim would be the wife of a decorated police detective. He'd find a way to let Jason know at a later date, after he'd ascended the 13 steps of the pyramid to the Eye of Providence and shut down the concert industry. Too bad Mrs. Duffy couldn't count as one of his steps.

An Irish crystal cross hung on the wall just beyond the statue of the Maltese Falcon.

CK said, "All done with the inspection. Before I go, I have to tell you how much I like that crystal cross on your wall."

"It was a wedding present from Jim's parents," she said, stepping to within two feet of the cross.

CK stood shoulder to shoulder with her. The Falcon sat on a table six inches from his right hand.

He said, "I love the shade of green in the main vertical crystal."

"I have no idea how they do it, if that's what you were going to ask me." Molly leaned slightly forward to have a closer look.

CK said, "It's really a shame about the crack that runs all the way up the middle. I was going to ask you how that happened."

Her eyebrows shot up. "What crack! This is news to me!"

Molly took a step forward. Her nose was less than an inch from the crystal. CK wrapped his fingers around the Falcon, letting his little finger encircle the bird's neck. Putting his weight on his right leg, he quietly sidestepped behind her.

"I don't see it," she said.

"Try tilting your head just a little," he said and brought the base of the statue up behind his ear.

Suddenly, there were several footsteps on the porch. CK heard a man slur, "Let go of me."

Molly quickly turned her head to the left and CK moved back to where he was standing, returning the Falcon to its original position. The door flung open and rebounded off of the doorstop. Dad had his arm around Kerrigan's waist and Fallon put his hand on the side of Kerrigan's head so he wouldn't bang it on the door frame.

"Get yer fuckin' hand offa my head. Yer treatin' me like a perp," Kerrigan scowled.

"What's going on?" asked Molly, stepping back from the cross.

Jim replied, "You should know. You sent me on this rescue mission."

Molly forcefully said, "You're not letting any bull-in-a-china-closet loose in my house."

Turning to Fallon, Jim said, "You and Gilhooley, take him through the side gate out to the backyard. I'll be along in a couple of minutes." Looking at CK he asked, "Who's this guy?"

Kerrigan yelled, "I'm not doin' no fuckin' intervention! Get yer hands offa me!"

Jim shut the door and Molly replied, "SDG&E is going to connect us to the Smart Grid. He's doing the pre-site inspection."

Jim asked, "How much longer is it going to take?"

CK said, "I just finished. Let me grab my ohm meter and I'm on my way."

I spent most of the morning debriefing Jeannine and Cory, then entered notes into the case file. I expected to have lunch with Shamansky to trade info on the suspects we tracked over the weekend. But after four phone calls to San Diego Metro, a detective told me that Shamansky would be out of town until tomorrow.

In mid-afternoon my mother called to fill me in on the scandalous Kerrigan intervention that would soon be the talk of the neighborhood. After I calmed her down she told me about her visit from SDG&E and when to expect an inspection at my house.

"I don't remember hearing anything about that," I said.

"Supposedly it was on one of those inserts they put in with the bill."

"Nobody reads those."

"That's what I told him. By the way, I hope you don't get the guy who came here."

"Why is that?" I asked.

"He told me he saw a crack in our crystal cross. I must have looked at it for a half hour after he left and I don't see even the slightest hint of a crack."

"Maybe he saw a cobweb get reflected in it."

"Cobweb! What kind of dive do you think I'm running over here?"

"I don't know, Mom. Rumor has it that you've got a drunk rolling around in your backyard as we speak."

"Goodbye," she said, and hung up.

Chapter 28

I woke up on Tuesday morning a little earlier than usual and heard Kelly in the shower of the master bathroom. Knowing that I'd have to take time out of my day to meet with Shamansky, I hopped out of bed for a quick start. I dismissed the notion of joining Kelly in the shower when my stomach reminded me of the ingredients that were added to the chili we ate last night.

I thought of the adage *Look Before You Leap* immediately after getting out of the shower in the hall bathroom and noticed that I had only a pair of blue terrycloth hand towels at my disposal. No sooner had I dried my hair when I heard the doorbell.

From the other side of the bathroom wall Kelly called, "Jason, can you get that? I'm indisposed." I wasn't the only one who had second helpings last night.

With my hands in the Old West gunfighter, *reach for it* position, I bridged the gap between the two hand towels I had strategically positioned, and moistened the hall carpet on my way to the front door. Glimpsing through the peephole I saw Kayleigh standing on our new *Wipe Your Paws* welcome mat. I now faced the perplexing conundrum of how to twist the deadbolt and turn the doorknob without looking like I was dressed for a day at Black's Beach. Luckily, my brain engaged without the benefit of caffeine.

"I'll be with you in just a minute, Kayleigh."

Wearing a black satin Everlast boxing robe with gold trim, I received our guest with my modesty intact.

"What brings you to San Diego on this bright and beautiful morning, Kayleigh?"

"Didn't Kelly tell you? She asked me to do a presentation for her class today. She also has a student whose new stepmom is in a band. The girl is having a lot of problems and Kelly thought it might help if I talked with her."

"That sounds like a great idea. I've been working on the case so many hours that we haven't talked very much lately. Calvin's such a slave-driver. You must know how that can be."

"I think I know why you two are such good friends."

Kelly appeared at the entrance to the kitchen nook. "Hi, Kayleigh. I see Jason's been showing off his Irish tan."

Boxing robes aren't known for their length.

I said, "If I answered the door in the two little hand towels you left in the bathroom she might have been seeing my blarney stones.

"I need a cup of coffee," Kelly said.

I said, "I have to get into the office early. I'll let you two work on your game plan. Nice seeing you again, Kayleigh."

I called my sister, Lisa, from the bedroom and confirmed that she still had a free-standing, dry-wipe, white board that I could borrow. I liked the visual effect from Jeannine's two-sided cork board. But with the victims on one side and the suspects on the other, there was no room for the project I had in mind.

Jeannine looked like a kid with a new toy when I rolled the white board into the office.

I said, "I need to get a handle on how John Murray is connected to every insurance company and rep related to this case. Did Cory photograph the registration book at the conference?"

"We did what Detective Shamansky suggested. Just as they were about to close registration, I got the two women staffing the table to follow me to the concierge desk, where

Detective Shamansky's friend told them about a special amenity the resort was extending to the conference guests. Cory shot the book while they were gone."

"Good job. Start with a list of the reps from the two insurers that covered the concerts, Gordian C. Knox and Keagle. Check and see if Diversified Risk Insurance Group had any reps in attendance. As a reinsurer they wouldn't have gotten much out of the conference presentations, but may have sent a rep or two for networking purposes."

Jeannine said, "I wrote down everything I could remember about the conversation Mr. Murray was having when Aaron Tesslerod accosted me. I put the notes on your desk. Unfortunately, they hadn't really gotten down to business before that horrible man grabbed my wrist. I still have a bruise." She extended her left arm to show me. "Yesterday, Cory printed a photo of Tesslerod next to a picture of my wrist, and I put it on Hoover's blankie. I think he'll know to protect me if that horrible man ever shows up here."

I didn't want to give her a mini-lesson on canine ocular sensation and perception, so I said, "Remember, Hoover's still a big puppy. You're doing a great job with him, but don't expect too much just yet. It isn't fair."

"I know," she said.

"Until the case is over we'll lock the doors and turn on the hallway security cameras."

She said, "Cory did a pretty fine job of protecting me at the conference."

"Yes he did. I was proud of him. Let him know that I want him upgraded from part-time to full-time status until we clear this case."

I knew about Cory's issues with physical confrontations from being his counselor prior to becoming his boss. I knew that Jeannine's perception of safety didn't always follow a logical track. I also knew that I didn't want her to speak the name Delbert Henson, a former client of mine and one-time short-term employee of Duffy Investigations, who suffers from Delusions of Grandeur.

I met Shamansky for lunch at a Chinese restaurant on the third level of Horton Plaza. The dapper detective was dressed for court, which explained why he hadn't pressed for his favorite budget busting bistro in La Jolla.

Shamansky insisted that I lead off with all of the details from the weekend conference at La Costa. I used my phone to do a show and tell presentation.

"I emailed these pictures to you just before I left the office."

Shamansky asked, "Do you have any idea who Murray met in Carlsbad when Cory lost him?"

"My best guess is that he got together with Lonnie to sign documents. With all of that cash flying around they probably needed to set up a dummy corporation or two."

"That makes sense. Was Cory able to find the guy with the thick-stemmed glasses who went up to Murray's room?"

I shook my head. "I'm working on developing a profile on all of the possible players in the insurance business. How did you make out with your ConcertMaster contact?"

"The reason I didn't want to meet at Larabee's is that my contact is Abbie Delison. She was our waitress a couple of times during the Terry Tucker case. At the time, she was a student at San Diego State and did an internship at ConcertMaster in her last semester. They hired her full-time after she graduated."

"How well does she know Manning?" I asked.

"They both work out of the San Francisco office. She provides support to his department, but isn't on a first-name basis with the guy. She said he's been riding the staff really hard the past few months."

"Since around the time the murders started?"

"I couldn't get her to commit to a particular month when it began. The thing I found to be most interesting was a comment she made when talking about the Christian rock band he's guiding."

"Guiding?" I asked.

"Her word, not mine. She said he acts like a saint most of the time that he's around the boys and their family entourage, but turns into a slave-driver as soon as they leave."

"Do you mean that he doesn't care if the support staff knows it's all an act?"

"She said he keeps the act up around his bosses and other sales people at his level, but doesn't feel the need to wear the mask in front of the peons." Shamansky said.

"Interesting. Did she have any other notable tidbits?"

"She said he asked her a million questions about how things worked on the SDSU concert committee."

"Calvin once told me that his company did a lot of partnering with colleges. The schools get the benefit of accessing dates for their favorite bands without having to worry about being in the right place at the right time to get the bookings. Calvin gets the benefit of free advertising on campus and an almost guaranteed gate."

"It sounds to me like Mr. Manning has designs on capturing Calvin's customer base."

"What else did she have to say?"

"Just that the guy is a workaholic and she's surprised at how far he's gotten at such a young age. She estimated that he's barely in his mid-20s."

"So, what made you extend your weekend an extra day? Is Abbie into May/December relationships?"

"We had backstage passes to a Divine Guys Dance concert on Sunday night in Sacramento. And, I'm barely through October."

"So is Halloween. Did she introduce you as her father?"

"Just for that, I'm ordering a dessert."

"Tell me about the concert."

"Manning was on his best behavior all night. I was hoping he'd show his dark side to Abbie when the boys weren't around. But there were so many of their relatives backstage that he didn't risk letting Mr. Hyde make an appearance."

"So why stay on through Monday?"

"Abbie promised to bring a flash drive to work and copy any documents that could help me figure out Manning's whereabouts on the nights of the murders. She was a little squeamish about giving me the flash drive or letting me copy the files."

I said, "She probably figures that ConcertMaster will eventually become a monopoly and she'd be permanently blackballed if the leak got traced back to her."

"Unfortunately, she wasn't able to access his calendar or tap directly into his computer. But she did get hold of the expense vouchers that he submitted. I took a lot of notes that I haven't been able to check out yet. I'll tell you this: The man does travel a lot."

At that point Shamansky was served his dessert and I cracked open my fortune cookie.

"It says: Man who can't tell winter from fall should stay away from fattening desserts."

Kelly called in the middle of the afternoon to say Kayleigh agreed to stay at the school until the girl she was helping got picked up from the afterschool program. They were hoping Kayleigh would be able to talk with the musician stepmom.

"I want to take Kayleigh out to dinner before she has to battle traffic," she said.

"Sounds like a good way to say thank you. Did you defrost anything for dinner tonight, or should I stop for take-out?"

"There's a package of turkey burger in the fridge. I was going to make a meatloaf. You ought to be able to take a quarter pound without messing up my recipe."

"I'll mix in a few corn flakes if I go back for seconds."

Kelly replied, "After last night's chili chow-down you'd better not or I'll have to start calling you Jason Puffy."

"Sticks and stones, teacher. Sticks and stones."

I exited the 163 Freeway on my way home when my smart phone made a noise at twice its usual volume. It sounded like a submarine going into an emergency dive. I was still a half mile from home, so I drove into a nearby convenience store parking lot and pulled the phone from my pocket.

I tapped an icon I never saw before and found myself listening to Colonel Hogan barking, and seeing a blurry image that looked like what a drunk would shoot if given a video camera. It had to be the collar-cam Drayton installed.

Suddenly, I heard a *plop* sound and saw a pile of uncooked burger on the screen. My first impression was to wonder how Colonel Hogan got into the refrigerator to steal my dinner. I was about to pop the phone in my shirt pocket and rush home when I saw a pair of feet on the other side of the chain-link gate that separated my driveway from the side yard.

The camera swayed hard to the right. I heard a thud, and could now see Colonel Hogan's paw sticking out. He was lying on his side, whimpering quietly.

I was about to throw the car into gear when I heard the gate open and a voice became audible. "What's that on your collar, fella?"

I saw the feet disappear, heading toward the street parking in front of my house. Whoever drugged Colonel Hogan obviously knew his electronics and was making a break for it. I gunned the engine out of the lot.

There's only one road in and out of this section of Serra Mesa. If I stayed north of the intersecting streets, the perp would have to drive past me. I had to make an important choice. If I remained nearly a half mile from the house it's possible I'd recognize the perp as he drove out of the development. Or, it's possible I'd see someone driving like he was trying to make a getaway. Either way, I'd have to give chase. That would mean leaving Colonel Hogan alone for an indefinite length of time. There was no way of knowing if he was given a roofie to knock him out for a while, or if he was poisoned. Poison is decidedly more readily available than knock-out drugs.

I drove straight home, hoping I'd spot someone in an oncoming vehicle that I'd recognize, and pursue after taking care of our puppy. But the only vehicle I encountered belonged to an elderly woman from the neighborhood.

I skidded into my driveway, nearly hitting the garage door in the process. By that point Colonel Hogan was unconscious, but still breathing. I scooped him up in my arms and placed him on the back seat. Then I drove like Billy Bob on White Lightning for two miles to the vet's office.

I didn't stop at the reception desk and walked into Dr. Nguyen's office while she was using a rectal thermometer on a Springer Spaniel. The doctor dropped what she was doing and managed to induce vomiting in a matter of minutes. Just as I was releasing a sigh of relief, Colonel Hogan stopped breathing. The doctor worked furiously for the next five minutes. Colonel Hogan would take a couple of breaths, then stop again.

"I'm afraid we're going to have to let him go, Jason," she said.

"No," I replied.

Wrapping both hands around Colonel Hogan's snout, I gave mouth to nose resuscitation. I took a Red Cross class in rescue breathing when my sister's kids got old enough to bring to the beach.

Dr. Nguyen watched without saying a word for a few minutes. She put her hand on my back, leaned her head close to my ear and whispered, "We've done all that we can."

I placed Colonel Hogan's head down gently on the metal examining table. I thought about the day Kelly insisted that he be picked from the litter of six pups. I thought about how he ran into Kelly's arms the day he was placed on Jeannine's hospital bed. I thought about …

"Ack! Ack!"

"Colonel Hogan!" I cried.

"Ack!" Colonel Hogan coughed again. He breathed in short bursts, and continued to cough intermittently. His eyes didn't open, and he heaved in a jerky motion with each cough. But he was showing signs of life.

I was hoping for a *Lassie Come Home* moment when he would lift his head, gaze into my eyes, and let me know that everything was going to be OK. After a couple of minutes I thought: *Hollywood be damned! Ack, ack will have to do.*

I reached Kelly shortly after she said goodbye to Kayleigh, and told her to meet me at the vet's without giving her any details. By the time she arrived, Colonel Hogan's coughs and heaves had subsided quite a bit. He still hadn't regained consciousness, but continued to breathe without disruption.

Chapter 29

CK had become frustrated during the past few days. He networked a referral to a new client that he hoped would put him over the top in his competition for advancement at his company. The deal that he just completed fell apart early that morning. He should have been holding his customer's hand through the process instead of spinning his wheels with the Duffy clan. It was nearly noon and he was still lounging in his room at the Hotel Del Coronado.

He realized that he needed to call his boss and tell him about the rescission email. But his confidence ebbed and he couldn't bring himself to come across as weak in their conversation. CK needed to take his mind off of the blown deal and the Duffys, so he took his complimentary copy of the paper out to the balcony and tried to immerse himself in the troubles of others. When that didn't work he turned to the entertainment section and his mood changed instantly. The perfect band would be appearing at the perfect venue that very evening.

CK's body took on a new feel. He moved from a slumped sitting position to an erect posture to a standing stretch. It felt as if he had awoken from a bad dream and was about to conquer new lands. The butler outfit he purchased in Los Angeles last month was neatly packed in the trunk of his car, along with everything else he would need for his sixth kill.

Using a combination of Bible quotes and heartfelt bravado, CK conveyed to his boss that his contract was looking shaky. He would try one more time to salvage the deal in San Diego, but that some are destined to never see the light. The boss echoed his sentiments and approved the plan. They would meet the following afternoon.

CK's phone alarm woke him from a nap at 8:00 PM. The warm-up act would be getting started soon. After he showered, he inserted hazel contact lenses and methodically applied a subtle make-up that made his complexion seem darker. He then put on an expensive blond wig that gave him a well-groomed, Nordic look. The butler outfit was authentic, even though a good costume shop knock-off may have sufficed. Finally, he used spirit gum to add a thin blond mustache with black roots spanning its entire upper border. He was certain that the clerk at the gourmet shop he'd soon visit would focus on this unique feature and ignore the other details that the police would be seeking. He had already determined that no security cameras would be recording his image.

CK arrived at the amphitheater shortly before the show ended. He was able to find parking near the band's RVs, thanks to one of the many concert-goers who skipped the encores to beat the traffic jam. It was just after 11:00 PM and the temperature had dipped into the mid-40s. The band would put in an appearance at the requisite backstage party after the show. But CK studied several of the band's fan websites before his nap. A groupie site was particularly helpful in noting that lead singer Cable Kincaid travelled in his own RV, and gave a description that made it easy to identify.

In spite of the thermal warming container, the smell of pheasant permeated CK's vehicle. As the crowd thinned he spotted a large man standing in front of Kincaid's RV. He was definitely a roadie and not security, as evidenced by his clothing and lack of portable radio. Two frail groupies stood next to him shivering. They hugged themselves, tugged at their short skirts, and tottered off after about twenty minutes.

At 11:45 Kincaid emerged from the stage entrance alone and was admitted to the RV. The roadie remained posted out front. CK removed the thermal jacket from his serving tray and carried it on his finger pads above his right shoulder. In his left hand he carried a bottle of Dom Perignon champagne in a thermal sleeve. A white linen napkin draped his left arm.

Upon reaching the roadie guard, CK used a British accent to say, "Delivery for Mr. Kincaid complements of CLAM Concert Promotions."

"Nobody told me nothin' about any delivery."

"Apparently, the gate receipts triggered a clause in the group's contract. As per the agreement, Mr. Kincaid is to receive one gourmet dinner featuring Chef Andre LeBlanc's famous pheasant under glass, and a bottle of Dom Perignon."

"You wait right here," he said.

Three minutes later he was granted entrance to the RV. The driver sat behind the wheel studying a road map.

CK stepped slightly past the driver before asking, "Where shall I set up, sir?"

"Bring it back here," called a voice from the back of the vehicle.

He walked past a sitting/TV area, kitchenette, and bathroom before reaching a well-appointed love nest. A bed took up at least 80% of the floor space. Kincaid sat in the middle of the bed. He was shivering and wrapped from head to toe in blankets.

"You can set the tray on the bed right in front of me."

"Very well, sir."

He did as instructed, and without asking permission, uncorked the bottle.

Kincaid said, "Don't bother with that. I'm too cold for champagne."

CK removed a flute wrapped in a linen napkin from his pocket. "I anticipated the inclement weather conditions, sir, and maintained the bottle at just a few degrees below room temperature. It should be just cool enough to balance the entree, which I assure you, is piping hot."

He turned his back on Kincaid, removed a corked bottle no bigger than a fingernail from inside the white glove on his left hand, and poured its contents into the champagne flute. He added the booze and placed it on Kincaid's tray. By that point, the lead singer was warming his hands over the steaming plate.

"Enjoy," CK said with a slight bow.

"Tell the roadie out front that I said for him to give you a tip."

"Already taken care of, sir. Bon appétit."

I met Kelly in front of our house when she rolled into the driveway. She had just picked Colonel Hogan up from the vet after school. Initially, we had no problem getting him settled into his bed. Dr. Nguyen told Kelly that he was on a sedative, but should be coming out of it fairly soon. We acted like new parents dealing with a child's illness for the first time. We turned in at 10:30 PM as a way of encouraging him to get a good night's sleep.

We both overreacted when the phone rang at 12:40 AM. By the second ring I didn't need Caller ID to realize it was Shamansky.

I made it to the crime scene by 1:30. Shamansky escorted me behind the yellow tape, briefing me on the reports of the roadie and driver on our way to the RV. The forensics team kept us from entering at that time, and we were directed to a police van by a uniformed officer who said the forensics supervisor was going to be setting up a grid in the parking spaces adjacent to the RV where the killer could have observed the victim's arrival.

"Is Darden in the van?" asked Shamansky.

The uniformed officer nodded.

Turning to me he said, "Let's get in my Crown Vic. I don't feel like dealing with him right now."

Shamansky went into greater detail on the reports from the roadie and RV driver. Less than five minutes after the butler departed, Kincaid made some gagging noises and the driver heard the serving tray and dinnerware crash. He opened the door and yelled to the roadie, and they rushed to the back of the RV.

I pointed to the forensics supervisor emerging from the RV. We intercepted him before he got to Darden's van.

Shamansky asked, "What's the story?"

"It was definitely poison. I'd say arsenic, but I won't know for sure until after I take a look in the lab."

"Any prints or hairs?" Shamansky asked.

"Nada. Both witnesses said the butler wore white gloves. It's apparent he wiped away the chef's prints as well."

I asked, "What kind of food and drink did he bring?"

"Pheasant, stuffing, chestnut soup, spinach, and celery root. The butler also brought a bottle of Dom Perignon."

Shamansky asked, "How was the pheasant prepared?"

"It was definitely braised. I couldn't identify the braising from my sniff test."

Shamansky asked, "Could you see any marking on the meat indicating that it was tied together?"

"Yes, I assumed some kind of cord held the stuffing in the pheasant and was cut away later," he said. "Look, I have to get this information to Detective Darden."

I asked Shamansky, "Do you think the poison was in the braising?"

"It was probably in the champagne. But we might get lucky if the perp isn't a gourmet cook. There can't be too many places that filled an order for Pheasant Ballotine last night."

"If you're not planning on tossing that bit of epicurean info at Darden, I can get Jeannine on it in about six hours."

He wrote the correct spelling on a scrap of paper, handed it to me and said, "I know that look on your face. You're holding out on me."

I asked, "Does the name of the victim's band, Aorta Event Invitation, ring a bell?"

"It's almost 3:00 AM. Let's not play games.'

"Victim #1, Delainya Tanner, died after their San Francisco concert."

Chapter 30

The last thing I did before going to bed at 4:00 AM was to send Jeannine an email explaining why I'd be late coming into the office, and telling her to start looking for an establishment that sells Pheasant Ballotine to-go.

I rolled into the office at 10:00 Thursday morning feeling surprisingly energetic.

"Any luck?" I asked Jeannine.

"I believe he used a place called Cordon Bleu from Me to You. It's the only high-end take-out place to advertise that entree online."

"Where is it located?"

"It's in the Banker's Hill section on 5th, near Laurel Street. Detective Shamansky called a half hour ago. He wants you to call the minute you get in."

Jeannine left a post-it with the epicurean caterer's name, address, driving directions and map on my desk. She added a recipe for Pheasant Ballotine from a gourmet website.

When Shamansky came on the line I gave him the details.

"Tell her I said she deserves a raise."

I asked, "Are there any new developments?"

"Our boy left us another message. It said, and I quote, 'Note to Santa: Got a singer, want a guitarist.' It sounds like he's feeling invincible and calling his next shot."

"If he's writing to Santa, it tells us he's planning another kill before Christmas. Did Darden pick up on the Aorta Event Invitation connection?"

"No, but Rappaport from SFPD called this morning and told him."

"Anything else?" I asked.

"Casey has decided to go public. He's called a press conference for 2:00 PM this afternoon."

I got angry. "There's only one big show scheduled in California between now and Christmas. It's right here at the Hooni."

"I hate that name. Why can't everybody just call it the Junipero Serra Arena. Our city's founder deserves better," Shamansky said.

"There are only two major acts and a warm-up playing that night, and we know he's looking for a guitarist. Why would Casey blow that kind of setup now?"

"The captain and I agree with you, Jason. But political pressure does some strange things to administrators who've been behind a desk too long. The captain wrote Casey an email this morning outlining your exact points."

"And?"

"He hasn't heard back and doesn't expect to."

"I've got to go," I said, and hung up.

I took five minutes before calling Calvin. Hoover followed me as I paced through the office suite. I decided that Shamansky wouldn't have told me if he didn't want me to do something about it. Considering my current lack of status with Lt. Casey, I had nothing to lose.

Calvin listened carefully as I brought him up to date. We sounded like a metal guitarist and drummer jamming on a screamer after the Casey revelation hit the table. Dueling rants.

Calvin said, "OK, let's settle down. There's got to be a way that we can prevent him from releasing that statement. We just have to come up with a plan and make it happen."

We spent the next hour hashing out possibilities. I switched to a hands-free phone and drove toward Calvin's office in L.A. while we talked. The call ended by the time I reached Mission Viejo. I refined the plan as I crawled through traffic.

The instant I walked into their suite, CLAM's receptionist put a finger to her lips, ushered me into Calvin's office, and shut the door on her way out.

Calvin said, "I haven't mentioned the plan to the other partners yet. They're all here and know about Kincaid's murder, but don't know about Casey's press conference. Although, I wouldn't be a bit surprised if Lonnie gets the word from one of this contacts any minute now."

"Then let's get right to it. I'm ready," I said.

Calvin handed me a phone and held one in his own hand. "I'll nod when Casey's secretary puts me through."

A minute later Calvin said, "This is Calvin Dawson of CLAM Concert Promotions. I need to speak with Lieutenant Casey." After 20 seconds of silence passed Calvin said, "I suggest that you tell him that if he refuses my call I will immediately contact the media myself and give a preemptory press conference that will contradict what your boss is about to say. Personally, I think we should be on the same page. But if your boss refuses this call, all bets are off." Calvin nodded and I clicked onto the line.

Casey's demeanor was decidedly gruff. "What's this all about?"

I said, "I'm prepared to tell the press that you're the one responsible for keeping the public in the dark about the Concert Killer."

"Why would you do something like that? You're the one who's been fighting to keep this thing under wraps."

I said, "The note to Santa tells us he's going to strike again before Christmas. There's only one large venue show between now and then. We even have a very short list of possible targets. By telling the public now, you'll either send him underground to a less conspicuous venue, or you'll ensure that every whacko in the state will show up at that event, making it impossible to spot the guy."

Casey said, "Nobody tells me how to conduct this investigation. You're not going to run to the press and say it was me who stopped the disclosure when three of the top papers in the state got the denial directly from your partner, Lonnie Cancelli, on the day the San Diego Sound Scene ran that article. Your credibility will be in the crapper on that one, Dawson."

"Actually, you're talking with Jason Duffy, and my credibility is just fine. By the way, it was CLAM partner, Mark Danby, who gave the story to Dee Martin Sandler. Once Danby has Sandler confirm that fact, you'll be the one dealing with the public relations fiasco."

"Why are you doing this, Duffy?"

"I'm not going to let our best shot at catching this guy be destroyed because you won't man-up to some politician. You don't seem to have any problem telling an old colleague who's dying of cancer to butt out, but you don't have the balls to say the same thing to some hack whose main concern is his reelection."

Casey asked, "O'Malley's dying?"

"He just signed up for a high-risk experimental surgery. It sounds to me like he wants to go out on his own terms with his dignity intact. I'd say your career is at a similar crossroads right here and now, Casey."

"O'Malley is a good man and a good friend. This news is very disturbing. Unfortunately, I'll be forced to postpone my press conference due to this medical emergency. But you can damn-well bank on the fact that it will happen the day after that Christmas concert if the perp is still on the street," Casey said, and slammed the receiver for emphasis

I phoned Shamansky on my way back from L.A. We agreed to a 4:00 PM meeting at my office.

Shamansky was fifteen minutes late. During that time I asked Jeannine and Cory to pull some information together and told them I'd be calling them into the meeting at some point.

I filled Shamansky in on my conversation with Casey. The captain informed him that an email was received by the task force instructing them to disregard the earlier announcement due to a development in the case that warranted continuation of the media blackout. It was apparent that Shamansky didn't want to discuss the particulars, preferring to keep his distance from what had transpired.

Cordon Bleu from Me to You was indeed the source of the Concert Killer's gourmet meal. Unfortunately, they don't have security cameras and the clerk's focus was primarily on the butler's two-tone mustache.

"Was she able to give you an approximate age?" I asked.

"She guessed he was in his twenties, but didn't sound very convincing. I'd categorize her as someone I wouldn't want to put on the witness stand."

"Why not? She had a one-on-one interaction with the guy from just a few feet away?"

"This is more your area of expertise, Jason. But there was something that wasn't quite right with that girl." Shamansky looked through the horizontal mini-blinds in my office at Jeannine, sitting at the reception desk. When it was clear that she wasn't looking, he tapped his index finger on his temple three times. "Let's just say her spice rack was missing a few key ingredients. I'm guessing she's the owner's daughter."

"I take it he paid in cash."

"Did you really need to ask?"

"Let's take a walk over to Cory's office."

As we exited my office, I waved for Jeannine to follow.

Cory placed the new whiteboard, detailing all of the players in the insurance industry, next to the corkboard listing the suspects. He added a picture of everyone below their vital info.

I said, "We've been crunching data all week trying to get a handle on the suspects. After the weekend at La Costa, as you can see, we've got an entire whiteboard full of possibilities. I could spend the next hour explaining how each one made it onto the board. But I think our time would be better spent cutting to the bottom line. Jeannine, how about if you pick it up from here."

"I wish I could say that we've narrowed it down to four suspects, but we've actually got it down to four suspect groups. Let's start with the insurance people. We have several known possibilities in this group, as well as the unknown man in the thick-stemmed glasses."

Shamansky said, "I see you have John Murray at the top of the list."

I said, "He's the common denominator, but it's also possible he's pulling the strings and Tesslerod, or a hitman, or different hitmen are actually offing the vics."

"What's his motive?" asked Shamansky.

I said, "We know he has an ax to grind with his old partner at Diversified Risk, and that they've taken a huge hit as the reinsurer of all of the events."

Shamansky said, "By the way, neither Keagle nor Gordian C. Knox covered last night's show, but Diversified again reinsured the company that did."

Cory's comment was censored by a Hoover bark-over.

I said, "Keep going, Jeannine."

"The second group includes three men affiliated with the Delainya Tanner murder. First is Ms. Tanner's boyfriend, Luke Milner. Even though Detective Rappaport cleared him as having an alibi, Jason wants to dig a little deeper and make sure it holds up. Second is her boss, Jorge Martinez, who promoted her. And, third, we have a wild card on the board, representing a loan applicant, stalker, old boyfriend, or someone else from her past."

I said, "We bumped this group up to the number two slot after the Aorta singer got killed."

Jeannine said, "Third we have Mr. Manning. He's the right age, and it looks like he gains from CLAM's loss."

I turned to Shamansky. "Did you get a chance to call your friend and find out what he was doing last night?"

"She didn't know offhand and said she'd get back to me."

Jeannine said, "Finally, we have the employees of CLAM. We've cleared Calvin and Ashley. Mark fits the religious profile. And, we know Lonnie's working some angle that looks pretty suspicious."

I said, "There are still a lot of possibilities. I was hoping you could cover Manning and keep me posted on the task force. I could cover CLAM and the insurance crew. And, I was hoping you and the captain could get the task force boys to turn over every rock connected to Delainya Tanner."

Shamansky asked, "Do you really want Darden working the angle you've ranked #2?"

I said, "Of course not. But I have a lot of confidence in Ike Rappaport, Maurice Johnson, and Harry Lutz. They're the ones who'd be doing the legwork in NoCal. Let Darden do what he's good at: Sucking up to people with the political clout to make it happen."

Shamansky said, "You realize there's cross-over in all of these groups." The Duffy Investigations trio all nodded. "But I like it. I hope you realize that I'm going to have to lead the captain to believe this was my idea."

"As long as Darden isn't sharing the spotlight, I have no problem," I said.

"That will never happen," Shamansky said, and departed.

Chapter 31

I stood in front of my wall calendar and realized it was exactly two weeks until the only major California concert before Christmas. Calvin told me that permits for shows were getting extremely difficult to secure due to the huge spike in liability caused by the Concert Killer. It seemed clear to me that the insurance people readily accepted what the mainstream press would not. But the insurers wouldn't block San Diego's longstanding tradition of the major colleges banding together to bring in at least two very hot bands the Friday before Christmas week. Even though The College Christmas Cotillion evolved into the politically correct Higher Ed Holiday Happening, it was a *bullet train* on the SoCal scene. Any politician, police commissioner, or insurance company that jumped in front of the train would surely suffer dire consequences.

The Junipero Serra Arena was San Diego's newest and largest indoor facility. Its nickname, the Hooni, came from a combination of the Spanish pronunciation of the letter *J* and a shortening of Friar Serra's first name.

Current college students would be seated on the floor and first tier. The general public and alumni would have access to a huge second tier. Corporate skyboxes, with both enclosed and open seats, ringed the top tier.

Before I could begin to formulate any ideas on how to protect my guitarist friends in one of the show headliners, Doberman's Stub, I got a call from Celia Bains.

She said, "I've got something to trade, but you have to go first."

"I think Jimmy tried poisoning Colonel Hogan on Monday."

"That bastard!" she exclaimed. "And I suppose Sergeant Schultz saw nothing."

"Colonel Hogan is my dog."

"I'm sorry to hear that, Jason. Is he OK?"

"He's doing a little better every day."

"I got you mixed up with Jimmy in the first place, so I'll let you know what I have. Do you remember me telling you about my cute cousin who hangs out at Jimmy's bar in L.A.?"

"What did she find out?"

"Jimmy got really wasted the other night and bragged to her that he was making a killing in the stock market. Normally, I'd think it was just drunken bullshit. But Jimmy pulled out a top-of-the-line smart phone and was wearing brand new leathers."

I said, "I can't imagine him reading the Wall Street Journal or watching a lot of CNBC programming. What do you make of it?"

"I was hoping you'd come up with an angle based on his association with Lonnie and that Tesslerod character. Does Lonnie play the market?" Bains asked.

"The last time I saw Lonnie he was asking his partners to vote me off of the case because he thought I leaked a story to the free press. We're not exactly at the tip-swapping stage of our relationship yet. I'll check with Calvin as soon as I can. Why would Jimmy poison my dog?"

"Maybe he wanted to snoop around your house and see what you had on him, and the dog looked intimidating."

I said, "It happened just before the time I usually get home. And, the dog is less than six months old."

"That really doesn't sound like Jimmy's style. In biker world, poisoning is a chick kill. A pink knife would have been a more manly way to do it. Jimmy's too much of a braggart to use a method he could never talk about."

"Thanks, Celia. I'll be in touch."

Shamansky called in the early afternoon to say the task force refocused its attention on the Delainya Tanner murder without any prodding on his part. The Aorta Event Invitation connection was the first solid link between any of the murders.

"Did you find out if Manning has an alibi yet?" I asked.

"Abbie said that his calendar was blank. She tried asking him if he did anything fun on Wednesday night and he told her he wasn't in the habit of swapping after hours stories with underlings."

"He sounds like a jerk, but not necessarily a murdering jerk."

"I finished analyzing his expense account entries and didn't find anything that would help us," Shamansky said. "What's happening with the insurance companies?"

I filled him in on my conversation with Celia Bains. "Is there a way to find out what stock trades are being made by our key players in the insurance group?"

"I don't know the particulars, but I'm sure we're pretty far away from establishing probable cause for a warrant at this point. I have a meeting on another case. Keep in touch."

I remembered my parents talking about a retired friend who never rose above the rank of desk sergeant, buying a huge cabin cruiser. Dad said he made a ton of money in the market. I phoned home.

"Mom, what's the name of the desk sergeant who made lots of money in the stock market?"

Mom started crying.

"What's the matter, Mom?"

"O'Malley passed about an hour ago."

I spent the next fifteen minutes consoling her. It was agreed that Kelly and I would meet my parents at the viewing on Sunday afternoon. I briefly considered asking my mother if she wanted to stay at my house tonight, knowing that Dad would be getting blitzed at Casey's. Instead, I simply said, "Call me if you need any help with Dad."

After getting off of the phone I pulled out a yellow pad with every intention of listing questions about the stock market that could relate to the case. But my mind kept wandering to my many encounters with the O'Malley family. The thought that O'Malley was only two years older than Dad made my efforts at critical thinking a fruitless exercise. I considered the prospects of stopping by Casey's to extend my condolences to Dad, but was sure he'd interpret it as an attempt to get him to go home.

I worked out of my house on Saturday rather than go into the office. I knew that my mother wouldn't ask for any help if she thought I was working on the case. Shortly before noon I reached Calvin at the CLAM office suite.

"I need to ask you a few questions about Lonnie. Can you talk?"

"I'm in my office with the door closed. What's up?"

"Do you happen to know if Lonnie has been making stock market trades?"

Calvin said, "He's been playing the market since we formed CLAM. I've been in his office a few times when he's gotten alerts on his computer about his holdings. One time he asked to postpone a meeting because he needed to talk with his financial advisor."

"So, he's not making the stock picks by himself?"

"I think he mentioned something about a golfing buddy getting him into the market. But I don't know any of the specifics. Why do you ask?"

I told him about my conversation with Celia Bains. "I've been wondering about why Lonnie would use Jimmy to transfer money to John Murray through Tesslerod. Do you think Murray could be Lonnie's stock advisor?"

"Lonnie's in his office right now. I'll try to snoop around after he leaves for the day."

I said, "Some people customize the home page of their computers with a stock market app that constantly updates while the market is open. If you see something like that, write down his current holdings."

"Will do," Calvin said. "By the way, Kayleigh enjoyed spending the day with Kelly."

"They definitely hit it off. We'll have to get them together over the holidays." After a brief pause I added, "One more thing."

"What?" asked Calvin.

"When you go into Lonnie's office make absolutely certain you leave it exactly the way you found it. If Lonnie's mixed up in this mess it means he's complicit in six murders."

Chapter 32

I hate attending funeral home viewings. I have no problem with paying my final respects to the grieving family members. But I have a big problem with the agendas of many of the attendees. Invariably, I'm hit on by one or more politicians, an insurance agent, a realtor, and at least one other salesperson. Then there are the elderly who attend strictly for socialization purposes. I feel very uncomfortable listening to a joke when the widow is within earshot. Idle banter unrelated to the corpse also seems inappropriate.

O'Malley's viewing was scheduled from 4:00 PM to 7:00 PM. We arrived at 5:30 and immediately made our way to the casket. Mrs. O'Malley's eyes were very red, but she appeared to be holding up reasonably well. She brightened when I introduced her to Kelly.

"You're every bit as lovely as Molly described," she said.

I checked in with my parents, and noted that Dad appeared to be hung over but sober. Uncharacteristically, my father did not maintain eye contact when we talked. Mom seemed on the verge of tears, so I simply gave her a hug and whispered a few reassuring words in her ear. An elderly couple headed our way, so I told my parents I was going to say hello to my sister, who sat a few feet away with her kids.

After exchanging pleasantries with Kelly, Lisa told her kids to move down the row a couple of chairs to make room.

"Sit," she said, tugging on my jacket and patting the seat next to her.

Lisa is two years older than me, and has an Irish temper that makes Kelly's occasional outbursts look like mild agitation. I passed her in height and weight when I was seven years old. Somewhere around that time our father made it clear to me that I was not to hit her, even though Lisa was very prone to slap, kick and punch as part of her feisty nature.

I tentatively took the seat next to Lisa and instinctively drew my elbows into my sides.

"What's going on?" I asked.

"Mom told me about the SDG&E man coming to the house about a Smart Grid survey on Thursday."

"She told me, too. So what?"

Lisa said, "I never heard anything about the program so I called SDG&E on Friday and was told that nothing of the kind is going on."

"Are you sure?"

"Of course I'm sure. Do you think I'd make something like that up?" Lisa's voice was getting loud and drew the attention of a few nearby mourners.

"I mean, did you ask to get confirmation from a supervisor?"

She said, "I didn't ask for one, but after I gave the customer service woman all of the details on the visit, one came on the line. After I told her what Mom told me, she said it was a good thing Dad came home when he did."

I asked, "Did you tell this to Mom?"

"She had just heard about O'Malley when I called. She wasn't ready to deal with anything more at that point. But I think you better do something about it."

"I agree," I said. "Can you keep Kelly company for a few minutes?"

"She can help me deal with the little monsters."

I stood up, scanned the room, and spotted Bob Kerrigan and his wife chatting with another couple about 15 feet from my parents. Instead of the usual formal greeting one usually gives at a funeral home, I clamped my hand on Kerrigan's shoulder and whispered in his ear.

"I need your help with something right now."

In response to Kerrigan's quizzical look, I angled my head toward my father. Together, we approached Dad, and I whispered the same words. My father looked annoyed, but noting Kerrigan's presence, followed me out of the main viewing room and into an empty room across the hall, where I repeated what Lisa had told me.

"Do you think it was a robbery that almost happened?" asked Kerrigan.

"It looks that way," said Dad.

I asked, "Did Mom tell you about Colonel Hogan getting poisoned the next day?"

"What does that have to do with anything?" Dad asked.

"Mom gave the guy my address."

We all looked at each other, contemplating the implications and trying to figure out how the incidents could be related.

Dad asked, "Is there some way this could tie in with the case you're working on?"

I replied, "My name did get mentioned in the free press article that tried outing the Concert Killer. But I have no idea how he could have gotten *your* home address."

"Your mother said something about him mentioning a crack in the crystal cross."

"She said she was leaning in to have a closer look when you two came rolling in the door."

Kerrigan said, "Holy shit! He was gonna kill her!"

"Why would he come after Mom?"

Dad said, "To take your mind completely off of the case."

I asked, "Are you sure it isn't some old perp from your past coming back for retribution?"

"You told me your suspect has been leaving religious clues, like the bloody cross and the St. Blaise medal. This guy made his move in front of the crystal cross."

"It sounds like we need to be on high alert until this guy gets put away," I said.

Kerrigan said, "As of now, the O'Malley sorrows drowning is officially on hold. Let me know what I can do."

Chapter 33

I attended O'Malley's funeral mass on Monday at 11:00 AM with my parents and sister. Kelly and Lisa's kids were at school. I sat in front with Dad on the ride from the mass to the cemetery and learned that his stock-savvy friend was currently fishing in the Gulf of Mexico.

While we waited near the grave for the mourners to assemble, I called Jeannine, who was working out of her apartment via call-forwarding and the high-end laptop computer she received after a recent client sent me a big bonus.

"What's going on?" I asked.

"Calvin called and seemed very upset. I don't know the details, but it has something to do with ConcertMaster horning in on the Christmas show."

"Did he mention the name Matthew Manning?"

"No, but he did say that he has a meeting with the SDSU Concert Committee tomorrow afternoon here in San Diego, and he wants to get together with you afterwards."

Lisa elbowed me in the ribs. "Get off the phone. The priest is ready to get started."

I disconnected the call. "Why do you have to keep hitting me? You're 30 years old. Do you put up with that from your own kids?"

She replied, "Shhhhhhhh!"

We attended the bereavement luncheon at O'Neil's Restaurant after the graveside service. I hoped to map out some plans with Dad on how to protect the family, but he was inundated with conversations from guys he knew on the force. Mom spent most of her time with the wives, leaving me quality time with my sister. She told me that she thought of her playful jabs as an endearing quality that made her feel young again. A couple of minutes of trying to get her to see things from my point of view reminded me of her bullheaded nature. So I used the time to focus on the case.

When I returned to my car it was 3:30 and didn't make sense to collect Jeannine and put in a brief appearance at the office. So I paid a visit to Bernie Liebowitz at the Dali Lama, Yo Mama.

"Bernie, I'm not even sure if you can help me with this one. But since you seem to know a little bit about everything I thought I'd ask you."

He replied, "Just don't start calling me Liebopedia. What's on your mind?"

I laid out the suspects from the insurance industry and their tie to Lonnie. I also told Bernie about Jimmy's claim to be making a killing in the stock market.

"I'm trying to figure out how Lonnie and John Murray could be using the market to make money off of the killings."

Bernie retrieved two bottles of water from his mini-fridge and handed one to me. He then sipped and walked slowly while running the fingertips of his left hand around the rails of his pool table. After one circuit he stopped, raised a finger as if to make a point, then lowered his hand and made another complete circuit.

"I'm no expert on the market, but I might be able to steer you in the right direction. Keep in mind, it's all speculation," he said.

"Tell me what you've got, Bernie."

"I have a friend who's a huge hockey fan, and has made his living day trading for the past 15 years. He once told me, 'You have to learn how to skate forwards and backwards if you want to make a living in the market.' Do you know what he was talking about?"

I replied, "Does it have something to do with bears and bulls?"

"It has everything to do with them. The market trends up and down like the ebb and flow of the oceans. You have general market trends and you have sector trends. I'm sure the insurance sector has been trending downward very steadily since the Concert Killer knocked the actuarial charts off of the wall for companies that insure concerts here in California."

I asked, "So how do they make money off of the downtrend?"

"There are a few possible ways to go. First, they could simply short the stock of a particular company if they were sure it was going to get hit. In laymen's terms, it's a flat-out bet that the stock is going down. Second, they could buy *put* options. This is a time-limited bet that expires on a particular date. It's substantially less costly than a short, but could work out to be worthless if the stock goes the other way. A lot of people use options as a hedge against long and short positions going the wrong way. Third, you have ETFs which represent a basket of stocks in a particular sector. These are purchased as longs rather than shorts, but you can buy ones that track to the downside."

I said, "At one point Dee Martin Sandler wrote a story speculating on the existence of the Concert Killer. Lonnie used his best media contacts to discredit the story. Why would he do this if he was betting that the stock would go down? Wouldn't it make more sense if Lonnie was the leak instead of the leak plugger?"

Bernie did a couple of more laps around the pool table, and returned to his desk chair. "I mentioned earlier that when you buy an option it has a specific expiration date. I'm guessing that perhaps on the date that the story broke, the short option (or put) had expired and they were stuck holding a long (or call) hedge. They would have taken a bath if that was the case."

"How could an experienced trader like John Murray get caught in that position?"

"Didn't you tell me that you saw Jimmy DeLong giving cash to Aaron Tesslerod?"

"What does that have to do with anything?"

Bernie said, "It sounds like Murray wants at least two or three layers of insulation between himself and the money. He could be using a third party to make his trades. In fact, it might look downright suspicious to the SEC if an insurance man was making a killing shorting stocks in his own sector."

I flashed on the man with the thick stemmed glasses that I photographed at LaCosta.

"Thanks, Bernie. You've been a huge help."

As I was leaving the club I got a call from Kelly. "Is it safe to go home?"

"I'll call you right back."

I called Jeannine. "Can you check the security system on my house and tell me what you see?"

Jeannine said, "This is really cool. Drayton set it up on a motion detector so that I can see snippets only when there are people in the picture. How come you couldn't use this to find out who poisoned Colonel Hogan?"

"He just added that feature a few days ago. He got into a little bit of a time crunch the day my dad was there to oversee the project. What are you looking at on the screen?"

"I see a couple of seniors taking a walk, a couple of mommies with strollers, and your mail man. Nothing unusual. Are we back at the office tomorrow?"

"I'll pick you up at 8:30."

Kelly answered her phone by saying, "It's about time. I'm parked up the street and our weird neighbor with the *Joe Dirt* haircut has been winking at me."

"Jeannine reviewed the security footage and we're all clear. I should be home in a few minutes."

Upon arrival I found Kelly in the kitchen chopping vegetables. A teardrop dangled from her chin.

"What's wrong?" I asked.

"I was just thinking about standing in front of O'Malley's casket and wondering how long it will be before it's one of my family members I'm looking at." Kelly sobbed, and I gave her a hug.

"I know I should be more involved—"

Kelly held up her hand as a stop sign. "After finding out that the crazy man you're after nearly murdered your mother and our dog, I don't want you even thinking about my family until your case is over. OK?"

I gave her another hug and whispered in her ear, "I love you."

CK's efforts to calm himself by staring into the Eye of Providence were futile. First thing in the morning he learned that his office nemesis had surpassed him in the competition that would determine who would advance to the national accounts position. He had convinced himself that he could win the competition while fulfilling his crusade to shut down the concert industry. As if the self-realization that he was spreading himself too thin was not enough, he was reminded of his status change by both his boss and his competitor.

He hoped to reclaim his rightful position quickly by applying just the right amount of subtle pressure to his top prospects. But found himself in no state of mind for subtly or professionalism after receiving an unexpected call from his father, Ezra. It seems that their last conversation upset his father so much that he aired much of that exchange with his Bible study group. Ezra was calling to convey the collective wisdom of the farming community from whence he came.

The most frustrating part of the whole experience was that CK received the call on his desk line, within earshot of Shane Wesley. CK felt like he was 10 years old, forced to listen to his father's views on life. He wished he had saved his most recent sacrifice for that evening to vent his frustration.

Chapter 34

Jeannine and I spent our day getting familiar with the basics of stock trading. I called Bernie once to clarify a few points, and afterwards felt like I had a rudimentary grasp on how it worked.

As per Calvin's request, at 3:45 I walked Jeannine home and returned to my office for a private meeting. It seemed like an unusual request until Calvin arrived and spewed more four-letter words in the first five minutes than I had heard from him in our entire friendship.

"It's absolutely great that you got that off of your chest. Keeping things bottled up can be hazardous to your health. But all I got out of it is that things didn't go well at your meeting with the college concert committee and it has something to do with ConcertMaster horning in on your turf. Did the name Matthew Manning come up in the conversation?"

"They've added Divine Guys Dance to the show and Manning was mentioned as the contact person to coordinate the logistics."

I asked, "Why in the world would they bring in a Christian boy band? They probably aren't even charting in the top 100 with college students?"

The question triggered rant number two that petered out after about three minutes.

Calvin asked, "How do you know about Manning?"

"He's actually charting high in the *suspects* hit parade, so his presence may not be such a bad thing. This move by the concert committee ensures that he'll be at the scene of the next crime. If he does turn out to be our guy, it will make ConcertMaster look horrible."

Calvin was still too worked up to smile. "How many suspects do you have?"

I brought him into Cory's office and did a show-and-tell, using the boards to explain the four suspect groups.

"Now that you're settled down, will you help me to understand why a college concert committee would want a band that appeals mainly to the 12 to 16-year-old market?" I asked.

"Dee Martin Sandler's free press article ran here in San Diego. The mainstream press gave it a lot of coverage and ticket sales are way down, especially in the deck where the general public sits. Their plan is to put the altar boy band on right after the local warm-up act, before most of the college students show up. A public relations advisor at State told them it would make the religious community believe the concert is blessed, and no harm will come to those who attend."

"Do you think it will work?" I asked.

"It worked with Mark. He asked to be put on the backstage pass list as soon as he found out about it."

"Who else is on that list? Can you get it to me ASAP?"

Calvin pulled out his phone. "If I can link this to your printer I'll give it to you now."

Two minutes later I was drawing circles around names on our *suspects board.* When I finished it included Mark, Lonnie, John Murray, Aaron Tesslerod, and Matthew Manning. I suspected that most of Jimmy's posse was also on the security crew.

"Were you able to get a look at Lonnie's desktop to see if he has a customized stock ticker?" I asked.

"I did, but it was password protected. When I typed in a word I thought might work, a strange tone sounded so I clicked off," he said.

"Uh-oh."

Chapter 35

I called Shamansky five minutes after Metro roll call normally ends. "Can I interest you in a breakfast meeting?"

"It must be pretty important to get you out of bed at this hour."

"I've got some big news on Manning and need your help on the insurance company angle," I said. We agreed to meet at an upscale breakfast nook.

When I arrived, Shamansky was sipping coffee and reading the morning paper. "You're late."

"I stopped at a Do-It-Yourself Office to copy a file for you," I said, dropping it in front of him.

"Give me the Manning news first," Shamansky said.

"He managed to cut his altar boy band in on the Christmas show and now has an *All Access Pass* for the event."

"I thought Calvin was running the show."

"So, did Calvin. He was in my office last night after meeting with the concert committee."

I told Shamansky about the other names on the *Backstage Pass* list. After a waitress took our orders, I told him where I was at on my stock shorting theory.

"I need to get an address on Tesslerod. I think he's funneling cash to the mystery man in the thick-stemmed glasses that I saw at La Costa. Once we find out who he is, I'm hoping you can get a court order to have a look at his stock trading account."

"I'm going to need more than you have here to make that happen."

"I was thinking that once we had an address on him, I might just drop by his office and provide a little free servicing of his computer," I said.

Shamansky replied, "I love Eggs Florentine, but it tends to block my ears every once in a while. Did you say something, Jason?"

"Just clearing my throat. Do you keep up on the stock market?"

"Enough to watch my retirement account, but not enough to do the kind of things you've mentioned in this file. I can certainly see how a person with inside information could clean up if he knew when an insurance company was going to take one on the chin."

"Do you have anything new on Manning?" I asked.

"Just that he's been acting more stressed than usual this week." Shamansky stood up. "I'll give you a call when I get an address on Tesslerod."

I called Calvin from my office. "When you met with the concert committee did you discuss how the inclusion of ConcertMaster will affect your insurance arrangements?"

"They slanted the profits in our direction to keep us from calling off the whole event. CLAM will be giving ConcertMaster a quarter of our take, even though we're supplying two bands and they're supplying one. ConcertMaster will, in turn, pay one quarter of our costs."

"Does that mean there won't be another insurance company involved in the event?"

"I imagine that ConcertMaster has some type of Lloyds of London specialty policy on the altar boys that includes everything from skateboard accidents to The Rapture." Calvin was getting irked. "Why do you want to know?"

"For two reasons. First, I think that if Lonnie caught wind that another insurance company was at risk he might double down on his stock play and I could follow the money to the guy who's placing his trades," I said.

Calvin replied, "I'd try scamming him if I thought he'd buy it. But he's too much of a businessman not to read the fine print, especially on this contract, which he can access at any time. What's your second reason?"

"I was wondering how Matthew Manning might react if he learned that the Concert Killer vowed to kill a guitar player at the event. Would he pull out? Would he beef up insurance? And, do you have a fiduciary responsibility to make him aware of the situation in lieu of the threat?"

"That is one very interesting question, Jason?"

"Since I brought it up I feel obliged to tell you that Matthew Manning is my police contact's number one suspect. While sharing that information might get Manning and ConcertMaster out of your hair for the time being, it might also alert the Concert Killer that he's walking into a trap," I said.

Calvin said, "It's not like the Concert Killer doesn't know that the cops are on to him. He's been hitting them over the head with clues since the fourth victim. He's vowed to kill a guitar player before Christmas and the Hooni show is the only event between now and then. What could be the downside?"

"If Manning isn't the killer he could leak the info to the press to screw up your relationship with the concert committee and get his band out of harm's way. If you want to make him aware of the situation I suggest you do it through Detective Shamansky. He could threaten Manning with criminal prosecution if the story gets out. If Shamansky can find out who insures the altar boys you could pass that info along to Lonnie."

"Set it up. When you're ready to go, I'll tell Lonnie and you can follow the money," he said.

"Did Lonnie mention anything about a security alarm going off on his computer?" I asked.

"He told me that one of his gangsta rappers wrote a song called *Curiosity Killed the Cat*, and wondered if his client could get sued when the person it was written for recognized it as a death threat."

"Watch your back, Calvin."

Chapter 36

I had a long phone conversation with Shamansky on Thursday morning. We agreed that Matthew Manning should be informed about the risks involved with the holiday show. He liked the idea of having a legitimate excuse for meeting with Manning and taking a reading on his top suspect.

"Didn't Manning see you at his office and backstage at the boy band show in Sacramento," I asked.

"He looked too busy to notice me. But so what if he did?"

"Won't it screw things up for Abbie if he remembers seeing you with her?"

Shamansky said, "We're getting short on time. Maybe a phone conversation will have to suffice. Did Drayton install anything on your phone lines that would allow you to record a conversation?"

"Yes he did, and you're welcome to use it. I take it you'd rather not have that conversation in the stationhouse."

"The walls have ears and squeaky little voices. How about if I stop by toward the end of the day?"

"That works fine."

Shamansky reciprocated by giving me more than I asked for regarding Aaron Tesslerod. Besides his office and home address, Shamansky conveyed that Tesslerod got into some major trouble in Iraq working for Safe-Ops Sentry, a Blackwater-type security contractor. A congressional oversight committee alleged that Safe-Ops Alpha Team employed a *shoot first, don't bother asking questions later* policy in specific zones for a period of two weeks after roadside bombings occurred. Numerous civilian casualties were attributed to this policy. To maintain their contract,

Safe-Ops Sentry fired their Alpha Team, including team leader Aaron Tesslerod.

Shamansky said, "I'm surprised that guy was the voice of reason at your run-in behind that bar in Ocotillo Wells."

"Maybe he's so far past *three strikes* that he couldn't afford to be involved in a missing persons investigation where a bar full of people saw both of us in the same place at the same time just before my disappearance."

"Or, he knows that Jimmy has a big mouth," Shamansky offered. "Either way, I want you to proceed with extreme caution when following this guy. Why don't you swap vehicles with Kelly since you know he's seen the RSX?"

"A schoolmarm ride? I don't think so. Michael is working his way across the south with Doberman's Stub right now. I'll see if I can borrow his Viper."

"Marinangeli has a Viper?"

"Touring is the most lucrative side of the music business when you're a headliner," I said.

"It's not fire engine red with white racing stripes, is it?"

"Just glossy black, and faster than a street hooker on rent day."

"Don't underestimate this guy, Jason. You might want to upgrade that .38 you carry to something with a little more stopping power, like a Mauser."

"I don't think I'll need an elephant gun, but I will run your suggestion past Dad."

"Extend my condolences."

"Will do."

I called Dad shortly after 11:00 AM. "Any sign of the Smart Grid man?"

"No, but I've gotten more exercise getting out of my chair every five minutes to look out the windows than I did when I was in training for the annual police physicals. What's going on?"

"Shamansky thinks I need to upgrade my .38 since I'll be tailing Rambo's evil twin. I was hoping to tap your armory for a loaner."

"Your mother made Maryland crab cakes for dinner last night and has plenty of leftovers. Why don't you stop by for lunch in about an hour?"

Shortly after I arrived at my parents' house Mom excused herself to tend to lunch. Dad and I immediately went to the gun cabinet where I selected a Glock 17.

"That was my weapon the last five years that I was on the force," he said.

"How about if I take this other one? It looks just like it."

"That's a Glock 31. It shoots .357 SIG rounds. You're better off shooting 9mm rounds with the 17. There's a new range over by the grocery store. Why don't we drop your mother off at the store after lunch, and I can give you a quick lesson on adjusting to this weapon?"

We kept our luncheon conversation off of weapons, the Smart Grid man, and O'Malley. Mom surprised us by sharing a talk she had with Lisa about why she continues to rough house with me. While it didn't appear that Lisa experienced any Zen-like moments of clarity on the topic, I was glad to hear she gave some thought to the notion that it was time our relationship evolved. The crab cakes were every bit as good as advertised.

Mom surprised us for a second time by not questioning why her husband and son were going off to a shooting range together for the first time.

"I'm glad you two are finally finding some common ground."

Shamansky must have been honing his gift of gab while I worked on my marksmanship.

"Jeannine, is that you? I thought Jason hired Reese Witherspoon's little sister when I walked in the door."

"I've been getting that a lot lately. Maybe it's my new haircut," she said.

Shamansky reached over from the side of her desk and lightly touched her hair. "Beautiful."

I heard this exchange and walked to the threshold of the reception area. What I couldn't see from that angle was Hoover beginning to hump Shamansky's leg in mid-lean.

"Bad boy! That's disgusting!" Jeannine scolded.

"I agree. Get in here before she calls the cops," I said, and turned back into my office.

Sitting in the chair opposite me he said, "Hilarious, Duffy. If that story gets back to the stationhouse you'll have a better relationship with Darden."

"What story?"

Shamansky glanced at his leg and changed the subject. "The best play, as I see it, is to assume Manning is the perp."

I turned on the recorder, activated the speakerphone, turned off Caller ID, and dialed. Two minutes after dealing with a receptionist, Shamansky was patched through.

"Matthew Manning, this is Detective Walter Shamansky of the San Diego Police Department. I want to start off by making you aware that I'm recording this conversation. I'm calling to notify you of a situation regarding the Higher Ed Holiday Happening. It's my understanding that a band you represent, Divine Guys Dance, will be performing at the event. Is that correct?"

"Yes, it is. What's this about?"

"Before I can go into that I need to have your word, on the record, that you will not share this information with the media, and will take personal responsibility for making sure anyone at ConcertMaster who is made aware of the situation will hold the information in the strictest confidence under penalty of prosecution. Do I make myself perfectly clear?"

"No, I'm afraid you don't. I'll need more clarification before I agree to anything."

"A statewide police task force has been withholding information from the public by imposing a complete media blackout. The information has been released strictly on a *need to know* basis. When you involved yourself and your band in the concert, you put yourself on the need to know list. At this point you can either withdraw your band from the concert or agree to cooperate with the info blackout and make an informed decision after hearing the reason for the secrecy," Shamansky said.

"You've peaked my curiosity, detective. I'll agree to maintain confidentiality, but reserve the right to pull my band if I think the risk is too great."

"Fair enough. I'm sure you've heard the rumor in the free press that a serial killer has been attacking victims at California concerts."

"I thought those rumors were debunked," said Manning.

"I'm here to tell you they're true. The Concert Killer has claimed six victims so far. He's threatened to kill a guitar player before Christmas, and the only major venue holding a concert between now and then is the one you just signed on for."

"A guitar player?"

Shamansky said, "We're 90% sure he'll try to strike outside of the arena. We'll have airtight security, and everyone entering the facility will pass through a metal detector."

Manning said, "It looks like there could be a huge downside to keeping my band in the show."

"I'm told that the concert committee agreed to your proposal partly because they feel a Christian band would bless the concert. If the Concert Killer is arrested at a show where your band performs, I'm sure the divine intervention aspect would become legend."

Manning was silent for a few moments. "I'll have to speak with my boss before giving the go-ahead."

Shamansky said, "I assume you have some type of comprehensive insurance policy for the band."

Manning said, "Of course."

"Who's your carrier?"

"Bressler Specialty Insurers. Why do you ask?"

"There's a possibility that the killer is able to access concert and specialty insurance data. I'll ask that you not make any adjustments to your policy before the show."

"It's certainly within my right to protect my company's assets. You can't expect me to increase our risk without increasing our insurance."

Shamansky said, "If you can't accommodate that directive then pull out of the show. If our main suspect is a no-show, the first thing I'll do is serve Reginald Bressler with a warrant to see if you or anyone at ConcertMaster violated that directive. If you ignore the directive you'll be arrested for obstruction of justice, and ConcertMaster will be blamed for a serial killer being on the loose. Do we understand each other, Mr. Manning?"

"Absolutely."

They concluded the call by Shamansky giving his contact information. "Let me know the minute your boss reaches a decision."

I asked, "What's up with the 90% certainty that the attack will take place outside the venue?"

"I want the attempt to go down backstage. When you told me that all of the players have backstage passes I saw it as a chance to limit the risk to the general public. Tell Calvin to pass the same ruse along to Lonnie."

"So, you're planning on putting Michael in the cross hairs?" I was clearly pissed off.

Shamansky said, "I was serious about everybody passing through a metal detector. That will include

maintenance men, security, everyone but sworn personnel –
and, every one of *them* will be ID'ed by a supervisor."

"Aren't you forgetting that this guy has already used
deadly force that doesn't show up on metal detectors?"

"Jason, we know his target. We know he's going to be
in close proximity to the target. Why not give him a false
sense of security in an area where we can go overboard on
protection?"

I asked, "What did you have in mind?"

"First, I thought we'd get our techs to wire the
backstage area to the max, and monitor it from the control
room on the skybox level. The backstage party wait staff will
be all cops, and we'll hide an armed cop in each of the
dressing rooms. We'll have eyes on every inch of the
backstage area at all times."

"What if he tries to make the hit onstage?"

"That's pretty unlikely, since he seems intent on
getting away with it."

"So far, he's been very imaginative. I need to see a
plan that includes providing onstage protection," I said.

"The best I can do in that department is get
authorization to allow you to carry a weapon on the stage. If
you think your pals in Doberman's Stub would let you join
them again, I think the captain will approve your presence as
a bodyguard."

"Let me think about it."

I called Michael in the early evening and summarized
my conversation with Shamansky.

"I don't know, Jason. It sounds pretty dangerous."

I replied, "I can see if they'll let Jack carry a weapon,
too."

"I'm not talking about that. My Viper's barely two
months old. This guy you're going to be following sounds
like he wouldn't think twice about putting holes in my baby."

"Your bambino will be fine. What about being on the stage? Where are you at with your personnel moves?"

"We're going to debut a new lead singer that night. It's Donald Quinn from the Irish band, North Sea Green Fire."

"Congratulations! Quinn is an excellent choice. I hope he works out."

Michael said, "We're making a big deal out of the debut. Derek came up with a grand entrance that should keep the Internet buzzing for weeks."

"Quinn doesn't happen to play guitar, too?"

"He's strictly a singer. We've been using a contract musician since Tony Belinni didn't work out."

"One paesano too many?"

Marinangeli replied, "More like one coke habit too many. He's talented and fully functional when he's high. But we figured he'd knock Ian off of the wagon in a matter of days, and we'd be out looking for another drummer, so we gave him the heave-ho."

"What does your play list look like?"

"We'll be doing mainly songs from *Cain & Abel.* That's what Quinn has been working on. You should be fine. We can keep the contract guy in the wings for the songs you don't know, and you can improv a synch while scanning the audience. I'm sure Jack and Ian will be glad to see you, especially under the circumstances. Do you want me to tell them about the situation?"

"Make sure they don't let it slip to anyone. And, speaking of slips, I suggest you talk to Jack first and make sure he thinks Ian can handle the pressure."

"You got it, Jason. Now it's your turn to impart some difficult news. I'm putting you in charge of telling Jeannine why she can't come to the show."

"Thanks a lot, Michael. I'll probably have to listen to Hoover barking all morning."

"What? Oh, the Cory bark-over thing. Yeah, she's gonna be plenty pissed. Gotta run."

Chapter 37

I arrived at my office earlier than usual on Friday morning. The Holiday Happening was one week away and I still had four groups of suspects. Cory arrived ten minutes after me and we worked out a plan for tag teaming the tail on Tesslerod. Shamansky had provided a home address in Descanso, a remote town east of San Diego, about half-way between Ocotillo Wells and the coast. We positioned ourselves at the entrance to Interstate 8 so that if Tesslerod headed east, toward Ocotillo Wells, I would have the lead. Instead, he drove west toward San Diego in his BMW Roadster. He exited at Alpine and I considered the possibility that he was meeting someone at Viejas Casino. But Tesslerod took Alpine Boulevard to Olde Highway 80, and quickly made a right onto Broad Oaks Road.

Cory made a right into the first development, and I picked up the tail. My GPS showed three 90 degree turns in the next mile. If Tesslerod was as careful as his dossier made him out to be, it was likely he'd pull over around one of the corners to make sure he wasn't being followed. Fortunately, I was able to see the first two turns from a distance and navigated past them without incident.

The final turn was preceded by a patch of woods that obscured my sightlines. So I pulled into a driveway and walked toward the corner. Ten seconds later I saw the tail of his Roadster backing up for a look down the road he just travelled. I dove into the tall grass that bordered the road and called Cory.

"Stay where you are till I call you back. Tesslerod is getting cautious."

I waited until he departed to retrieve Michael's Viper. A close look at the GPS told me he was relatively close to Lake Jennings Park. So I closed the windows, turned off the car stereo and quietly proceeded forward. After a couple of hundred yards I called and told Cory to maintain his position for the time being.

Rounding another turn I saw the unique maroon metallic shading of Jimmy DeLong's Harley glinting through a thin stand of trees. I proceeded another 300 yards and pulled far enough onto a private road that I couldn't be seen. I told Cory what was going on while doubling back on foot.

At that point, Broad Oaks Road ran north to south. It appeared that Jimmy and Tesslerod were in a cabin that wasn't visible from the other direction. I skirted the tree line that bordered the north side of the property. A small field of healthy grass that stood about 18 inches high separated me from the cottage. Considering SoCal's climate, it must have once been a lawn that's sprinkler system was never shut down after the cottage was vacated.

I dropped to my belly, elbowed my way to the edge of the house, and settled in under an open window.

"Aaron, it ain't like that! I been doin' just like Lonnie told me!"

"Ya got greedy, Jimmy."

"No. I swear. I didn't touch a thing. I got Lonnie's envelope in my saddlebag. Let's go outside and I'll show ya," said Jimmy.

"Yeah, let's go out and have a look."

I crawled to a spot where I could see Jimmy's bike. Tesslerod shoved Jimmy as they came through the door. He held an M-11 submachine gun with a silencer. Lying on my stomach, I pushed myself up to the top of the grass where I could see what was going on.

"There's no need for the gun, Aaron. I been good. I swear."

"Let's see the envelope, Jimmy. And, that better be the only thing I see coming out of that saddlebag or you'll be dead before your gun barrel clears those studs."

"I'm using two fingers, Aaron. Just like the queen at teatime. Just the envelope – see."

"Toss it over here, and move away from the bike," said Tesslerod. Jimmy complied.

"Do you see how the envelope looks lumpy on the back. That's what happens when you steam it open and reseal it."

"I musta spilled beer on it," Jimmy pleaded.

"Jimmy, you're a thieving partner, a bad liar, and you have a big mouth. That's a combination we can all live without."

Before he could react, Tesslerod squeezed off a short burst that flung Jimmy into a death spiral. He landed in a position where his dead eyes drew a direct bead on me. I instinctively dropped to the ground.

"Who's out there?" Tesslerod called.

I pulled the Glock and considered my options. I could try shooting at Tesslerod from fifty feet away. But my accuracy, shooting through grass while tentatively propped up by my left arm, might not be as sharp as I would like. Considering that Tesslerod led a commando force, I decided not to initiate a confrontation.

Tesslerod asked, "Is that you, Clarkie?" He took three steps in my direction. "I got no beef with you, Clarkie. In fact, my boss thinks you might be the right guy to take over for Jimmy. C'mon out and we'll talk about it."

Tesslerod held the M-11 in a ready position, and started walking directly at me. I figured I'd get one shot and better make it count.

Suddenly, I heard a noise to my left, and looked up in time to see Tesslerod eviscerate a little brown bunny.

"Cwazy fuckin' wabbit," he said, and walked back to his car.

I called Cory. "He's seen the van. Go back down to the gas station on Olde Highway 80 and park where he won't see you. If he heads east, stop on the rise just past Hawley Road, where you can see the interstate and watch for the Roadster."

I briefly considered calling Shamansky, but he'd be compelled to tell me to stay put. Meanwhile, Tesslerod and the evidence he was transporting would connect with the middleman, who would remain unknown.

Judging from the speed that the Roadster left the crime scene, I deduced that I wouldn't have to worry about Tesslerod being parked around any corners. I ran back to the Viper and travelled as quickly as possible back the way I came. When I passed Hawley Road I saw Cory shaking his head. Just as I spotted the freeway entrance ramps, Cory called to say Tesslerod was heading west on I-8 at a fast pace.

I was about to test the limits of Michael's dream acquisition when Cory called back to say a Highway Patrol car just set up a speed trap at the base of the hill, about a mile from my entrance ramp.

The info saved me from a ticket, but the cop may have cost me any chance of catching Tesslerod. Once past the Chipper, I ran the Viper up to 125 mph for about 6 miles. I cut it back to the low 80's when I reached El Cajon, but was feeling very anxious as I passed another freeway that connected to the South Bay and Mexico. I opted to stay the course and gripped the wheel tighter as I crested the ridge by San Diego State University and headed down the hill toward San Diego's Mission Valley. It would be less than a couple of minutes until I hit heavy traffic. I took a deep breath as I approached the Charger's stadium, and was looking off in that direction when I spotted the Roadster turning onto Interstate 15 North.

I barely had time to cut over three lanes and catch the exit. After relaying the info to Cory, I followed Tesslerod to one of the Rancho Bernardo exits. The Roadster passed the Carmel Mountain Ranch Golf Course and continued another mile or so to the perimeter of the Glazier Canyon Golf Course, a smaller public course bordered by condos, duplexes, and older mid-priced homes. About a quarter mile before the clubhouse, Tesslerod pulled into the driveway of a duplex that bordered the course. I saw the man in the thick-stemmed glasses greet him at the door.

I earned the money for my first electric guitar by caddying at a private course when I was in junior high. In the summer, caddies could play for free on Monday during non-peak hours. I continued to play about once every couple of months while I was with the band. Although I wasn't familiar with this particular course, I knew that if it was like most of the others, the duplex would be two floors, with bedrooms on the bottom floor and the living room and deck overlooking the course on the second floor.

After pulling the Viper around the corner, I spotted a maintenance walkway along the side of the duplex and followed it to a hot tub on a slab just below the deck. A set of French doors led into a large bedroom with an unmade bed on the ground floor. A moment later I heard the two men enter the deck above.

"Look, Steiner, my job isn't to give you explanations," said Tesslerod.

"I'm not really sure what he wants me to do."

"Call him at his club at 5:00 PM and tell the person who answers that you're Elvin Wexler."

Steiner said, "He usually wants me to have a chart in front of me when I talk to him. Did he say the name of the company he's looking at?"

"I heard him mention Bressler Specialty Insurance on the phone just before he gave me the money. I'm not sure if that's it, but I'd guess so."

"Thanks. Did he say anything about a strangle option to you?" Steiner asked.

"Aaaahhhh!" A high pitched scream spun me around. Three feet away was an attractive blond in her early twenties, passing through the French doors toward the hot tub. Her choice of tub-wear left no doubt about her natural blond status.

"Another snake?" called Steiner.

"Daddy, there's a man down here listening to you!"

I sprinted for a section of hedges where I could see the fairway through a gap, and was suddenly propelled backwards when I hit a three foot chain-link fence obscured by foliage. The sound of feet hitting concrete and a second scream from Steiner's daughter told me that Tesslerod was less than thirty feet away. I took a second run at the fence and dove over, like a halfback trying to vault a goal line stand. I managed to tuck my shoulder at the last second and rolled through the landing.

When I stopped, I reached for the Glock and realized I left it in the Viper.

A combination of willow trees and privacy hedges provided some cover as I ran south on the course. But I was about to run out of cover soon. To my right was a creek running through the middle of the course, separating two fairways. Shortly after cresting a rise, I dashed across the fairway into the foliage surrounding the creek bed. Glancing to my left I saw Tesslerod on the south side of a willow tree, sighting his pistol. Before he could shoot, a golf cart passed in front of him, and I ran as quickly as possible through the creek.

I reached a clearing near one of the greens and saw Tesslerod casually jogging across the fairway, as if he was heading back to his cart for a different club selection. This gave me time to pass through the clearing and back into the heavy rough that, once again, lined both sides of the creek. I was about to chance a sprint across the other fairway when the course marshal's cart came to a stop fifteen feet ahead of me.

I couldn't risk being detained by the marshal, who might possibly be carrying a weapon because of the number of rattlesnakes in the area. Dressed in a camouflage T-shirt, black jeans and sneakers, I couldn't pass for a golfer. So I quietly skirted the opposite side of the creek, moving very slowly.

Fortunately, the marshal was in the middle of tapping a kidney and preoccupied with the daunting task of trying to squirt a gecko. I reached a bend in the creek where it widened into a pond that served as a water hazard bisecting a fairway. Just before I rounded the corner I heard an unnatural groan and a splash. The marshal wouldn't be giving any more golden showers to reptiles, and Tesslerod was closing fast.

Hastening my pace, I nearly knocked over a Vietnamese man holding a pail full of golf balls in one hand and a cup of soda in the other.

"Brand new balls, $1 each."

I grabbed my wallet, pulled out two twenties and said, "I'll give you $40 if you'll tell the guy who's following me that you saw a man in a green shirt run across that fairway and jump over that fence."

"Yes sir. I can do that," he replied.

I said, "I'll also need your straw."

"Of course," said the young entrepreneur.

The water wasn't very deep, but had quite a bit of algae. I hoped Tesslerod wouldn't see me at such a shallow depth. I worked my way through the mucky bottom of the pond to the shade of a bridge that enabled the carts to cross over. From the shade, I risked bringing my eyes and nose up out of the water in time to see the Vietnamese man pointing in the correct direction. To my horror, I saw Tesslerod crack the handle of his gun over the man's head, then turn him so that he was face down in the water. Tesslerod walked directly toward me, and I slipped back under the water.

I waited until I could hear Tesslerod approaching, then put my tongue on the base of the straw and, feeling reeds to my right, pulled myself to the bottom of the pond, about three feet below the surface. I gripped the base of the reeds with my right hand and laid my left arm on the bottom of the pond, palm down, trying to minimize the visibility of my fair Irish skin.

I felt a wave ripple past me and realized that Tesslerod was just a few feet away. Suddenly, I heard a noise and saw something streak past. I was sure Tesslerod saw me and took a shot. Then I saw a hand reaching down into the water and struggled for comprehension. My lungs tried involuntarily to breathe, but I managed to push the feeling down. Somehow my instincts told me to remain perfectly still even though my lungs were about to explode. Just as I reached a semblance of calm, Tesslerod's hand passed in front of my face holding a golf ball. In a moment of clarity I realized that Tesslerod was about to toss a golfer's ball away from the hazard to avoid a foursome confrontation that would mean witnesses or gunfire.

Pulling myself to a point where I could see Tesslerod, I poked the straw through the surface, blew out slightly and drew a breath as Tesslerod tossed the ball past the far post of the bridge. I lowered myself to the bottom once again and flashed on a yoga breathing technique that Kelly had mentioned. It was working very well until I heard golf carts on the bridge above, then felt a stabbing pain in my left pinky. Tesslerod repositioned himself, and my natural reaction to shout opened my mouth enough that the straw escaped, floating to the surface.

Muffled voices of the golfers seemed to last forever. My lungs were again screaming, I couldn't dare risk trying to slide my finger out from under Tesslerod's heel, and I wondered if the Special Forces expert noticed the straw suddenly appear under his nose. Death by drowning was not an option. I needed to make a move. I visualized letting go of the reeds, reaching into my pocket for Michael's keys, gripping them so that they stuck out of my fist …

The heel was no longer on my pinky. I lifted myself to within an inch of the surface and could see Tesslerod peeking over the rim of the hazard, then passing under the bridge in the general direction of Steiner's house. As my lips broke the surface I vowed to add "Sometimes All I Need is the Air That I Breathe," to my iPod. If anybody gives me any shit about it, I'll blame Kelly.

After taking a circuitous route back to the Viper, I risked certain death from Michael by replacing his baby's new car smell with that of pond scum. On the plus side, I would be able to testify against Tesslerod as an eye witness to two murders.

Chapter 38

The first order of business on Saturday morning was to drop Michael's Viper off at an auto detailing shop in the Mission Gorge area. I then picked up Jeannine and got her started on a thorough Internet search of Aaron Tesslerod.

I barely finished entering notes on yesterday's activities when I spotted Shamansky in the hall on my computer security-cam. With Tesslerod still on the loose, my home and office were in full lockdown mode.

Shamansky grumbled a greeting at Jeannine as he passed her desk, and shut my door after walking into my office.

He said, "Get Cory in here. I need a few new adjectives to describe what went down at Metro this morning."

"What's going on? I thought we caught a major break."

Smashing both fists on my desk, Shamansky bolted to an upright position.

"Darden rifled my desk while I was at the coroner's office last night. He bypassed the captain and gave everything in your insurance file and in my report from yesterday to Dean Casey. As of now, neither of us is to go anywhere near Tesslerod, John Murray, Jimmy's gang, or anyone mentioned in your LaCosta report. You're also ordered, under penalty of obstruction charges, to refrain from discussing these matters with any and all CLAM partners, employees and acquaintances."

"They're my employers! Tesslerod could pose a threat to Calvin's life!"

"Those assholes violated the sanctity of the stationhouse. They broke protocol by going over the captain's head. Everybody's furious about it. But for now, an interdepartmental state task force takes precedence."

"Are you being shut out, too?" I asked.

"They're treating it like they identified the Concert Killer and yesterday's murders were victims 7, 8, and 9. Darden told Casey that if I had turned over the file on Tesslerod and the insurance boys to him, that yesterday's deaths could have been prevented."

"Was he buying that line of crap?"

"Casey clearly doesn't like you and was glad to find a way to push you out of the way. The captain showed me a copy of Darden's report. He made it look like we were conspiring to grab the glory by stealing the case out from under him."

"Did anyone pick up Steiner?" I asked.

"He left in a hurry. Some of he and his daughter's clothes were still there, but his laptop was gone."

"What are you going to do?"

"Continue to look at Manning. You have four different groups up on that suspect board. I'm not convinced that Tesslerod is definitely the guy."

"Why?"

"It sounds like Jimmy's bosses figured out what he was up to and cut their losses. Killing a thieving underling, then going after you for a cover-up, makes sense for a soldier of fortune. Whacking innocent people at concerts and leaving notes does not," said Shamansky.

"I'm still not sure if Lonnie and Murray orchestrated the murders to short the concert insurers, or if they merely tried to benefit financially from something they picked up on before everyone else," I said.

He opened my door and Hoover appeared. Shamansky drew his gun.

"If that fuckin' dog goes for my leg again I swear I'll neuter him right here and now."

I grabbed Hoover's collar and said, "I say we offer the same service to Darden."

Shamansky smirked and departed.

Since Celia Bains wasn't on the *do not call* list I gave her a full rundown on the events of yesterday and this morning. She listened without comment. When I finished she said, "I'll see what I can do behind the scenes, but don't expect much."

I called Jeannine into my office and explained the situation. "I want you to go back to our flowchart of suspects and come up with one question you feel needs to be answered for each one."

"Do you want me to include the insurance people?"

I said, "Absolutely. I wouldn't trust Darden to find Hoover's missing chew toy."

Over the next few hours I assembled my own list of questions, focusing on the two groups that were no longer getting police scrutiny. In the mid-afternoon, Jeannine appeared in my doorway.

"Michael's on the phone and wants to talk with you."

"Thanks again for lending me that sweet ride, Michael."

"You didn't scratch it, did you?"

"The paint is as perfect as the day it rolled off the showroom floor. What did the band say about playing the concert?"

"Jack thinks he's James Bond, and Ian asked if I had any Imodium AD."

"What about Donald Quinn?"

"He said his homeland would ban him from his favorite pubs if he backed away from a fight. I was hoping maybe you could coordinate with the police and security about the setup for his grand entrance. I don't want Derek to be in any danger," he said.

"Just how does he fit in?"

"The last time I was in town Derek told me about his latest engineering project. He's doing some amazing things with holography."

"What are you planning to do at the show?"

"As you know, Donald Quinn will be joining us for the first time since leaving North Sea Green Fire. He's always been a bit of a showman."

"I think he makes Mick Jagger blush."

"He asked if we could design something special for his entrance that he could put out on the Internet to win over his old fans and convince them that Doberman's Stub wouldn't be clipping his tail."

"Is it something like Disneyland's old Michael Jackson 3-D show or more like Avatar?" I asked.

"Neither one can compare to what we'll be doing. Derek is going to make Donald appear in a block of Plexiglas that's seven feet tall and three feet wide. He'll have green flames shooting up all around him. The block will run on a rail attached to the ceiling from the control center in the middle of the skybox section at the far end of the arena to the left end of the stage. There'll be a matching immobile block on the right end of the stage, too. Donald will actually be filmed in front of a blue screen just offstage. When the block crosses the front of the stage, a wall of green smoke will shoot 20 feet in the air, obscuring everything long enough for Donald to walk on stage, and for two live Doberman Pinschers to appear in the blocks."

"Will everyone have to wear 3-D glasses?"

"You won't believe this technology, Jason. There are no glasses, no multi-colored sparkly dots. You'd swear Donald was really in the block. You'll be able to see his lips move as he talks to the crowd while making his entrance."

"How does Derek do it?"

"If you really want to know, do what I did and bring a six-pack over to his house and be ready for two hours of techno-talk. Better make it a twelve-pack."

"Amazing."

"The only thing we'll need to watch out for are the rods that come out of the four corners of the block's base. One holds a projector and the other three hold small mirrors. You'll be on the side where Donald touches down and I'll be on the right. The contract rhythm guitarist we've been using will be behind a curtain a few feet away from you. He'll be playing your part simultaneously. If you need him to go live just give him a nod and step on the red pedal on your pedal board. Step on green and you're back in control. It'll work out fine."

"I've been playing a lot of your songs with Derek and Kyle up at Aunt Esther's. We were getting together about every six weeks until I caught a couple of time-intensive cases," I said.

"I know. Derek told me. That's why I'm going along with the onstage protection. I want you to make sure Derek gets protection while he's setting this up. He'll need to get started on Monday if he's going to be ready for Thursday's dress rehearsal."

"I'm sure Shamansky can get a detail to cover the setup crew. When do you get to town?"

"Thursday afternoon. When will you tell Jeannine that she can't come to the show? We just had a very awkward conversation."

"I'll tell her today."

At 4:30 I called Jeannine into my office and gave her the bad news. I expected anger, but got tears instead.

She stopped crying when I asked, "What was the best suspect question that you came up with?"

After dabbing both cheeks she replied, "Why did Mark put Mary Eliason on the backstage pass list?"

"Who's Mary Eliason?"

"It took a half hour of intense digging to find that out. She's Matthew Manning's sister-in-law."

My eyebrows arched. "Mark Danby? CLAM's Mark?"

Jeannine almost smiled. "Pretty good question, wouldn't you say?"

"That's a very good question."

"I found that Mary Eliason chaired a concert committee for a huge church in Dallas. She booked Divine Guys Dance to play in a diocese-sponsored event and later introduced them to her brother-in-law. One of the altar boys told a Christian rock blogger that Mary discovered them."

Chapter 39

The Chargers were playing on the east coast, which meant a 10:05 AM kickoff in San Diego. I met Shamansky at a sports bar in Kearny Mesa that featured numerous big screens and a terrific brunch buffet. Shamansky was sipping a Bloody Mary when I arrived at 10:30.

"What did I miss?" I pulled my stool alongside his to have a straight-on view of the screen.

"Shrimp omelets and blueberry blintzes."

"What's the score?"

"10-7 Chargers. I suggest you grab a plate now. They put out the high quality stuff before the alcohol kicks in."

Ten minutes later I returned to the table with two plates. "A few days ago you mentioned setting up the backstage monitoring. Is there any chance you could talk the captain into approving Drayton Claymore for the technical security job?"

Shamansky said, "I know how you like to patronize your old clients, but I think it would be better if we just let an SDPD tech work with the arena people?"

"The top manufacturers are now sending Drayton their newest inventions for testing and critiques. My friend, Derek, is going to be setting up the latest in holographic technology that will run from the stage, across the arena to the skybox next to the control room on the third tier. This setup is so new there aren't even any manuals for it yet. Drayton's the only one I know who could piggyback Derek's system onto the current electronics configuration and still have room for all of the security enhancements we'll need to cover the place."

The Chargers scored a touchdown and the room went wild. Shamansky used the interruption to mull my proposal.

"I haven't seen this guy in action, but I heard he's off the charts on the weirdo meter."

I said, "He'd never make it as a diplomat, but he was Kitzer & Kitzer's top designer for two years. I'll bet if you pitted Drayton's recommendations against SDPD's top tech it would look like the Chargers against Kearny High."

"I'll see what I can do. Tell me more about this connection between Mark Danby and Manning's sister-in-law."

I reached into my back pocket and unfolded an article Jeannine printed on Mary Eliason's role in discovering Divine Guys Dance.

When Shamansky finished reading, I asked, "Do you think Abbie could find out if Mark made any overtures to ConcertMaster?"

"That sounds like it would be more for the benefit of Calvin's business interests and less like it would pertain to this investigation."

I replied, "Only if you've ruled Mark out as a suspect."

"Do you really think he's a suspect?"

"Let's see. We're looking for a religious fanatic with a profound interest in the concert industry. If it turns out that Lonnie isn't directly behind the killings, we're also trying to find out how he and his stock market advisor got onto the fact that we're dealing with a serial killer before anyone else. How could Mark possibly fit into that equation?" I asked.

"Abbie told me that Manning had a blowup on Friday with his main rival on the corporate ladder. She hasn't been too thrilled with her dream job over the past few weeks. I get the impression that Manning would fire her in an instant if he found her snooping around."

"Yeah, but he's on the road quite a bit," I said.

"It's a corporate environment, Jason. People fight over even the lowest rungs on that ladder."

We watched the game until halftime. When Shamansky returned from a restroom break I asked, "Did you find out why John Murray lost his partnership in Diversified Risk?"

"I tried the usual channels and hit a roadblock. So I asked the captain to look into it. He told me that some politician managed to get the court documents sealed."

"Does that mean there's no way of finding out?"

"The captain called the Assistant DA who handled the case. He said that Murray pleaded guilty to domestic violence after some fanciful tap dancing by the lawyers," Shamansky said.

"Why would Murray give up a huge share of a very profitable business over a criminal charge?"

"Murray was married to the niece of Diversified's senior partner at the time."

I said, "I'd sure like to know what's sealed in that file."

"The captain managed to find out that the fight that sparked the violence had something to do with the niece being a stock broker."

"I suppose the captain had to give this info to the task force," I said.

"Of course. The captain thinks it was some kind of underhanded stock deal that resulted in Murray getting caught with his hand in Diversified's till."

"That would explain why the records were sealed. If Murray was borrowing from Diversified's funds and the shortfall left the company below the government's mandated limits, he'd never be allowed to work in the insurance industry again."

"And, Diversified could have been punished as well for leaving itself open to that kind of problem."

"How did they manage to sweep it under the rug?" I asked.

"Campaign contributions through insurance industry lobbyists would be my best guess."

I called Calvin in the late afternoon and gave him an update. "I came up with an idea that might help us to locate Steiner or Tesslerod or both."

"What can I do?" he asked.

"As I recall from your pool party, Lonnie's girlfriend won't be earning any money on Jeopardy in the near future."

"The last time I saw her she asked me if the Rolling Stones made more money from their concerts or their magazine."

"I think you should call her and tell her you're throwing a surprise party for Lonnie," I said.

"He actually has a birthday coming up next month."

"Good. If she manages to remember, it will add some credibility. Tell her you want to hold it in San Diego County, and ask her if Lonnie or any of his rapper buddies has a secluded place down here where a bunch of his friends could make a lot of noise without the cops being called."

"Why do you think they're in San Diego County?" Calvin asked.

"Tesslerod's from Descanso and Steiner was living in Rancho Bernardo. I think they'll stay as close to familiar territory as possible. It would also make it easier for them to have friends run errands."

"I don't have Chanel's phone number. It might take a couple of days for me to get it without raising a red flag with Lonnie."

"I don't want you to do anything risky, Calvin. Lonnie is the task force's number one suspect at this point. Even if he didn't commit the murders himself, they think he's in it up to his hair gel."

"I'll call you as soon as I have something."

Chapter 40

CK started Monday morning with an unexpected surprise. He was called into his boss's office and told that Shane Wesley's most recent deal fell through and he was back on top for the time being. He was also reminded that, with so few days remaining in the year and the caliber of his competition, every minute was to be used wisely.

Unable to contain his glee, CK sang *Jesus Loves the Little Children* as he sat at his cubicle across from Wesley. "How are you on this glorious morning, Shane?"

"Enjoy the big smile while you can. I'm closing a blockbuster deal today that will put your holy roller act down for good."

"I'd watch the blasphemous comments. Judgment Day could be right around the corner."

Ten minutes later CK walked into his boss's office and said he just received word that his father suffered a stroke.

"I'll need to take a few days to be with my family."

"Take all of the time you need. You know how I feel about your work ethic. I'm sure you'll have other opportunities to move up in this company. Don't give the contest a second thought."

"I'm glad you feel that way, sir. I'm going back to my cubicle now and tie up a few loose ends with pending clients. Then, I'll head home."

"God be with you."

He returned to his cubicle and considered his options. For his grand scheme to work, it was imperative that he be promoted to National Accounts Manager. The state task force was severely limiting his opportunities to fulfill his destiny. National travel would allow him to spread the word on a much larger stage. But Shane Wesley stood in his way. His blasphemous comments made CK's decision to count him among the martyrs less difficult.

The biggest problem was his inability to give Wesley's demise the due diligence he performed with all of the others. He planned to make a big splash at the Hooni by detonating a small bomb in the middle of the performance, eliminating a guitarist and the false denial that a serial killer was stalking the concert industry. Every time he tried to imagine a way to eliminate Wesley, all he could think of was the bomb that was resting comfortably in the trunk of his car.

Since Wesley's territory was out of state, today could be the last time he would be able to eliminate his nemesis. It also seemed right that CK win the competition while he was still in first place, rather than have it handed to him as some type of benevolent inheritance extended posthumously by the man he loathed.

CK rose from his cubicle and walked toward the exit. He saw Wesley glance up at him, but neither man spoke. If Wesley was informed of his father's stroke, he made no effort to offer support or condolences.

The transfer of the bomb from his trunk to beneath the seat of Wesley's company car was no problem. The company vehicles were washed and vacuumed every Monday by a contract service, and everyone was instructed to leave them unlocked. They were both parked in a special section near the elevator, and away from the entrance guard. He pushed the *Stop* button on the elevator to avoid surprises while making the switch. CK was pleased that the cleaning service had completed their work.

The bomb was not on a timer, but triggered by a transmitter. The previous week he planted a duplicate of the transmitter at the Hooni, inside the hinge housing on a fold-down baby changing table in the most remote men's room in the complex. There would not be time to order and assemble another bomb. But he had four days to come up with an alternative. The window of opportunity for killing Shane Wesley was closing by the minute.

Five blocks from his office, CK pulled into a *Park & Ride* lot where commuters met before entering the adjacent freeway. From his parking spot he could see the road he had just travelled, along with the north and southbound entrance ramps to the freeway.

About two hours later he spotted Wesley approaching the northbound freeway entrance. A California Highway Patrol car was three car lengths behind him and also turned onto the entrance ramp. CK briefly considered the unwanted collateral damage, as the CHP vehicle closed to less than two car lengths behind Wesley. The freeway was busy and a multicar pile-up was a distinct possibility if he waited.

CK said, "I hate tailgaters," and pressed the button.

He rolled up his windows, ignored the sights, sounds, and smells of the explosion, drove to the southbound freeway entrance, and began putting together a new plan for Friday night.

Calvin phoned at 10:30. "I just got a call from the concert committee. They said Manning called this morning and told them that ConcertMaster wants a full share of the profits instead of the reduced fee they originally proposed."

"What did you say?" I asked.

"Instead of getting the call from my usual contact, this one came from a faculty advisor who chairs religious studies. She made it very clear that she's a big fan of the altar boys and felt it was only fair that her favorite band get an equal share."

"Did you have any luck contacting Chanel?"

"I figured out a way to get her cell number, but won't have it until tomorrow night. If I do it any other way, Lonnie's liable to find out about it."

"Keep me posted, Calvin," I said, and hung up.

I called Shamansky and told him that the altar boys were in the show.

"Did you ask the captain about Drayton yet?"

"At first he was a bit hesitant. The department likes to keep security on special ops in-house. But I explained Drayton's role with Kitzer & Kitzer, and he started coming around. When I told him the referral came through you, and that Darden will shit a brick when he finds out, I got the thumbs up."

I called Drayton and gave him the good news, along with twenty minutes worth of dos and don'ts on police relations and the importance of containing his sense of humor.

Just after 2:00 PM I received an unexpected call. Jeannine said, "Detective Rappaport on line one."

I said, "Don't tell me Casey finally lifted the *cone of silence.*"

"I'm not in the mood, Duffy. If you want to crack wise you'll be doing it to a dial tone."

"To what do I owe this unexpected pleasure?"

Rappaport replied, "The aforementioned Chipper-in-Charge has seen fit to put me on John Murray full-time because of my proximity to Monterey."

"And you're calling to find out what I know about him?"

"I read the file you gave to Shamansky. Murray's up to no good, but I don't think he's the killer. I was finally starting to make some headway on the Delainya Tanner case when I got stuck with this detail. I carped to Maurice Johnson about how my lieutenant won't assign anyone else to the case, and he put me in touch with Celia Bains. She suggested you might be in a position to follow up on a couple of leads that look promising."

"What have you got?"

"First, I found out that Tanner's boyfriend, Luke Milner, might not have the airtight alibi we once thought. It turns out there were only two employees in the building the night of the murder and they were on separate floors."

"Interesting," I commented.

"Second, I found out Tanner might have been having an affair with her boss at the bank."

"What gave you that idea?"

"I sweated her tramp girlfriend, Amanda Dorian, after the security guard who worked the stage entrance identified her as a regular groupie. She said that Jorge Martinez told her if she was interested in working her way to the top, like her old friend, she'd need to work her way down to his zipper."

"Did she go for it?"

"She told him to take a hike. But I got the feeling it was more about her not wanting to work overtime than it was about moral compromises. I think the three of them know things about the night of the murder that they're not telling. Unfortunately, actual detective work conflicts with my babysitting duties."

"I'll fly up tomorrow morning and let you know how it goes," I said, and disconnected.

I briefed Jeannine and Cory on my plans. While Jeannine went to her computer to book the flight, Cory asked me to bring a camera along so that he could compare Milner and Martinez to his database of faces. I assigned Cory to watch the Hooni service entrance to make sure Derek was safe while he started setting up the holography rigging.

Chapter 41

I managed to catch a morning flight out of Lindberg Field and landed in San Francisco at 8:30 AM. Experience taught me the value of the pop-in. Giving suspects an opportunity to prepare for one-on-one meetings puts me at a disadvantage. After renting a car and making my way through downtown traffic, I arrived at the reception counter of Luke Milner's employer, Clean Air LNG.

"May I help you," asked an attractive blonde, whose embellished updo featured beaded threads through loose chignons.

"My name is Jason Duffy. I'm here to see Luke Milner."

"Do you have an appointment?"

"No, I don't. I was hoping to catch him at his desk."

"Mr. Milner is on the road more than half of the time. Let me see if he's in today," she said, and picked up the phone. After a brief conversation she said, "I'm sorry. Mr. Milner is out of the office and not expected back until next week."

"Do you happen to know where he went? It's very important that I see him."

The receptionist gave my casual attire the twice over.

"Are you a client of ours?" she asked.

"I'm a private investigator working on the murder of his girlfriend."

"It was certainly tragic what happened to that poor girl. Don't you have Mr. Milner's phone number?"

"I do, but I'm in town for the day and was hoping it would be a good time to bring him up to speed on the investigation. Do you happen to know where he went?"

"I'm sorry, Mr. Duffy. If you were to drop in on him while he was doing a presentation for a fleet customer it could cost us a major account, and cost me my job. I suggest you give him a call and arrange a meeting. Good day, Mr. Duffy."

I was confident that the bank employees I needed to see would not be on the road. I hoped to speak with Amanda first, since I knew the sensitive nature of my conversation with Martinez could get me booted from the premises. But I spotted Amanda staffing a teller slot, and knew she wouldn't answer my questions with her coworkers just a few feet away. After a stop at the Information Desk, Jorge Martinez led me into his office.

"I don't have a lot of time today, Mr. Duffy. Please be brief."

"I'm going to tell you something about Delainya Tanner's murder that the police are keeping from the press. I need your word that you'll keep it completely confidential."

"You have my word," Martinez replied.

"Delainya's murder wasn't an isolated incident. She was the victim of a serial killer who is expected to kill again before the end of the week. I'm here instead of Detective Rappaport because he was sent to the city where the killer will probably strike next."

"That's very disturbing, Mr. Duffy. How can I be of assistance?"

"Detective Rappaport recently learned about your affair with Delainya just prior to her receiving the promotion into the Loan Department. That put you on the lower half of the suspect list. I'm here to see if I can clear you from the list."

"I categorically deny any such relationship with Miss Tanner. If that ridiculous charge goes any farther than this room, I'll see you and SFPD in civil court." Martinez crossed his arms, lowered his chin, and glared at me through thick black eyebrows.

"The department knows that this wasn't an isolated incident, and there are other employees willing to come forward and press charges. But you're the least of their worries at the moment."

"I think I should call my attorney."

"Here's how it's going down, Jorge. If you don't cooperate with me here and now, I'll immediately call your regional director." I reached into my pocket and pulled out a small spiral notebook. "That would be Marshal Roscoe. I programmed his number into my phone. I'll tell Mr. Roscoe that due to your unwillingness to cooperate with a major murder investigation, the SFPD will be making your arrest the media event of the season."

Martinez asked, "How could this alleged affair possibly help your investigation?"

"Before we get into that I need to clear you as a suspect. The killings took place all over the state. A look at your calendar and a couple of phone calls should clear you, provided you're not the killer."

"If I admit to an affair, it will be the end of my job and my marriage."

"I can't guarantee that you won't be prosecuted. But I can tell you that sexual harassment is decidedly lower on the priority list than murder. Rappaport will either see you as a guy who cooperated, and helped catch a killer. Or, he'll see you as the guy who made him drop what he was doing and fly back to San Francisco, making it easier for the killer to get away."

"Can we talk hypothetically?" he asked.

I handed him a slip of paper. "Let's start by pulling up your calendar and finding you a credible alibi for at least one of the nights that the killer struck."

Martinez took a deep breath as he looked at the list. "Six?"

"Most of these were weekend nights. I assume your social schedule will yield a night where you were seen in public."

He held the paper to his computer screen. "I recognize the night Delainya was killed. I was home with my wife. Here! The very next date. I represented the bank at the Dudley Foundation dinner. It started at 8:00 PM and I left between 11:00 and 11:30. I sat next to Dr. Michaela O'Toole."

"Are you sure she'll remember you?"

"We danced at least three or four times. We also walked out together and collected our cars from the valet at the same time."

I said, "Put the phone on speaker. Give her a call now and tell her you found a ding in your fender the next morning. Tell her that the banquet facility originally agreed to pay for it, but now they're saying you didn't even use valet parking."

Martinez was able to reach her, and she corroborated his story. Her manner suggested he may have done more than share a few dances with her that evening.

I said, "First, I need to know if Delainya was working on, or turned down, a loan to any type of religious organization."

He looked as though he was about to parrot the bank's rules on confidentiality. After a brief silence he began tapping his keyboard.

"None of the businesses she dealt with since the promotion appear to have a religious affiliation, and none of the individuals seeking a personal loan have the doctor of divinity initials following their names."

"Will you scroll through one more time and check the purpose of the loans she handled?"

After five minutes he said, "Nothing remotely related to the religious community."

"Do you happen to know if Delainya attended church?"

He ran his fingers lightly over his black pompadour. "I asked her to come in on a Sunday to help out with an audit about two months before she died. Miss Tanner told me she could do so after services."

"Did she happen to mention which church she attended?"

"It was one of those unique spin-off sects, custom-made for the rich."

"I'm not up on the Bay Area religions."

"It's run by a female minister. I forget her name. She attracted the national press a couple of times because of her belief that God rewards the most worthy with the most money."

"Did you ask Delainya what attracted her to that religion?"

"I simply told her that the parishioners could certainly help with her self-generated loan referral numbers. She didn't respond to that comment."

"How about pillow talk?"

Martinez said, "Bear in mind, I haven't admitted to any of your allegations. But I can tell you this: Miss Tanner never initiated any discussions with me regarding her religion, personal finances, personal relationships, or anything that might explain why she was killed. Her conversation was always goal oriented. Personally, I think she was buying what the reverend was selling, and trying to earn her way into heaven."

"How long until Amanda gets off of the teller window?" I asked.

"She should be in the lunchroom in about five minutes."

I exited the office and made my way to Amanda's slot just as she was putting the *Window Closed* sign into place.

"Hi, Amanda. Do you remember me?"

"You're the private eye looking into Lainy's murder."

"Can I buy you lunch?"

"Sure. I'll be around in a minute," she said.

Amanda wore a somewhat more appropriate business outfit and toted a Coach knock-off purse as she walked briskly toward me. I wondered if she had accepted Jorge's offer of a spot on the loan officer casting couch.

"Where are we going?" she asked.

"What's good?"

"For the amount of time I have for lunch we better just go to Russell's at the end of the block."

I opened the front door to the bank and was about to comment on her wardrobe upgrade when she asked, "Did you tell Mr. Martinez what I told Detective Rappaport."

"He knows that somebody gave him up, but I got the impression he has a long list of suspects."

We were immediately seated in a booth. Amanda fingered what appeared to be a rough-cut emerald in a small cage, on a gold chain.

"That's a beautiful necklace," I said.

"It was a present."

"It looks pretty expensive."

"The guy who gave it to me could easily afford it."

I said, "It sounds like the relationship might be getting serious."

Amanda leaned forward and said, "Yeah, right. He was drunk and probably doesn't even remember my name."

I gently wrapped my fingers around the cage and said, "Let me see how my psychic powers are working today." After closing my eyes and taking a deep breath I said, "I'm getting that this was given to you by a rock star."

Amanda's eyes went wide as I let go. "That's incredible. How did you know?"

"I played in bands for 10 years. I know what kind of women rockers find irresistible. You probably break hearts on a regular basis."

"Did you play with any band's I'd know?" she asked.

"I'm on one of the tracks of the Doberman's Stub CD, *The Metal Musings of Cain & Abel*."

She replied, "You're full of shit."

"Let's hope not," said the waitress, with pen hovering over her pad. "What can I getcha?"

After she took our orders I said, "I'll bet Lainy was popular on the rocker circuit before she found religion."

Amanda said, "She was a star magnet. Partying with the headliners got a lot tougher when she dropped out."

"Did she really believe in what Reverend Big Bucks was selling?"

"I think her boyfriend got her into it. But it wasn't long before she started acting like a true believer."

"Then why did she go back out on the party circuit the night she died?" I asked.

"We had the radio on in the bank's lunchroom a few days before the show. Lainy was complaining about how her boyfriend just broke his word about a weekend getaway. We were both chomping on our sandwiches when the radio station asked a trivia question about a drummer that Lainy scored with a couple of years ago. She called in and won two tickets to the show. She thought it was karma telling her she needed to have one last fling."

"Do you think she was just punishing her boyfriend for blowing off their plans?" I asked.

"I'm sure that played a big part in it, but she'd never badmouth him to me. I'd been telling her to dump him since she traded in her stilettos for a pair of goodie two-shoes."

"Did you ever meet him?" I asked.

Amanda reached into her purse and pulled out her phone.

"Lainy made him pose with me at last year's Christmas party. Wait till you see the expression on his face."

"You're right. He looked pissed. Can I send this to my email account?"

"Sure."

"Do you have a good one of Jorge?"

Amanda retrieved the phone, pushed buttons, handed it back to me, and I forwarded that as well.

Returning the phone I asked, "What happened after the show that night?"

She replied, "Prove to me that you really played with Doberman's Stub and I'll tell you."

I used my phone to get online, pulled up the band's website, and showed her my rhythm guitar credit. Amanda spent the next 10 minutes in groupie gossip mode. She split time between describing her own tryst in the back of an equipment truck, and speculating on what was happening in the adjacent vehicle with Lainy.

"Are you sure she was alive and well when you left the parking lot with Chase?" I asked.

"I can assure you that I heard her *fun with foreplay* voice while we were walking to Chase's car. She definitely wasn't in any danger at that point."

I asked, "Did you see anybody standing around, or sitting in a vehicle nearby?"

"One of the roadies was standing guard outside the RV that she was in, which is common practice. But I didn't see anybody else."

"Are you sure?"

"Chase was tickling me and I was a little loaded," she said, glancing at her watch. "I have to get back to work."

On the return trip to the bank I asked, "Has there ever been any rumors about Jorge getting rough with the girls?"

"He's just a playful horndog. The only thing that pisses him off is when slackers make him look bad to his boss. Believe me, Lainy was no slacker. Besides, Jorge is a yeller, not a hitter."

Chapter 42

I used my key to enter Duffy Investigations on Wednesday morning. My staff has been taking extra precautions ever since the incidents with Mom and Colonel Hogan. The hallway and outdoor security cameras that Drayton installed over the summer were tiling matchbook-sized live feeds on all of the office computers.

Jeannine said, "Cory wants to see you right away. He's in his office."

Hoover sniffed at my feet and looked up for a reassuring pat on the head. He followed me into Cory's office and sat in a position where he could see both of us. I suspected that he put himself on censorship detail.

"Hoover, your mommy wants you," I said, and closed the door after his tail cleared the threshold.

Cory immediately went into a description of how he compared footage of the four concert venues we were able to secure. He found three matches without the use of the "disguise" software he installed, and four more with the enhancements.

"Let's see what they look like," I said.

Cory asked for the photos from my trip to San Francisco before presenting his findings.

"They're in my email." I stood up. "I'll forward them to you in a minute. Can you print out some side-by-side comparisons for me to look at?"

In a vernacular thick with expletives, Cory conveyed that the software could only do so much for my photography skills.

"I didn't take these, but they were taken on a cheap cell phone. Also, Milner is making a face in his shot. I hope the recognition software will still work."

Cory looked doubtful.

"Print them out anyway, and let me look at them next to the other possible matches."

I wheeled Jeannine's suspect board out of Cory's office and into my own.

"Jeannine, can you come in here for a few minutes?"

She was obviously pleased that I focused on her board. "It looks like your trip was worthwhile."

I ran through the various pieces of information I learned in San Francisco. "I've been trying to figure a way that the murders all somehow tie together, starting with Delainya Tanner. But finding out that she's an ex-groupie who's into a religion where the rich shall inherit the earth, is making me lose my perspective. I need some fresh eyes on the new pieces to the puzzle."

Jeannine said, "I think it will take me a while to digest it, too."

I received a message from Shamansky that Drayton Claymore was approved to engineer technical security for Friday night. I spent the next two hours on the phone coordinating access and security during the preparation stage. After learning that the Concert Killer tried to murder my mother, I wasn't about to allow anyone else in my circle to be vulnerable.

With that in mind, I called Mom and asked to be invited to lunch. I wanted to bring Dad in on the security detail, but would only do so if he felt that Mom was safe.

Jeannine walked into my office without addressing me. She flipped the 4'x6' white board from the *suspects* side to the *victims* side, and drew a line down the right side of the board with a black grease pencil. She labeled the column: #7 *Possible Targets*. Down the column she wrote: Jason,

Michael, Jack Pascal, and the remainder of the guitar players scheduled to perform on Friday night.

I said, "I thought you were working on how my information from yesterday fits into the big picture theory."

"I am, and most of it does make sense. At least it does until I get to the note at the last crime scene. I have no idea why he wants to kill a guitar player."

"I think you're right on the money with your first name on the list. He was at my house. Obviously he wants me out of the way."

Jeannine angled her head at the victim's board. "You're an obstacle that could get him caught. You had nothing to do with the Delainya scenario. You're in the mix, but not part of the overall scheme. I don't know how to explain it."

I said, "In most of the rock songs that I play there's usually an outside chord that isn't part of the key that the song is written in. It typically shows up around the bridge, and adds a unique flavor. But it's also the toughest one to suss out because it lies outside of the key."

She said, "Not one of the usual suspects."

"Exactly."

Cory walked into my office carrying a trifold poster board. Jeannine excused herself and Hoover followed.

"Do you need me to sign off on your science project?" I asked with a smile.

Cory laid it on my desk and unfolded the flaps. He had printed side-by-side comparisons of all of the matches he found from the venue footage. The larger middle section contained all of the ones found by using the software that eliminated wigs, glasses, and facial hair that could potentially be disguises. On the left wing were the matches found without the software enhancements, along with the San Francisco pictures from yesterday. On the right wing were pictures of insurance men of interest that he took at La Costa.

We discussed the reliability of the software for a few minutes. I excused myself to leave for lunch with my parents, and took the poster with me.

Mom greeted me with a big hug. "I'm glad you're here. Your father has been acting more-and-more depressed every day since the funeral."

"Do we have a few minutes before lunch? I have something I want to show him."

"Actually, you're a little late and everything is ready."

"It can wait."

Mom usually avoids shop talk over meals. She knows how obsessed Dad becomes over active cases, and feels that by providing a respite she helps him to gain some perspective. However, today she prompted me to talk about the case.

Dad asked, "Since when did you start caring about police work?"

She replied, "Since the guy we're talking about nearly killed me in my own home."

I said, "That seems like a good reason to me."

Dad shook his head, and dipped a piece of French bread into his soup. In spite of our best efforts, Dad spent most of the meal staring into his bowl.

When we finished Mom said, "Why don't you two go out in the living room while I clean up?"

"Dad, how about sitting on the couch with me? There's something I want to show you."

The poster was folded shut and flat on the coffee table in front of us.

"Before we open this up I want to ask you about a case you worked a long time ago. Do you remember busting a child molester in Balboa Park when I was about eight-years-old?"

"Of course I do. That guy was a sonofabitch to catch. I'm surprised you remember it," Dad said.

"Actually, it came up at the picnic table I was sitting at during one of our backyard barbecues a few years ago. I think you were tending the grill at the time. O'Malley was at our table and said the reason the guy was so hard to catch was because he wore a different disguise every time he went out on the prowl," I said.

Dad looked pained at the mention of O'Malley. "So?"

"I've got a similar dilemma and was hoping you could help."

"I can't leave your mother alone till that guy is put away."

"Then help me get him. You don't have to leave the house." I unfolded the trifold poster and explained what Cory had done.

Dad said, "I'm not as focused as I should be, son. I don't think I'm gonna be much help to you on this one."

"How about if I leave the pictures with you until tomorrow? Get the big magnifying glass out later and see if your experience gives you a gut feeling about any of these guys. Also, have Mom check them out. Even though he's been clever about his disguises, she might recognize one of the SDG&E man's features."

"I'll take a look, but my eyes aren't what they used to be. In spite of our lunch conversation, I think your mother has been trying to put the whole incident out of her mind."

I briefly considered asking him if he'd like to come along to the concert venue and advise on security needs. But a flash recollection of Dad's last encounter with Drayton made me immediately dismiss the notion. Instead, I said goodbye to both parents.

The Hooni featured the ultimate in modern design and technology. Located in Mission Valley, it shared a parking lot with the adjacent football stadium.

True to his word, Shamansky had a uniformed officer on every open entrance. I was admitted through the stage door, and spotted Derek as he walked out onto the stage. He was directing a forklift operator on the distribution of boxes that were piled in front of the stage.

Derek turned to me and said, "I heard you're tagging along with the Doberman again."

"I'm just playing pin the stub on the big dog to keep an eye on Michael."

"Has he been misbehaving?" Derek asked.

"The killer is calling his shot this time, and informed us he's going after a guitarist."

"Well, at least it's good to know he isn't after drummers, and I can run out to my car for tools, as need be."

"I wouldn't count on him recognizing you as the former drummer of Tsunami Rush. He got into my parents' house and nearly snuffed my mom."

He said, "Maybe you're the guitarist he's after."

"I always thought I was better known for my singing," I said, then pointed at the bolt of paper in Derek's hand. "Are those the plans?"

Derek rolled them out on a large waist-high wooden box. "What do you need to know?"

"Michael gave me an idea of the basic stage layout, and where I'll be standing. I'm concerned that your Plexiglas blocks will give me an obstructed view to my right."

"If it's any consolation, those blocks could easily stop a bullet."

Over the next 15 minutes Derek showed me the monorail supporting the mobile block, which he installed yesterday. He noted that it was anchored between the control booth on the third tier and the first skybox to the right, where CLAM and friends would watch the show. He used the plans to show me where the two blue screens would be located in the wings of the stage. They were separated by about 40 feet. Donald Quinn would stand in front of one while his image was projected into the mobile block as it descended onto the stage. The other would be where the first Doberman Pinscher would be videoed. A second Doberman would be brought in as soon as Donald walked onstage.

"Why the big distance between the blue screens?" I asked.

"The official answer is so the dogs don't get into a fight."

"What's the real answer?"

"I was sworn to secrecy, but I'll give you a hint. It has something to do with a new Doberman being deathly afraid of real Dobermans?"

"I can see why the band wouldn't want that to get out."

Walking toward the middle of the stage, I commented on the nice job the concert committee was doing with their Christmas decorations. Suddenly, we heard the PA system boom.

"Ho, ho, ho. Santa's got a big lump of coal for Jason Duffy this year."

Startled, Derek asked, "Who the hell is that?"

Before I could reply we heard, "Jason kept Drayton from becoming an Internet millionaire this year. So no toy for the bad boy."

I said, "That would be our security engineer, Drayton Claymore. Don't worry, he's harmless." Then I yelled, "I need to talk to you, Drayton."

Insisting on keeping up his improv, Drayton cranked the reverb to the max. "Santa is in the control room with his elves. Take the elevator next to the churro stand."

The control room reminded me of the bridge on the Starship Enterprise. Drayton had four crates of electronic gizmos in various stages of assembly strewn about the room.

"I was kidding about the coal," he said. "This is my dream room. If the killer plugs me in this room I'll die a happy man."

"You're here to make sure nobody dies."

Over the next 10 minutes I prodded Drayton to give me the CliffsNotes version of the cornucopia of technology at his fingertips. Just as he was transitioning into the minutia, I was spared by a phone call.

"It's Calvin. I just got off the phone with Chanel, and I got what you wanted."

"What did she say?" I asked.

"Lonnie's got a hip-hop buddy named Snaggles with a place near the border, in Jacumba. According to her, it's so far out in the boonies that, and I quote, 'Jimmy the Cricket' couldn't even find it," Calvin said.

"How are we supposed to find it?"

"She saved the Mapquest that Lonnie sent her. They spent a long weekend there over the summer."

"Perfect. Forward the map to me. I'll get in touch with Shamansky and call you when I have something to report. You don't think she'll tell Lonnie, do you?"

"I told her that if I got even the slightest inkling that she let the secret slip, I was going to cancel the birthday party and give Lonnie season tickets to the Dodgers instead. She hates baseball. Believe me, her lips are sealed."

Shamansky stopped the Crown Victoria at a stand of scrub pines guarding a barely visible driveway, obscured by darkness, and partially overgrown by indigenous flora. The only reason we stopped was because the GPS unit was telling us to turn right, in a female voice with a slight Irish brogue.

I asked, "Why didn't you get the Slavic sweetie model?"

Shamansky replied, "Your father was probably on the purchasing committee before he retired."

He continued driving another hundred yards, turned left into a field, and parked behind a huge boulder.

"It looks like the hip-hop hideout is the only building for miles," I said.

We approached the house with caution after passing through the scrub pines. It was a massive combination of glass and log cabin architecture.

"What do you make of that crib?" Shamansky asked.

"It looks like Jethro Bodine tried cramming the Glass Chapel inside his dream home."

"With all that glass, I'd hate to be paying the air conditioning bill in the summer."

I said, "Maybe he bought it from a pot farmer. It'd make a great grow house."

"Since we're not sure how many people are here, let's split up. You go left, I'll go right, and we'll meet on the other side of the house in 10 minutes, unless the backyard is occupied."

I rounded the corner on the left side of the house and found a small yard and very few windows, none of which were low enough for me to see into. Although it was late afternoon, darkness had fallen. A half moon in the cloudless sky provided the only illumination of the side yard.

Peeking around the rear corner of the house, floodlights lit a multi-tier party area. The near deck held an elaborate barbecue that could easily feed the largest of entourages. The next tier held a DJ set-up that was now encased in a white and clear tent. The largest tier held a huge dance floor, covered by a giant plastic sheet.

I worked my way around the back of the dance floor, toward Shamansky's side of the house, and encountered the last of the tiers. It consisted of flooring that appeared uneven and the color of a hippie tie-dyed T-shirt. On the far end was a three foot log wall holding a sign that read, "Rolling Room." I saw one of these on a television show about weird toys of the rich. It was called a Squishy Room. The show's narrator said it simulated the sensation of an acid trip and was nearly impossible to cross without falling.

I reached the back wall of the house, just to the right of the Squishy Room, when I heard a voice on the other side of the wall say, "Don't move."

I raised my hands and glanced over my shoulder, but no one was there.

On the other side of the wall I heard Shamansky say, "Snaggles sent me out here to get the house ready for a Christmas party. I take it you're his security man."

I lowered my hands, got down on all fours, and crawled to the far wall of the Squishy Room. I struggled into a crouching position and dug my fingernails into the wall logs to inch my way upward. I was grateful that I had been practicing my guitar for the show, since it always stimulated nail growth on my left hand.

Tesslerod asked, "If you're the party guy why are you carrying a Glock?"

I grasped the top of the three foot wall, pulled up to where I could see them twenty feet in front of me, and tried spreading my feet for stability. I teetered mightily. But as long as I held on with both hands I would remain upright.

Shamansky asked, "How long have you been working for Snaggles? Everybody in his posse carries. It's part of our job description. Anybody that doesn't pass his monthly test at the shooting range is out the door."

I admired Shamansky's ability to sling the cow caca in the face of adversity. I took one hand off of the wall and removed my gun. This caused me to sway side-to-side and drop into a football down lineman position. Fortunately, all of this was happening on the other side of the wall from Tesslerod, and was not making any noise.

"It sounds like Snaggles way of telling me you're expendable. I hate to be a bad houseguest, but I don't have time to check out your story," Tesslerod said.

I pulled myself to a position where I held Dad's Glock 17 with both hands and pushed my forearms into the shelf at the top of the wall. Just as I was stabilizing I saw Tesslerod extend his pistol hand toward Shamansky. I lurched forward as I pulled the trigger. Tesslerod grabbed his right buttock, spun toward me, and squeezed off three rounds. By that point I had already performed a gymnastic move on the Squishy floor worthy of a gold medal, and crept back toward the wall.

While Tesslerod was focused on the wall, Shamansky took one big step sideways and lifted a glass lantern off of a lawn jockey. He flung it with an exaggerated overhand motion, and it shattered on Tesslerod's shoulder.

By the time Tesslerod turned his attention to Shamansky, I was back on my feet, gripping the shelf with one hand while trying to aim the gun with the other. I got off two poorly aimed rounds before hitting the deck once again. One went into a pile of leaves and the other capped the lawn jockey.

Tesslerod limped to the wall, reached his gun hand over it and blindly fired one round before Shamansky shot him just above the ear with a round from his backup piece.

"Jason!" Shamansky shouted.

He stuck his head over the wall and peered down. I was lying on my back with the Glock pointing up at him.

"Jason, are you alright?"

"Just get me off of this floor. I think I'm gonna puke."

Over the next half hour we searched the house and grounds to make sure Steiner or any other hostiles weren't on the premises. Shamansky then called his captain and we waited for the bevy of officials to show up before heading back to Metro.

We arrived just after 9:00 PM and expected most of the fireworks to be delayed until the following day. But, along with the captain, Darden and Casey were eagerly waiting for us.

Casey led the charge. "What the hell were you two doing confronting a task force suspect?" he yelled at Shamansky.

Shamansky said, "Tesslerod was wanted for three murders that had nothing to do with the concert killings. Duffy witnessed him killing a man at a golf course in Rancho Bernardo."

"Shamansky, you're looking at me filing charges against you for insubordination. I gave a direct order that you were to have nothing to do with my case," Casey bellowed.

Shamansky's fingers balled into fists. "Guess what, Lieutenant. I take my orders from my captain. I think this assignment has you on such a power trip that you believe your running all of law enforcement in California. You go ahead and file your charges, and I'll make sure the FBI knows the level of incompetence you've demonstrated so far."

The captain jumped into the conversation before Casey could return the volley. "In less than 48 hours we'll be in the middle of a show where the killer is expected to strike. I'm here to make sure it doesn't happen in my city, on my watch. Casey, you either start cooperating or I'll pull my men from the task force and set up my own detail to handle the show."

Casey replied, "You can't do that. I'm in charge. This is a statewide case."

"If I back Shamansky, and formally request FBI assistance, you'll be gone in a matter of hours, and you know it."

Casey said, "I also know that you and your men will be totally off the case if you make that call."

Shamansky said, "Put me on the task force, without having to answer to this idiot," pointing at Darden, "and we'll call it even."

Casey mulled the suggestion for a minute. Darden opened his mouth, but stopped when the captain raised a finger to his lips. Casey said, "I'll do it on two conditions: First, that Duffy doesn't set foot on the floor of the Hooni until after the case is solved. And second, you agree to follow my orders."

Shamansky and I began to protest, but the captain said, "Deal!" and returned to his office.

Shamansky asked Casey, "Why are you so down on Duffy's participation? He's come up with some of our best leads so far."

Casey said to Darden, "Tell Shamansky what you learned from the tap on Murray's phone."

"One of Duffy's employers, Lonnie Cancelli, called Murray a half hour before you two got here. They knew Tesslerod was dead. How do you suppose they came by that information?"

I said, "I haven't called anyone since the shooting."

Darden said, "It was probably the assistant coroner checking in with his old buddy, Lonnie."

Casey said, "Until we plug this leak you're out, Duffy. That's why the captain didn't go to bat for you. Maybe you're telling the truth; maybe not. We just can't take the chance. Now if you'll head on home we have some work to do."

Chapter 43

My first order of business on Thursday morning was to try and find out how Lonnie learned of Tesslerod's death so quickly. At 7:15 AM I called Calvin at his home.

"Sorry to wake you up, but I need you to get on something right away."

Calvin said, "I saw a band in Cleveland last night and didn't get to bed until after 4:00. Give me a minute to clear the cobwebs. I'm on my way to the coffee maker. What's up?"

I gave him a full rundown on last night's activities, including the wiretap and Casey banning me from the show tomorrow night because of my connection to CLAM.

Calvin said, "The killer hit outside the venue a couple of times. Maybe you'll be just as valuable in the lot."

"Forget that. I'll be onstage with Doberman's Stub. The Concert Killer said he was taking out a guitarist. I'm guessing he meant either me or Michael. If I'm not in the arena I paint a target on Michael's chest."

"Won't Casey throw you out the minute he sees you?"

I asked, "Did you get a look at the rhythm guitarist who's been temping for them the past two months?"

"Can't say that I have."

"I'm guessing ZZ Top is his favorite band. If I wear a Billy Gibbons disguise there's no way any of them will recognize me," I said.

"Are you sure you can play with that much beard blocking the view of your strings?"

"I can play by touch just fine. If I can avoid getting the beard in between the strings and my pick, I'm home free."

Over the next ten minutes I told Calvin the information he'd need in order to determine how Lonnie learned of Tesslerod's death so quickly.

At 8:30 AM I received a call from Dad. "You've gotta get over here right away!"

"Is it Mom?" I asked.

"Right now!" Click.

Cursing La Jolla traffic, I slowly made my way to the freeway. I was tempted to call Dad back and ask for details as I inched along. But if my mother was having a medical problem the call could be a major distraction.

At 9:15 I burst through the front door and called out for my parents.

"In the kitchen," Dad yelled.

I took a deep breath when I saw my mother seated at the kitchen table with Dad hovering over her right shoulder. But she was as pale as an east coast visitor at a May beach party.

"What is it?" I asked.

Dad replied, "Come around the table and have a look."

I posted myself over Mom's left shoulder and looked down at the trifold picture array that I dropped off the previous day.

Mom tapped the picture of Luke Milner posing with Amanda. "That's the man who said he was here to do the Smart Grid upgrade."

I said, "That's a pretty weird expression he's making. Are you sure?"

"I'm absolutely positive."

Dad said, "By the time I found the magnifying glass yesterday afternoon it was too dark to get a good look at the pictures. So I sat them here on the breakfast table. When your mother brought my eggs over she damned near dumped them in my lap after she spotted the guy. Do you know who he is?"

"His name is Luke Milner. He's the first victim's boyfriend."

Mom used her index and middle fingers to tap the two adjacent pictures Cory identified using the disguise removal software. "I get the same chill when I look at the hippie and the man in the brown wig. I think they're all the same man."

"You better call Shamansky right now. It definitely sounds like this is your guy," Dad said.

"I'll call him from my car. You might want to get Mom out of town for a couple of days. We're sure he'll be in San Diego for a Christmas concert at the Hooni tomorrow night. He knows Mom can identify him."

"I saw him, too. I was just a bit too distracted with Kerrigan to get a good look at him," Dad said. "I can keep an eye on her just fine."

"Then why was the front door open when I got here?" I asked.

"Kerrigan's house sitting across the street, and watches our property like it was the latest episode of his favorite TV show."

"Even so, no more chances, Dad. This guy's killed at least six people, maybe more."

Mom said, "We'll be fine dear. You go do what you have to do, and take those pictures with you. I don't want to look at that man anymore."

After trying unsuccessfully to connect with Shamansky at his desk, cell, and home numbers, I called the main number at Metro and was put through to Darden.

"I need to talk with Shamansky right now." I said.

He replied, "I thought Lieutenant Casey made your status perfectly clear last night, Duffy. Don't bother trying to reach Shamansky. He's out of town and carrying a different cell phone. We don't expect him back until about an hour before show time. You can talk to him then. Oh wait. You're on the black list."

"I know the identity of the Concert Killer."

Darden said, "I consider any of your theories to be a smokescreen defense for your employer, Lonnie Cancelli. Be a good boy and take a seat on the sidelines, Duffy. Otherwise you could become even harder to reach than Shamansky." A dial tone followed.

I called Clean Air LNG and asked for Luke as soon as I returned to my office.

"I'm sorry. Mr. Milner will be out of town for the remainder of the week."

I recognized the voice of the attractive receptionist who gave me the runaround when she learned I was a private investigator.

"This is Nelson Wilkes. A member of my club recently converted his fleet to liquefied natural gas and worked with Mr. Milner. I'm in the process of putting together an agreement with one of your competitors, but I promised my friend that I'd speak with Luke before signing off on the deal later today."

"Let me connect you with his manager."

I listened to the elevator arrangement of *We Are the World* for the next minute.

"This is Anson Parmeter, Mr. Wilkes. I understand you received a last minute referral to Luke Milner."

"That's correct."

Parmeter asked, "May I ask who referred you to us?"

"I don't put my friends in a position to be pressured by salesmen, Mr. Parmeter. Can you connect me with Mr. Milner, or not?"

"I'm going to be candid with you, Mr. Wilkes. Luke's father suffered a stroke on Tuesday. He's flown home to be at his bedside, and provide moral and spiritual support. I tried reaching him this morning to inform him of the death of a coworker, but had to leave a message. He's undoubtedly turned his phone off. I take that as a bad sign regarding his father's prognosis. I'm afraid Luke won't be much help to you today. But I'll be glad to assist you personally."

"What happened to his coworker?" I asked.

After a brief moment Parmeter said, "He died in an explosion. It was very tragic."

"Was it a liquefied natural gas explosion?"

"No, nothing like that. His car exploded as he was getting on the freeway about a mile from our headquarters."

"I'll bet your liquefied natural gas was in his tank. I'm starting to have some serious second thoughts about this conversion," I said.

Parmeter cleared his throat. "He was killed by a rather sophisticated bomb that had nothing to do with liquefied natural gas."

"And, Mr. Milner worked closely with this coworker?"

"They are, or were, my two best sales executives. They sit next to each other here at headquarters, but Luke's territory is California, and Wesley handled the Pacific Northwest. The police don't see any business-related motive. Let's talk about your fleet."

"OK, here's what I've got," I said. In a different tone, with the receiver half-covered I said, "Hello." Returning to my normal voice I said, "My fiancé just walked into my office. I'm going to have to call you back later."

I walked out to Jeannine's desk. "I need you to research two things right away. First I need everything you can get on Delainya Tanner's boyfriend, Luke Milner. He works for Clean Air LNG. I'm especially interested in his parents' address. Then check out a hip-hop artist named Snaggles. Try to find out about his property in Jacumba, including all building permits, security company contracts, insurance, and see if he's had any run-ins with local law enforcement."

"I heard what you said to Detective Darden a few minutes ago. Is Luke Milner the Concert Killer?" she asked.

"Yes, he is. Let's take a look at your victims board and see if we can spot the connection you've been talking about," I said.

Using one of Derek's old drumsticks as a pointer I tapped the index card at the top of the cork board. Delainya Tanner was strangled by her boyfriend, Luke Milner. Rappaport was right when he called it a crime of passion."

"Let's put the puzzle together," said Jeannine.

"OK. She went to a concert to relive her groupie days. She drank beer, took drugs, and had sex with a rock star while a roadie stood guard. After killing his girlfriend, Milner killed a beer vendor, a roadie, a groupie, a drug dealer, and the very rock star who defiled her. I'd say you were right on the money about them being related, Jeannine."

"How does a guitar player fit into the mix?" she asked.

"Good question."

"Speaking of guitar players, Michael called this morning. He needs you to be at the Hooni tonight at 7:00 for the sound check and a practice session," she said.

"Got it," I said. "I need you to call Guthrie's costume shop and ask them if they still have the Billy Gibbons hair and beard kit. If they have it, ask Cory to run over and pick it up right away."

"Anything else?" she asked.

"There was a bombing in San Francisco on Tuesday. The victim was named Wesley. I'm not sure if it was his first or last name. I think Milner planted the bomb. Read whatever was printed and give me a quick summary after you take care of the other matter."

Twenty minutes later Cory popped into my office to see if I needed any spirit gum from the costume shop.

I told him about my mother's discovery and confirmed that he had run a comparison of Luke's picture through the disguise software.

"I take it that means Luke is very skilled at applying disguises," I said.

Cory said that the software wasn't perfect, but that he gave the photo of Luke a close comparison to his top suspects and saw no resemblance. Milner was indeed very good at changing his look.

"That means we're going to have a hell of a time spotting him tomorrow night."

Cory's excited response drew barks from Hoover in the next room.

"At this point all I can plan for is what we can do after he makes his move, provided he doesn't kill his guitar player before we get a chance to respond."

Cory nodded slowly, and Hoover peeked around the corner of the door.

"Bring a picture of Delainya Tanner with you to Guthrie's and see if you can find a wig that matches her hair. Also, pick up some zombie make-up along with extra spirit gum."

Cory cocked his head, hoping that I would explain. Instead I picked up the phone and waved goodbye.

"Kelly, I want to hire your friend, Lynette, to reprise her haunted house role tomorrow night at the Hooni. See if she's interested and tell her I'll supply the costume and the make-up."

"Do you want me to wear one, too?" Kelly asked.

"You can wear whatever you want, but you won't be at the Hooni tomorrow night. It's too dangerous," I replied, flashing on an image of a bomb turning a car into a fireball.

Kelly's Irish temper flared. "You wouldn't ask one of your employees to do something that was too dangerous for you. Don't expect me to ask that of my friend."

I said, "Fine, forget it."

"I thought we settled this argument when I moved in with you. By the way, I haven't thrown away my Miss Frumpington outfit. Maybe I'll wear that to the show tomorrow night and have Kayleigh get me a pass to the backstage party."

I started to protest when Kelly cut me off. "You need Lynette, I'm not staying home, and you don't have time for an argument. I'll call you if Lynette can't make it," she said, and hung up.

I looked at Hoover and said, "Stay away from the Irish Setters. They're pretty and playful, but when those Irish eyes aren't smilin' they can flare up like a canyon fire in August."

He put his head in my lap and gave me a mournful look.

"It's OK, boy. Go help your mommy." Hoover tottered off toward Jeannine's desk.

I called Rappaport at SFPD. "You were right about your gut feeling. Luke Milner is the Concert Killer."

"How do you know?"

I spent the next ten minutes explaining how I reached that conclusion, as well as my inability to convince Darden.

"Do you think I should bother trying to talk with Casey?" I asked.

"Casey's scared shitless that he'll do something wrong. That's why you've been banished from his little fiefdom. If I call him and say I know that Milner's our guy, he'll pump me for details to put in his report. The minute your name comes up, I'm off the case with an official reprimand, and he dismisses the information as a tip from a suspect's employee, who's passing it on to direct suspicion away from Lonnie."

"How could he dismiss the fact that the first victim's boyfriend was in my parents' house? That his coworker was blown up in a bombing two days ago? And, he went incommunicado immediately afterwards?"

"I saw a transcript of the tap on Cancelli's land line last night. Around midnight he had a conversation with Murray and said to tell Steiner that he doesn't care what happened to Tesslerod, make sure the strangle is still on. Casey and the brain trust assume Steiner plans to strangle a guitar player or hire a hitman to do it."

"Lonnie's definitely up to something that reeks. I'll see what I can do to find out. In the meantime, I have a favor to ask, if you're coming to San Diego for the show tomorrow night."

"I wouldn't miss it for all the rice in Chinatown."

"Can you bring the outfit Delainya Tanner wore the night she was murdered?"

I shared my reasons for the request, and Rappaport agreed.

Jeannine popped into my office in the early afternoon. "I have some background on Luke Milner."

"Have a seat," I said.

Jeannine wore an attractive lilac mini-dress that accentuated her figure, knowing that her boyfriend's plane would be arriving in San Diego during the workday, and it was possible he could stop by the office.

"Luke Milner was born and raised on a farm near Eureka, California. He's the son of Ezra and Matilda Milner, who are both still alive. I have an address and phone number."

"Good going. What else?"

"I found an interesting article about Ezra in a Neocharismatic religious newspaper. It said that he routinely stirs the congregation with his incredible gift for glossolalia," she said.

"What's that?"

"Speaking in tongues."

"As in, speaking a foreign language without prior training?" I asked.

"No. That's xenoglossy. I just looked it up," Jeannine said. "Glossolalia is unintelligible language."

"What good does that do?"

"According to the article, it's God's way of speaking directly to the congregation, and the preacher is able to interpret the message."

I said, "I wonder if Cory could fit in with that crowd."

"That would be grossolalia," she replied, and we laughed.

"Does Ezra's church have a website?"

"Yes, it does. They list all of their parishioners, and Luke's not on the list."

"Maybe they dropped him when he moved out of town," I said.

"I don't think so. There were listings for other parishioners with adult children who moved out of the area, noting their current location in parenthesis."

"So, we have the son of a very religious farmer who leaves the boonies for one of the most socially liberal cities in the United States, where he's hired as a sales executive."

Jeannine says, "Before was hired he worked his way through Berkeley, earning a Bachelor's in Business Administration."

"That's quite a leap for a small town farm boy. I wonder if he keeps in touch with either of his parents."

"There were no *Local Boy Makes Good* articles in the religious or Eureka community papers."

"What did you find out about Snaggles?" I asked.

"He contracts with an electronics security company to do video monitoring of his property in Malibu, but I haven't been able to find out if it also monitors the Jacumba property."

"That would certainly explain how Lonnie found out so quickly. If the security company saw Tesslerod go down, I'm sure Snaggles was alerted and immediately called Lonnie. I think that's what happened, we just don't have any proof."

"Cory picked up your ZZ Top disguise," Jeannine said.

"Get some pictures from Doberman's latest shows and see if you and Cory can modify it into looking like their rhythm guitar temp, whatshisname."

"Ignatius Danzig."

"Seriously? OK, you've got to make me look like Iggy D. That includes clothes, jewelry, and tattoos. Also, have

Cory make me a five minute video montage of Iggy's stage moves. I'm sure YouTube will have clips from the recent shows."

Jeannine said, "That's how I've been following Michael while he's on the road. But they don't spend much time showing Ignatius."

"Do what you can," I said, and Jeannine returned to her desk.

I spent the remainder of the afternoon asking a favor of Celia Bains, talking about the stock market with Bernie Liebowitz, and getting transformed into Iggy D by my staff. Once I achieved the desired look, Cory took my photo and emailed it to the fake ID craftsman that I used over the summer. I then called Drayton to make sure the name on the fake ID would appear on the Hooni stage door admissions list.

I planned to walk into the arena in a few of hours with at least one of the members of Doberman's Stub at my side, catching a ride past Darden's parking lot watchers. But Michael was having a romantic dinner with Jeannine; Jack's voicemail said he was meditating at the venue where he'd be practicing tonight, and would return calls after practice; and Ian was at an AA meeting. I would have to park a couple of blocks from the arena and make my way past Casey's guardians.

Chapter 44

Luke Milner was wrestling with a conundrum of his own. There was no time to make another bomb. In spite of the fact that he brought three very serviceable weapons to San Diego, that were sure to make it past any metal detector, he was stuck on the mental image of the explosion in the Hooni. He planned to stay at a hotel in Mission Valley, not far from the concert site, in case he had to make a getaway on foot. Instead, he opted for a small motel in the Mission Gorge area, a mile east of the arena. This gave him the opportunity to walk the surrounding neighborhoods while planning his alternate strategy.

The further complication that perplexed him was the addition of the Christian boy band to the entertainment roster. Luke's perverse moral gyroscope couldn't adjust to the notion of subjecting those fine young men to the horrors of martyrdom. He feared they would give up their mission and stop carrying the message to impressionable young adults.

Walking up Zion Road, Luke considered the notion of killing the guitarist before the show. This could possibly result in a cancellation, or at least cast a pall over the concert to follow. He read that many bands perform their sound checks the night before the event. Perhaps he could find a spot outside the venue where he could avoid assaulting the sensibilities of the Divine Guys, while furthering his objective.

I parked my RSX at a shopping center on Friars Road, just west of the Hooni, and walked southwest to the point where the shopping center abutted a condo complex. I slowly made my way along a chain link fence on the east side of the property, dividing the condo's lawn from a finger of scrub brush reaching up from the San Diego River basin. Fifty feet of undeveloped land separated it from the Hooni parking lot. I hoped to find an existing opening in the fence, but carried a pair of wire cutters in my guitar case should they be necessary. At 6:30 PM the moon was obscured by clouds, and all that illuminated my way was a halogen floodlight from the condo complex.

Pausing to get my bearings relative to the Hooni, I heard the faint rattle of chain link up ahead. My first thought was that it could be teenagers from the condo having a little impromptu party. Then I flashed on the rather sizeable homeless population that resided farther down the bed of the river, and the stories I'd heard about how fiercely some of them have defended their squatter's rights. I briefly considered removing the wire cutters from the case, but realized that the blunt tip would offer very little intimidation value.

I reached a small clearing where I could see forty yards in front of me, and saw no sign of makeshift tents or lean-tos. In the middle of the clearing I caught sight of the Hooni for the first time. About a quarter of the light fixtures in the parking lot were illuminated, making it a little easier to see as I made my way along the fence. Immediately after leaving the clearing, I found what I was seeking - a cut in the fence that was large enough for me to squeeze through. I noticed that there was no rust on any of the jagged edges where it was clipped. Pulling at the fence to widen the opening, I recalled the sound I heard five minutes earlier.

Luke found the perfect spot across from the stage door entrance to the Hooni. It was located between the south and west entrances, and housed a fenced lot for VIP parking. He set up behind a willow tree that sprouted off in six directions from the main trunk. Luke rested the barrel of his Bushmaster Optics Ready Carbine Rifle where the tree's two center-most branches diverged. A lower branch on the west side of the tree had been trimmed, and provided a fine seat for Luke to sit on.

While Luke pondered the possibility of divine providence providing the perfect hunting blind, he heard a rustle of bushes fifty yards to his right, and saw a bearded man holding a guitar case, tentatively step onto the macadam of the parking lot. He was certain that God was showing him a sign that He was fully onboard with Luke's plan to kill the guitarist. Why else would a martyr appear so readily out of nowhere? Lifting his rifle from its resting place, Luke considered the possibility that the devil was placing a temptation in his path. With the scope of the rifle to his eye, Luke could see that the man had scraggly hair and a very full beard. This man did not resemble any of the guitarists his Internet search had turned up while doing research on the guitarists that would be performing at the show. The man in his crosshairs could easily be a homeless beggar hoping to play the parking lot for beer money. Besides, he still had hopes of taking out his original target. He was obviously moving slowly and cautiously. Luke slipped an iPhone from his pocket and typed: *Doberman's Stub.*

I emerged from the bushes and scanned the periphery of the parking lot for Darden's men. I spotted a cop seated on a tall metal stool next to the VIP parking entrance, holding a clipboard. A lone gray van, parked about half way between myself and the stage door, shielded me from the cop's view. Perhaps I could wait there until I spotted one of my friends from Doberman's Stub approaching, and flag him down before he reached the VIP lot.

Just as I reached the south side of the van I briefly thought I saw a red flash on the tip of my nose. Looking up, I saw a huge picture of Rudolph the Red Nosed Reindeer on the graphics board above the west entrance. I shook it off and continued up the right side of the van. When I reached the passenger side window, I started to peer around the corner. Suddenly, the window dropped, and I was staring at a .44 magnum.

"Freeze, motherfucker!" screamed the voice behind the gun. Then I heard, "Ignatius, is that you?"

"Jack, is that you? It's me, Jason. What are you doing out here?"

"Holy shit, Jason. You're lucky I didn't blow your head off. Get in here."

Climbing into the passenger seat, the smell of pot answered my question about why Jack was in the lot. He extended a half-smoked joint.

"No thanks. I'm gonna need every available brain cell tonight."

I proceeded to tell him why I approached on foot, and that my credentials say I'm Aloysius Danzig, Iggy's brother and newest member of the band.

"They're gonna think ZZ Top was added to the bill."

"I thought you'd be in there checking out the competition," I said.

"Maximum Trone? I'm not a big alternative rock fan. I'd rather smoke a little Kush and get in the mood," he said.

"Don't get too far gone, Jack. This guy left a note that he's looking to kill a guitar player. We're on a very short list."

"Doesn't he understand what concerts do for people?"

Laying out Luke's motives would have prompted Jack to roll another joint. "I don't think the guy realizes why fans go to concerts instead of just listening to recordings. It's like taking your girlfriend out on a date instead of just calling or texting her," I said.

"That's right," he said. "It also gives fans a chance to see if their favorite groups are really great musicians, or if most of the magic happens in post-production."

I added, "And, the fans are able to interact. They get to clap, dance, sing along, mosh, cheer, and represent their cities."

Jack stubbed out his roach with a smile on his face.

Luke managed to find information on Ignatius Danzig. He decided that Danzig was a relative nobody. He also recalled that St. Ignatius was the founder of the Jesuits. While neither the religion of his youth nor the one he now practiced thought highly of the Jesuits, Luke wasn't sure God concurred with their assessments. Ignatius Danzig would be an inadequate martyr. Besides, the night was young.

While I explained to the cop on the door that I used the wire cutters to trim my strings, the scream of tires snapped everyone's attention toward the south entrance. Around the corner flew Michael's Viper, followed closely by a silver Hummer. They screeched to a stop at the entrance to the VIP parking lot.

Luke noted the grand entrance, and correctly assumed they were band members, and certainly not any of the Christian rockers. Luke looked through his rifle scope and scanned the back of the Hummer, which was completely blocking the Viper from his view. A bumper sticker read: *Snare A Drummer – Bang All Night Long*. The Viper would either be driven by a guitarist or their new vocalist. Once they pulled into their parking spots he'd have a clear shot as they walked to the stage door.

Jack crooked his finger when the Viper moved forward. Michael pulled all the way up to the stage door. Before he could exit, Ian Davis was cleared by the VIP gate guard and stomped on the Hummer's gas pedal. He roared to the left of the Viper, and cut the wheel hard to the right, sliding sideways to within three feet of Michael's rear bumper.

Luke spat on the ground when the Hummer completely obscured his view of the Viper and the stage door. Closing his eyes he whispered, "Patience is a virtue. Good things come to those who wait."

Ian snatched Michael's keys out of his hand and dropped two sets on the door cop's clipboard. In his cockney accent he said, "Be a good bobby and take care of our wheels for us."

Jack rolled his eyes, and I wondered if a return trip to the Betty Ford Center was in Ian's immediate future. But the cop's expression had *NASCAR fan* all over it, and we were admitted immediately without a hassle.

Inside the arena, Jack led Ian away from the others for a brief chat. Michael, Jeannine, and I continued on toward the dressing rooms.

Michael said to Jeannine, "Nice job. He does look like Iggy's brother."

I said, "I can't believe you brought her after making me tell her she had to stay home."

Jeannine said, "He's looking for a guitarist. I can't even play the opening to *Iron Man.* Please don't make a big deal out of it, Jason. I haven't seen my boyfriend in almost two months."

Michael added, "C'mon, Jason. Even Delbert Henson can play *Iron Man.* Let it go."

The debate ended abruptly when we walked into the Doberman's Stub dressing room and shocked an obviously uninformed Ignatius Danzig.

"What the fuck!" he yelled.

Michael made the introductions and briefed Danzig on the plan.

"I don't want any trouble from the cops," he said in a way that suggested he wouldn't be cooperating.

I said, "Look at it this way: There's a maniac out there who's promised to kill a guitar player at tomorrow night's show. Who would you rather have out there on the stage, me or you?"

He replied, "I think it might be a good time to go back to Anaheim."

I said, "It sounds to me like you're hiding something from the cops. If you screw up this plan I'll make it my business to find out what it is and return the favor."

"Ignatius, Jason is the best private investigator in California. If you've got a skeleton in your closet this is not the guy you want as your enemy," Michael said.

Ignatius opened his arms and said, "Brother Aloysius, as I live and breathe."

Before I could revisit the topic of Jeannine's presence at the arena, Donald Quinn walked through the door wearing an emerald green cape with a black satin lining, and attached hood. A red goatee accented a Leno-like jaw that protruded from the hood, as the hood's shadow obscured his other facial features.

"C'mon. I'll introduce you," Michael said.

In a voice that could fill the Hooni without the benefit of a PA system, Donald made a huge fuss over Jeannine, and thanked me for providing protection onstage. In spite of his warm welcome and thick brogue, Jeannine was obviously wary of this huge man whose face remained ominous in the backstage lighting.

"'Tis not a druid before you, dear lady," said Donald, pushing back the hood, "merely a giant ginger who was vaccinated with a phonograph needle."

Jeannine smiled nervously and squeezed Michael's arm as if they were about to take the big plunge on a roller coaster.

"I can't wait to hear that voice power-up the Doberman catalog," I said.

As if on cue, the backstage squawk box announced: "Doberman's Stub to the stage, please."

"I guess you won't have to," Donald replied.

Once everyone was assembled, the stage director announced that they would start with the entrance, in case the techs needed to tweak their rigs.

I asked Iggy to stand in as my placeholder on the stage while I ran up to the control booth.

"Good evening, Mr. Claymore," I said, entering the control room. The arena engineer and the new Doberman's Stub sound man sat behind control boards to Drayton's left. Both of them swiveled quickly to look at me, obviously on edge. Drayton continued to face the stage.

Drayton asked, "What sounds like Jason Duffy, looks like Billy Gibbons, and smells like a jasmine bush?"

"I give up," I said.

"Don't give up yet. You should at least wait until you stumble through the rehearsal before hanging up your strings."

I flashed on our unbearable therapy sessions during my two-year career as a mental health counselor. The worst ones involved Drayton trying to act like the *King of the Improv*. Rapid topic change was my only effective defense.

"Who will be in the empty chair to your right?" I asked.

"Your buddy, Shamansky, provided Lonnie comes to the show as planned."

To the right of Shamansky's seat were six unlit monitors.

"I thought you used computer tiling instead of monitors," I said.

Drayton punched a few keys and the monitors lit up. Each one looked like a tic-tac-tow board, divided into nine squares.

"Won't it be hard for Shamansky to recognize a face when the mini-screens are so small?" I asked.

The stage director's voice came through the control room squawk box. "Dexter, you missed your cue. What the hell are you doing up there?"

The tech on the far left tapped out a command and poised his finger over a button. "Sorry, Lou. All set to go."

A few seconds later he hit the button. I noticed Derek's refrigerator-shaped Plexiglas block start down the monorail. Donald Quinn appeared to be trapped inside the block, engulfed in green flames. Quinn was a born showman.

Drayton asked, "Now that you've seen the big toy block would you care to see how we're going to spot the bad guy?"

"Dazzle me, Drayton," I said.

"Let's say Shamansky sees Murray in tile number one of monitor one. We'll pretend your old friend Detective Darden is John Murray."

"When did he get here?" I asked.

"Before you. Pay attention." Drayton massaged his temple briefly. "If Shamansky wants a closer look he just touches that tile and it fills the screen."

I asked, "What if he's scanning the crowd from across the arena, looking for a guy in a disguise. Can you get any closer?"

Drayton stood up, stuck his nose an inch from mine and said, "I wanna hear *Sharp Dressed Man*."

The sound tech laughed and I rolled my eyes. "Can you zoom in closer?"

Drayton sat down and tapped the monitor at five second intervals. Each time Darden got bigger and bigger.

"He really needs to prune those nose hairs," Drayton said.

"Drayton, are you sure you'll be able to feed anything on your monitors through the Skype connection to our people on the Bluetooth network?"

"I'd bet my YouTube millions on it if somebody hadn't killed my golden goose."

The squawk box once again came to life. "Aloysius Danzig to the stage."

I took the elevator to the main concourse and reached the seating entranceway in time to see the twenty foot high green pyrotechnic display as the block imprisoning Donald Quinn crossed the stage. When the smoke cleared Donald was at his microphone, and live Doberman Pinschers were occupying both blocks.

Considering that we never played together as a fivesome, the Doberman rehearsal went surprisingly smooth. It was obvious that Donald did his homework. I learned most of the Doberman catalog with my old band mates shortly after Michael became a member of the band.

From his hunting blind behind the willow tree, Luke contemplated his options as Doberman's muffled sound leaked out of the arena. An unmarked bus rolled up to VIP Parking and into a slot to the right of the stage door. The bus's exit door faced Luke, affording him a clear shot at anyone who emerged. Without activating his red dot, Luke trained the scope on the door as soon as it opened. Calvin Dawson was the first one off the bus, followed by Kayleigh, Mark and Matthew Manning. Luke slid his finger on the red dot button. Suddenly, a gleeful burst of shouts rang through the open parking lot as the Divine Guys poured out of the bus. Luke tapped the safety and took a deep breath. The boys would practice next, and the hedonists would be exiting soon.

Doberman's Stub was nearly finished with its session. I practiced switching over with Iggy on a couple of songs that Tsunami Rush rarely played. It was as simple and seamless as I had hoped.

When the final song ended I heard Iggy yell, "Get your hands off of me!"

Ten feet away, next to a huge black curtain, Darden's partner held Iggy's arms from behind.

"This guy's dressed up to look like the guitarist," he yelled. Darden strode toward them from blue screen area #1.

The partner let go of one arm, grabbed Iggy's beard and said, "I'll bet this is fake."

"Aaahhh!" screamed Iggy.

Using a deep voice I yelled, "What are you doing to him!"

Darden shouted, "Let him go. Don't you recognize ZZ Top?" Smoothing Iggy's beard he added, "Sorry about that, Mr. Gibbons. My partner is a country fan, and doesn't know about you and your brother. He thought you were a maniac strangler."

I said to Iggy, "C'mon, bro. Let's get our lawyer to call the police commissioner. Those two will be directing traffic the next time you see them."

Walking back toward the dressing room Iggy said, "I can't believe *the cool one* thinks Dusty Hill is Billy's brother."

"I can't believe you just called that numb-nuts *the cool one*." My phone buzzed, and I glanced at Caller ID. "I need to take this. I'll catch up with you later."

"What's going on, Celia?"

"For starters, Ezra Milner is as healthy as a heifer, and hasn't seen his son in over a year."

"How much did you tell him?" I asked.

"That his son got in with the wrong crowd and might be in a bit of trouble."

"Do you think he'll call Luke?"

Celia said, "He told me that he wouldn't, and he strikes me as a man of his word. Although, he also strikes me as the kind of guy you'd see in a revivalist's tent with a fist full of poisonous snakes."

"I guess the fruitcake doesn't fall far from the tree."

"What's happening in San Diego?"

I gave her a five minute summary. Then I got her to reluctantly agree to remain in Eureka until after the concert by reminding her of my close encounters with Jimmy DeLong and Aaron Tesslerod.

Celia noted, "Whoever coined the phrase *payback's a bitch* must have been one of your old debtors."

Nearing the dressing room door, I heard a familiar voice from behind.

"What did you think?" Derek asked.

"Very impressive. I liked it."

"What was wrong?" Derek asked.

"I just told you that I liked it. Why would you ask me what was wrong?"

"It's me, Jason. I know you. Your tone of voice tells me you have a problem with something."

I said, "OK, there's one thing I'd change, but it's not a big deal."

"What?"

"I don't like the way you can see how the Plexiglas attaches to the monorail. It's like seeing the puppeteer during the show."

"That's very fixable. A little skirting would do the job."

"It was hard to believe Donald Quinn wasn't really in that box. I was blown away," I said.

Luke heard Divine Guys Dance start their session, and knew his targeting choices were just moments from walking through the stage door. His phone buzzed, and he checked Caller ID. It was his father. Normally, he'd let it go to voicemail. But since he told his boss a lie about his father, Luke thought it best to confirm that he didn't have a problem on that front.

"Good evening, Father."

"I knew it was just a matter of time before Satan held you in his hand."

"What are you talking about, Father?"

Ezra Milner began speaking in tongues with a fury Luke never experienced. The drummer with the Hummer walked out the stage door.

"Speak English or I'm hanging up!"

Ezra said, "The police were here a few minutes ago. They know that you've sinned against God and man. Come home, Luke. You can be reborn. No matter what man's punishment shall be, God will forgive. Move out of Sodom, and return to the virtues of the common clave—"

Luke hung up. The rest of Doberman's Stub and the CLAM contingent exited the arena. If the police knew he was the Concert Killer, he no longer needed to worry about taking a low-risk shot in a parking lot. It was time for his mission to be the lead story on CNN. That meant moving the action into the arena during showtime.

Chapter 45

I woke up at 6:30 Friday morning and was half-way through my shower when Kelly popped into the bathroom.

"You're up early," she said.

"I have the feeling it's going to be a very long day. Did you talk with Lynette?"

"Move over," Kelly said, drawing back the shower curtain. "She'd love to, but doesn't get out of work until 5:00. Is that going to be a problem?"

I ran the soap across Kelly's back.

"It starts at 6:00, but I don't expect any problems while the warm-up is on. The boy band starts at 7:30. I don't think the killer would try anything with them on the stage, but you never know."

"Woo! I think the Irish Spring is getting fresh."

"Would you prefer to get zestfully clean?" I asked.

"I'd prefer to get to school on time since I have to take off early to meet Detective Rappaport at the airport," she said. "I don't see why he can't just bring Lynette's outfit to the Hooni."

"If Casey or Darden got a look at it, he'd be in a lot of trouble. I promised that someone would meet him at Lindberg Field. Are you going to be able to make it on time?"

Kelly soaped her feet. "Yes, I'll be there; and that better be the loofah."

My first order of business upon arriving at the office was to call Lt. Casey. I took it as a good omen that I was being patched through immediately. Casey listened without interrupting while I told him about my theory on how Snaggles tipped Lonnie about Tesslerod's death after hearing from his security company. I was cut off before I could transition into identifying Luke as the killer.

Casey said, "Let me see if I can summarize your argument. You want me to lift the ban because you came up with an unsubstantiated guess on how your boss found out about Tesslerod's death around the time you were free to make a phone call. I'd say 'nice try' but I'd be lying. Every cop in the facility is going to see a picture of your face before going on duty. If I see you in that arena you're going down for felony obstruction of justice." Click.

Luke stood in front of his bed looking down at an array of weapons that could pass through a metal detector. He had moved to a rundown motel in Ocean Beach in case the police were conducting a manhunt. A little research would establish his propensity for booking five star accommodations. Luke selected an acrylic tent peg with a razor-sharp point.

Parting his curtains a few inches, he looked out at morning beach-goers and wondered why society tolerated such lack of ambition. He also wondered how many of those beach bums would be at the arena later on, and if the significance of his mission would change their lives.

Moving to his cheap dresser, Luke gazed at the back of the dollar bill he had taped to the mirror and ran his finger over the words above the Eye of Providence. "Annuit Cœptis," meaning: He approved our undertakings.

Luke had plenty of money in an offshore account that would enable him to continue his mission. But he always assumed that he could maintain his anonymity and resume his life at any time. This new development would change his existence forever. He decided to take a walk and contemplate his future. Should he continue forward with the mission he carefully designed, by sacrificing 13 martyrs and shutting down the concert industry? Or, should he alter his plans now that his identity was no longer a secret?

Stepping out on his second floor balcony, Luke hiked his shoulders and turned away from a brisk wind. Before starting his walk, he added a sweater and sports jacket to fend off the chill of December on the San Diego coastline.

Luke trudged along the water's edge, contemplating his situation as he neared the Ocean Beach pier. There were no pretty girls sunning themselves in scandalous bikinis this morning. All of the action was just north of the pier, where several surfers in wet suits bobbed on small waves waiting for one worth riding. Luke stopped beneath the pier and stared out at them. Both of his cold hands were buried in his pockets, and he bounced a bit to keep his aerobic exercise going.

He thought about how the surfers before him were wasting their time waiting for a three foot wave. The real action would be a monster wave in Hawaii. Luke was bored with the three foot waves. He longed for the big one that would be remembered forever.

Suddenly Luke felt someone hit him from behind, and careened forward into the surf. Turning around he saw four wetsuit-clad boys in their late teens. Three of them were laughing at him, but the muscular blond who hit him with his surfboard wore a stern look.

He said, "We don't put up with your kind coming down here, jacking off to boys in wetsuits."

"I was just watching them," Luke protested. He briefly considered charging the leader. But with three backups holding pointy surfboards, he opted to run away.

At 11:30 AM I joined Calvin and Kayleigh for brunch at their hotel on Mission Bay. The spectacular view of the bay did little to calm our nerves.

I said, "I couldn't believe my eyes when I saw you walk into the arena last night with Matthew Manning. Isn't that considered consorting with the enemy?"

"We met at the airport. Mark was with them, and chatting with one of the Divine guitarists at Baggage Claim. It was a bit awkward at first."

"I'll bet. Do you think Mark's looking to jump ship?"

Calvin said, "I think he's had it with Lonnie."

Kayleigh added, "He's been withdrawing into his religious texts since he leaked that story to the press."

"Did you get a chance to meet Matthew Manning on the bus?" I asked.

Calvin said, "It was everything I expected from a ConcertMaster clone. He kept his Bluetooth conversation going while Mark was introducing us."

Over breakfast I brought Calvin up to speed on the investigation and the contingencies I prepared for the evening. We speculated on Lonnie's role, discussed the task force's position, and concluded that it would be best if Calvin and Kayleigh distanced themselves from Lonnie as much as possible during the evening.

Calvin said, "He'll probably spend most of the night backstage. We'll go up to the skybox when the Divine Guys take the stage. I'd like to get a look at them anyway."

"Do you think Lonnie and Murray will head up there, too?" I asked.

"Lonnie's strictly a backstage guy. In fact, there should be no more than a handful of people in our skybox," Calvin said.

Kayleigh said, "Tell Kelly to come up and join us if she gets a chance."

At 4:00 PM I entered the stage door as Aloysius Danzig. Drayton met me in front of the Doberman's Stub dressing room.

He said, "Your buddy, the hairless detective, is up in the control room."

"Can you get me in to see him?"

"He's joined at the hip by the cop who talks like Michael Jackson."

"Darden," I said.

"Here's your Bluetooth. Besides the two of us, I'll also have Shamansky, Kelly, Lynette, Bains, and Amanda Dorian on the network."

I said, "Milner strikes me as being very computer savvy. Is there any chance he could bluejack us?"

"I personally handled the encryption coding. What do you think?"

"We're good. What else is going on?"

Drayton said, "It's beginning to look a lot like Christmas. The decorating committee came in after you left last night and there are candy canes, Santa hats, and reindeer everywhere."

"Do they pose any security problems?"

Drayton said, "I'm a little concerned about Prancer. I saw a movie about him once, and his decoration alter-ego came crashing down onto Main Street, nearly smashing a windshield. You don't suppose the Concert Killer might try a *death by antler* move?"

"Did the security force check all of the committee members on their way in?"

"Not only that, they x-rayed the decorations."

"Any other problems?" I asked.

"Just a bit of an Indian problem," Drayton replied.

"What's that?"

"I drank a large cup of Earl Grey a half hour ago, and I have to take a tea-pee."

I cringed. "Did you get Kelly and Lynette on the backstage pass list, and entry through the stage door?"

"They're in like Santa in the sand," Drayton said.

"What?"

"You know – sand sculpture. Ocean Beach, Imperial Beach. Try getting in the Christmas spirit, Jason."

"I'll get in the Christmas spirit once I'm sure the Grinch isn't going to blow somebody away."

Derek joined us. "Jason, come with me. I want to show you the tenting I put on the Plexiglas block."

"I've got to deal with a tenting issue myself," said Drayton, and he walked quickly toward the men's room.

I handed Derek my Bluetooth. "Can you put this on me so that my Billy Gibbons hair keeps it hidden?"

"I think I could hide my drum set in there."

In three minutes I was on the wireless network and heading into the arena.

"It's nice to see somebody looked in the suggestion box," I said.

Derek had placed what appeared to be a large black cloth bag on top of the Plexiglas block, hiding the metal arms that connected it to the monorail, and the large red button that enabled him to start and stop the device manually during the trials.

"I couldn't hide the poles that stick out of the bottom, holding the projector and mirrors. But the top looks a lot less conspicuous."

"Yes it does. Now I have one more request. Can you show Kelly how to work the blue screen when she gets here?"

"Why?" asked Derek.

I filled him in on my contingency plan.

Luke purchased a throw-away cell phone and placed a call to Westerhill & Weis Trucking, a liquefied natural gas client he established a few months prior. The CEO shared his religious fervor and struck Luke as a kindred spirit.

"Mr. Westerhill, this is Luke Milner of Clean Air LNG. Have you gotten a delivery in the last couple of days?"

"Hello, Luke. I'm expecting one this afternoon. What's this about?"

"I just found out that one of our trucks bound for San Diego County might hold a contaminant that could make the

LNG unstable when the valves are opened up. I just flew into Lindberg Field, and I'd like to accompany the driver back to our warehouse for testing."

Westerhill said, "I'm surprised this call is coming from you instead of someone from operations management."

"I'm sorry to tell you this Mr. Westerhill, but management is trying to sweep this under the rug. They say there's only a 10% chance that the truck could blow up, and that a scare of that magnitude could put the company out of business. As a good Christian, I can't take that chance. I promised that I'd take care of you when we signed our contracts. I'm in town right now to live up to that commitment," Luke said.

"I trust you Luke, and appreciate how you're putting your future with the company on the line for me. But this makes me uncomfortable about continuing my relationship with Clean Air LNG."

Luke said, "I promise you that everyone involved in the decision to send that truck to your business will be exposed and out of a job by the middle of next week. What time is the shipment scheduled to arrive?"

Chapter 46

Luke pulled a rented truck into a warehouse facility recently leased to Clean Air LNG. Upgrades to the facility were not scheduled to begin for another month. He helped his company find it six weeks ago in between sales calls in SoCal. One of the other warehouses that he looked at in the neighborhood served as temporary storage for the annual Christmas Parade floats. Luke was pleased to learn the realtor hadn't changed the combination on the lockbox since his last visit. Using a rented truck, Luke transferred some of the parade float items to the new Clean Air LNG warehouse.

Giving Mr. Westerhill a knowing nod, Luke pulled his company LNG driver aside upon arrival and explained that they were to quietly visit the company's new San Diego facility where a chemist would run a quick test on his load before delivery. The driver was aware of Luke's reputation as both star salesman and devout Christian.

Luke zapped the truck driver with a stun gun as soon as they arrived at the facility, and injected him with a powerful sedative that would keep him out for at least 12 hours.

He disguised the 10,000 gallon LNG cryogenic tank truck to look like Santa's sleigh. Inflatable reindeer and a massive inflatable Santa were added to a gigantic red & green plastic tablecloth-type covering, designed to convert the sides and back of a double-long flatbed into a festive float.

Luke rented welding equipment to seal the vent on top of the LNG tank. He dumped half of the LNG payload behind the warehouse to create better conditions for detonating a BLEVE (boiling liquid expanding vapors explosion). He thanked his employer for his many hours of company-sponsored training on the subject. To his surprise, he had never been asked a single question about this topic in his numerous sales calls.

First, Luke welded the tanker's vents shut. He then installed a small explosive device to blow the cooling system, and linked it to a series of propane-fueled burners to engulf the tank in flames. He set up his controller to mesh with the frequency of the triggering device he planted in the Hooni last week.

I entered the Doberman's Stub dressing room and nodded at Jack Pascal who was sitting on the floor in the lotus position, chanting quietly. Taking a seat on the other side of the room, I said, "Shamansky," and was quickly connected via Bluetooth.

Instead of his usual phone salutation Shamansky said, "Darden, how about getting us a couple of coffees? It looks like it could be a long night."

In the background I heard a familiar high-pitched voice say, "I'm not your waiter, Shamansky. You can send that idiot security geek if he ever gets back here."

I asked, "Any chance you could fill me in without Darden knowing you're on the Bluetooth?"

Shamansky said, "If I wasn't off shadowing Lonnie the past couple of days I could have arranged a waitress that's a hellufa lot more attractive than either of you."

Darden said, "Somebody had to sit on him. Check the monitor and see if he's at the backstage party yet."

Shamansky said, "There he is with the staff security chief. He's not being very social at the moment. Did Casey ever find out if he talked with Snaggles the night I shot Tesslerod?"

"You can ask him yourself when he stops by."

I asked, "Is Darden going to hold your hand all night?"

Shamansky asked, "Darden, what does it tell you when the brass decides that the best use of your talent is to watch me look at security monitors all night? I wouldn't stick a rookie patrolman with that duty unless he was being punished for screwing up."

"If you're a good boy, maybe I'll take over your monitor and let you watch me for a while," Darden said.

I said, "OK, just listen and I'll bring you up to date on what's been happening while you were out of town."

I spent the next five minutes telling Shamansky how I identified Luke as the Concert Killer, and about my Billy Gibbons costume.

"Did you tell Casey?" Shamansky asked.

Darden replied, "Tell him what?"

Shamansky said, "That you want to be promoted from shoulder watcher to security monitor watcher. Frankly, I don't think you're ready yet."

While Darden carried on, I filled Shamansky in on Casey quoting Lonnie about making sure the *strangle* was still on.

"Lonnie and Murray have been gaming the stock market since Lonnie figured out that a serial killer has been attacking the concert industry. They've been using Steiner to short the stocks of insurance companies that indemnify California concerts, and the reinsurer, Diversified Risk."

Shamansky whispered, "Strangle," while Darden continued his rant.

I said, "Bernie Liebowitz told me that a *strangle* is a stock market term used to describe an options strategy that can be very profitable if there is a big movement in the stock price, either up or down. If the killer gets caught, the stocks go up substantially because the risk that was driving claim incidents is over. If he gets away, and the public finally gets wind of the fact that he's out there, the insurance stocks plummet. It's a win-win for the stranglers, unless the insurance company stock prices remain relatively unchanged."

Shamansky asked, "Why did Lonnie tell all of his media contacts that the killer didn't exist when the free press ran that story?"

Darden replied, "He was trying to get them off of his trail. Geez, Shamansky. How did you ever make detective."

I said, "Bernie thinks they were hedging with long positions and got caught with their shorts down after the options expiration date."

Michael, Jeannine, and Donald entered the dressing room. Michael said, "C'mon, you two. It's time to watch Donald play *meet the press*."

I said, "I gotta go, Shamansky. I sent you an email with Luke Milner's picture attached. Maybe if you tell Casey a little white lie and say that he met with Lonnie yesterday it will get circulated to the sworn officers. Then again, Milner is pretty clever with his disguises. Call me if your shadow takes a restroom break."

Donald boomed, "It's good to see our undercover protection is already on the job." Turning to Michael he added, "Either that or we've hired a loony who talks into his hair."

Michael said, "We got the best of both worlds with this guy, Donald."

The six of them entered the backstage party room after being patted down by SDPD. The media quickly surrounded them and shot questions at Donald Quinn."

I said to Michael, "I need to talk to Calvin. Let me know if you see anything suspicious."

Calvin was standing between Kayleigh and a Frosty the Snowman shrimp bowl. Without the top hat it looked like Frosty met up with Hannibal Lecter. Casey and Lutz were noshing ten feet away.

Calvin smiled and said, "The shrimp is delicious, Aloysius. Why don't you give it a try?"

I said, "Don't mind if I do," and nestled in close. I then passed a picture of Luke and said, "See if you can get this circulated among your security personnel. Shamansky's getting it to SDPD."

"The team captain should be checking in with me any minute. I'll give it to him." Nodding to his left Calvin added, "By the way, isn't that guy in the corner with the derringer tattoo one of your suspects?"

"I think he's taking over Jimmy DeLong's gang."

"Shouldn't someone be keeping an eye on him?"

"See the Korean woman that he and his posse are talking to? That's Michele Ko, the primary on the Irvine case. I heard her tell him that she's Yoko's cousin," I said.

"Don't they know that Yoko's Japanese?"

"Calvin, you do realize we're talking about Jimmy's underlings. Those guys would probably copy SAT answers off of Chanel's exam."

I noticed all of the members of Divine Guys Dance exit the party room. The warm-up act had been playing for about a half hour at that point. Mark emerged from the altar boy huddle and headed straight for Calvin.

"I can't believe that Matthew Manning is actually trying to pick up the teenage cousin of the Divine Guy's bass player. I'll bet he's on drugs. Manning's sister is a saint, but her brother walks on cloven hooves."

I said, "See those two cops shoveling down the goose pate?"

"Yes."

"Wait until they split up. Then tell the big one what's going on. His name is Detective Lutz. He'll keep an eye on that sleazeball for you, Mark."

"Jason?"

Calvin said, "He's not supposed to be here, so don't mention his name."

The words were no sooner out of Calvin's mouth when a firm hand slapped my back and Doberman's Stub drummer,

Ian Davis bellowed, "Jason, what are you doing over here. I want ya to meet somebody."

I nodded at Calvin and slipped into the middle of a line in front of the bar, which had just been invaded by the entourage of the other headline band, Maximum Trone. Casey spun around and strode purposefully toward them.

Calvin put his arm around Kayleigh and boomed, "Jaylynn! Look, its Ian!" He stepped on Ian's toes before he could verbalize the quizzical look on his face. "Jaylynn, Ian wants you to meet someone! Lead on, Ian."

Casey scanned the crowd and returned to the buffet table.

I exited the party room just in time to catch a call from Celia Bains.

"I'm afraid I've got some bad news," she said. "I had my partner pull Ezra Milner's phone records, and a call was made to a Clean Air LNG cell phone less than five minutes after I left his house last night. I think it's safe to assume that Luke knows we're on to him."

"Are you near the Milner's farm right now?"

"I can see the farmhouse lights from my car window."

"Did you test your Skype connection?" I asked.

"It's working fine."

"How about giving a call to Detective Rappaport? See if he can reach Luke's boss, Anson Parmeter. Find out if he had any contact with the company, or if anything unusual has happened over the past couple of days."

"Why don't I just call him directly?" she asked.

"Rappaport's got jurisdiction, and could cause a lot more problems for them if Parmeter gets more concerned with the sales implications than how his answers could help the investigation. I have a feeling Rappaport knows which politicians could cause him the most problems if he gets a whiff of bullshit."

I got a call from Shamansky immediately after disconnecting. "The altar boys just took the stage a few minutes ago, and there's a huge backup at the four entrance gates because of the pat-down and metal detector scans. Darden told Casey what was going on and got the OK to bypass some security measures since they're looking for a strangler."

"Tweedledum and Tweedledumber," I commented.

Shamansky said, "The brain trust took a look at the fans getting loud about missing the altar boys and decided they might start a riot. They'll still go through the metal detector, but the pat-downs are over."

"They think the Christian rock fans will riot?"

"That was my point, too. But no one has been listening to me since the Tesslerod shooting, so be prepared."

"Is there anything else I should know?" I asked.

"I just saw Calvin, his wife, and Doberman's new manager sit in the skybox next my security perch. You might want to have Calvin pass the word to his security staff about what's going on at the door. Also, Mark, is standing in the wings watching the altar boys."

"I'll tell Calvin about the door. Don't worry about Mark. But Manning was last seen putting the moves on a teenager in the 15-will-get-you-20 age range. If you see him doing anything lewd or lascivious on your monitor give Lutz a call," I said.

"Gotta go."

After telling Kelly I was on my way, I popped into the "Referee Room" that was serving as Lynette's dressing room. "You look awesome, Lynette."

Smiling at Kelly she said, "We went to the wig store on Broadway and found a perfect match for Delainya's hair."

I said, "That's a big upgrade from what Cory picked up at the costume shop. Did Derek show you how to operate the blue screen?"

Kelly replied, "He introduced us to the stage tech in charge of the equipment. Derek told him to go to a live feed of Lynette on my say-so."

Lynette said, "The script that Kelly gave me is in bullet points. I take it that means you want pauses in between each one."

I said, "I highlighted a keyword in bold for each bullet. I'll give you the keyword on the Bluetooth when I want you to recite that bullet. I may also feed you some lines on-the-go. Can you handle that?"

"I took an improv class last semester. I'm ready for anything."

Kelly said, "I told you she was good."

Luke drove the converted tanker to the Hooni's commercial entrance and convinced security that he was woefully late in getting the only Christmas prop that could be seen from Friar's Road into position. He had added a massive bolt of white cloth tied with a thick rope to the white tanker, covering the company name. It made Santa appear to be sitting on the biggest toy sack in the world.

The gate guard called his supervisor since the truck was not on his list of vehicles approved to enter through the commercial entrance. He was told that SDPD was looking for a strangler, and approved the truck to enter the lot.

Luke said, "It's supposed to sit between the sidewalk and the north wall, beneath the flood light to the left of the north entrance. Can you call perimeter security and make sure no one is blocking my access?"

"Will do. Merry Christmas."

Outside security waved Luke into the spot he had described. Upon exiting his cab, Luke hooked Santa up to an air compressor and placed two spotlights on the patch of lawn in front of the tanker, illuminating the massive decoration.

Chapter 47

Doberman's Stub took the stage at 9:25, minus Donald Quinn. They led off with a three minute instrumental intro to a song from their *Don't Bury Your Bone Alone* CD. From the control room, Shamansky saw lead guitarist, Michael Marinangeli, on the far right. Two uniformed SDPD officers stood on the floor below the stage, within ten feet of Michael. Bassist Jack Pascal stood to his left, about six feet farther back from the edge of the stage. Ian Davis sat behind his drums on a riser in the middle of the stage. Donald's microphone stood unmanned to the left of Ian, and I was on the far left.

Ian had added a second bass drum for the opening, and began to create an effect that sounded like thunder rolling through the arena. Shamansky's chin shot over his left shoulder when Derek's Plexiglas block started to move. Since it was anchored to the back wall of the adjacent skybox, where Calvin and his guests were seated, Shamansky was one of the first to see the surrealistic sight of Donald Quinn beginning to float out across the arena, engulfed in green flames.

Drayton said, "My doctor once gave me pills that made me feel like that."

"When do you come off of them?" Darden asked.

A loud murmur started at the back of the arena, followed by shouts of, "Look!" and much finger pointing. When the block crossed the quarter mark, Ian reached a crescendo with his drums and crashed his cymbals mightily.

Donald used every nuance of his powerful voice to deliver a speech about an ancient druid who compelled him to bridge the gap between the US and the Emerald Isle. It was amazing how animated he appeared in that block.

Looking beyond the block, I spotted Dean Casey talking with Calvin and pointing to the arena floor. Before the block made it to the edge of the stage where the wall of green smoke would obscure my view, I saw Calvin follow Casey and a uniformed officer out of the skybox. This left Kayleigh and Doberman's manager as the sole occupants of a suite that could comfortably hold 50 guests.

The crowd erupted when the twenty foot wall of green smoke obscured the stage. The moment the block touched down I became concerned about how it limited the view to my right. Knowing that there were two sworn officers on the floor just beyond the stage did little to settle my uneasy feeling.

I switched over to Iggy in the middle of the third song when a group of uniformed officers stormed down the main aisle and grabbed a young man wearing a large overcoat in the 10th row. The man was thrown to the aisle floor and handcuffed. I noted a tube the size of a small RPG rocket launcher sticking out of the bottom of his overcoat, and sighed audibly when the tube turned out to be a three-foot bong that was duct taped to the coat's lining.

Before taking rhythm duties back from Iggy, I glanced up at Shamansky who was shaking his head and pointing his thumb at Darden. Off to the right I saw Doberman's new manager exiting the skybox. Kayleigh was on her phone, probably trying to find out what was going on in front of the stage.

Over the next four songs Michael went out of his way to synch his lead to my rhythm. It was like a tribute to our Tsunami Rush days when Michael crossed the stage behind Donald Quinn to draw attention to a key track written by former bandleader, Terry Tucker, to accent his own rhythm guitar prowess. When the song ended, I glanced up at

Calvin's skybox, hoping he had returned and recognized what Michael had done.

Instead, I saw a skybox waiter approaching Kayleigh with a large beer on his tray. I did a double-take when I remembered Calvin saying that she hated the smell of beer. Standing in profile, I could see that the waiter was holding something with a sharp point under his tray.

Lunging to my mic I shouted, "Kayleigh! Look out! He's got a knife!"

Kayleigh flipped the tray up in the air, splashing Luke's face with beer. She jumped over a couple of rows of seats, and headed up the aisle toward the exit.

"Shamansky!" I yelled into my Bluetooth.

He said, "The control room door is sealed shut. It won't budge."

"Does your front window open?"

"No, it's like a recording studio in here."

I could see that Kayleigh was not able to exit the skybox door. Luke bounded up the stairs two at a time and reached the inside part of the skybox, where the bar, buffet, and lounge chairs were arranged around circular tables. Kayleigh looked back in time to see Luke approaching, and moved to a point directly across the center table from him.

I asked, "Can a cop get over there from the next skybox?"

Shamansky replied, "They all have eight foot glass partitions."

I dropped my guitar, jumped on top of the Plexiglas box, and pushed the red manual start button.

"Derek," I said into my Bluetooth.

"I see you, Jason."

"Can you make this thing go any faster?"

Luke tried shoving the table out of the way with his free hand. Fortunately, it was bolted to the floor.

Derek said, "I have the controller, and can bump it up another 50%, but the track can't handle much more than that, especially with your added weight. It could come crashing down on the audience, killing you and everybody else it hits."

"Do it!" I screamed, and felt it surge forward.

I heard the track make a sound that confirmed Derek's assessment about the strain.

Luke dove across the table, and Kayleigh ran out of the interior suite into the open seating area. Using her right foot to push off a side aisle armrest, she leaped to gain a finger hold on the top of the glass partition separating her skybox from the next one. She missed by a couple of inches, bounced off of the partition, banged her knee, and fell to the concrete flooring.

I pulled the black cloth skirting up over me, allowing just a peek hole, when I saw Luke in the doorway assessing the situation. His disguise included conservatively cut red hair and a matching goatee. I passed the halfway point, alongside a digital scoreboard that was still showing a view of the stage. I needed a distraction to buy some time.

"Kelly," I said.

"We're in front of the blue screen."

"Start from the top of the script and go now."

Luke held the acrylic tent pole in front of his chest and walked toward Kayleigh. Most of the crowd on the third tier could see that Kayleigh was in imminent danger. Their reactions caught the attention of almost everyone else.

I was briefly startled when the cube below me flickered, and I found myself looking straight down on a very animated rotting corpse. The crowd reacted an instant later.

Lynette said, "Luke, it's me, Delainya. Why did you choke me, Luke? I only went to that concert because you lied to me. You said you'd take me away for the weekend. Then you tossed me aside to spend more time at your job."

Luke was momentarily stunned when he focused on what appeared to be his dead girlfriend in the approaching Plexiglas block. Kayleigh used the distraction to drag herself over a couple of rows of chairs, but it was clear that she wasn't moving well, and would not be able to make another run for it.

"You're not Delainya!" Luke shouted.

"Amanda," I said.

"I see it on my computer. This is really creepy, Jason," Amanda said.

"Are there any phrases Delainya used that Luke would recognize?"

"She called him her green giant."

I said, "Lynette, go to the *miss you* bullet and call him your green giant."

Luke jogged down the row where Kayleigh crouched, two rows from the edge of the balcony.

Lynette said, "I really miss having my green giant by my side."

Luke screamed, "You don't sound anything like Delainya!"

"A crushed larynx will do that to you – thank you very much!" Apparently Lynette aced the improv class.

Kayleigh crawled over another row.

"I don't believe you." Luke stepped over the row that Kayleigh had just scaled. He looked at her and said, "Now it's time for me to sacrifice that guitar player I mentioned in my last note."

"Celia," I said.

"I'm with Luke's father. We can see him."

"Give me five seconds and put him on."

"Drayton," I said. "Put the Skype feed on the Big Screen now."

Kayleigh no sooner climbed over the last row when Luke grabbed her red sweater and pulled her to a standing position. I was three-quarters of the way there, and couldn't possibly reach the skybox balcony with my best leap.

Luke raised the tent pole to a strike position. The crowd gasped.

At full volume Ezra Milner said, "Thou shall not kill, Luke."

The Concert Killer looked up to see his father's face filling the Big Screen above the band. He let go of Kayleigh and faced his father's image. Kayleigh scrambled for the front left corner of the suite. She hoped to climb over the rail and into the next suite, but the glass partition extended a foot beyond the rail to protect celebrities from unwanted intrusions.

Ezra Milner said, "Son, you've brought shame to the Milner name. You were raised to respect the laws of God."

The hologram block was nearly at the docking port against the wall separating the interior suite from the control room. I could see Shamansky and Darden's faces pressed to the window.

The moment the cube came to a stop I grabbed two of the rods at the base of the block and lowered myself down to the walkway as quietly as possible. Luke was shouting at his father, but with his back to me, I couldn't hear a word. My peripheral vision picked up rapid movement on the other side of the glass separating the skyboxes. I turned to see Calvin rushing down the stairs.

I moved down the center aisle as quickly and quietly as possible. When I reached the halfway point Luke noticed Kayleigh trying to climb over the railing toward Calvin's outstretched hand. Putting his fingers down the back of her pants, Luke yanked Kayleigh back and spun her around. He glanced at his father as he drew the tent spike to the ready position by his ear.

Kayleigh screamed.

I used my left arm to implement a move I learned over the summer. I got Luke in a sleeper hold, and grasped his right wrist. Luke spun to his left and pulled his legs up off the floor. This caused me to lose my grip on his wrist, and fall backwards onto the balcony railing. I managed to keep my left arm wrapped around Luke's neck.

"Go, Kayleigh!" I yelled. She crawled back toward Calvin.

A red hot searing pain rippled through my body when Luke plunged the tent spike into the back of my upper left arm. Before I could regain my composure, Luke pushed down on my neck with his left hand while trying to wiggle the spike out of my humerus bone.

Luke said, "I tried sending your mother on ahead of you, Duffy. I guess you'll have to go it alone."

Kayleigh stood on the balcony wall. With her left hand on the glass partition she reached for Calvin's hand. Luke spotted this, gave me a hard shove, and yanked the spike out in one motion. His strength from growing up on a farm was apparent. The only thing keeping me from plummeting twenty feet, head-first was the iron railing below the back of my knees. I flexed my calves to firm the grip, and pulled my feet toward the balcony wall with all of my might. The crowd below me scattered quickly.

Kayleigh's right hand folded into Calvin's powerful grip when Luke lifted both of her feet off of the balcony wall and yanked violently. Calvin's wrist slammed into the corner of the partition and he lost his grip. Luke flung her toward me, thrusting her feet outward to send her plunging to the deck below. But her momentum spun her around, and she was able to catch the railing with both hands, four feet to my right. She looked like a gymnast grabbing one of the uneven bars.

There was no way I could pull myself to an upright position without a foothold. I looked at the candy cane decorations alongside Kayleigh and realized one was within reach. I slipped it through a loop of wire, and was surprised to find it was actually white PVC pipe with a *U* fitting on the end, coiled by a red ribbon. I hooked the U over the railing and pulled like I was the point man in a beach fire pit tug-of-war.

I came up fast while Luke was extracting the tent spike from his belt. Before he could bring the spike down on

Kayleigh's hand, I smashed him on the bridge of his nose with the PVC cane. Luke fell backwards into the second row of seats, and I pulled Kayleigh over the rail.

I said, "Go to Calvin. I'll keep him away."

For the next two minutes I battled Luke with the cane while Kayleigh played the ultimate game of "Trust Me" with Calvin. Immediately after she was safely on the other side of the glass, six SDPD officers came up behind her with a couple of maintenance ladders.

I said, "Give it up, Luke. It's over, believe me."

Luke reached into his pocket with his free hand and came out with his radio-controlled detonating device. Turning it toward me, he pressed a red button, and two green LED lights illuminated.

Luke said, "No, it's not. Believe *me*. Or should I say, be-levi me."

I immediately understood the implications of Luke's last comment.

"Where is it!" I screamed.

The feet of a ladder dropped down next to me.

"Everywhere!" Luke yelled, and ran toward the interior suite.

I lunged forward and hooked his ankle with the cane. Hopping to my feet like a shortstop who just laid out for a hot grounder, I knocked Luke unconscious with a knuckle to the temple. While the crowd cheered, I ripped two sets of keys from his pocket, and turned toward the ladder. Two officers were on their way down.

"Shamansky," I said, but got no reply. I touched the ear where my Bluetooth used to be, and flew up and down the ladders on each side of the glass wall.

"Tell Shamansky to look for an LNG tanker in the lot," I yelled to Maurice Johnson, who was examining Kayleigh's ankle. Without waiting for a response, I ran up the stairs of the suite and into the upper deck concourse.

Sprinting toward the escalator I recalled an article I read about LNG before calling Luke's boss. I clicked on the BLEVE link in the article and saw the massive destruction of a huge storage facility. I also saw an example of how the vent on top of cryogenic tankers should alleviate enough of the gas buildup to avert an explosion. I was sure that Luke somehow disabled the vent.

I nearly lost my balance quick-stepping down the escalator stairs. I ran past door security at the south entrance so fast that two of the officers left their post to pursue me. Upon hitting the parking lot I scanned my field of vision and turned left toward the east entrance.

"Stop! Police!" I heard coming from behind.

I quit scanning and ran at a full sprint. Two more officers joined the chase as I passed the east entrance. One of the officers was threatening to shoot when the huge cryogenic tanker was suddenly to my immediate left, and engulfed in flames. Santa had been cremated into a red goo, but the reindeer, anchored to the outside of the tanker platform, remained surprisingly intact. The flames seemed to emanate from the bottom of the tanker, completely surrounding it in a blue flame.

One of the east entrance officers tackled me hard, as if he was preventing the winning touchdown.

The older of the south entrance officers caught up to them and yelled, "The captain said to let him go."

My right arm was bleeding from the stab wound. A cut on my right eyebrow from the pavement abrasion dripped blood into my eye.

"Get some fire extinguishers," yelled the same officer. Both east entrance officers ran back toward their posts. The other south entrance officer ran toward the north entrance.

"There's no time for that," I yelled.

I looked down at the two sets of keys in my hand. One key ring was made of sterling silver. The other displayed the number 5 encased in plastic. I dropped the sterling ring and climbed into the cab.

After starting the truck and roughly jamming it into first gear, I flashed on an image of the Oklahoma City bombing, and tried to recall more details from the BLEVE article. I couldn't remember any mention of the amount of time it would take once the tank was surrounded in flames. There was also no mention of whether or not an explosion could be triggered by sudden splashing in the tank. Relieved that it didn't blow as I eased it off the curb and into the parking lot, I headed due south toward the dry bed of the San Diego River.

Immediately after hitting third gear I spotted backup lights moving into my lane from behind a large black SUV with tinted windows. I stayed on the horn and continued to accelerate. The driver saw me at the last instant, threw it into drive, but couldn't get out of the way before getting clipped on the rear bumper. His green Volvo banged into the pickup on his left while the front end hit the passenger door of the SUV. I saw the airbags deploy, and thanked God the man was driving a sedan tank.

Focusing forward I saw two big problems. First, a row of cars was parked in front of the chain link fence separating the parking lot from the scrub brush leading down to the river bed. Maybe if Mark had been allowed to warn everyone about the Concert Killer there wouldn't be a need for so many people to park illegally. Second, I saw a trolley at the platform in front of the football stadium beginning to pull out of the station in my direction. It would be practically overhead at the time I smashed into the cars in front of the fence.

I locked in on a four foot gap between two economy sedans just to the right of the end of my lane. I had no idea how much the collision would slow me down, but figured that by splitting them at least one wouldn't serve as a giant brake by getting stuck in front of the bumper. I hit fourth gear and floored the accelerator.

Passing under the trolley trestles I said, "God help me."

The front bumper of the cab took out the two economy cars like hitting a 4-6 split in bowling. The cars flew away in opposite directions, and a big section of ten foot fencing bent to the ground like a sapling in a hurricane. I felt a powerful wave of liquefied natural gas surge forward.

Kelly stood on the stage with Jeannine and Lynette while I battled Luke in the skybox. Once I disappeared from her view she couldn't comprehend my urgency after knocking out the Concert Killer. She connected with Shamansky on the Bluetooth in time to hear him say that I was running toward a burning gas tanker parked between the north and east entrance.

"He's out here," she shouted, and ran for the stage door.

Jeannine, Lynette and the band followed her. Unfortunately, they were on the opposite side of the building. Kelly turned left and ran as fast as her footwear would allow. She was glad she passed on the stiletto heels when getting dressed. Jeannine was paying the price and lagging behind while Michael kept pace by her side. Jack Pascal sailed past Kelly while Ian huffed and puffed a few feet behind her.

Rounding the south entrance she saw Jack pointing at an immense truck, engulfed in flames, and heading toward the trolley tracks.

"He's driving that truck!" Jack shouted.

Kelly gasped when the truck clipped the Volvo.

Pointing, and with a cry in her voice Kelly said, "Jason's in that truck," when the rest of their group arrived.

"Shamansky – what's he doing?" she said into the Bluetooth.

"He's saving over 14,000 people, Kelly. I lost sight of him. What's going on?"

At that moment the truck hit the parked cars and the fence.

"Oh my god!" she screamed, and ran toward the truck. Everyone followed, but this time no one passed her.

Just as she ran by the crippled Volvo an earth-jarring explosion knocked everyone to the ground. A fireball larger than the stadium to their left rose hundreds of feet in the air. The wave of heat that followed made them feel as though they were getting instant sunburns.

Kelly was the first one to her feet. She ran until she reached the opening in the fence, then fell to her knees and screamed, "Jason!"

A couple of hundred yards down the hill she could see a few minor brush fires. What made the pit of her stomach feel like zero gravity was the massive circle of blackened earth at the foot of the hill, illuminated by the moonlight.

A parking lot security cart pulled up next to them. Dean Casey and Ike Rappaport exited.

"I'm so sorry," said Rappaport, who had given Delainya's outfit to Kelly a few hours earlier.

Hearing those words, Jeannine became hysterical. Michael tried comforting her, but she pulled away. Her hands shook uncontrollably until Kelly wrapped her arms around her. She tried to speak, but all that would come out were loud sobs.

"The show couldn't have been that bad."

I walked out from behind a lone Torrey pine. In my grip, a deflated plastic reindeer dragged by my side. It served me well when I jumped from the truck after hitting the fence. The back of my shirt smoldered, and the distinct aroma of singed hair followed me.

"Jason!" shouted Kelly, and she threw her arms around me.

Jeannine wasn't yet able to verbalize, but threw her arms around the back of me.

"It's still a little warm back there, Jeannine," I said.

When I reached the parking lot, Dean Casey stood next to the security golf cart. An officer's two-way radio was on speaker, and we all heard the unmistakable voice of Darden.

"If Duffy's still alive put him in handcuffs."

Casey said, "Disregard that order." Turning to me he said, "I was wrong to try to run you off of this case. I've had some bad experiences with PIs in the past and I allowed them to cloud my judgment. Duffy, I'll be recommending you for the civilian Medal of Valor. I hope you'll accept my thanks for what you did here this evening."

I nodded my head, and Casey departed in the cart.

Rappaport said, "Lieutenant Casey missed his calling. He should have been a politician."

At that point Shamansky's captain stepped out from behind a parked SUV. "He's probably looking for the media to take a few bows. I can't do anything about that. But I just found out we're opening a new community outreach office in Logan Heights. I'm going to use *my* political clout to make sure Darden lands that assignment."

I said to Rappaport, "Logan Heights is our equivalent to East L.A."

Rappaport replied, "Maybe the altar boys can hire him when their voices change."

Chapter 48

Over the next few days I enjoyed the rock star status that I once hoped to attain through my music. By the third day I fully grasped the meaning of the phrase *be careful what you wish for.* Along with what seemed like every media outlet in the country, Jeannine and I heard from every conspiracy theorist as well. I gave an in depth interview to Dee Martin Sandler before accommodating any other requests. Cory graciously offered to talk with the conspiracy theorists for us.

I gratefully accepted an invitation from Shamansky to join him for lunch at Larabee's. With Christmas less than a week away, Larabee's waiting area was a madhouse. The hostess who reminded me of June Cleaver was on duty, and parted those waiting for a table to give me a big hug.

"Look everybody, it's our hometown hero, Jason Duffy," she shouted above the din. Enthusiastic applause followed, and no one complained when she seated me immediately.

Shamansky was already at the table. "Did one of the Chargers just walk in?"

"I think it was the San Diego Chicken," I replied, and Shamansky shook his head. "What's going on with Milner?"

"He used his one phone call to get in touch with that Minister of Money who's been filling his head with the notion that riches are God's way of saying He loves you."

"That's messed up."

Shamansky said, "The call lasted all of about 30 seconds. It ended with Milner telling her that the Eye of Providence sees through her gilded façade. Speaking of which, we found a dollar bill in his wallet where he was keeping score of his kills on the pyramid under the Eye."

"He would have needed an actual pyramid to keep score if his last plan worked as well as his first six. Do you think his insanity plea will hold up?"

"Are you kidding me? If they gave Oscars for that kind of acting he'd be a shoo-in. I caught his impression of his father speaking in tongues, and he nailed it."

I asked, "What's going to happen with Lonnie and John Murray?"

"We're hoping to get them on conspiracy to commit murder in the Jimmy DeLong case. Detective Ko got Doogan Clark on tape saying that he heard Lonnie threaten to have Tesslerod treat Jimmy like a roadside bomber if he opened any envelopes."

"How did she get him to say that?"

"She told him Yoko was looking for a new bodyguard; that she hated Lonnie; and if Clarkie had any info that she could hold over Lonnie's head, he might be interviewing for a six figure job in the near future."

"I heard Tesslerod accuse Jimmy of steaming an envelope just before he killed him," I said.

"That'll help. But finding Steiner and getting him to roll over would be even better.

"What about the insider trading? Is the SEC going after them?"

"Technically, it wasn't insider trading. Even though it's clear that Lonnie figured there was a concert killer out there before everyone else, and opted to profit from this knowledge instead of helping the police, the SEC feels he was acting on a theory, like most investors do. Unless he was getting tips from Milner, he's in the clear with them."

"Last night I kept thinking about how the first five concert kills were insured by just two companies. Did you ever find out why?" I asked.

"Gordian C. Knox insured the one where Delainya was killed, so Milner went after them for the next two. I found out yesterday that Amanda Dorian's father works for Keagle Insurance. She had it posted on her Facebook page."

I said, "I heard the control room door got super glued.
"

"Milner bonded the jams and left a glue injector in the lock. How is Kayleigh doing?"

"A little shaky, but she's going to be alright. Who would have thought she was the guitar player that Milner was after?"

Shamansky said, "I spent a half hour with Jeannine while you were in the ER. She told me about how you two were looking at the big picture relative to the details of the first murder. As I understand it, Delainya Tanner got the tickets for the show through a radio promotion put on by CLAM. Milner must have figured Calvin was the top man since he's the C in CLAM. I think he wanted Calvin to suffer the death of the love of his life."

"Good call," I said. "Now let me ask you this: Why do you think Milner went on to kill all of those people after murdering his girlfriend?"

"I think he wanted us looking for a serial killer instead of putting the usual suspects under the microscope. As Tanner's boyfriend, he would have been usual suspect #1."

"I think that might have been his initial plan. But there's no way he could reconcile those murders with his religious convictions unless he fit it into a master plan that he believed to be guided by the hand of God," I said.

"Justification after the fact? I see it all the time. So what's happening over at CLAM?"

"Lonnie and his acts will be doing a solo by mutual consent for however long he stays out of jail. Mark upped his status by landing the altar boys tour after Manning got busted."

"Good call, putting Lutz on that guy. The girl turned out to be 14 years old, and blew a .0185 an hour after the show. I just hope this doesn't put Abbie Delison out of a job."

I said, "I'll ask Calvin if he has any openings."

After suffering through another afternoon of nonstop phone calls I wanted nothing more than to go home and veg out on my couch. Instead, I pulled into the parking lot of a small family restaurant owned by Tyler Pierce, a former band mate from my high school years. Tyler was dropped from the band when his drinking resulted in the group being banned from playing at area Catholic schools. He was the first person I knew to incorporate Alcoholics Anonymous into his life.

I walked in the front door, spotted Kelly and walked to her table.

She said, "Jason, I'd like you to meet my parents and my brothers."

ACKNOWLEDGMENTS

The author gratefully acknowledges the assistance of the following people: Pat Brazill, Kristen Brooks, Tim Conklin, R. Glenn Cooper, Craig Correll, Kim Escobar, Carol Gillern, Pat Gillern, Darcia Helle, Marie Lumsden, Maryann & Mike Nebraski, Donna Riviello, and Vince Shumski. Your contributions and expertise helped make this novel possible.

OTHER ROCK & ROLL MYSTERY SERIES NOVELS

By RJ McDonnell

Rock & Roll Homicide:

Jason Duffy's first murder case could easily be his last. Hired by the widow of a slain rock star, he quickly learns about an unhealthy tie between the victim's recording company and the Russian Mafia. But his suspect list is not limited to the bent-noses of the Borscht Belt.

Midwest Book Review: "A brilliantly told tale of sex, drugs, rock & roll, and the Mob."

Beverly Ford, 20-year veteran Boston Herald crime beat writer: "As an avid reader, I've found McDonnell to be one of the most engaging, enjoyable, and funniest writers I've come across in a long, long time."

BookPleasures.com: "RJ McDonnell's enjoyable style is somewhere between Carl Hiaasen's in *Basket Case* and Michael Connelly's in *Chasing the Dime*."

Rock & Roll Rip-Off:

Premier Book Awards: 2010 Mystery/Thriller of the Year

Jason Duffy thought he had accepted a routine burglary case when a career studio musician hired him to recover a stolen memorabilia collection. But Jason quickly finds himself at the top of a hit list that has nothing to do with The Top 40 and everything to do with a table for one at the San Diego Coroner's Office.

Once again, Jason's staff of former outpatient mental health clients contributes a large measure of humor to this musical mystery novel. He reluctantly adds to his payroll a paranoid security expert who fancies himself as *King of the Improv.*

Compounding his troubles, Jason must deal with major girlfriend issues after his father meddles in his relationship with Kelly. Female readers are treated to a peek at the unique logic men apply to crises of the heart.

The Classic Rockers Reunion with Death:

San Diego private investigator, Jason Duffy, travels to Scranton, PA, in January after his uncle's best friend is murdered. He learns that Uncle Patrick and the victim were members of a rock band that nearly made it to the national scene in the early 1970s, and were about to play a reunion concert in their hometown when the murder occurred.

The investigation leads Jason back to an "almost anything goes" era that is exacting a huge price more than 40 years later. To mix & master this musical mystery, Jason fills in for the murdered guitarist and soon finds himself struggling to avoid filling in a cemetery plot.

Someone doesn't want that reunion concert to happen and is willing to do anything to cancel it forever. The case teaches Jason how easy it is for all of us to fall victim to our assumptions. It's a lesson that could exact a tuition that may never be paid back.

Follow and Friend RJ:

Author website: http://rjmcdonnell.com

Facebook:
https://www.facebook.com/profile.php?id=100000152963997

Twitter: @RJMcDonnell7

Goodreads:
http://www.goodreads.com/author/show/1861538.R_J_McDonnell

www.ingramcontent.com/pod-product-compliance
Lightning Source LLC
Chambersburg PA
CBHW060521180626
46817CB00002B/444